FORGETTING
AUGUST

FORGETTING
AUGUST

J. L. BERG

FOREVER

New York Boston

Copyright © 2015 by Jennifer Berg
Excerpt from *Remembering Everly* copyright © 2015 by Jennifer Berg
Cover design and hand lettering by Elizabeth Turner
Cover photograph by Claudio Marinesco
Cover copyright © 2015 by Hachette Book Group, Inc.

Forever
Hachette Book Group
1290 Avenue of the Americas
New York, NY 10104
hachettebookgroup.com
twitter.com/foreverromance

Printed in the United States of America

RRD-C

First published as an ebook in 2015
First trade paperback edition: April 2016
10 9 8 7 6 5 4 3 2 1

Forever is an imprint of Grand Central Publishing.
The Forever name and logo are trademarks of Hachette Book Group, Inc.

The Hachette Speakers Bureau provides a wide range of authors for speaking events. To find out more, go to www.hachettespeakersbureau.com or call (866) 376-6591.

The publisher is not responsible for websites (or their content) that are not owned by the publisher.

Library of Congress Cataloguing-in-Publication Data is available upon request.

ISBN 978-1-4555-3673-3 (trade paperback edition)
ISBN 978-1-4555-3671-9 (ebook edition)

For Chris
Thank you for being the beautiful chaos in my life.
You are my everything.

FORGETTING
AUGUST

Prologue

Sound roared in my ear like a freight train as I fought against the rushing tide.

I clawed, gripping and pawing my way to the surface. Where it led, I didn't know—only that I needed to get there. Somehow.

In the distance, I heard an echo of a laugh. Soft and feminine, it disappeared like a feather drifting and dancing in a violent windstorm.

Sharp colors and fuzzy images danced around my head, confusing me, enticing me—motivating me to push ahead.

Where was I?

The sound of a siren blared in the distance as a murky green light seemed to move in and around me. It flowed like water and pulsated through me like it had a purpose. The color looked so familiar. I reached out to touch it and suddenly everything stopped, making my heart stop in its tracks.

I need to get out of here.

The woman's voice called out once more and I instinctively chased after it, determined not to lose it.

But once again, like everything else, it faded and I was left alone in a dark tunnel with nothing but myself.

Sometime later, the soft green light returned. I watched it intensify, swirling and changing until it morphed into a single stone. It fell to the ground with a solid clink just as I glimpsed a wisp of red hair around a corner.

"Wait!" I yelled. "Come back!"

My lungs heaved and my body ached as I tried to catch up.

"Don't leave without me!" I begged.

One tiny plink, then another. I looked down to find several green stones hitting the earth. As I looked up to the heavens, it began to pour. Thousands of stones fell from the sky like rain, filling the streets as if they were a giant glass bowl. I tripped and stumbled over them until I fell face forward and hit the ground. Reduced to a crawl, I still didn't give up.

"August!" the woman yelled.

The stones piled one on top of another, surrounding me until I was choking and nearly gagging on the dazzling brilliance as each stone slowly buried me alive.

"Please," I cried, clawing my way to the top as the stones began to cover my head, "Don't leave me here."

My next breath broke the surface and I opened my eyes.

I was awake.

Finally.

Chapter One

Everly

I saw him again today.

It was at the mall this time.

He was wearing a gray suit and it was just seconds this time before he disappeared around a corner and my life returned to normal once more.

It had been two years and yet I still saw him. Everywhere.

The day after that fateful night, I saw him in our neighborhood walking a dog. Months later, he was next to me at a stoplight when I went out for groceries. Two weeks ago when Ryan got down on one knee and placed a dazzling diamond ring on my left hand, I swear I saw his face the minute I said yes.

He was like a ghost—my own personal poltergeist.

I knew it wasn't really him. My therapist had reminded me of that simple fact over a thousand times, but that didn't stop my heart from skipping a beat or my lungs deflating of air every time I saw someone that looked like him pass in my direction.

It could be the color of a person's hair or the way someone laughed that set my body on edge.

Today, it was simply a suit.

Tailored, dark gray with a small pinstripe. The style had been his favorite, and even though the man who wore it looked nothing like him, I still found myself frozen in the middle of the food court.

Still as ice, unable to move.

Because life really didn't move on from a person such as August Kincaid.

No, you simply learned to adapt and above all, you survived.

And that was what I had been doing for the last two years.

Surviving.

"Hey, you went blank again. Are you okay?" Sarah asked.

I looked around, and the world suddenly shifted back into focus. Children cried and begged for ice cream, teenagers laughed and flirted as they walked by us. The smell of cinnamon rolls and cheap Chinese food mixed and mingled, as people pushed and shoved their way around to get in ridiculously long lines. Life went on around me as I returned to the land of the living.

"Yeah, I'm fine," I assured her. Concern was written all over her beautiful, trim face. Her hand lifted briefly as if she were going to offer a hug, but quickly decided against it.

"Okay," she answered, defeat clearly written all over her face. She knew I wouldn't talk about it.

I never did.

There were certain things that just didn't need to be shared.

Specific memories of my past were one of them.

She already knew I was a nutcase yet for some reason became my friend despite this. I guess we had that specific trait in common. We'd met in the waiting room at my therapist's office. She was a recovering purger, or at least that's what she called it. Since the time Sarah was barely old enough to vote, she'd been suffering from a variety of eating disorders. She attributed her illnesses to a dance mentor who'd never thought she was thin enough to be a ballerina.

"When all you want to do is be the Swan Princess in *Swan Lake*, you make sacrifices," she'd told me that day in the office very matter-of-factly. Sarah was at peace with her issues. She'd gone through years of counseling and this year would finally be the swan princess she always dreamed of being—fully in control of what she considered her "livable flaws."

Me?

Well, I guess we all had issues that lingered. Some had visible flaws they could see in the mirror, touch with their hands…measure on a scale. Others, like me, had memories that woke us from sleep and haunted our waking hours, making normal, well—different.

I doubted there would ever be any glorious end of the rainbow moment that would somehow magically cure me of all my flaws.

But I was working on it, and Ryan had made a world of difference in my once bleak outlook on life. Now I saw possibilities where there once was only darkness. He brought hope to my sadness and light to my life. There wasn't a day that went by that I wasn't thankful for his persistence in seeking me out.

I'd been a hard one to nail down, or so he told me.

"So, are you ready?" she asked, grabbing my hand and moving away from the frozen yogurt and fried food.

"As I'll ever be," I sighed, taking one last longing look at the exit.

"Oh come on. Most girls are excited to do this. Hell, I've been excited for this day for weeks!"

"Then say you're me," I begged, as we turned the corner and my eyes spotted the brightly lit sign at the end of the walkway. I could feel the groan already forming, the deep rumbling sound vibrating through my lungs as it made its way up to express my displeasure.

"Everly Adams. You will not ruin this for me! This is your day and you will enjoy it!"

"I thought *my* day was several months from now," I joked.

"As the blushing bride-to-be, you will have lots of days between now and then. Get used to the attention."

I groaned again, looking at the floor-to-ceiling windows that displayed more tulle and sequins than I'd seen in my entire life.

"We should have eloped."

*   *   *

"This is horrid, Sarah," I whined, shuffling out of the dressing room in a gown that could only be described as a cross between the Little Mermaid and that scary Alfred Hitchcock movie with all the birds.

"It's beautiful! And so fashion forward," she practically squealed, clapping her hands together like a happy toddler who had just been given a lollipop for supper. "Look at the way the fabric gathers together, making it look like tiny feathers at the bottom of the skirt. So dramatic."

"That," I said, pointing to my calves, "is also where my legs are supposed to be able to move back and forth. It's called walking. I look ridiculous!"

"Walking is so overrated. Besides, how much walking are you planning to do in this thing?" She rolled her eyes, kneeling down to play with the skirt some more. It resulted in the tulle or whatever the puffy stuff was called doubling in size.

"There, perfect."

"I'm not wearing this," I said firmly, trying to look anywhere but at the three different mirrors all reflecting my ridiculous image. "Pick another one. And for the love of God, pick something less... well, less you!"

I once again attempted to walk back into the dressing room, doing more of a waddle than a walk. Once there, I was joined by an attendant to assist me. There was no way I could get out of this monstrosity by myself.

"Your tattoo is lovely. Quite unique," the bridal attendant said, as she stood behind me and removed the clamps that held the dress in place. My thin, boylike frame never did fit into sample sizes well. The lack of hips and boobs kept me in sizes most women would die to wear, but the lack of aforementioned body parts sometimes sucked. A lot.

Especially when trying on wedding dresses. Or anything remotely feminine. I felt more like a prepubescent boy trying on drag than a beautiful, curvy woman.

"Thank you," I answered awkwardly, as my hand instinctively reached behind my shoulder to touch the piece of me that I rarely shared with others. The walls of mirrors put my body completely on display, highlighting every rough curve and jutted angle, exposing the harsh black lines of the branch as it wove up my back and around my shoulder.

"Why doesn't the bird fly away? She's free," she said absently, her head cocked to the side as she stared at the birdcage etched on my right shoulder. It was intricate and beautiful as it hung on the barren branch, the door swung wide open for the world to peer in on the tiny bird inside.

"Maybe she's not ready yet," I answered quietly, looking away.

"Okay, I've got another one, Everly! And I promise, you're going to love it!" Sarah's singsong voice seemed to break the spell hovering above us, giving us both a startle. The attendant straightened, turning quickly as I retreated into the corner to grab the satin robe. I'd just fastened it around my waist when she opened the door to let Sarah in.

"Tell me you love me," Sarah said as she waltzed into the room, holding up a simple ivory-colored empire-waist gown with a small amount of beading around the neckline and not a single bit of organza or tulle in sight.

"I think I love you," I said, as my eyes widened at the understated elegance of the dress. Simple and understated. Everything I wanted to be.

"Let's try it on," she suggested, handing it to the attendant who motioned for me to come forward.

Nodding, I agreed, knowing it was unnecessary.

It was perfect and as I glanced around the room, I caught a glimpse of that tiny bird on my shoulder. The one too afraid to jump out of her cage and discover the world outside.

Soon, I would be perfect, too.

Or as close as I could be to the word.

*   *   *

"You are mine, Everly," he whispered. "Mine and mine alone. I own every part of you, every inch of your body…every breath in your lungs. You. Belong. To. Me."

"Everly," another voice murmured. "Everly, wake up. You fell asleep right at the good part again." Ryan laughed.

My eyes cracked open as the glow of the TV made me turn my head toward the comfort of his warm chest.

"Hey, sleepyhead," he said, pulling me tight against his body. "You'll never know who the winter soldier is now," he joked, his head leaning forward just close enough that I felt the heat of his breath against my neck.

"I saw that plot twist ages ago," I answered, covering a quiet yawn with my palm as I stretched in his arms.

"You always do."

"I can't help it. The story lines are always so obvious."

"And if you had written the story," he said, pulling back slightly with a boyish grin lighting up his face, "what would you have done differently?"

"I don't know—I'm not a scriptwriter," I answered with a shrug.

"Maybe you should be." His brow arched, challenging me to answer.

"Who's being the obvious one now, Ryan?" I asked with a huff, rising from my comfortable spot on the couch in order to create some much-needed distance. "And seriously? Scriptwriting? Pick something a little less insane next time. When have you ever seen me pick up a pen? Or sit in front of a computer?"

Whenever the subject of where I was going with my life came up, I needed space.

Unfortunately our apartment was only so big, and right now a football field or two didn't seem large enough.

"I don't want to start an argument, Ev, but I just want you to think about it."

"I have been thinking about it," I answered, stepping into the kitchen as the lights flickered on. I pulled open the refrigerator and grabbed a bottle of water. Roughly twisting the cap off, I upturned the bottle and chugged half the contents in one gulp. Water was definitely not my first beverage of choice, but right now I didn't have the patience for anything else.

"And what have you decided?" he asked cautiously, rising from the couch to take a seat at the kitchen island across from me.

"That I'm still deciding." I held my head high, avoiding his eye contact.

I was not in the wrong here.

He sighed long and slow, and I let the silence settle between us, setting the half-empty bottle down on the counter in front of me. A quick glint of light caught my attention as I turned my head and I swiveled back around toward my left hand, noticing the way the overhead lights reflected on the small diamond centered in the middle of the thin gold band.

Three weeks ago he'd asked me to marry him and I'd said yes.

Despite everything I'd put him through—the cold indifference and the numerous rebuttals to his advances, he'd loved me. When I'd told him there would always be a part of me unavailable...that I just couldn't share, he'd accepted me. For who I was.

And what I was willing to give him.

"I'll look at the brochures again," I said, offering up an olive branch as I stepped forward and held out the rest of my water bottle. His warm smile returned as his fingers encased mine around the plastic.

"I just want to see you succeed. In whatever you choose, Ev. Hell, you can major in basket weaving for all I care. I just want you to feel like you have a purpose in life beyond working at that coffee shop you refuse to quit."

"I know, and I love you for it," I replied, feeling the deep gaze of his eyes settle on mine. Needing to be closer to him, I walked out of the kitchen and walked into his arms at the counter where he sat.

He pulled me into his large frame, where the world felt safe and measurable again.

"I do make a mean cup of coffee," I said, my lips curving into a smile.

His fingers cupped my chin, tilting it toward his dark brown eyes.

"I know. Why do you think I kept coming back every damn day? It wasn't your charming personality."

"I thought it was my ass," I laughed, shaking it as his hands closed around each cheek and squeezed.

"Ah yes. The ass of a porn star and the mouth of a mime. No matter how hard I tried, I could never get you to talk to me."

"Such a sweet talker, and besides—I was told to never speak to strange men," I said, quickly hating myself for saying it. My face slipped slightly as my stomach turned, rolling and churning as my mind replayed unwanted memories from my past.

I never, ever want to see you speaking to another man again. Do you understand me, Everly?

The words rolled around in my head as I tried to shake them out. In the last two years of my life, I'd had a thousand moments like this. A glance, a turn of phrase—anything could bring them on. I'd learned to recognize the symptoms and process the reaction quickly.

So quickly that Ryan didn't even seem to notice anymore.

"Well," he said, grinning, his hands slipping underneath my shirt, "I finally did wear you down. And now you're mine."

A weak smile spread across my lips, seconds before his mouth touched mine.

No matter how much he loved me.

No matter how much I loved him in return.

I would never, ever belong to another person.

For as long as I lived.

*   *   *

The movie had been long forgotten, as had our clothes.

They were strung out all over the apartment, leaving a trail toward the bedroom. Little breadcrumbs of debauchery.

"Hey, it's still early; do you want to order a pizza?" Ryan yelled from the shower as I took a long breath and snuggled deeper into the covers on our bed.

"Does it require me to get out of this bed?" I whined, moving my legs back and forth against the smooth sheets. Ryan always said it looked like I was swimming in bed when I did this.

Growing up, I never had nice sheets. Hell, sometimes there were foster homes that didn't even give me sheets—just a blanket and a dirty bare mattress.

Luxuries like Egyptian cotton sheets were things I would never grow accustomed to, no matter how many times my legs touched them. Every night, I'd sink into bed and run my legs back and forth against the smoothness, loving the way it felt against my skin.

Like Ryan, it brought me peace and made me feel safe—two things I'd struggled with the majority of my life.

"Please, babe. I'm hungry. So very, very hungry," he said, sticking his head out the door of the bathroom. His lips turned downward, making him look years younger. I laughed, unable to resist his boyish charm.

"Okay, okay," I said, stretching one last time, before I rose to grab my robe.

"On second thought, I might need to work off a few more calories first," he said, stepping out of the bathroom in just a towel. His tanned skin was slick and wet from the shower, and I couldn't help but lick my lips as I watched a tiny drop of water skate down his chiseled chest.

Who knew nerds could be so hot?

His gaze turned heated as he stalked forward and I watched the towel drop to the floor. I stepped backward, feeling the edge of the bed hit the backs of my knees.

Our bodies met once more as his hand cupped the back of my head, tilting it upward. "I love you, Everly. I love you so much," he whispered, touching his lips to mine. I moaned into the kiss, feeling every hard inch of him press into me.

Always aware of my needs, he was gentle as he lowered me to the bed. As my head touched the pillow, I heard the sounds of a cell phone ringing throughout the apartment.

Ryan's head dipped forward, shaking back and forth.

"Just ignore it," he said.

I was already pushing at his shoulders, begging him to let me answer it.

"It can't be that important, Ev," he said, his eyes dancing with amusement. "I'm right here."

I rolled my eyes, grabbing my robe as I raced to the living room.

"It could be Sarah," I said. "She had her first rehearsal tonight."

I picked up the phone, not recognizing the number, and paused.

"Babe," Ryan said, standing in the doorway of our room. "Come back to bed. Whatever it is can wait."

I didn't listen. Instead, I answered and heard the words I had begged God to never allow to come true.

"Miss Adams?" a woman said on the other end.

"Yes," I answered.

"This is Doctor Lawrence from St. Marcus Hospital."

My heart began to beat frantically as my hand sought out something solid to hold me up. I knew it was coming. Like a freight train in the middle of the night, I could see the light off in the distance...I knew what was coming.

Who was coming.

"He's awake."

The phone hit the floor seconds before I did, and then the world went black.

Chapter Two

August

"I need a doctor in here!" someone shouted. I felt my lungs expanding, gasping for air. "Breathe! Look at me!" she yelled once more. My eyes opened, as blinding white light burned my retinas, making the room blurry and distorted. Instinctively lifting my hand, I tried to block it out, but felt held back by cords and wires.

"I'm Nurse Amy. Do you know where you are?" the woman asked. "You haven't spoken in a very long time—your throat will be hoarse. Please don't try to speak."

Long time? Nurse?

I blinked, looking around, as I waited for the spots and auras to dissipate. Fuzzy white walls came into focus as I looked down to see my own limp body below, covered in stiff bleached blankets. I flexed my hand and felt my bones cracking like ancient tree branches. I looked down at my arm, noticed the tape around the crook of my arm—for an IV, perhaps?

"Sir, are you all right? Do you understand what I'm saying?"

I looked up to see Nurse Ally or Amy, a young blonde, staring at me with concern and perhaps what might have been a bit of shock. I nodded, narrowing my eyes as I tried to gauge her appearance. Did I know her?

"Do you know where you are?" she repeated. "Just shake your head for yes or no."

I shook my head no, the muscles in my neck feeling tight and thin.

Just then an older man dressed in a white lab coat and scrubs appeared in the doorway.

"You called for his doctor," he said absently, searching through a paper chart as he sauntered in. His eyes lifted and met mine.

"Good god," he whispered, the clipboard falling to the floor with a clatter. Leaving the mess of papers where they fell, he stepped forward as his wide look of surprise and wonder stayed solely focused on me.

"I was doing chart updates and he suddenly took a large gasp of air. I thought he was flatlining, but then his eyes popped open and he was fully awake. I've never heard of such a thing."

The man just stared at me, eyes full of shock.

"Doctor, are you all right?" The nurse asked, glancing over at the aged man with concern. His gray eyebrows furrowed together as his frozen statue of a frame narrowed in on me.

"Yes. Yes, of course. We need to run vitals right away," the old man said, still seeming to be stuck in some sort of trance.

"Amazing," the doctor managed to say as I watched him and the young nurse hover over me like some crazy science experiment.

It made me suddenly wary of my situation.

The nurse scuttled away and I was suddenly left alone with the ancient doctor.

"Do you remember how you got here?" he asked, pushing a chair toward the bed. He took a seat, resting a clipboard on his lap as he calmly folded his legs and held a pen ready for notes.

"I—" That single word felt like sandpaper and sent me into a sudden coughing fit that had no end.

A hand pushed me forward and patted my back, attempting to calm me.

"Take your time," he said, rising to walk toward the sink. He returned seconds later with a paper cup filled with water.

"Just small sips at first," he directed, as I brought the cup to my lips. The process, although it should have been second nature to me, seemed clumsy and new. My hands shook, and my arms felt tired from the strain. I nearly missed my mouth and had to look down as the cup met my mouth, drops of water spilling all over my thin hospital gown.

I was like a child. A feeble, helpless child.

The cool water soothed my aching throat, though, and provided much-needed relief as I finally found the words I'd wanted to say since my eyes cracked open.

"I…remember…nothing," I answered hoarsely, the truth hurting more than any pain or ache could.

*　　*　　*

Nothing.

My former life was an endless tunnel of oblivion, where there was no beginning or end. There were no ups or downs or signs to tell me of the twisty turns up ahead. There wasn't a highlight reel—no cliff notes to remind me of what had occurred or transpired.

It all came crashing down to one singular word.

Nothing.

No matter how many questions they asked, my answer remained the same.

I remembered absolutely nothing.

What did I do with that?

The doctor—he called himself Lawrence—said the memories I'd lost might return with time. I asked the probability of that happening.

His response was that he honestly didn't know.

"After a certain amount of time, the chances of a patient reawakening after a brain injury such as yours become slimmer and slimmer. We honestly didn't know whether you would ever wake up, August. This is rare. We're all treading on uncharted ground at this point."

August.

That was my name—August Kincaid.

But a name couldn't tell me what kind of man I was—what kind of life I'd led. I would have said I'd never felt so lost or alone in my life…but had I?

My eyesight now well-adjusted to the fluorescent lights above, I stared ahead, trying to figure out a way to make sense of my new reality. My focus drifted toward the window, where the city spread out before me.

The nurses had explained to me I was in San Francisco. As I looked out onto the city below, it felt foreign and cold. Nothing stood out. Had I really lived here?

The door creaked open as Nurse Amy crept in once more.

"I brought you some food. Unfortunately it's only applesauce and broth—but it's a start," she said with a subtle smile, setting the tray beside me. "I also managed to unearth your box of belongings, if you'd like to look through them?"

"Belongings?" I asked, my attention now completely wrapped around the small cardboard box in her hands.

"Yes. When you arrived, you had some things with you. We saved them in case... well, I'll just leave them right here."

The doctor had mentioned I'd been in some sort of attack—a mugging, but hadn't given me the details. He'd said it was best if we just started with the basics for now.

Placing the box on the bed next to my leg, she turned.

"Amy," I said quietly, needing to know something... anything.

"Yes?" she asked, rotating back around. Her amber eyes brimmed with sympathy.

"Did anyone ever come to see me? Family, friends—anyone?"

Her lips pursed together as her face fell. "No, sir. Not since I've been here."

"And how long has that been?"

"I've been working this wing for a little over a year and a half, sir."

I swallowed the giant lump in my throat as I quickly thanked her. Listening to the door quietly click closed behind her, I glanced once more out the window to the thousands of streets and houses below.

Dr. Lawrence had told me I had been "asleep" for a little over two years—twenty-six months, to be exact. It was like falling asleep on a plane ride and waking up three hours later as the pilot announces your final descent—only you're still stuck at the beginning, wondering where your complimentary beverage and peanuts are. Everything seemed to have happened in a blink of an eye because you were asleep during all the action.

I'd missed over two years of my life—a life I didn't remember. A life no one wanted to be a part of.

I was already learning about the type of man I had been.

No family or friends—I was either a loner or an asshole. I didn't know which was worse.

*   *   *

My hand shook as I pulled the box into my lap, preparing myself for what may lie hidden within. I felt nervous and sick with anticipation. I suddenly wanted to flee, but where would I go? And how would I get there? Moving my leg took more concentration than I was willing to admit and I was still attached to what looked to be a hundred monitoring devices.

The box stared back at me, waiting…wondering when I would crack its lip and finally divulge the secrets it had been keeping for so long.

What if I didn't like what I found? What if I did?

Taking a deep breath, I placed my hand on the lip and pulled, knowing there was only one way to find out.

All neatly arranged inside, I found clothes, a wallet, and a scattering of other personal belongings. I immediately went for the wallet, knowing it would hold the most information. With everything else forgotten, my fingers traced the smooth edges of the soft leather as I bent it open.

There staring back at me was a picture of my own face. Because of the mirror across the room near the sink, I'd managed to catch a glimpse of my reflection a time or two since awaking here hours earlier.

The man looking up at me from the California driver's license photo was a stark contrast to the person I was today.

Cold, empty green eyes looked through me, as if the world and everything in it were beneath him. The me in the photo wore a crisp white shirt and flawless green tie and jacket, but there was no smile permeating the lens—not even a hint of emotion showed. My now long, unkempt hair had been trimmed short and neat, matching the impeccable persona that could be seen even through the tiny picture.

My attention turned toward the address.

1023 Sea Cliff Lane, San Francisco.

I looked out the window, trying to see if anything beyond its paned glass brought back any hints or memories of a life I'd once led.

San Francisco.

Even though the driver's license confirmed what the nurse had already told me, I still felt no connection with the city below. Nothing called out to me; nothing held my attention.

Was there anyone down there that would remember my name?

I dug further through the wallet, finding a couple hundred dollars in cash, as well as several credit cards and a few membership cards to places I'd never heard of, but apparently belonged to.

Or had belonged to.

What happened to your life when you went into a coma? Did you disappear? Cease to exist, or did life carry on? I looked at the address on my driver's license and wondered if I still had a home...a bank account? I wasn't dead, but who had been paying my bills for the last two years?

Did I have money to pay the bills?

Fuck.

Suddenly, all I wanted was to slip back into that coma and never wake up again.

And then I saw her.

It was just a glimpse at first, the edge of a picture sticking out from inside the wallet—a wisp of hair that had me pulling at the picture to see it properly.

With the Golden Gate Bridge as our backdrop, a much younger, carefree version of myself held a girl in my arms and suddenly the world didn't feel so lonely anymore. Copper red hair tumbled down her back like a fiery mane. Her bright blue eyes sparkled as if she held untold secrets waiting to be revealed. In my own eyes, I didn't see harshness or the rigid void of nothingness. I saw her, reflecting back in spades, the love radiating between us.

I flipped the photo over, hoping for something…anything that would tell me who this girl was.

There was nothing but a date and a name.

August and Everly—2005

Everly.

She had a name.

Now all I had to do was find her.

Chapter Three

Everly

A soothing hand caressed my forehead and my eyes fluttered open; that's when reality came crashing back to the forefront of my mind.

August was awake.

Oh, God. Did he know?

Would he find me?

I bolted upright, nearly knocking Ryan out in the process. My heart kicked into high gear as my fight-or-flight response took over.

Too weak to fight. Must flee.

Need to leave.

Should never have stayed here.

I should have left. I should have moved far…far away like I'd always planned. But plans have a way of getting muddled and as my breath evened out and my eyes once again opened, I found the reason for my muddled plans staring back at me with nothing but concern and love written across his handsome face.

"It's okay," he said softly, gently pushing back a piece of my hair as he leaned in close. "I'm here. You're going to be okay, Ev."

Unshed tears stung my eyes and I fought to keep them in place. He pulled me into his arms and I willingly let him, gripping his shoulder as if it were an iron anchor. My body felt like someone had just dropped a hundred-ton lead weight into my arms, like I was carrying every single worry and panicked thought I'd stowed away over the last two years.

They all rose to the surface. All at once.

"Oh god, Ryan. I can't do this," I cried.

"You don't have to do a thing. No one is making you do anything at all, Everly. He's awake; that doesn't have to mean anything to you."

I knew he meant well, but he didn't understand. He'd never understand.

"I can't exist in a world where he does, Ryan," I whispered, as the walls began to close in around me. Panic settled in my bones, had me pulling my knees close to my chest, rocking back and forth in Ryan's strong arms. The tears continued to fall as I felt myself growing weaker, knowing August was mere miles away, growing stronger by the minute.

How long until he came for me? How long until he found me and ruined the little life I'd created? What happened then?

"Yes, you can," Ryan vowed, turning me in his arms as he pulled me from the darkness and growing fear in my head. "This changes nothing."

I shook my head, not so easily convinced. The only reason I'd carried on in his absence was because I'd convinced myself he was gone. For good.

Denial really was a cold-hearted bitch.

"What happened…after…I mean—did you talk to the doctor more?"

I felt him nod. "I hung up to take care of you, but after I got you in bed, I did call him back."

"What did he say?" I asked, my breath barely audible as I waited for his response.

He pulled back, our eyes locking as he smoothed away the crimson hair from around my face. Warmth and tenderness met me as he spoke. "He wants to see you."

Fear flooded my system and I immediately tried to retract from his hold, needing space as the room once again began to shrink around me.

Flee. Must flee.

"I can't," I managed to choke out as I got up and paced the room. "I won't."

"No one is making you, Ev. I already told Dr. Lawrence no."

My body tensed at his admission. I came to an abrupt standstill in the middle of the living room. "You had no right to do that!" I shouted, my hands flailing as anger coursed through my veins. Ryan looked at me as if I'd lost it, and maybe I had.

"What are you even saying?" Ryan yelled back at me. "Do you see yourself right now? How can you say that when you just know I'm right? You couldn't in a million years visit that guy. He's a monster!"

"It's my decision, Ryan!" I spat. "I've already spent enough of my life with someone who felt the need to make decisions for me without consultation. I won't do it again."

His hands made a worried run through his hair. "I was just trying to protect you."

Deep down I knew he was, but part of me—the profoundly damaged part that grimaced every time he uttered words like "mine" or jokingly said "don't ever do that again"—hated being protected. I loved the safety I felt nestled in his arms, but it was it was another man's love and overwhelming need to protect that had gotten me into the mess I was in now.

"I need some air," I said finally, walking hastily toward the front door of our apartment.

"Please don't leave angry with me, Everly," he begged.

"I'm not angry—I just need some time."

"Okay," he answered, the sound of rejection and defeat clear in his voice. He'd learned not to argue when I uttered this phrase. Needing air was my way of pressing pause, or asking for a time-out. Sometimes I just needed to get away and I tried not to think too critically about what that meant.

I don't know how long I wandered around the city. Everything passed by in a blur until I found myself in that familiar spot by the bridge. It was nearly spring, and the bluff was blooming with wildflowers. As the rest of San Francisco went on with their busy lives, new life was blossoming right here on this hillside.

From here, things seemed much simpler.

The Golden Gate Bridge rose high into the heavens, its red pillars a stark contrast to the grayish blue sky. As I found a seat among the tiny yellow buds, I reached out my hand. The bridge felt so close, its enormity giving it an almost unworldly appearance to the world below. But my fingers only grasped the cool air. Nothing else. My mighty bridge was where it always was, stable and secure in the water beyond.

I'd been coming to this spot since I was a tattered little girl, moving from one foster home to another, wondering when my real mom and dad were finally going to rescue me from the hellhole of a life I'd become accustomed to. I wondered how many foster kids secretly watched *Annie* late at night, hoping they'd be just like that little redheaded songstress, only to find out that dreams like that never happened outside of the movies, and real-life heroes are never what you expect them to be.

I guess at some point I could have figured out why I'd been placed in foster care, but after so many years of being considered a problem or a paycheck to others, I stopped caring. That *Annie*-like hope eventually leaks out like dirty car oil and all you're left with is remorse; remorse and regret for the life you could have had if your real parents had been someone else. Someone kind and loving—someone better.

I'd thought my someone better was August. Turned out he was just another version of something even worse.

* * *

I met August when I was eighteen. I stumbled into a nightclub — I was too young to be drinking—too young to be doing a lot of things that night—and when I saw him, he was like the knight in shining armor I'd never had.

Or at least what I'd always envisioned one to be.

He was four years my senior, and at the time he'd seemed so mature and sophisticated. Twenty-two was old enough to drink legally and walk into hotels without a second glance.

It was love at first sight. For both of us. From that singular moment, as the bass boomed in the club and we took our first dance together, we became inseparable.

I never had a mother growing up. Or a big sister or brother. Sometimes kids are lucky and find a good foster family in it for the real reasons.

I wasn't one of those kids.

I did all right by myself, and had a good head on my shoulders—most of the time—but there was never anyone around to tell me that you should be consumed by love, not the other way around.

Within months of meeting August Kincaid, I was consumed. So consumed, I couldn't remember where he began and I ended. He became the family I never had, the lover I'd always dreamed of and the friend I'd longed for. He was my everything. He took care of me and made me feel safe. He never made me feel trashy or let my shitty past define me. He was all I'd ever wanted, and soon I couldn't remember what life had been like without him.

We could have floated away into our perfect fairy-tale love story and that would have been the end. The newspapers could have printed our perfect wedding announcement and everything would have been wrapped up in a neat tidy red bow.

But nothing having to do with me is ever neat. Or tidy.

And that's where my fairy tale derailed and I found myself living something closer to a nightmare.

Several years into our romance, August became very successful in business—very quickly. Whenever I asked what he did he always just smiled, patted me on the head, and answered with something vague and ambiguous.

"I'm a stockbroker—you know that," he'd said.

But part of me worried that whatever "business" he'd become involved in was illegal or at least not legit. I should have listened to that part more—she's one smart bitch.

With the addition of wealth he began to change. He became more possessive, more clingy and domineering. A sideways glance at a party and suddenly I would be pulled into an empty room and fucked ten different ways just to be sure I understood who owned me. If another man looked at me, I was immediately taken home, like an errant child.

My fairy tale became a nightmare and I lived in a constant state of fear. Each and every day, his behavior worsened. It was as if success had made him crazy—pushing him into some sort of manic behavior where he believed everyone in the world was out to get him and I was their means to do so.

Parties and social events became a thing of the past, and I eventually became a prisoner in my own home, unable to leave because he was too paranoid to take me anywhere.

"You're mine. Only mine," he'd chant over and over as he pinned me against a wall and came hard and long inside of me. "I love you, Everly. Forever."

Ryan once asked why I'd never run, why I didn't seek help.

I knew the answer, but I just shook my head and said I didn't know, averting his gaze.

Because sometimes the truth hurts worse.

* * *

"How are you feeling about your decision today, Everly?" Tabitha asked, in that soothing tone that used to drive me up the wall but now seemed to have the opposite effect.

I curled my feet under me on the worn couch, holding a cup of hot tea in my hands as I contemplated my answer. We were never supposed to blurt out an answer in therapy. *Think before you speak*—that was Tabitha's motto, and as much as I'd despised it and everything about this place years ago, when I'd entered and found her sitting in front of me with her weird, frizzy gray hair and long, flowing skirts, I had to admit it worked.

Because of this woman and her soothing ways, I'd managed to break out of the rock-hard tortoise shell I'd buried myself into after August vanished from my life. Although his coma had been something of a blessing—pulling me out of a life no one should ever have to live—suddenly I'd been forced back into a world I no longer understood.

As much as I hated to admit it, I'd been lost and alone without him. The world was scary and far too big. I wanted nothing more than to run back to the confines of my prison and never come out again.

But somehow, I'd found Tabitha. Attempting to venture past my own driveway, I'd gone for a walk that turned into more of a hike, and found her sign in a little neighborhood not too far from the one Ryan and I currently live in. Her eclectic ways and throwback looks were mind-boggling at first, but I soon found a home with her, or at least a place to return to once a week.

Slowly, she gave me a direction in life. I got a job at a coffee shop nearby and months later, I met Ryan. I took each day as it came, and eventually I stopped wondering when life was going to come crashing down again.

And then it did—or it was about to.

"Everly? Your decision regarding visiting August? How do you feel?" Tabitha asked once more, bringing me back to the present.

"Honestly?"

"That's all I ever ask for," she stated.

"I don't know."

"It's okay to be unsure."

"Even about this?" I asked, biting my bottom lip with uncertainty.

"What are you unsure about?" she questioned, tapping the butt on her pen against her crisp yellow notepad.

"Everything. What will happen if I don't go? Will he come find me—invade the life I've made for myself? If I go see him in the hospital, can I avoid all of that, or am I just perpetuating it? I feel like I'm stuck in this damned-if-you-do, damned-if-you-don't scenario. No matter what I do, he's going to destroy everything."

"So you've thought about seeing him?" she asked.

"Yes," I admitted reluctantly.

"You don't have to feel ashamed in front of me," she consoled, the smooth tone of her voice giving me the comfort I'd come to find within these four walls.

"It's more than that. Admitting it makes me feel like I'm betraying Ryan. Just saying the words—Hell…even thinking about the action of doing so makes me feel like I'm cheating on him somehow."

Silence settled between us as I let my words evaporate into the air.

"Have you ever thought that maybe this is the closure you need?"

"What do you mean? I've had my closure—you went with me. You held my hand as I said good-bye to that man," I pressed, my hands wrapping around my knees like a child.

"I know, but perhaps you need to hear him say the words as well. See his face as he says them," she suggested.

The idea of seeing him again made the air seem to dissipate around me. What would he look like? What would he say? And how would I react?

My hands shook just thinking about it. It scared the living hell out of me.

And yet, a small part of me still wanted to go. To get in the last word maybe, or to see him weak and fragile in a hospital gown...or maybe just to see him after all this time.

That was what scared me most of all. That after everything, there was still a fraction of me somewhere deep down that missed him as much as the rest of me hated him.

* * *

I'd finished up my session with Tabitha and had been staring at my cold cup of coffee for hours when Ryan walked in after a long day at the office.

Cold coffee...such a waste.

"Did the coffee do something to piss you off?" he asked, loosening his tie as he set his keys and wallet into the glass dish on the counter.

"I'm thinking about going to the hospital," I blurted out, unable to look up at him. I took the coward's way out and instead chose to continue reading the words on my mug over and over again.

Just call me Sassenach. I loved this mug. It usually made me smile and giggle like a giddy schoolgirl. Ryan would just groan and roll his eyes at my obsessive fascination with a certain Scottish book series.

The door to our bedroom slammed, telling me exactly how he felt about my remark.

Obviously that wasn't happening today.

Moments later, he reappeared, ready to fight. Sleeves pushed up, with his eyes set straight ahead, he was ready for business. Ryan never walked away when it came to me. I'd pushed him away more times than I could count, fleeing arguments and needing air more times than I could count, and yet he still came back.

He'd always fought for me.

"Why, Everly, why? After everything we've been through together, can you at least do me the courtesy of giving me an answer?"

"I need to see him."

The look of devastation on his face was like a blow to my gut, making me feel like the worst kind of human on the planet. If there was an award for that type of thing, I was pretty sure I'd be in a three-way tie with whoever invented the selfie stick and those pants that look like jeans but really are pajamas. That's just all kinds of wrong.

"I need him to hear it from my own lips that it's over between us—that I've moved on, that I survived after everything he put me through. I don't want him interfering in our lives, Ryan."

"He doesn't deserve it," he said through gritted teeth.

"No, he doesn't. But I do," I pressed, my emotions taking over as I gazed up at him.

He ran his hands through his wavy blond locks and finally nodded. "Okay."

I went into his arms, letting him believe he'd just won an argument and granted me some sort of blessing over the situation.

"Don't sweat the small stuff," Tabitha had once told me when I'd come to her complaining about the way Ryan left the seat up and never washed the dishes. I guess this fell in that category.

I would have gone to the hospital regardless of his opinion on the matter. I needed this for me. Having his agreement obviously made the situation easier, but by no means swayed my decision.

I would never be owned again.

Chapter Four

August

In the few days since my miraculous awakening, I'd managed to make several leaps and bounds toward my eventual recovery and release.

Release. This was what Dr. Lawrence had called it.

Soon I would be released back into the world. Like a fish, or a wild animal set free into the wild again.

"What will I do?" I'd asked, like a puppy looking to its mother for guidance.

"Whatever you want," he'd suggested.

Whatever I wanted... The thought lingered in my mind like a loose thread in the wind. What did I want? How would I even know?

What I'd learned over the last seventy-two hours wasn't much, but it was enough to know I at least had some security when I left this building. My house was still mine.

In my former life, I had been a wealthy man. While I'd wasted away in this hospital bed, my estate and finances had been taken care of.

How? I didn't have many personal details, but according to the paperwork I'd been sent from my law firm, there was nothing to worry about. At least I had someplace to return to when the hospital deemed I was fit enough to be discharged. Until then, I celebrated such successes as moving on from applesauce and chicken broth for breakfast to oatmeal.

I briefly wondered if the old me had hated oatmeal as much as the new me did.

The watery, tasteless applesauce suddenly didn't taste nearly as bad as it once had.

Pushing the oatmeal aside, I grabbed the file box that held the contents of my personal belongings once more. I'd opened and looked over each item a dozen times now, choosing to bury myself in my unknown past rather than dwell in the confusing present I'd currently been thrown into.

Dr. Lawrence said the brain is a curious and complex thing. While I couldn't remember anything about myself and the life I'd led, I did somehow recollect trivial things such as what a Starbucks was or when the Gulf War occurred. I understood modern living, could write and speak, but had had to ask what day and year I'd been born.

It turned out I'd had a birthday last month. I'd breezed through the end of my twenties and landed in my thirties without a party or hangover to show for it. The only thing I had as proof for the milestone was a hospital bracelet declaring my age.

If my life wasn't my own…whose was it?

I reached into the box, shuffling around the neatly folded clothes I had not previously touched. Something fell out of one of the jacket pockets. I pushed the suit jacket and slacks to the side until I found it. Wedged into one of the corners was a tiny green stone.

I picked it up, rolling it between the smooth pads of my fingers, and held it up to the light. It was drilled through as if it had once been a set on string, and appeared to be a raw emerald or perhaps a piece of jade.

Why it was in my pocket the night I ended up here, I'd never know.

Much like everything else.

Feeling the familiar feeling of frustration seeping through my pores, I decided there had been enough show and tell time for the day and set the box aside. Closing my eyes, I tried to block out the world and my thoughts but was abruptly interrupted when the door swung open and I found myself staring into a familiar set of blue eyes.

It was her.

Everly—the girl from the picture.

I'd asked the nurse on duty if she could find her and she'd assured me she'd try, but after several days, I'd assumed she'd been unable to complete the task or had simply placated me to keep the unpredictable coma patient calm.

Yet, here she was.

She entered slowly, her steps hesitant and timid, and I took the extra time to absorb every detail.

Her hair was different—shorter maybe, but still that same fiery copper color. She'd aged since the photo was taken, and rounded some, transitioning from a gangly girl to a waiflike siren.

"You're here," I managed, grasping at straws. I didn't know what to say. I didn't know anything about this woman beyond her name.

"Yes," she answered curtly, her lips barely moving as she formed the word. "Dr. Lawrence called me."

"I didn't know if they'd be able to find you after I found the photo."

She looked slightly confused by my statement but didn't say anything more. I looked around the room awkwardly, feeling like a showpiece at the zoo. Her eyes roamed all over me, no doubt noticing my lack of muscle and reduced appearance. The insecurity I felt in that moment was tangible.

"Why don't you take a seat? I know I must look different from the last time you saw me."

She silently took the seat farthest from me, but didn't relax in the slightest. Her posture remained rigid and on edge. Was she afraid of me?

"I'm sorry to have bothered you by asking you to come here, but I just wanted to—" I started, but was quickly interrupted.

"August, please don't. I came here for one reason and one reason only."

"Okay." My eyebrows furrowed in confusion as I tried to sit up properly. Setting the box on the metal tray, I placed my hands on the bed and pushed myself upright. The effort caused trickles of sweat to form at my temples.

"I wanted to tell you we're over. All of it. Done. I've moved on. I'm engaged. I have a new life—without you. Please don't contact me anymore."

I looked up at her, and while I should have felt nothing but confusion, her words caused me a physical pain I wasn't prepared for. My heart jolted and I reached up, touching my chest as her words sank in. I didn't know this woman but my heart obviously did, because in that moment—it was breaking.

"I don't understand," I muttered.

"Of course you don't. Do you remember anything?" she replied, her voice heated with raw anger and annoyance.

"No," I answered simply.

Her hands went up in frustration as she rose to her feet. "I knew this was a stupid idea."

"Please, let me speak," I begged.

Her eyes met mine briefly and she nodded, turning away as she began to pace the room.

"The doctors are calling it a dissociative fugue—or at least that's what they're thinking today. I'm sure they'll come up with something new next week when they bring in more consultants, seeing as I'm now their newest lab rat."

She turned around, her face contorted in confusion.

"I don't understand anything you just said."

"You asked me if I remembered anything and I said no. I mean it, Everly. I have no memories of my life before I opened my eyes a few days ago. I asked the doctors to call you because I found a picture of you in my wallet and thought you might be able to help me figure out who I am. I have amnesia."

I saw the words hit her like a battering ram; her eyes widened and her breath accelerated. It was as if her body seemed to reject the idea, and suddenly everything went blank. She checked out.

"Nurse! Help!" I screamed as I watched Everly's body crumble to the floor.

*　*　*

The look of her soft skin so close to mine was familiar, yet new at the same time.

After the nurse and attendants rushed in and I explained what had happened, they'd quickly lifted her and placed her frail body on the empty bed next to mine. Suddenly my isolation and lack of roommate was paying off. Nurse Amy looked a little wary when I'd made the demand to have her near me, rather than moving her to another room, but quickly complied when she saw the look of distress in my eyes. I wasn't ready to say good-bye to this mysterious woman.

After a quick assessment, Nurse Amy announced breathing was even, her vitals normal—there was nothing wrong with her, other than what she could only guess was an overwhelming amount of stress.

Stress caused by me.

My fingers reached out, wanting to slowly trace over the curve of her shoulder as I memorized the shape of her pouty pink lips and the slight flush of her cheeks.

How could I forget a life with someone like her? It was as if I'd forgotten something as magnificent as the sun rising over the horizon.

Her eyes fluttered open and locked with mine. Suddenly, realization set in and she pushed upright and bolted away, jumping off the bed and putting as much distance between us as possible without actually leaving the room.

"You passed out," I stated, trying to explain the situation as best I could.

"So they left me in here…with you? Alone?" she hissed. Her face was beet red with anger as she glared at me from across the room.

"I thought you'd be more comfortable."

Her gaze narrowed as her arms folded across her face and tightened.

"Look, August, you obviously have the doctors fooled and I can see why—you play dumb well. But I'm not falling for it."

I shook my head in confusion. "I don't understand."

She raised her voice as her hands flew over her head. "Cut the shit! This won't work. I'm not falling for it. If this is some sick way to get even with me for—" Her gaze turned away as her words cut off mid-sentence.

Dragging my fingers through my long hair, I nearly laughed at the irony of this moment. "You think I'm lying?"

"No," she said, wrapping her arms across her chest as a small chuckle escaped her throat. "I *know* you are."

"Amazing," I muttered.

"I've got to go," she said, shaking her head. "I'm not coming back. Don't come for me. Don't try and find me."

I watched in a daze as she marched toward the doorway, her angry footsteps echoing through the silent room as she walked away—forever.

And still I had nothing. Nothing but more questions, more confusion—and even more frustration.

"What did I do to you?" I blurted out, stopping her in her tracks as she reached the door. "What kind of man was I, Everly?"

She spun around, her face filled with shock and raw awe as she took a single step back.

"Are you kidding me right now?"

"No, I genuinely want to know. I was here for two years. Two years and not a single visitor and now you've come and treated me like I'm a viper. I need to know."

"Fine." Her hands clenched by her sides as she briefly closed her eyes. "You want to play this game. Let's play. You want to know what kind of asshole would deserve this kind of animosity? What kind of cold-hearted jerk could be in a hospital for two years and yet no one gave a fuck."

"Yes," I whispered.

She took a few steps closer and answered, "The controlling, manipulative kind. August Kincaid is a monster who takes what he wants out of life, no matter the cost. The only thing that matters to him is money, and greed is his ultimate idol. He's the type of man who keeps his girlfriend imprisoned in their own home for two years because he's so batshit crazy he believes the entire world is out to get him and they'll do anything—including taking her. August Kincaid is jealous, domineering, and—"

"Stop. I've heard enough," I said, holding my hand up. I suddenly felt sick, as every word she'd said settled deep in my chest.

"It's enough," I echoed, feeling like I'd just been gut punched.

My mind reeled as I processed everything she'd just said. I'd imprisoned her? For years?

"Did I ever hurt you? I mean, did I ever physically abuse you?" I asked, turning my face away from her, too ashamed to even look in her direction.

"No," she answered softly. "But I've since learned that abuse comes in many forms."

I nodded, unable to speak.

"You really don't remember, do you?" she asked.

"No," I managed to say, the word harsh against my throat.

"Anything?"

I shook my head, tears stinging my eyes as the reality of my life swept over me. I'd been a horrible, horrible man.

"I think I've had enough visiting for today," I said, still turned away from her.

"Right. Of course. Good-bye, August."

I looked up and her eyes met mine, and I saw her clenched fists loosen. She lifted her hand as if to offer it to me in some way. Maybe a handshake, or a simple touch...She might not have even realized she'd done it, but I did.

I also noticed her hand quiver and shake as she reached for me.

"Good-bye, Everly," I said, ending her trancelike movement toward me.

She stopped, blinking briefly as her face went blank. I didn't watch her walk away, but the door clicked shut seconds later.

I was once again alone.

After learning about the real August Kincaid, I decided that was exactly what I deserved.

Chapter Five

Everly

I should have gone straight home.

Ryan was a worrier and I could see him now, pacing an uneasy path back and forth through our worn carpet as he counted down the hours wondering when I would return home safe and sound.

I'd woken up this morning nervous and agitated, wondering what I was doing and why I'd made such an enormous, stupid decision like this one. I wanted to cave—to dive under the tranquility of my covers and live the rest of my life from the safety of my bed.

It was a legitimate idea; I doubt I was the first female who'd considered it. Beds were safe. Beds were understanding and never neglected you.

Rather than talking me out of the decision I'd made, Ryan had pulled me out of bed, made me French toast and the one thing that always cheered me up.

Coffee. Blessed, wonderful coffee.

As I'd sat down, wondering how I'd managed to find a man as wonderful as him, he'd solidified my faith in him even further.

"You can't back out now," he'd said. "You'll regret it. You'll always wonder what life would have been like if you'd taken this chance. So, even though I hate the thought of you being in the same room as him—go. You'll be better because of it."

I sat there in awed silence, staring up at him, amazed by his supportive nature, until he leaned forward and placed a tender kiss on my lips and reminded me my breakfast was getting cold. I'd quickly slathered my French toast with peanut butter while he made gagging noises and grimaced as I'd poured half a bottle of maple syrup on top of the peanut butter.

"That's seriously disgusting."

"No," I'd corrected him, "It's delicious."

He'd dodged and weaved my attempts to airplane-feed him a bite and instead made himself a plate of "normal" French toast, which consisted of plain butter and syrup. So boring.

We ate in enjoyable silence and got ready side by side. I listened to him hum top-forty songs off-key in the shower.

When it had been time to go, he'd given me a kiss and said he would be here when I got home.

"But you have to work," I'd argued.

"I'll work from home until you get back."

I knew he probably hadn't worked a single productive minute since I'd left for the hospital, which was why I felt incredibly guilty as I went in the opposite direction, toward the coast, rather than taking the freeway home.

The traffic congestion lessened and the houses grew larger as I drove closer to the cliffs. Each street I passed reminded me of the life

I'd once had. The little organic ma
particular kind of juice every week…
The smell of the salty air reminded me
when life had been simple and sweet—befo
crashing down.

I pulled up the driveway and parked. Hidde
of my glove compartment, in a tiny manila envelo
single key—one I'd hidden years ago when I'd walke
this place and my life with August. It had been my respo
take care of our home, to nurture it and keep it flourishin
absence.

Two months after he went into a coma, I handed everything ov
to his attorney with directions on maintenance and financial care, and
walked away.

And yet, here I was. Again.

I should have tossed the stupid key over a cliff years ago.

Standing in front of the house, I felt small and insignificant before
its high walls and grand exterior. The first day he'd brought me here,
I had been blindfolded. There had been a giant red bow wrapped
around the front, just like in a movie. At that moment, I'd been so sure
he was my happy Hollywood ending.

*　　*　　*

"Are you serious?" I squealed as the blindfold fell to the ground and I
got my first glimpse of the colossal house standing before me.

"Very," he answered with a devilish grin.

*"We can't afford this, August. It's too much! Shit," I swore, "I don't
think Oprah could afford this."*

nt, spinning in cir-

d. "I promised
ired."

ve both."

...ndscap-
...nance required of
...r guilty that this magnificent
... because of me. Because of us.

...beautiful as the day I first saw it. The sprawling
... gave way to a beautiful garden and entryway. The color of
the flowers had changed since I'd last been here, but it all still felt
the same. At first glance, you'd never know no one had lived in it
for years. Yet as I grew closer and peered in the windows, I could
see the white sheets scattered throughout the first floor, covering and
protecting the expensive furniture we'd spent months picking out.
The house resembled the Spanish architectural style California was
known for, with rounded windows and doors that reminded me of
field trips to old missions along the El Camino Real, and an ornate
red-tiled roof that gave it character and charm. The multi-million-
dollar view of the Pacific didn't hurt, either. That view was what
made this area of the city so sought after. The waves crashed below
as the sun set over the crystal blue water. Each and every day. It had
been a life most people only dreamed of living, and one I'd run away
from long ago.

My hand shook as I held the key up to the lock in the large wooden door, and as its first tooth locked into place, I stopped and took a hesitant step back. The key fell from my fingers, clattering onto the stoop, and I fled, my heart pounding in spades. Quickly unlatching the gate to the backyard, I ran. I ran until my lungs burned and my cheeks reddened from the gusts of wind rushing over the jagged cliffs. The house faded into the background as I stood there and let the roar of the ocean drown out my thoughts and memories, pushing back the sobs that were threatening to force their way out.

I would not cry over this man.

Not again—not ever again.

And I would not allow his presence to ruin my life.

*   *   *

"This weeks of not seeing each other thing? It has to stop—you're my best friend and I feel like I barely know you. It's been ages…ages, woman! So, come on with the details. Tell me, how are you?" Sarah asked, her words all strung together like the chaotic strand of pearls she wore wrapped around her neck. Every color imaginable, without rhyme or reason. That was Sarah. A hurricane wrapped in pink ballet tights.

We settled into the cozy corner booth at the local coffee shop I'd been working at for the past two years. I unwrapped my apron, which resembled a large burlap sack, and sank into the cushions a few more inches. My feet hurt from standing all day and sitting felt like the most amazing luxury in the world.

"It hasn't been ages. Stop being so damned dramatic. And I'm fine," I said, waving her off as I stretched my aching back.

Her critical brown eyes searched mine. "If I had a dollar for every time you said the word 'fine,'" she said, raising her eyebrow in challenge. I ran my tired hands down the front of my plain white shirt, a stark contrast to the vibrant flowery dress she was wearing. Sarah's personal taste was a tad diverse. Having formerly been a perfect ballerina the majority of her life, dressing in whatever she was told to wear from frilly tutus to sparkling tiaras, she now tended to steer clear of anything that had crinoline or lace and hovered closer to the outlandish.

"I know. Tabitha would have my head if she heard it, too. She hates the word 'fine.' She says people use it far too often and it generally means the opposite of what it's used for."

Sarah placed her strong arms on the table and bent forward, her lean muscles bulging from years of training.

"So, is that what you're doing then? Saying you are fine when you're actually not?"

"No. Yes. Maybe," I said all at once, hating that she saw underneath all my protective icy layers. It was impossible to lie to her. I don't know why I tried.

"That's better." She grinned. "Confusion is at least an emotion."

I shook my head as my coworker Trudy brought over our coffee and I checked my watch. I still had most of my break left. Trudy gave me a quick wink before running back behind the counter, her way of telling me to take my time. She didn't know how badly I suddenly wanted to get back to work.

Talking about my feelings seemed to be the highlight of everyone's life lately. Except mine.

"I know you don't have much time, so start talking. I want to know everything."

"Everything? Starting where?" I asked, trying to appear cool and levelheaded. Because I was definitely anything but.

"The beginning," she said, stirring a packet of zero calorie sweetener in her plain black coffee, but adding nothing else. She'd come far since her purging days, but she still watched every calorie she put into her body and probably would until the day she died.

Some habits were hard to shake.

Much like my past—it just sat there, over my shoulder, reminding me of my failures and regrets. Knowing it would always be there if I let it, I took a deep breath and decided to tell her about the phone call and Tabitha's words of advice.

"She was right, you know," Sarah said between sips. "It might help you move on."

"Let me finish," I said. "This is the part I left out from our phone conversations. I guess I was still coming to terms with it myself."

Her face fell as worry took over.

"He wants you back."

"No." I shook my head. "Or at least I don't think so. I already went to the hospital."

"And you're just telling me now?" Her voice rose and then fell again as she looked over her shoulder, suddenly remembering where we were.

"What happened? What does he look like—I bet the fuckwit isn't nearly as threatening with his ass hanging out the back of his robe!"

"Sarah! Would you focus for just one second and listen! He doesn't remember me. He came out of that coma and doesn't remember a damn thing."

Her expression remained neutral as she slowly stirred a wooden stick around the edge of her mug. The silence started slowly driving me insane. Sarah was never quiet and hardly ever kept her opinions to herself for long. As the wooden stick went round and round, I began to regret even mentioning August's condition.

Of course she would have seen through that, too.

"He's lying," she stated, knowing just what kind of man August Kincaid was—or had been. She may not have known me when I was with him, but she'd been there for the aftermath. Tabitha and Sarah and been there for me when I picked up every single scattered piece of my life, but unlike Tabitha, there was still much I hadn't shared with Sarah.

She had enough burdens without being weighed down with all of mine.

"I thought so, too, but then he asked me what kind of man he'd been in his past life to deserve such treatment."

A snort escaped Sarah's lips as she shook her head.

"So I told him exactly the type of man he was."

"And?" she asked.

"It was like watching a mountain crumble. As his face fell, I saw the life drain from it as well. That wasn't something that could be faked, Sarah. The old August isn't there anymore, or at least not right now."

She studied me for a moment or two, trying to gauge my expression before replying. "Could he come back? Will the memories return?"

"I don't know," I answered honestly. It was something I'd been thinking about a lot lately, as I lay in bed, too restless to sleep, too tired to get up. What if that monster did return one day? What happened then?

"Wow, Ev, I don't know what to say. How is Ryan handling it all?"

she asked as her warm gaze met mine. She leaned forward to take my hand.

Looking down at our joined fingers, I smiled, grateful to have Sarah in my life. She always brought me out of my tortoiselike shell. "Like he always does—in stride. First he was shaken a bit by the news, and then he went into defense mode, figuring out the best way to keep us secure. You know how logical he gets in situations like this."

"And what did he come up with?" she inquired.

"He said we should just keep the status quo. Go about our lives like usual—ignore August. And if the time comes that it becomes a problem, we'll deal with it."

Her eyes met mine and as usual, I know she saw more than most.

"And what do you think? Do you believe in the status quo?"

As much as it pained me to admit it, I shook my head.

"No," I answered honestly. "Not with August back in our lives."

*   *   *

I saw him again.

This time he was bending down to tie his shoe. His short brown hair fluttered in the salty sea breeze and my lungs began to burn and soon I was gasping for air. No, it wasn't him, couldn't be him. The build of his body was all wrong, the shape of his nose was different—and yet I faltered, all because of a stupid pair of shoes. Shiny, black—expensive. Exactly the type August would have preferred.

There once was a time when he hadn't cared about the type of shoe that covered his feet. Shoes, clothes...none of it had mattered. Back when things had been simpler—easier.

Happier.

The man who wasn't him turned slightly, his face catching the light from the sun high above us as he rose, the untied laces now fixed, and went on his way down the street while I still stood unmoving, cemented to the ground.

Lost in a memory.

*   *   *

"How is he today?" I asked the maid as she quietly shifted around the room, trying not to disturb me as she set the morning tray beside the bed.

Her troubled eyes met mine and I knew instantly that it was another bad day. There had been a string of bad days that bled into weeks now. There had once been a time when he would confide in me—ask me for advice when it came to his life, no matter what the cause. We had been a team—a strong partnership.

Now he just disappeared into that damned office of his and paced. Paced the floor like a man awaiting the gates of Hell. For all I knew, maybe he was. With Trent by his side, he very well could have done a deal with the devil himself. August swore Trent was a great guy and an even better partner, but I had my reservations. Trent seemed like a snake, waiting for his moment to strike.

"He's in a mood, Miss—I won't lie. I heard him on the phone earlier this morning shouting. It didn't sound good."

I nodded and thanked her before she stepped out. This had been our routine for the last several days. A phone call, a visit, an early morning meeting—there was always something.

Maybe hiding out in my room wasn't the answer anymore. Perhaps I just needed to be there for him—like I once was.

Feeling invigorated for the first time in a while, I jumped out of bed and quickly dressed, leaving the tray of food completely untouched. I applied a small amount of makeup, pinned my hair back, and spritzed on a little of the vanilla perfume I knew August liked. Feeling eager, I raced out in search of him, my mood lifting high and light in anticipation of our morning reunion.

As expected, I found him downstairs, tucked away in that dark office he loved so much. What I didn't expect to find was August surrounded by a crowd of people. They were buzzing back and forth between racks of designer clothing, dodging between each other as they grabbed jackets and pants, one after another, each trying to best the other in their display of overpriced fabric.

No doubt there would be a hefty tip for whoever pleased him the most. I resisted the urge to roll my eyes as one of them fluttered past me, the sharp smell of expensive cologne in their wake.

August caught my gaze in the reflection of the mirror as he adjusted a plum-colored tie tightly around his throat. The jewel tone went nicely with his hazel green irises, bringing out the slight variation of color that sometimes went unnoticed by others.

Not by me, though.

I saw everything. All of him. I had since the very beginning.

His smile lit up the room when he saw me standing by the door, and in that moment I felt my belly alight with fire and an anxiety I hadn't felt in a long time. It felt good. And right.

"You look happy this morning," I said, stepping forward to stand behind him, watching his reflection in the mirror.

"I am," he replied. "Had a bit of a rough start, but that's all behind us now." He turned around, a glimmer of excitement in his eyes as his hands reached for my waist.

"Anything I can help with?" I asked as his warm fingers dug into my skin.

"No, just a misunderstanding. Nothing you need to worry about. Besides, there's something I wanted to tell you. We've been invited to the Hope Gala next weekend."

My nose wrinkled in disappointment. "I thought those types of things weren't really based on invite but rather on donation." I quickly skimmed the room, seeing rows and rows of what appeared to be the same stuffy, boring pants and jackets over and over. Out of the corner of my eye, I caught a glimmer, but my gaze was quickly brought back to August as he tugged on my chin.

"Oh, it is. And a hefty donation was made in our names." He grinned. "But even though they say it's for charity, they're still pretty stingy on who they let through the door at one of these events. And I've been trying to get us in for weeks."

"Why?" I asked, trying to remain positive. He seemed happy for the first time in weeks. I should be, too.

"Why?" he repeated, as if the answer were plainly written across his flawless face. "Why? Because, Everly. We're one of them now. It's only fitting they know it. Having this house, wearing the clothes, and living the lifestyle isn't enough. I want them to know who we are."

The lighthearted mood I'd had when I'd entered his study finally fell to the floor. I'd hoped I would be the one to light his spirits and wash away his troubles, but someone had already beaten me to the punch.

Or something.

The one thing that had managed to weasel its way into our life without ever making a sound. It was sneakier than a mistress and more addictive than the priciest cocaine.

Money.

It was the one thing August worshiped now. Above God, and family.

And me.

Nothing brought him out of the darkness more than a new suit or a fancy pair of shoes. As I watched him turn back around, the attendants flocked back to him to show him everything they'd brought. His happy eyes met mine and he waved me toward the corner, where my stash was.

The glitz I'd seen out of the corner of my eye.

"Try something on, babe. Try it all on. Hell, take it all!" He laughed as he bent down to tie a pair of shoes that matched the jacket he'd just pulled on.

"Perfect," he said, standing tall and broad in front of the mirror. "Just perfect."

As I sulked back into the corner, my fingers skimming the fabric of the priceless designer gowns, I felt like the life we'd built together had become something less than perfect.

It was broken.

So very broken.

* * *

I blinked once, twice as Ryan's familiar voice pushed through the haze. Traffic noise rung in my ears as the bright afternoon sun warmed my chilly cheeks.

"You ready to go?" he asked as he stepped out of the sporting goods store he'd been rummaging through. Looking around, I slowly returned to the present, the salty sea air reminding me of where I was and everything I'd accomplished and left behind since that moment I'd realized I'd been replaced in August's gilded world.

Blinking back into reality, I quickly looked down the street. The man with the fancy shoes was gone, a ghost of the past, much like the memory I'd allowed to take over just now.

Turning back to the gentle man before me, I smiled, snaking my arm through his as we stepped onto the street to continue our lazy stroll down the wharf.

"Ready," I answered, resting my head on his shoulder.

Ready for what, I wasn't certain. But I had a feeling that our idea of keeping the status quo was about to be obliterated.

Chapter Six

August

The next couple of weeks in the hospital became a whirlwind of activity as the doctors and nurses prepared for my release. Everything revolved around making sure I was healthy enough, both mentally and physically, to assimilate back into the real world.

No one knew when or even if my memories would ever resurface, but everyone agreed—there was no point in waiting.

Life had to go on—with or without them.

I was placed in physical therapy, counseling, and psychotherapy. The toll my body had taken from being practically listless for two years was staggering, and although my caregivers had done everything in their power to prevent as much atrophy and deterioration as possible, it had occurred anyway.

From the few pictures I'd found of myself scattered among my personal belongings, I knew I barely resembled the man I once was. Where broad shoulders had given way to tight lean muscles now only pale skin remained. My hair had grown out, unruly and disorderly, as if each little hair was rebelling against the well-manicured man who used to occupy this body.

In between sessions intended to help me relearn how to move my weary limbs, I was shoved into counseling sessions where I spent hours having my mental health assessed.

I silently wondered if my hatred for psychiatrists was new or old.

I was given homework by the crazy loon the hospital assigned to me. Like a damned child. After each session, I was sent back to my room with a loaner laptop to research the time I'd spent away from the world, as he called it. Dr. Schneider—or as I liked to call him, Dr. HappyFeelGood—wanted me to adjust, first to the outside world, and then when I was released we could work on reacquainting me with, well…me.

So after another brutal session with Dr. HappyFeelGood, I lay back in my hospital bed, my eyes searching out the city below, wondering what life outside might be like now.

It'd only been two years. Two fucking years.

It seemed insignificant and insurmountable at the same time.

It wasn't like I was one of those coma patients who awoke after decades and found the entire world completely altered—family and friends dead or aged beyond recognition—with an entire lifetime of history behind them.

Two years really wasn't that long—a couple of iPhone upgrades. Maybe a few missed holidays. But for someone who'd been asleep for those twenty-four months, I wondered just how much I'd missed. My fingers itched to turn on the television, to binge watch the news and late night TV. But I had been instructed not to do so.

"Only research the time you lost for now," the doctor had instructed.

Why? I had no idea. Probably to keep my weak, fragile brain from overloading. The way everyone tiptoed around me in here, that seemed a real possibility. Like I was a recently found nuclear bomb no one knew how to defuse. The nurses and doctors all spoke in hushed tones when they entered my room, as if anything louder than a whisper might set me off into some deranged fit. Hell, even the woman who brought in my food looked fearful of me.

Was I that much of a freak?

Didn't people wake up from comas all the time?

I guess not.

I knew I was a rarity. I understood the situation was unique and they were treading in uncharted territory when it came to treating me, but it still hurt.

The loneliness. My solitary life.

I was a man brought back from the brink of death to what? Usually you read these amazing stories of coma patients waking up to be reunited with their families...wives and loved ones.

I had no one.

Nothing but a box of memories I didn't understand.

I pulled closer the ancient laptop the hospital psychologist had loaned me and rested it on my lap. Booting it up, I tapped on the Internet icon and waited for it to load. Staring at the blank screen, I tried to decide what to search—knowing full well my session would be monitored later.

Sneaky doctor.

"Major events in 2013," I started with, feeling good with my decision. Might as well go with the headlines first.

Thirty seconds later, I regretted my decision and made a mental note to never watch the news again. Boston Marathon bombing, typhoon in the Philippines...the U.S. government shutting down. Hell, couldn't anything good headline the news every once in a while?

I scrolled down and saw the Pope had resigned. I found myself chuckling.

Couldn't really blame him.

I couldn't continue. For once, I realized Dr. HappyFeelGood might actually know what he was talking about. That simple search solidified so much for me.

Life really had gone on without me.

People had been born, died...fought for our country, all while I lay helpless in this bed.

And here I was, still so incredibly helpless.

How did I get it back?

I wanted it all back.

* * *

Several days later, I found myself back on the other side of the hospital, in the familiar office of Dr. Schneider. From the floor-to-ceiling wooden bookshelves to the impressive Tiffany style lamps, I could tell the happy doctor was a lover of the classics. Even the couch he offered me was like something right out of a Sigmund Freud museum.

"Did you use the laptop?" he asked, fully aware that I hadn't. After my initial perusal on the Internet, I'd decided the past was better left there. I couldn't handle any more bad news.

"No," I answered casually.

It'd been less than a week since I'd last seen him and I think, based on the way his forehead creased together and the annoying way he tapped his pen against his notepad, he didn't believe I was making enough headway in my recovery.

Of course, as he put it, every brain injury was unique, so how he could definitively decide what was normal or "enough" in this case was beyond me.

But then again, I was just the patient.

He was the guy sitting in the fancy leather wingbacked chair, in an office littered with diplomas and plaques all singing his praises and educational accolades. He obviously should know better.

I sat back with my arms folded tightly across my chest, an unconscious response to my personal distaste for being here. I was frustrated to my very core—with the man sitting across from me. With this hospital.

With myself.

If I'd been given an option, shown what life would be like minutes before my eyes fluttered open in that hospital room weeks earlier, I'm not sure I would have chosen to wake up.

Who would choose this life?

"You seem more agitated today," Dr. Schneider commented, writing something down on his notepad, before lifting his foot up to rest on his opposite knee.

I stared at the yellow pad of paper for a moment, the dark black chicken scratch of his writing illegible from where I was sitting.

Did all doctors have messy handwriting?

I shook my head, trying to clear the cobwebs.

"Just frustrated…"

More scribbling.

"I noticed you didn't utilize the laptop much." He looked up, waiting for a response.

"I didn't really see a point."

His face scrunched together in that way that told me he was displeased, or maybe even a little disappointed. Perhaps this was what a child felt like when calling out answers in a classroom, over and over—watching the teacher shake his or her head, let down by the failure of her pupils.

I had no memories of my childhood, so I wouldn't know.

Maybe I had been one of those kids—the defiant ones who never gave the right answer, unwilling to conform to the norm. Or had the guy with the perfect hair and blank stare been an exemplary student—scared to step a foot out of order?

Perhaps a mixture of both?

What if I never found out?

"What are you thinking about?" Dr. Schneider interrupted my thoughts, sending my gaze upward. I met his pointed look as I tried to decide which type of pupil I wanted to be in that moment.

Teacher's pet or non-conformist.

"What if I never get the memories back?" I finally asked, ditching the idea of games in search of answers.

"It is possible they may never return, August. That is a reality you must face."

For once, I appreciated his honesty.

"How will I know what kind of man to be?"

"Does it matter?" he asked, before adding, "You have a gift, August. I know you don't see it that way, but you have to find the silver lining in your situation. Not many people are given a second chance in life—a do-over, if you will. That is exactly what you have. If you aren't liking the type of man you are discovering you were before—become someone else. Do whatever you wish. Find new talents, discover new ambitions. Live, August."

I wasn't quite certain I agreed with him, as I remembered the haunting pain of Everly looking back at me that day in the hospital. I had a feeling the shadow of the man I once was would follow me no matter where I went.

But as I sat there, I knew there was only one way out of this place, and that was through Dr. Schneider.

So it was time to start playing it his way.

"How do I start?" I asked with an encouraging smile.

He looked down at the laptop I'd brought back, and I knew I had my work cut out for me.

No more sullen attitudes or gloomy meetings. From now on, it was nothing but hope, rainbows, and sunshine springing forth from this mouth. I was getting out of this place, and once I did—I was going to figure out just who the hell August Kincaid was.

Chapter Seven

Everly

Since when had coffee become so damn complicated?

Granted, this frothy, overly complicated beverage was currently keeping me employed, but as I hollered back orders to my fellow coworkers...I failed to understand why someone would screw up a perfectly good drink with caramel and soy milk when it was like heaven on earth all by itself.

The line of eager caffeine addicts currently cleared the door, as each person stared at our unfamiliar menu. I suspected they were each nervously comparing it to the big box chains they knew and loved, secretly wondering if that two-block walk down the street was suddenly worth it.

We mostly catered to the locals, but being close to several hotels the cute little family-owned coffee shop I'd been working at for the past two years tended to get a rush of business professionals and tourists early in the morning as they rushed off to start their individual days.

I knew Ryan wasn't pleased with my career choice, but I enjoyed working here.

The tourists could get a little intense, but I had my regulars and a lifetime supply of coffee. What wasn't there to love? And I genuinely enjoyed my coworkers' company. They were eclectic and wild, something I was used to growing up in foster homes.

My life hadn't exactly resembled a *Leave It to Beaver* episode.

"Nonfat mocha latte with extra whip!" I shouted back to Simon, who continued to slow jam to the quiet jazz playing over the sound system. His rhythm was completely off, telling me he was actually dancing to his own tune—probably something he was working out for his reggae band in his head.

The only acknowledgment I got for my shout-out was a slight raise of his eyebrow as he continued to work the machines, dancing backing and forth between them like he was seducing a woman rather than working at a frantic coffee house.

But everything came out quick, on time, and correct. I had no idea how he did it, especially considering the amount of medicinal marijuana that had to be running through his system, for a recurring migraine he never seemed to have. When I asked him about it, he just smiled and said, "Well, it must be working," as he moved on to the next coffee order.

I continued to work our morning rush, saying hi to our many loyal customers. Trudy, another coworker on shift that morning, worked pastries, warming and toasting everything as I took orders and Simon brewed. I backed him up when things got tight.

It was a well-oiled machine and we all worked well together.

Why would I want to leave?

We worked tirelessly until the morning rush passed, thoroughly earning our mid-morning lull. As Simon cleaned the espresso machine and restocked milk, I roamed through the café, emptying garbage and checking the creamer situation up front.

Trudy peeked up from the pastry case, a brownie in hand.

"Hey, feel like splitting?"

"You know we're not supposed to take from the case in the middle of the day," I reminded her, folding my hands across my chest.

"I know, but this one might have fallen on the ground," she said, scooping some peanut butter frosting off the corner with her index finger. I watched in fascination as she dipped it in her mouth.

That bitch knew peanut butter and chocolate were my ultimate weaknesses.

"You're putting something that was on the floor in your mouth?" I asked, refusing to budge. Even for a brownie.

A really gooey, yummy brownie.

"No, but when I report to Sherry at the end of our shift, it will have fallen to its death on the floor. Very sad." Her lips formed a little pout as she dangled it in front of me, the last shred of restraint melting as I caved.

"Okay, fine," I answered, looking around the vacant store, "but I want coffee to go with it."

"Deal!" she exclaimed.

Knowing I didn't go for anything fancy, she poured us two freshly brewed cups of coffee and I watched her carefully split the brownie down the center with a knife.

"Yours looks slightly bigger," I complained.

"It does not!"

"Does too," I fought back with a slight smirk.

"Oh stop, and get back to work. I gave you chocolate, and coffee—you should be happy."

Kissing her smooth cheek, I grinned. "Thank you, Trudy. This makes my day."

The three of us finished up our little odds and ends chores, and I helped the few stragglers that managed to find their way in. The late bloomers, I called them: the tourists that moved to the beat of their own drum—setting their own pace as they relaxed their way through vacation—or the shift workers who kept odd hours and needed a pick-me-up or a relaxing cup of tea to help end their day while others were just starting out.

I liked these people. They moved slower. Life always seemed to be a bit calmer for the late bloomers. That's exactly how I wanted my life to be.

Calm. Carefree.

Simple.

Looking down at my engagement ring with its small cluster of diamonds surrounding a glittering center stone, I knew I'd have that with Ryan.

He was my anchor.

We quickly made it through our midday rush, which wasn't as hectic as the morning's but still quite busy. We had a partnership with a deli downtown. They delivered gourmet sandwiches and salads to our door every morning, so even though we didn't have the equipment to prepare food on our own, we were able to serve lunch to the merchants and businessmen stopping by.

It earned extra revenue for the shop and kept us all gainfully employed.

Win, win.

As I was finishing with my last customer, and dreaming of diving into a large bowl of split pea soup from my favorite bread store down the street, I saw him.

Only it wasn't a vision or a dream…or even a ghost this time.

It was really him.

Walking into my place of business.

Dressed in a loose-fitting T-shirt and designer jeans I recognized from years ago, he appeared disoriented, sweaty, and tired as he stepped through the doorway. So different from the many visions I'd had of him over the years, and yet I still froze like a statue.

I couldn't breathe. I tried, taking quick sips of air through my lips and swallowing them in an attempt to force the air down, but it just felt like gravel against my throat.

He couldn't be here. Not here with my coworkers, who had no idea of the life I'd once had. Snapping back into reality, I moved. Pure survival instinct flowed through my veins now. I needed him away from here—out of my life.

"I'm taking my lunch!" I hollered, grabbing my purse from under the cash register as I stepped forward, taking a ragged breath that seared a fiery path down my windpipe.

"What are you doing here?" I said through gritted teeth.

His eyes met mine and a brief moment of shock mixed with surprise moved through his features.

"Everly?" he said, an acknowledgment that almost seemed a confirmation.

"Yes, who else would it be?" I answered with annoyance, grabbing his arm. I tugged him out of the building.

I glanced back and tried not to notice the way his eyes could look straight into me, like he had a direct line to my soul. It unnerved me—still.

He seemed unaware of his effect on me as his gaze darted from me to the street and back toward the building. I let go of his arm, not wishing to hold on to any part of him for longer than necessary, and watched as he pushed his hands into his jeans pockets.

He was thinner than before, the jeans hanging looser on his body than they once had. But he was still August...still formidable and...

Look away, Everly. Look away.

"Is that where you work?" he asked, motioning toward the tan apron I still wore. I looked down and huffed, mad that he'd made me rush out and miss out on my date with my soup.

"Yes," I answered, undoing the ties and neatly folding it into my purse. "Isn't that why you're here?" I folded my arms across my chest, a clear indication of my less-than-hospitable attitude.

His hands flew up in a defensive gesture.

"No, god no. I'm sorry. This...shit. I'm sorry. I'll go. I didn't mean to." A frustrated huff flew from his lips as his hand ran through his messy hair. One last glance and he turned.

"August," I called out, hating myself for getting involved. I was an idiot.

A moron and a schmuck.

No doubt, this was exactly what he was hoping for, and I was falling for his scheme beautifully. But as it had always been with all things August-related, I just couldn't stop myself. "What are you doing here?"

He stopped and I watched his shoulders fall in defeat as he pivoted back in my direction.

"I'm lost," he simply stated.

"What?"

"I decided to go for a walk, you know, to clear my head, and before I knew it one block started looking like another and I couldn't remember my address, and suddenly I was going in circles." He let out a frustrated breath. "I've been walking all morning."

"Are you serious?" I asked.

He just stared.

"But your house is at least five miles from here," I stated.

"You know where I live?" he asked, before he remembered our earlier conversation. "Oh, right."

Part of me—the untrusting cynical side that still remembered the August who'd locked me in the house when he went to work during the day—doubted his sincerity.

That part of me really wanted to believe that this was an elaborate hoax he'd concocted to get me back.

Because the other part of me—the trusting, loving side—knew I was in big trouble with a brand new August in my life.

*   *   *

"You really don't have to do this," he said again as I clicked the "unlock" button on my little blue Kia sedan.

"I know," I grumbled, hating myself already for deciding to drive him home. "Get in."

I'd blame it on my good upbringing, but that certainly wasn't it. God knows the host of foster parents I'd had over the years hadn't taught me many values besides *eat everything in front of you as fast as you can* and the art of learning to re-wear clothes several days in a row without anyone noticing.

Maybe it was something hardwired into my DNA—the same reason I wanted to save every kitten and stray dog that I saw wandering down the road, or why I felt the need to give every spare dime I had to the old man on our street corner even though he reeked of alcohol.

Whatever it was, here I was—driving down the road toward the cliffs.

In a car with a man I loathed.

Ryan would kill me if he knew what I was doing. This definitely did not fit in with our status quo plan. It didn't fit with any logical plan—at all. Yet, here I was, driving my psycho ex who had just been discharged from the hospital after waking up from a coma that no one had ever thought he'd recover from.

And that's when it hit me. He might never remember anything. Not a single kiss, a happy sigh, or a night spent in bed. The good, the bad—it was all gone.

Guilt hit me square in the gut as we drove, and my fingers loosened slightly as I tried to relax and calm myself.

Status quo, I reminded myself.

Looking over at him, I tried to feel sorry for him. I tried to feel remorse.

But all I saw was the man who'd locked me up.

And here are the days of our lives, folks.

Yeah, so much for simple and carefree. My life was totally fucked up.

My palms suddenly grew sweaty as we turned down the block, closer to the ocean. A salty mist blew through the winter air, reminding me of lazy evenings spent eating dinner out on the spacious patio, where the view seemed to go on for miles. Long ago, I'd thought we'd raise our children in that house.

I'd thought a lot of hopeless things back then.

Turning into the driveway that was no longer mine, I put the car in park, not bothering to kill the engine.

"Well, here you are," I said, averting his gaze. I couldn't look at him. Not here. Not with the flood of memories that were threatening to assail me.

"Thanks," he answered, moving toward the door. He paused

briefly as if he had something more he wanted to say, but then seemed to decide against it and stepped out. The door shut and I felt air rush back into the small compact space.

I took one huge gulp, then another—willing myself not to cry.

August Kincaid would not make me cry.

He was awake, but he would not rule my life.

Not ever again.

When I looked up, my gaze settled on the glove compartment—the place where I hid the key to my past. The key to this place.

What had been a mere duty I'd carried on in his absence now felt dirty and shameful.

The key was my last physical connection to him…to this place. I needed to get rid of it. Now.

I ripped open the glove compartment, pulling out manuals and registrations for years back.

Wow, I needed to clean this thing out.

Finally I found it, in the very back where I had shoved it the last time I'd visited—when he'd first awakened. Feeling resolved and settled, I jumped out of the car and stomped toward the front door, intent on my decision.

He opened the door even before I had the chance to pound on it.

That was a little disappointing—I had some pent-up frustration to let out.

"Sorry, I was watching from the window. I wanted to make sure you got out of the driveway safely. It's steep," he said lamely.

I rolled my eyes and let out a frustrated sigh. "You forget I used to live here."

"Right," he answered, rubbing the back of his neck nervously. Stepping back, he motioned for me to enter, which I hadn't planned on. Hell, it was the last thing I wanted to do, but before I had the chance to decline he was gone—disappearing around the corner toward the living room.

"What the—" I huffed as I quickly followed him. Had he forgotten manners during his two-year slumber as well?

"Listen, I'm not here to hang out. Believe me—that's the last thing I want to do with you. I just wanted to give you my key."

As I rounded the corner to catch up with him, I nearly gasped. What had once been a warm, beautiful room was now full of dusty boxes, old papers, and god knew what else.

"Your key?" he asked, turning around, his gaze searching the piles as if he were looking for something specific.

What exactly, I wasn't sure.

"What is this?" I asked.

"Oh, um—everything I could find in the attic. I brought it all down, hoping I could make sense of…well, anything."

I stepped forward, picking up a sheaf of pages from the top of a stack. It was an old term paper from his days at Stanford. I held back the smile that wanted to break through, remembering what a brainiac he used to be.

He wasn't that August anymore. He wasn't anything anymore.

And I needed to get out of this situation.

"Well, I wish you good luck with that," I said politely, placing the key on the stack of papers. "This was my key to the house. I had it while you were—absent—just in case, but now that you're back, well—there's obviously no need. So I'm returning it to you. Also, if you could remove me as your power of attorney, now that you're able—I would appreciate it."

His eyes met mine—those intense hazel eyes I'd fallen in love with at the tender age of eighteen, when life was easy and monsters were things of legend.

"Good luck, August," I said softly, before he had the chance to respond.

It had turned out monsters came in all shapes and sizes—and right now, I needed to remember that.

*   *   *

Starting work in the wee hours of the morning had very few perks, aside from super fresh coffee, clear streets, and free afternoons.

Today, I was thankful for one of those in particular as I clocked out at three and headed home.

I had two hours to figure out what I was going to say to Ryan.

Two hours to formulate my story about how my encounter with August wasn't a big deal.

My fingers tapped nervously on the steering wheel as I waited for the stoplight to turn green. As I turned into the Whole Foods around the corner from our apartment, I knew Ryan wouldn't agree.

To him, this would be a huge deal. Which was why I shouldn't tell him.

It would be so simple—easy. And after all, wasn't easy what I wanted?

Placing the car in park, I took a deep breath as my head slumped forward.

It would be easy—so easy to just omit the entire event. He would never have to know.

But how many relationships were built on tiny white lies? How many heroines had I read about, watched on TV—screamed at for making the same mistake?

No matter how small, lying is still just that—lying. And secrets have a way of revealing themselves over time.

Ryan was the man I'd chosen to spend the rest of my life with. He was good, decent, and kind. The exact opposite of August and everything I'd left behind. I would not let the echoes of my past pollute the possibilities of my future.

Taking a firm step forward, I got out of the car and began carefully planning out my night.

* * *

I was just putting the finishing touches on the table when Ryan walked in, causing me to nearly jump out of my skin.

Calm down, Everly, I silently chanted, turning to face him.

The look on his face was priceless as he wordlessly stared down at the candlelight and then back up at me. It was that scared, fearful look guys get when they see the house is set a certain way, and suddenly their minds start flashing through dates and memories as they try to remember if something significant happened on this particular day.

"Relax, you didn't forget anything," I assured him, an amused smile pulling at my lips as my pulse slowly returned to normal.

His eyes wandered up and down my body shamelessly. "Are you sure? Because I can't remember the last time I saw you pulling a casserole out of the oven, dressed like that."

I guess I had gone a little overboard. Guilt will do that to a girl. But I just wanted him to know how much I loved him and when I got stressed, I tended to act out in odd ways. Particularly in ways that involved food.

"No—no anniversaries. No special celebrations. I just thought it would be nice to have an evening together. We always eat in a rush, gathered around the TV. Isn't this better?"

The coppery flecks of his eyes caught under the lights, turning a dazzling gold as he walked toward me. A casual smile tugged at his face.

"Yes. Very nice." Placing a slow, soft kiss upon my lips, he lingered, grabbing me around my waist to pull me closer. I could smell the familiar scent of his aftershave mixing with the fruity scent of my own shampoo. He'd run out of his own brand, so he'd been using mine for the last few days. The thought made me smile as I rested my head on his shoulder, loving the fact that I had someone to share my shampoo with.

"Now, what can I do to help?" he asked, stepping back to admire me one more time. I hadn't really done much to my appearance—just a little more makeup than I usually wore and a nice pair of jeans that hugged all the right areas. I appreciated the attention, though.

"Nothing, really—oh, maybe pour the wine?" I suggested, pointing to the bottle I'd just uncorked.

"How was your day?" I asked, hoping he'd have some stories worthy of discussion—lengthy discussion. Although I did want to tell him about my day, I didn't want to do it right away.

Maybe after he's had a glass of wine…and a bite of pasta. That might make things better, right?

Cheese and wine always put me in a better mood.

"It was good—okay, I guess."

I laughed at his muddled response. "Can't quite decide yet, huh?"

I asked as I watched him finish pouring the merlot. He set the bottle back down on our small dining table and turned back around, leaning against a chair.

"Just frustrating, I guess. This new client I have. They're—"

"Frustrating?" I guessed with a smirk, as I finished stirring veggies that were sautéing over the stove.

"Yes. One minute they want one thing. The next minute they want something else. And then they decide they don't like something but they're not sure why."

Ryan was a graphic designer—a pretty good one, and he worked with one of the top website companies in the area. He was used to picky clients.

"And they're different from your last client how?" I questioned.

"I guess I'm just tired," he sighed. "Ready for a vacation."

"You mean a honeymoon?" I corrected him with a grin. He stepped forward and slid his hands around my waist again, resting his chin on my shoulder.

"Yeah, that would be nice. Any thoughts on my ideas for that?"

Reaching forward to shut off the burner, he stepped back and allowed me to plate everything.

"Paris? It's just so much, Ryan. Can we even afford that?"

"Ev, I've been a bachelor for a long time. Which means, I've basically had myself to care for. I don't know if you've noticed but I'm not exactly high maintenance."

I snorted, remembering the hint of raspberry shampoo wafting from his hair. No, definitely not high maintenance.

"With my job, I've managed to save up quite a lot over the years. I don't want to go crazy, but let me do this for us. We only have one honeymoon."

Turning to face him, I couldn't help but smile. He brought that out in me—simply by being him. From the moment I'd met him, he'd always managed to bring out the best in me.

"Okay, but only on one condition," I said. "I want to pay for half from my savings."

His mouth opened to protest, but I stopped him, holding up my hand to silence him.

"My choice," I pressed. "You already take care of more than your share of the rent. Let me do this."

"Fine," he grumbled, obviously hating the idea, but a small smile escaped from his lips before he pivoted back toward the table. "But soon, it's not going to be yours or mine...it's just going to be ours. That's what this whole marriage thing is about."

"Oh yeah?" I teased. "Is that what I got myself into?"

I pulled the few remaining items out of the oven and headed toward the table. When I'd arrived at the grocery store earlier, I had no menu planned and little to go on but the guilt eating at my gut, so I'd decided to stick with what I knew best. Looking at the table as I set everything down, I wondered if I should have planned better.

"It looks great, babe," Ryan said, taking his usual seat by the window. We didn't sit here often, but when we did, we tended to migrate toward the same two chairs. Mine was closer to the kitchen since I liked to flutter between the two areas for forgotten items like butter and extra knives.

"Are you sure?" I asked. "It looks kind of strange." I was always my worst critic when it came to cooking.

"Are you kidding? This is every man's fantasy. Meat loaf, mac and cheese—hell, even the veggies are floating in butter. It's great."

"I guess I was in the mood for some comfort food." I shrugged, scooping mac and cheese onto his plate. He helped himself to the meat loaf and we dug in. Thankfully, it was all pretty tasty and Ryan was reaching for seconds within minutes.

All those hours watching Paula Deen and every other Food Network star over the years seemed to have paid off.

"So, are you going to tell me what's going on?" he asked after a third helping of meat loaf. He pushed a piece of a roll around his plate, catching the leftover bits of cheese and meat.

Our eyes met and I knew my ruse was over. Suddenly the idea of shoveling food into my face didn't seem appetizing anymore. No amount of sinful casseroles or dolled-up outfits could cover up the fact that I was hiding something. He knew me too well, and I might as well have stamped it on my forehead—he'd seen it coming a mile away.

I sighed, my head falling forward into my hands.

"Am I that obvious?" I asked.

"Well, the dinner was a little much." He grinned.

"Okay, yeah…you got me there."

Smooth fingers gripped my chin, tilting it upward until I found myself swimming in the warm glow of his gaze.

"What is it, Ev?"

"I saw August today," I answered, feeling each word as I tried to maintain eye contact.

His hand fell, the warmth from his touch dissipating like thin air. He slumped into the seat, as I watched his eyes lose focus.

"Did you"—he paused—"seek him out? Did you want to see him?"

And this was why I should have never told him—why I should have never done any of this. The hurt in his words, the anguish he felt in that very moment cut me to the core. That ultimate trust we'd had—it was gone. I could see the first fragments of doubt in his eyes now.

"No, god no, Ryan," I answered, moving to take his hand in my own. "It was an accident."

He finally looked at me—an encouraging sign—so I decided to continue. "He was lost. He's been released from the hospital, and I guess he decided to take a walk. He wandered into the coffee shop. He wasn't looking for me."

A pained laugh escaped his throat as he shook his head.

"I bet he wasn't," he said quietly, under his breath.

"Ryan, I honestly don't think he was trying anything."

"And what did you do—when he showed up at your door, lost and alone, Everly?" He asked as if he already knew the answer.

"I—I gave him a ride back home."

He smiled, a tortured smile, as he pulled our joined hands close to his lips. I watched in confusion as he kissed each of my knuckles, slowly. Reverently.

"You're too damn nice for your own good. Don't let him get under your skin. Don't forget, Everly. Don't ever forget the person he once was."

I felt him tug gently on my arm and I willingly went to him, just followed him into the bedroom later that night and willingly gave myself to him, promising myself I would do anything to make him forget the pain and distrust he must have felt from the reappearance of August in my life.

I wouldn't let August come between us.

And yet, later that night...as Ryan slept in our bed, I couldn't help but think of August sitting among those boxes, wondering. Always wondering and never knowing. And it gnawed at me.

Until I couldn't stop myself.

I was too damned nice.

Too damned nice and a whole lot of stupid.

Chapter Eight

August

It had been fifteen minutes.

Fifteen of the longest fucking minutes of my life.

Or at least I think it had.

How the hell was I supposed to know? It wasn't like I had a memory of my life to compare it to.

But as I sat there listening to the latest shrink's sound machine, as he tried to lull me into a sense of security with the fake sounds of ocean waves and birdcalls, it surely felt like the longest damn time ever in that room.

Was he ever going to talk?

I continued to look around the small but tidy room, taking in the hip gray walls and modern suede couch he sat on across from me. All very different from Dr. Schneider's preferred dark wood and leather. The furnishings obviously weren't the only things that differentiated the two men. The lack of communication from this guy was high on the list.

Weren't psychologists trained to speak? Or was this guy special because he'd been labeled a therapist? Great, I'd probably been stuck with the college dropout. Just like that, the chorus line from "Beauty School Dropout" started running through my head on repeat. I really needed a few good friends around every once in a while to tell me when the Internet was dead wrong about movie suggestions.

I glanced up at him and he gave me a polite, encouraging smile but remained mute. I resisted the temptation to let my head fall back in frustration but finally decided one of us needed to say something. At the very least, I wanted to know if he could indeed speak words. Actual words. From his happy, smiling mouth.

"So, are you going to say anything in this hour...or are we going to just stare at each other for the next"—I glanced at the clock and nearly rolled my eyes. Only two minutes had passed since I'd last looked at the damn thing—"forty-three minutes?"

The gentle smile returned to his face as he simply shrugged. "This is your session. You can choose to use the time however you wish, August."

Well, huh—the man could actually form complete sentences.

"So, I'm just supposed to talk? About anything?"

"If that's what you want," he responded. His voice sounded very passive, as if he really couldn't give a fuck whether he was here or not.

"What if I wanted to sit here and do nothing?" I challenged, crossing my arms in front of me defiantly.

Poker-face just continued to smile. "Again—your session, your choice. I get paid no matter what goes on in here so it doesn't really matter to me one way or another."

"Isn't that kind of a crooked way to conduct business?"

His grin widened, and little wrinkles appeared around his dark brown eyes. I'd gotten to him. Good.

"Not really. Why try to help someone who doesn't want it? It's frustrating for everyone involved. You don't have to be here—no one is mandating you seek therapy. It was just highly recommended, and yet here you are. So I've got to figure some part of you wants help; otherwise, why bother showing up? So until you figure out what kind of help that is, I'll just be over here waiting—earning money while I plan my grocery list."

My mouth hung open for a moment as I tried to formulate my comeback, but I had none.

The damn asshole was right.

No one was forcing me to be here. When I'd been released from the hospital, Dr. Schneider had written down names and numbers for a few therapists and psychologists, underlining this particular one. Schneider had said he was highly recommended, but nothing was required of me after I walked out those doors.

So, why was I here?

I didn't have an answer.

And neither did Dr. Abrams—that was his name, this crazy doctor with the sound machine, who didn't speak unless spoken to.

The crazy doctor who was charging me to stare at the dark gray walls of his office until I figured out what was wrong with me.

Me…not him.

This man was a fucking genius.

*   *   *

The boxes from the attic had been scattered across the living room for weeks now.

I'd unpacked every single one of them and so far hadn't made any headway into my past by doing so. It was a fool's errand and I was definitely the fool. Nothing was dated or labeled, and half of the boxes didn't seem to have any sort of organization whatsoever—as if I'd just thrown random shit into boxes, uncaring whether any of it made any sense whatsoever.

Of course, the younger version of me had probably also figured I'd have all my faculties intact and would be able to make sense of all of it down the road.

Yeah…funny how that all worked out.

There were some nights I contemplated lighting every last box on fire, and roasting marshmallows while all the confusion went up in smoke. But the rational side of me knew I'd regret it. Besides, rational people didn't start fires in their living rooms, and I was supposed to be proving I was sane. Or at least somewhat sane.

Running a frustrated hand through my hair, I picked up a picture I'd been staring at for the past few hours and sat down on the couch. As I reached for the half-empty bottle of beer I'd been nursing for over an hour, I flipped over the picture once again, somehow hoping that a date or timestamp had magically appeared since the last time I'd checked. But no, the only thing printed over and over diagonally across the back of the print was the word "Kodak," like so many of the others.

Turning it back around, I skimmed my thumb over the surface as I stared at the younger version of myself.

How odd to recognize yourself in a picture, but have no memory of ever being there.

But there I stood, probably no older than ten. I was standing by the ocean, holding a giant caramel apple in my hand. As I held the picture close, I couldn't help but notice the huge smile on my face. I wondered who I'd been looking at. My mother or father, maybe? I'd seen pictures of them—or at least I assumed I had, based on what I could deduce from everything. Had I loved them? Where were they now? Were they dead? Had they abandoned me like everyone else when I'd become too volatile to be around?

Looking at the picture, I held it close and noticed something I hadn't seen before. The hand that held the caramel apple had a tiny bandage—cotton, white and large, wrapped around my left thumb. Maybe I'd climbed a tree or tried my skills as a chef? Wondering what had happened, I instantly glanced down and saw a faint scar just below my thumbnail I'd never noticed until that moment.

The discovery made me feel ill. The sudden realization was like a tidal wave and I felt like I might drown in the deluge of memories from my former life.

It was too much.

I'd been up late the other night and caught the last few minutes of this old film where an entire town had been taken over by body-snatching aliens. That's how I felt. I wasn't August Kincaid. I was just someone who inhabited his body, and somehow I was expected to take over as if nothing had ever happened. Go on as if life were normal.

Life for me would never be normal again.

Not unless I started getting my memories back, and I couldn't bank on that. It had already been weeks since I'd come out of the coma and not a single memory had surfaced. Every day that passed just felt like further proof I'd never regain anything that was lost.

Finishing my beer in one long swig, I threw the picture back on the pile and rose to my feet. I needed air and I needed to be away from this house. I'd done nothing but comb through this mess for the last few weeks and suddenly the air in here felt stifling and stale.

I headed for the front door intent on walking out my frustrations, but made sure to grab my cell phone. With my address now programmed into my phone's GPS app, at least now I wouldn't get lost in this maze of a neighborhood I lived in.

Shaking my head as I locked the deadbolt, I remembered the awkwardness between Everly and me on the day she'd driven me home. How much had I hurt her to cause so much pain and tension between us? How could love have become so excruciating? I honestly wasn't sure I wanted to know. What would I learn about myself? Some things you can't unlearn.

When I took a deep breath, the salty air seemed to help clear my thoughts. I walked down the street. It was a weekday, still early in the afternoon, so the only sounds were the waves pounding against the nearby cliffs and the occasional bird or passing car. I'd realized shortly after moving back into this house of mine that this wasn't like the neighborhoods I'd seen on TV or movies, where children played in the streets and neighbors talked between driveways.

After a bit of hunting around on the Internet, I'd realized I was living among movie stars and millionaires. Sea Cliffs was like the Beverly Hills of San Francisco, and somehow I'd managed to snag a little piece of it for myself.

How? I still had no fucking clue.

After several walks like this, I'd discovered the rich didn't water their lawns and talk gossip over their rose bushes like I'd seen on the sitcoms in the hospital, nor did they allow their children to play basketball in the driveway.

Everyone kept to themselves. It was eerily quiet.

Which was both a blessing and a curse.

For moments like right now, when I needed to clear my head, it was perfect. I could simply step outside my door and not have to worry about walking into a single soul. I imagined my self-indulgent neighbors were either too busy making or spending money to worry about anyone but themselves, so I had the entire neighborhood to roam away my cares.

But when it came to seeking answers…well, it flat-out sucked.

No one knew me. Hardly anyone had even noticed I was gone. I'd made the mistake of trying to introduce myself to the guy next door—a musician of some sort—only to be politely asked to leave. Turns out he didn't know who I was and really didn't care.

So much for being neighborly.

After an hour or so, I made my way back to the house and stopped to check the mail. Bills had found their way to me once again, including ones from the hospital and my new therapist.

At least someone knew where to find me.

As I fumbled through the junk and a handful of bills, my eyes fell upon a familiar-looking envelope. My fingers caressed the words as I remembered where I'd seen the handwriting before.

August and Everly…2005

Everly's handwriting. Forgetting everything else, I raced inside and dropped the rest of the mail on the kitchen counter. I had no idea what to expect, but I felt exhilarated from anticipation alone. I knew nothing of our past, knew we had no chance of a future, but the mere sight of my name written by her hand did something to me.

And I had no idea why.

Could the heart remember what the mind couldn't?

This was something I contemplated as I pulled the letter out and fell back into my spot on the sofa—the only place free of boxes, photos, and dust. There was no greeting—no pleasantries or how do you dos.

Just a simple listing of dates and the milestone or event that corresponded with each:

June 8, 2001— Graduated from San Marcos High School,
Santa Barbara
May 14, 2005 — Graduated from Stanford University, BA
Business Management

Many other dates were listed, including my birthdate, my parents' birthdates, and the date of their deaths: February 10, 2003. In parentheses, she'd noted the cause. Car accident.

No other details.

My eyes blurred as I finished reading through everything she'd given me, which was more than I deserved.

I should have been happy. I should have felt elated. This list was my start—my step into finally figuring out what all this shit sitting in my living room meant. But instead, all I felt was loss.

Loss for the parents I'd never know. Loss for a life that had to be written on paper instead of remembered and lived.

As much as I hated to admit it, perhaps the quack doctor at the hospital hadn't been too much of a nut after all. Maybe it was time for me to look at this as a second chance rather than as a recovery.

After all, I couldn't recover what I didn't know, and I definitely didn't want to be a man everyone hated. So now I just had to figure out who the new me was and go from there. Perhaps one day I could become someone Everly could be proud of, even if she didn't know it.

Yeah, that sounded easy enough.

Looking around the chaos of the room, I knew without a doubt that I was already screwed.

Chapter Nine

Everly

Secrets.

Secrets have a way of digging into your soul, into your mind until all you can think about is that one simple thing you omitted from a conversation or the tiny white lie you told to keep the peace.

Secrets.

Everyone had them.

Mothers, husbands, priests, even. We all walked around carrying them on our shoulders like lead weights, smiling and going about our lives as if nothing was amiss.

Yet on the inside—we were screaming.

I had secrets and they were literally burning a hole in my gut.

I'd told myself to learn from the sins of those I'd watched before me. Never keep secrets from those you love, and god, I'd tried. Over macaroni and cheese, I'd come clean to Ryan, spilling the details of my uncomfortable afternoon with August to him because I knew that keeping it from him would only tear us apart.

Because with secrets and lies always came trouble.

I should have known better, and in truth—I did. I'd seen secrets tear people apart, so why hadn't I chosen a different path?

I'd known better when my shaking hand had reached for the pen in our desk drawer so late at night. I'd known better as I wrote each date out neatly, one by one, on the sheet of paper as Ryan slept soundly down the hall. I knew I was causing deceit and turmoil in my near-perfect relationship when I dropped that letter to August into the mailbox the very next day.

But I did it anyway.

Why?

I still didn't know.

A part of me knew it was my need to help—that part of me that couldn't turn away from a wounded bird or an abandoned puppy—but I knew that wasn't all.

Deep down, the part that wasn't willing to admit it knew I wasn't ready to let go of that part of my life.

And that was the biggest secret of all.

* * *

A warm hand slipped around me, pulling me from my dream. The dark room came into sight as my eyes focused and I felt August's hard body pressed against mine.

"It's late," I said, rubbing the sleep from my tired eyes.

"I know. I'm sorry." His fingers dug into my hip, and even though I was angry at him for leaving me here, my body responded, arching into his as his heated breath moved over me.

"Did you eat the meal I left for you? I had it brought in from

that restaurant you love. And the wine, it was imported from France."

"You mean the restaurant I never get to go to anymore?" I asked pointedly.

"Don't be angry, Everly," he whispered. "You know I can't stand the thought of you out of this house—unprotected."

"Unprotected from what?"

"Shh—just let me love you," he begged, dipping his hands between my quivering thighs.

* * *

My eyelids fluttered, and the distant sound of running water tugged me out of a dream.

Not a dream, but a memory.

The first rays of morning light cascaded into our quiet bedroom. The last remnants of my dream drifted away, leaving my body quaking with need as I remembered exactly how it felt to be loved by August.

I could hear Ryan humming in the shower as sweat dripped from my pores. Every movement, every twist of the sheets left me reeling. I was writhing; still trapped in the holds of a memory I couldn't escape.

Even now, August still owned me.

Would I ever escape?

My eyes darted to the half-open bathroom door as my hand traveled the length of my body. As Ryan continued to hum, completely unaware in the bathroom nearby, I gave in to myself.

Parting my slick folds, I rubbed my clit long and slow. My head fell to the side as a moan escaped my lips. Needing this release more than my next breath, I clamped my mouth shut and plunged two fingers deep into my core, knowing I wouldn't need much more to send me over.

As my fingers worked in and out, I flicked my clit once...twice, and I came. Hard. Curling into a ball, my body shook over and over as the waves of my orgasm spilled out around me. I heard the water shut off and slowly pulled the covers over my head and hid as tears streamed down my face.

I didn't move a muscle as Ryan moved around the room getting dressed for work. I lay there in my sweat and tears, the weight of my guilt overwhelming me until I thought I might drown.

*   *   *

"Son of a bitch!" I cursed as the simple white envelope fell to the floor. I'd just gotten home from my shift at the coffee shop and had stopped at our mailbox to pick up our daily dose of magazines and bills when I found a letter addressed to me from the bank.

Normally this wouldn't have really piqued my interest much, except for the fact that it wasn't from my normal bank; it was from the bank August and I had shared—the bank I no longer did business with. Like many things I'd shared with August that connection was in the past. No more big bank accounts and investment portfolios. Nowadays, saving for a new couch or a vacation could take years.

But my money was all mine and I earned every single penny.

As I held the check in my shaky hand, I looked down at the amount one more time.

Yep, there were really that many zeros attached that that three.

Shit.

I looked at the letter one more time, hoping it would give me some answers, but it was just a formal greeting and statement about what was enclosed. No reason, no justification for why a man who'd just come out of a two-year-long nap would suddenly decide to send his ex-girlfriend half of his entire estate.

I needed to sit down.

While most people would have likely jumped up and down, run up and down the block, and then proceeded to the nearest Audi or Cartier dealer, I felt nothing but rage.

Absolute blinding rage.

Who did he think he was, and what the hell was the purpose of this? Guilt money? Did he think he owed me something? Because I had words for him and they definitely did not include "thank you" or any other form of praise. Grabbing my keys off the counter, I didn't bother changing out of my coffee-soaked clothes. This needed to be done now and, as I looked at the clock, before Ryan got home.

Secrets.

They definitely had a way of worming their way into every facet of your life.

As I hopped back into the car, I thought about the letter.

That stupid, damned letter.

Had I not sent it, would I still be in this mess?

I knew without a doubt the answer was yes. I'd shown August a kindness, and now in his own weird way he was showing me one in return. Only, he could never fully understand what this money meant to me—because he didn't remember. Anything.

My mind whirled, spiraling into the past as I flew down the highway toward the home I'd once shared with August. Toward the life I'd once had—one that had started out like a beautiful fairytale only to end in misery. But despite everything I'd gone through, I'd picked myself up, dusted off the dirt, nursed my wounds, and come back stronger than ever and no one, especially not him, would ever drag me back to that hell.

*　*　*

"It's just a party, August," I urged, putting the finishing touches to my makeup. I'd spent hours getting ready, making sure I looked perfect for him. Over the past few weeks, I'd barely seen him and when he was home, he was always locked away in his office, shouting and barking commands at some poor peon on the other end of the phone line. As proud as I was of him and the rapid success he'd gained over the past few years, I secretly did miss the tiny house we'd shared on the other side of town. It had been drafty and cold during the winter and sometimes the stove didn't work, but no one ever yelled.

Life had been much simpler.

"I don't want you to go, Everly," he replied sternly, his eyes meeting mine in the vanity mirror.

This wasn't the first time he'd tried to keep me at home, but I'd always won out in the end.

Turning, I met his stare, but when I'd usually see him soften, now I saw nothing but hard edges and cold lines.

Where did you go, August?

"But I've spent hours getting ready." I faked a pout, giving him a coy smile that was sure to melt his grumpy attitude.

But he didn't budge.

"Oh, come on, August," I said, standing so I could slide my arms around his shoulders. He didn't reciprocate my movements and held

his posture rigid. So I tried harder, pressing my body closer to his. As my breasts molded against his chest, I felt his breath hitch. His head turned toward mine, and for the briefest moment his nose touched my neck, inhaling the scent of my perfume before he pushed me away.

"You will stay here, Everly," he said firmly and then he was gone. And I was left alone.

* * *

I don't know how long I sat in front of his driveway, staring at the massive house, holding the steering wheel of my old beat-up Kia like it was a symbol for the new life I'd forged out of the ashes of the one I'd left behind.

Wiping a tear I hadn't realized I'd shed, I picked up the check lying on the passenger seat and took a deep breath.

No time like the present, I told myself.

Pushing the door open, I stepped out of the car and took several sure strides toward the door, hoping that the rage and anger I'd felt back at home would resurface as I stepped closer and closer to his doorway.

Tears weren't allowed at this gathering.

Pressing the buzzer, I wrapped my hands around the folded piece of paper and waited, trying not to notice the brass knocker and how it so beautifully displayed our intertwined initials.

A housewarming gift from his partner. The man who'd made all his dreams come true.

Or so he'd said.

Prior to landing the job of the century, August had worked at a large, well-known firm. He'd interned there during his senior year and been offered a job before graduation. He earned a base salary and decent commission on sales. It had been a nice life for the two of us. Nothing compared to the drug-induced haze of the stockbroker life depicted in the movies, but we were happy.

Or we were until August became reacquainted with his old friend Trent. Trent and August had been fraternity brothers, and from the moment I met him I knew Trent was trouble.

He was slimy. There was no other word to adequately describe him, and the longer I knew him, the better the word fit.

He managed to pull August out of his quaint little job and lure him into bigger, greater possibilities. Suddenly, August and Trent were partners, working night and day on the start-up company Trent had founded just a year prior.

I'd never been one to believe in the old saying, "If it's too good to be true, it generally is," but when our bank account starting doubling, and we were celebrating crazy deals with champagne that cost more than a month's rent, I started to get worried.

August assured me everything he was doing was legal, and I believed him—at first. But the money just grew and grew, seemingly without end.

Along with my panic.

I tried to ask him to be cautious.

That's when our open line of communication had ended. Much like everything else.

The door flew open, severing my thoughts of the past.

"Everly," August said in surprise. I said nothing. Just stared. Stared because speech was impossible. The man looking down at me was a ghost and I was stumbling back into history.

Just let me love you. My dream came roaring back, along with every ounce of guilt. Suddenly I felt ill, weak, and nauseous all at the same time.

"Are you all right?" he asked, taking my elbow, only to feel me yank it back. I reached out toward his face, wanting to grasp a piece of his hair, but stopped myself short. I couldn't touch him. I would not touch him.

He watched my movements in fascination and smiled. "Oh, the haircut?" His hands raked through the neatly trimmed locks. "I figured it was time to get rid of the hobo look and try something a bit tamer. Do you like it?"

Still no words, so I merely nodded. He looked just like himself now. Like the old August. Neatly trimmed hair, vibrant hazel eyes. It was hard to look at him and yet I couldn't turn away.

"Would you like to come in?" he offered, motioning toward the hallway.

I simply stepped forward, clutching the check in my hand, telling myself I just needed a moment to collect myself before handing it over. Just a moment to stop the hammering in my chest and I'd leave.

The house still smelled the same. I didn't know how that was possible after all this time, but each time I'd entered since he'd returned, I could close my eyes and still smell the hints of lavender and the soft tones of vanilla tempting my nose. I had always loved the combination.

Now it just made me feel more nauseous. And guilty.

We rounded the corner into the living room, and I was surprised to see the living room had been cleared. The boxes and stacks of paper were gone, leaving nothing but the warm, inviting space I'd decorated years earlier.

Taking a seat in the paisley blue arm chair felt warm and inviting.

It suddenly made everything about this wrong. Sitting here, in this house…with him…was wrong. Completely wrong.

Nothing about the two of us together could ever be right. Before, he'd looked different and acted different. It was easy to compartmentalize what had happened and to almost treat him as if he were another person.

But he wasn't. He was and always would be August.

Cold, unfeeling August.

Memories or not.

"I just wanted to stop by and return this to you," I said calmly, placing the now-wrinkled check on the coffee table. I slid it toward him, keeping my posture stiff and unyielding.

Sitting across from me, he bent forward, grabbing the check and quickly scanning it.

"But why?" he asked as our eyes met.

"I can't take your money."

"As far as I'm concerned, it's *our* money, Everly. I thought it was only fair." He shrugged, leaning back once more against the plush sofa cushion. So casual. So relaxed.

"Nothing about that money is mine. We were never married. I don't want a single penny of it."

"Look, I'm just trying to get a hold on my life—or at least what's left of it. I will never need that much money. Ever. I thought you might enjoy starting over with your future husband. But if I've overstepped my bounds, please let me know."

Gritting my teeth, my words barely audible, I said, "You overstepped, August."

His eyes rounded as he leaned forward. "What did he do to you?"

It was the first time he'd referred to his former self as someone else.

For a moment, I almost fell for it. Had it not been for the new haircut and the fancy clothes I guessed he'd pulled out of his old closet, I probably would have broken down right then and there, allowing him to hold me as I told my story through tears and sniffles.

But I couldn't. Not with those eyes looking at me.

"Thank you for your generosity, Mr. Kincaid, but I will have to decline."

Rising to my feet, I walked briskly to the door and turned to see if he'd followed me.

"Have a nice day," I managed to say before turning the handle and stepping out into the fresh air. I took a deep breath, closing the door behind me, and found myself face to face with the brass knocker.

A&E.

I fled before the tears found their way to the pavement.

Chapter Ten

August

"I tried to give away several million dollars to a woman the other day," I blurted out, severing the tense silence we'd been sitting in for over half an hour. This was my third visit with the mute counselor and barely a word had been said since the first day. It was getting damn frustrating, and I think he knew this.

He knew that eventually I'd crack.

And crack I had. Like a damned nut.

One dark gray eyebrow rose slightly in amusement…intrigue, maybe…as he chose his words.

"Well, that was generous."

A sort of snorted laugh escaped my throat. "You would think. But she turned me down. Cold. Basically threw the damned check back in my face."

Now I was pacing the room like a caged tiger.

When had I gotten up?

"And this makes you feel agitated?" he asked.

I turned to him in shock.

"Aha! I knew you were one of those!" I pointed my finger accusingly.

"One of those?" he questioned, looking mildly entertained.

"You play it all cool, with your passive–aggressive attitude and the crazy sound machine, but I knew deep down there was a normal, predictable psychotherapist in there just waiting to get out."

He sighed in what I assumed was defeat, and I waited in silence for his confession. Everything he'd done to this point had been just a hoax—a thin veil to make me feel comfortable. And I'd almost fallen for it, but he was no different from Dr. HappyFeelGood at the hospital. They all wrote in their little notebooks, judging their clients on all their faults, only to go home to their own little fucked-up world.

We were all head cases—some of us just a little more so than others.

"You want to go out for a beer?" he finally said, as my eyes flew up to his.

"What?"

"Well, I figured we're probably done here, and I could really use a beer and a big plate of nachos. There's a place down the street that has the best nachos in town. You in?"

This guy was nutters.

"You paying?" I asked.

"Nope, you are. Seems you're loaded."

I burst into laughter, agreeing to his lunatic proposal.

Maybe a crazy loon was what I needed after all.

* * *

"So what's your story, Dr. Abrams?" I asked the shrink as we settled into a quiet booth in the corner of what could only be considered the smallest restaurant I'd ever seen.

At least as far as I knew.

God, my life sucked. Every thought, every comment that ran through my mind, I was constantly second-guessing. *Was* this the smallest restaurant I'd ever been in?

Fuck if I knew.

Had I ever been out of the country? I had no idea. Did I like chocolate or vanilla better? No idea.

"Brick—call me Brick," he replied, avoiding my vague question altogether.

"Okay—Brick, what's your story?" I asked again.

"Not much to tell," Dr. Abrams fired back, taking a long gulp of the microbrew he'd ordered. "Midwestern boy who fell in love with old surfing movies."

"Like *Gidget* and *Beach Party*?"

His eyebrow rose in surprise.

"I've had problems sleeping," I admitted, before he let out a laugh. "So I've been watching a lot of bad old movies."

"More like *Endless Summer* and *Morning of the Earth*," he replied. "Seeing films like that changed me—made me see something far greater than our tiny farm. I begged my dad for a surfboard when I was ten, not caring that the closest ocean was fifteen hundred miles away. He wasn't so keen on the idea. When it came to applying to college, I picked schools in Florida and California, although I ended up taking a slight detour before I actually got to classes."

"The waves were calling you," I interrupted, grinning.

"Yeah, something like that. An unbridled hatred for snow didn't hurt either."

We both chuckled as we continued to nurse our beers.

"So, how did psychology play into all that?" I finally asked after a long lull in conversation.

He shrugged. "Nosy, I guess."

I shook my head in amusement as I studied him. Dark brown eyes the color of milk chocolate stood out against tanned skin that had aged through years under the sun. His jet black hair and laid-back attitude gave him the appearance of a man with not a care in the world, rather than someone who carried the secrets of so many.

"Come on. There's got to be more to it than that." I pushed harder, hoping he'd hand over an answer.

"Oh, there is, I'm just not ready to share it yet."

And you're not ready to hear it. He didn't say it, but I could feel the afterthought clinging to the air like unsettled dirt making its way back to the earth.

We sat in awkward silence after that, waiting for our food to arrive. As I fiddled with my drink coaster and wiped away the condensation that had formed around my glass, I suddenly wondered what secrets Dr. Abrams—Brick—had of his own.

You couldn't carry around the baggage of so many without a little of your own.

And somehow, the more I got to know him, the more I thought he would agree with me.

Thankfully, our food arrived just a few minutes later, delivered by a perky young woman who had long red braids and a million bracelets jingling on her wrists. They reminded me of one of those bells attached to house cats. *Jingle, jingle, jingle...* all the time. Day or night.

Maddening.

Well, at least she couldn't sneak up on us.

"Can I get you two anything else?" she asked, eyeing me affection-ately.

"No, I think we're all set for now, Meg," Brick replied politely. She nodded, her eyes finally tearing away from my direction as she scur-ried back to the kitchen.

As we dug into our plates of nachos, the conversation resumed. This time Brick started it: Mr.-I-Don't-Talk-Until-You-Do appar-ently broke his own rules occasionally.

Or at least he seemed to when it involved food. And beer.

"So what went through your head—what exactly was your thought process when deciding to give away—how did you say it? Oh yes; sev-eral million dollars."

Smart ass.

"Was it a random choice? Or did you have a specific woman picked out? How does one choose such a recipient?"

"My, you're chatty tonight."

"Just making conversation." He shrugged again, taking a swig of beer before diving back into his dinner.

"It wasn't random," I answered. "She's my ex—from before, when I…"

"Had your memories—yes, go on," he said very matter-of-factly, between bites.

"And, I just wanted to give her something."

"Why?" he pressed. I sat back in the booth and just watched him as he continued to eat as if nothing was amiss. As if we were just talking about football or the weather.

Not something as sensitive as my life—or Everly. Just the mention of her name made my stomach twist in knots, and I had no idea why.

"Because I—I don't know."

"Yes you do. Otherwise you wouldn't have done it. How many million?"

"What?" I asked.

"You said several million. I'm asking for clarification."

"Three. Three million," I answered.

He paused, taking a moment to drink from his nearly empty bottle. "Sane people don't give away three million dollars without a reason."

"But I thought that was the point to all this. I thought I wasn't sane."

"I've worked with a lot of crazy people over the years, August, and I'm pretty damn good at spotting the signs and symptoms of mental illness."

"And?"

"And…you're not insane. You're unhappy."

"And how do I fix that?" I asked, looking at him from across the table.

"That's for you to decide."

*   *   *

"So, you don't find all of this insane? Not even a little?" I asked, motioning to what had once been my pristine living room, but now was cluttered with large brown grocery bags, sacks of clothes, and stacks and stacks of DVDs, books, and magazines.

"Not if it gets you where you want to be," Brick answered, sitting in the only seat that was free of clutter. The seat that Everly had occupied only days earlier.

She'd barely been able to look at me that day, her hands shaking as she slid the check in my direction.

It had been as if she were seeing a ghost.

Is that all I'd ever be to her? A reflection of her past?

It hurt to know that every time she looked at me she suffered, and yet I fought back the urge to comfort her from the pain she must feel—to protect her from...me.

Could someone really change? Or would I always be him, deep down?

I guess it was time to find out.

"Okay, let's do this," I said, rubbing my hands together in anticipation. "You got the notebook?" I asked Brick. He held up the leather journal I'd bought to track everything, and after I'd birthed this brilliant plan—after several Coronas in that tiny Mexican restaurant—I'd naturally put him in charge of writing everything down.

He was a counselor. He should be good at keeping notes.

"Where do you want to start?" he asked, glancing at me as he bobbed the pen up and down between his fingertips. I still couldn't quite figure him out. Like why, on a Tuesday night, he was hanging out with me, rather than at home with his family.

Did he have a family?

Other than his first name and the fact that he liked surfing, there wasn't much I knew about the good doctor's personal details. Hell, I wasn't even exactly sure he was a doctor. I just kept calling him that. His title on his office door said "therapist," but I wasn't sure what that meant. However, for the first time since checking out of the hospital, I felt like I'd found someone I could call a friend.

Or something as close to a friend as possible, since I wasn't entirely sure what this relationship was, and whether I was being charged for it. Honestly, I didn't care.

Scanning the sacks and large stacks of books and movies, my eyes settled on the brown paper bag in front of me. "Here. I think ice cream sounds good right about now." I pulled out pint-sized containers of Ben & Jerry's, gallon-sized tubs of Dreyer's, and various other brands and flavors.

When we'd checked out at the grocery store, walking away with enough candy, ice cream, and booze to supply a small frat party, the girl at the counter had taken one look at us and asked, "Pregnant wife?" I glanced down at the tequila and rum, shaking my head, and she just laughed.

"I see this combo at least twice a week, but it's usually from tired, worn out dads-to-be."

We shared a chuckle, then thanked her as we gathered our bags and headed for the car. As we made several other stops along the way, I thought about her assumption—that I could be a father, or at least a husband preparing to be a father. When I looked in the mirror, I just saw a man—an empty shell of a man staring back at me. He had no past, and for the most part, no future.

But that checker had seen something else. Maybe she didn't know me at all, but when she looked at me, she'd seen possibilities.

Maybe I should, too.

Setting all the different types of ice cream in front of me in a neat little row, I looked at them. Each container looked as if it was awaiting its turn.

Tonight, I was going to decide once and for all what type of ice cream August Kincaid liked best.

This was my brilliant plan; the one I'd concocted and managed to involve my therapist and now pseudo friend in. Slowly, I was going to create a life for myself. It might be different. It might be new. But the point was that it was mine. I was done mourning a life I might never get back, and frankly wasn't sure I wanted.

I'd been told this was a gift, and I was going to start treating it that way.

Starting with ice cream. Other guys might start with the booze, but I was still damned hungry, and I was pretty sure if I started with the booze I was going to be like most guys and just like whatever got me buzzed first.

Lifting the lid of the first ice cream carton, I took a spoonful and brought it to my mouth, only to grimace a second later.

"That's fucking horrible," I managed to say, glancing down at the label.

"So apparently mint chip is off your list," Brick laughed, scribbling in the journal.

"Do you want it?" I asked, putting the lid back on and offering it to him.

"Sure; my wife loves it."

So he *was* married. I stuffed that detail away in the small box of information I knew about Dr. Abrams and continued. Strawberry, Cherry Garcia, and chocolate were all okay but vanilla topped the list as my absolute favorite.

"Of all the flavors in the world, you picked the most boring one of all," Brick commented, setting the notebook down to help me clean up.

I shrugged. "Can't help it. Maybe I just like the classics."

"You want to try anything else or are you done for the night?"

Looking back over the piles, part of me just wanted to race through it all—fill that notebook to the brim with all of my new likes and dis-likes—but I knew now that that was part of the adventure.

"Nah, I think I'm good for now. I'm going to grab one of those movies, make myself a giant bowl of vanilla ice cream, and spend some time relaxing."

He nodded, a genuine smile painting his weathered face. "Well, pick a good one. Sounds like you've been watching shit lately."

I thought back and remembered my *Gidget* comment and laughed. "Will do. But how will I know if it's any good?" I questioned with a smirk.

"Guess that's half the fun, huh? But word to the wise, August."

"Yeah?"

"Stay away from musicals. No one likes those. No one."

My laughter followed him all the way out the front door. If he only knew. The lyrics from *Grease* still haunted me.

Chapter Eleven

Everly

"Wow, those fancy light-up mirrors really exist outside of TV shows?" I announced as I entered her dressing room. Her gaze met mine in the reflection and lit up brighter than the round bulbs that surrounded her. Sarah looked stunning in full costume makeup, her hair pulled tightly into an intricate bun with dazzling jewels wrapped around it.

This was how she was meant to be seen—ready to light up a stage and dazzle an audience.

Turning, she stood, still wrapped in a satin pink robe and with her feet in fluffy slippers.

"Look at you! Tomboy turned seductress," she exclaimed, gazing at me in a way that made me completely self-conscious and awkward. What she didn't know was that I used to dress like this all the time. For a brief period, parties, charity events, and galas had been my life. It had been fun for a while—having a new dress every day and a different bag for each occasion—but none of it had mattered when

August fell from my grasp. And now, fancy clothes and jewels just felt awkward and out of place.

Kind of like me.

"I'm so proud of you," I said softly, taking her in my arms. We hugged long and hard, resting our heads on each other's shoulders with the ease of two friends who'd been there for each other through the best and worst of times.

"Who would have thought?" she finally said.

Stepping back, I found her bright blue eyes and smiled warmly. "I would have. I did. I always knew you'd make it here one day, Sarah. You were meant to wow people and turn heads."

"I'm so glad we met in that lobby," she sniffled, trying to hold back tears.

"Here's to being fucked-up mental cases!" I laughed. We hugged briefly again before taking a seat. She sat in front of her vanity, finishing up last-minute touch-ups to her makeup, and I took the empty seat across from her and watched as more mascara was applied to her long, false lashes and sparkling white eye shadow was added to her lids.

She looked radiant—just like the swan princess she'd always wanted to be.

"So, how is everything?" she asked as I tried not to giggle. She was doing that weird opened-mouthed "O" thing women do when applying mascara. Had someone taught us to do that, or was it instinctual? I'd never had a mother or anyone to instruct me on matters of proper makeup application and yet I did the same thing.

"Everything is good," I answered. "*Really* good," I emphasized, hoping I'd slide by without any scrutiny.

"Oh yeah? Decide on a wedding location yet?"

Damn it. I should have known. This was Sarah. Glitz and tutus aside, she was still my best friend and like a shark, she'd always be able to seek out my issues.

"No. Not yet, but I've narrowed it down."

"How many?"

"What?" I asked, playing dumb as I watched her fuss with a tube of lipstick.

"How many have you narrowed it down to? Three...two?" she questioned.

"Ten?" I guessed, before sighing. "Okay, so I haven't really looked since that day we browsed the bridal magazine together. But I've had a lot of stuff going on, with—"

"August?" she guessed.

"No...yes," I said softly. "It's complicated, okay? He's just there...all the time. In my thoughts, my dreams...constantly invading everything. Again. I don't want him to be, but there it is. I just feel distracted and worried and anxious all the damn time," I finally confessed.

It was a confession I hadn't even admitted to myself, and having the courage to finally say it out loud made me feel like a heavy weight was being lifted off my shoulders.

Whether I wanted him to be or not, August was back in my life. I had to figure out how to deal with that. Did I terminate all contact with him? That would be the healthier option, the clearer path, yet when I thought about never talking to him again, my chest tightened and I didn't know why. This man—the one who'd caused me so much pain...why couldn't I walk away?

Sarah's warm hand touched mine and I looked up to see her tender, searching gaze. "Don't let him delay your life—again. Pick a place, marry Ryan. Live, Ev, and finally let your past go."

I nodded, knowing every word she spoke was true. She was right. I needed to let go. I needed to walk away. For good.

"Well, I did really like the little rustic church you showed me," I replied with a sheepish smile.

"Now you're talking." She grinned. "Now let's talk centerpieces."

My head was already spinning.

*　　*　　*

Nervously glancing down at my phone again, I checked the time and sighed. I'd promised Ryan I wouldn't be longer than twenty minutes, tops.

That had been almost forty minutes ago. God only knows what he was doing in this place without me. There were many reasons why I loved Ryan—his sweet nature, his devotion, and even his quirky shyness. He might have relentlessly pursued me, but only because he'd thought I was even more introverted and standoffish than he was.

Little had he known I was just scared and broken.

He figured that out soon enough, though; but still, he didn't run. That was when I knew he was a keeper. I'd been holding on ever since. And now I had to find my shy nerd of a man and rescue him from the San Francisco elite.

I moved quickly through the crowd. People mingled in the lobby, grabbing pre-show drinks and talking amongst themselves. It was opening night and everyone was dressed to impress. Designer gowns, fancy shoes, and of course jewelry were on display as I dodged and wove my way, trying not to choke on the expensive perfumes as they muddled the air. My eye caught a little girl clinging to her mother in the corner. The two of them, although nicely dressed, appeared far more conservative than many of the others, and seemed to be in their own little bubble. The mother reached down to adjust the child's dress, smoothing out the skirt so it lay flat over many layers of crinoline. She smiled, placing a small kiss on her daughter's forehead. Excitement and anticipation sparkled in the little girl's eyes as she waited for the doors to open and the show to begin.

I was so lost in the moment, wondering what it must be like for her to have that cherished memory to hold on to, that I stopped watching the path in front of me, and suddenly two hands gripped my shoulders, ceasing my movement.

"Everly?"

I looked up and saw the last person I'd expected to be here. My eyes moved down to where August touched me and I immediately pulled back, putting space between us, but the heat from his touch felt like a brand as my hand raced up to feel it.

"What are you doing here?" I asked, taking one last look at the mother and daughter before the crowd consumed them and their happy faces disappeared.

"Apparently I donate to the arts," he answered with a shrug.

"Yes, you do," I replied. "For many years. When you—after the coma, I was named the executor of your estate, so I just continued your charitable contributions." A twinge of guilt felt like it was gnawing at my side.

He nodded, a warmth in his eyes I wasn't sure what to do with, so I averted my gaze and looked at my nails, the ceiling, the floor. Anything but at him.

God, I want to look at him.

"Thank you. I truly appreciate everything you did for me—I know it must have been...difficult."

I didn't have an answer for that. Or at least a short one, so I let the awkward silence between us answer for me.

"Anyway, since I'm a large contributor, I was invited to tonight's event, and I thought why the hell not?"

A small chuckle escaped my throat, and I tried to cover it with my hand.

"You find that funny?" he asked, excitement lighting his hazel eyes.

"It's just you were never one for ballet," I commented.

"Well, I'm trying out new things. Many new things. Like peanut butter...Do you like it?"

My brow peaked in amusement at his random question. "Kind of?" I answered.

"I love it. I could put it on anything. I think I ate an entire jar yesterday. And watermelon—I really like watermelon."

I couldn't help but laugh. It had been so long since I'd seen any emotion other than anger or jealousy from this man.

"So this is what you're doing with your time now? Taste-testing foods and going to the ballet?"

His eyes lifted toward the bar, and I followed his gaze. A curvy redhead wearing a low-cut dress and a ton of jewelry smiled and waved.

"Ah, I see. Sampling other things as well?" I asked, as a sharp twinge of jealousy burned through my chest.

"Trying, I guess. Actually, I really can't stand her," he admitted with a laugh.

A smug smirk tugged at the corner of my mouth and I instantly tried to stop it. "Why? Not into redheads anymore?"

Why do I care?

His gaze settled on me before he spoke. "Not that particular one."

Butterflies blossomed in my belly.

As if she'd been called, August's date arrived at his side at the same time as I caught sight of Ryan. Seeing him was like being hit with a splash of cold water, and suddenly I realized who I was standing next to. Ryan's eyes immediately narrowed on August, and I felt my heart jump into my throat.

"Everly." Ryan's hand slid possessively around my waist as he approached and he pulled me tight against him. The two men eyed each other but said nothing, and I couldn't help but notice the way August watched Ryan's hand as it slowly moved back and forth over the fabric of my dress. Finally he grabbed his own date for the evening and muttered, "It was nice seeing you, Everly. Enjoy the performance," before disappearing into the crowd.

"What the hell was that all about?" Ryan barked, turning me to face him as he looked me over from head to toe. His eyes were full of worry and concern. I linked our hands together and placed my head on his shoulder.

"Nothing. It was nothing. I just ran into him on my way to finding you."

"I don't like seeing you around him," he said through gritted teeth as I felt his lips touch my forehead.

"I know. I don't like it either," I answered. I avoided his gaze as I wondered if I'd just added one more lie to the ever-growing pile.

"So, who is she playing?" Ryan asked, looking down at the playbill. I rolled my eyes and giggled at his ignorance. He'd never been to a ballet in his life and probably never would have gone if I hadn't made him come tonight.

"Odette," I answered, pointing to the first page, where the principal cast was listed. His eyes lit up in recognition, and he watched as I flipped toward the middle where the bios and pictures were.

"Hey, look! There she is," he said, a note of pride in his voice. Although Sarah and Ryan didn't hang out all the time, they had grown closer over the last year and a half, and a mutual friendship had blossomed. I was glad to see him here supporting her—even if I'd kind of had to drag him out the door when he'd found out he had to wear a suit.

Support was support—even if it was forced, right?

I managed to pop a breath mint and stow my purse under the seat only seconds before the lights dimmed and the orchestra began their opening notes to tune up. The conductor entered the orchestra pit and took a bow, then quickly raised his hands and began. My eyes were fixed on the stage, ready for when Sarah might enter.

I really should have checked the playbill.

Snagging it out of Ryan's hand, I turned it toward the stage for light and realized she wouldn't come on for several scenes. My excitement died down a bit and my eyes began to wander.

Don't look for him, Everly. Don't do it.

But I didn't need to look.

I already knew where he was. He'd always sat in the same seat—the best in the house.

*   *   *

"August—why do we always sit here?" I asked, glancing around at the large, private box seats set high above the stage. The first time we'd sat here the height had been a little alarming, but as soon as the show

began I'd forgotten all about it. I loved everything about the performing arts—the songs, the passion of the actors, and the technique and dedication of the dancers. I'd never once done anything so daunting in my life, and yet I was fascinated by it.

"Because they're the best," he'd simply answered, taking my hand in his and squeezing as we both watched the modern ballet unfold below. So different from the classical pieces I was used to, this performance pushed boundaries and brought a completely new style to dance. I was mesmerized watching the couple as they moved together across the stage. He lifted her with ease, sliding her down his body, until she fell gracefully to the floor. As he moved to hover above her, I felt August's hand cup my knee. His mere touch sent fire through my veins.

I glanced over my shoulder but August shook his head. "We're alone," he whispered, motioning to the tightly pulled curtain behind us. My heart hammered in anticipation of what he had planned as I glanced down at the hundreds of unsuspecting patrons below.

I'd tried to keep my focus on the beautiful couple as they'd moved through the passionate routine, but the farther his hand moved up my thigh, the harder it became to breathe at a normal rate.

"Spread your legs wider," he instructed, his voice hoarse and commanding.

As I did as he requested, I thanked the heavens the balcony was high enough to cover my less-than-ladylike posture. And that it was dark.

I was very, very glad it was dark.

"Let go, Everly," he whispered as his hand slowly disappeared between my thighs.

I exhaled deeply, and my eyes fluttered shut for the briefest moment as I did exactly what he said.

I let go.

And it was exhilarating.

* * *

"Everly, did you hear me?" Ryan's voice cut through the memory like a sharp knife, reminding me of exactly where I was. I blinked several times and sat up straight, looking right at the stage.

Sarah had made her grand entrance.

And I'd missed it.

"Is that her?" he asked, obviously for the second time.

"Yes," I said softly, watching her every movement as she danced across the stage.

I'd missed her entrance.

Because I'd been thinking of him. I willed myself not to glance up, not to give in to the curiosity that was churning inside me to know what he looked like up there without me.

Was he doing the same thing up there with her?

Why did it matter?

Pay attention to Sarah.

I made it through the entire first act without a single glance upward. The heavy red curtain pulled tightly closed and the applause died down, and people made their way out to the lobby for refreshments and bathroom breaks. I finally gave in and found myself looking into the eyes of the man I'd sworn I'd never love again.

The man I'd walked away from years ago.

The same man I couldn't stop thinking about.

* * *

"She did great, didn't she?" Ryan boasted as we made our way out of the theater.

"Yeah," I smiled, remembering her beautiful body twirling and spinning with ease across the grand stage. "She was beautiful."

"Are all ballets that long?" he asked, squeezing my hand, making me laugh as I leaned my head toward his.

"Yes—and I promise I won't take you to another."

"Thank you!" His voice rang out in reverence, causing me to roll my eyes. I caught a whiff of his hair as we took the last step toward the sidewalk. He still hadn't switched back to his normal shampoo yet and smelled like strawberries.

"Are you ever going to go to the store and get shampoo?" I asked, with an amused smile.

His hand reached up to his head, running his fingers through his messy hair. "Probably not. You never forget to buy that fruity shit you're always using and I kind of like smelling like you," he admitted with a wide grin.

"You're weird," I said, shaking my head as we turned the corner. There were tons of people flooding out of the theater. The sidewalks were packed—people were waiting for taxis, climbing into limos, and walking to distant parking spaces like us.

My eyes began to wander, looking over the crowd, searching for someone. I hadn't even realized who I was looking for until my eyes settled on him.

Without thought, I'd managed to find August in a crowd.

Instantly, regret filled my belly, but I couldn't turn away as I watched him carefully escort his date into the back of a sleek, black car. His hands lingered around her waist, casually dipping lower as he followed her into the car, severing my connection right before I took a nosedive into a gigantic pothole.

"You all right, Ev?" Ryan asked, catching me as I stumbled. Brushing it off, I gave him a sideways smile and nodded.

"Just fine," I answered. "I'm just fine."

I looked back one last time as the car carrying August and his date pulled into traffic. Wrapping my arm around Ryan, I tried to tune out the mental images that were threatening to drive me insane.

I've moved on and so should he, I told myself.

Even if it is with a floozy redhead.

As we silently approached our car, I wondered how many lies you could tell yourself before you went insane. Because thanks to August, I was definitely starting to believe I was on my way to being committed.

Chapter Twelve

August

No words were said between Meg and me on the drive back to my house.

I didn't even bother asking if she wanted to come home with me—I just assumed, or didn't give her the opportunity to say no. After the evening I'd just had, I didn't want to be alone, and even though I'd rather be with just about anyone else on the planet, currently she was my only option.

So, the car drove on.

And I thought.

Tonight had started off harmlessly—another experiment in life to discover who the new August Kincaid was. But the moment I ran into Everly, I knew the carefree night I'd envisioned was gone.

She made everything complicated.

Just seeing her made me confused, and it wasn't something I could fix by simply picking out my favorite amongst a few options—because she was definitely off the menu. And somewhere deep down—that bothered me.

A lot.

The black sedan came to a stop, and I looked up to realize we had made it back to the cliffs. Meg's eyes were wide with wonder as she took in the large house and affluent neighborhood.

She was probably thinking she'd just won the fucking lottery.

Too bad I wouldn't be calling her after tonight. Apparently I wasn't too different from my old self after all.

I paid the driver, thanking him for his service, and we both stepped out, then I led her to the front door. "Beautiful house," she commented before she'd even crossed the threshold.

"Thanks," I replied dryly.

Taking a look around, I watched as she most likely mentally re-arranged the furniture and planned our destination wedding in the Caribbean.

Even knowing all that didn't stop me from offering her a drink. She was my distraction, and as Everly's beautiful face flashed across my mind once again, I knew I needed one.

Fast.

Even her drink choice annoyed the shit out of me.

Sex on the Beach—who asks for that outside of a college bar?

"I have no idea how to make that," I admitted. "Maybe a glass of wine, or a rum and coke?" I offered.

"Rum and coke would be fine," she smiled, her eyes batting like crazy.

"One rum and coke coming up."

I really had no idea how to make anything, honestly. I wasn't sure if that was something I'd lost or if it was just something I'd never learned. Either way, I just improvised and threw in a good amount of rum and twice as much coke and hoped it tasted all right. I'd learned over the last week or so that I was more of a beer guy. Fruity drinks had been put into the same category as mint-chip ice cream.

"So, what did you say you do again?" she asked.

"I didn't," I answered, taking a long swig from my beer before adding, "It's complicated."

"Okay," she said softly as she walked slowly around the living room with her drink. Her long legs took one deliberate step at a time. She was beautiful, especially tonight, with her hair out of those ridiculous braids. The black dress she wore left nothing to the imagination, showing ample cleavage and every round curve.

But nothing compared to the elegant gown Everly had worn, that accented and hinted but never screamed "sexy."

In a way, that made it so much more.

"That couple you were talking to tonight—old friends?" she asked, as if she were able to pick up on my exact train of thought.

I glanced up at her, leaning against the fireplace like a male fantasy come to life.

And I was thinking of another woman.

I set my beer down and walked toward her.

"I guess you could say that. It's—"

"Complicated?" she guessed.

"Yes." I gave her a weak smile as I reached her, sliding my hand up her curve of her waist.

"Let's un-complicate things—shall we?" she said softly.

"Yes."

And for the rest of the night, the only redhead I thought of was the one nestled between my thighs.

* * *

Hopefully, the lack of breakfast in the morning dashed any future wedding plans for Meg, but I did promise to call her.

A promise I didn't plan on fulfilling.

I was starting to see why no one liked me.

But that was what single guys did, right? One-night stands—with no plans of repeat performances.

Although I would miss those tacos.

I definitely couldn't go back to that place now.

That was truly unfortunate.

But right now, I had greater things on my mind. Today marked one month since I'd been discharged from the hospital. One month since my life had started over. As I took what would hopefully be one of my last cab rides back to the hospital, I thought back on the last four weeks and how much I'd accomplished.

Or how little.

Sure, I now knew several foods I liked, and that I preferred comedy over horror when it came to movies, but it all felt so superficial. I was a multimillionaire with no career because I had no fucking clue how to do what it was I'd been trained to do. If I planned well, I could probably live comfortably on the large amount money I had in the bank for the foreseeable future.

But what would I do with the time? Taste-test food and watch bad movies?

There had to be more.

Thoughts like this brought back the fear of nothingness, the sense of loss and the overwhelming feeling that I was no one.

Absolutely no one.

When, if ever, would I feel like someone again? And would it ever
be the same?

I finished checking in at the hospital, got my awesome white
bracelet again, and was ushered back into a room so I could be eval-
uated by my doctor once more. If all looked good, I would be given
a clean bill of health and my driver's license would be restored—
something I'd been longing for.

No more cabs or long, tedious walks to the grocery store. Ultimate
independence was almost mine.

I sat waiting for the doctor to arrive, then started pacing back and
forth rather than sitting on that uncomfortable paper-covered exam
table. Several brochures on brain injuries and neurological conditions
lined the walls and my eyes briefly roamed them, wondering how they
would summarize my specific situation.

Coping with total memory loss in three hundred words or less.

Reclaiming a life you don't remember.

Starting over—a brief guide to living with amnesia.

Yeah, none of those sounded great. Pretty sure I could check "mo-
tivational writer" off my list of possible career choices.

Finally the door creaked open and my fragile old doctor appeared.
With his white hair and wrinkled, thin skin, Dr. Lawrence looked like
he was about twenty years late to his own retirement party, and yet
when he spoke, you couldn't help but pay attention. He demanded attention, owned a room, and was as sharp as a tack.

I was still afraid to be alone with him, for fear that he'd drop over
dead and I'd be somehow blamed for it, but I was also glad to have
him as my doctor.

"Well, look who it is!" he greeted warmly, taking my hand in his
in a friendly handshake. His cold palm felt small in mine but I gladly

took it, aware of everything this man had done to keep me alive over the past few years.

It might not seem like much to others—I was just one of his patients, part of his regular duties. But to me, those routines he'd performed had kept me alive. Checking to make sure my muscles hadn't atrophied, monitoring my brain waves, and running tests…and everything he'd done after I awoke. I had no idea why I was here—why I'd come back, but I knew for a fact I wouldn't have even had the option had it not been for this man, right here, doing his job.

Sometimes the simplest things we do in a day have the greatest impact.

"How have you been?" he asked as he ushered me to the exam table. I took a seat, ignoring the awful crinkling sound beneath me.

"Good. Not too bad," I answered as he began checking my heart and lungs. I took breaths when he directed and let them out at the proper time. Everything must have sounded like he'd hoped because he moved on to my eyes, flashing a light back and forth between my pupils.

"And are you adjusting well?" I caught his gaze briefly before his attention centered, and he held up his index finger and told me to focus on it.

"I guess—I mean, as well as can be expected."

The flashlight disappeared and it was just the two of us once again.

"Any blackout periods or dizzy spells? Any points you can't remember since you woke up?"

Nope, those were crystal clear…

"No," I simply answered.

"Well, then I don't see any reason we need to hold your license any longer. Just continue to take it easy, August," he advised, placing his hand on my shoulder. "This will get easier."

I took a deep breath and nodded.

"And the memories?"

He shook his head in uncertainty. "I don't know. I wish I could give you an answer, but I just don't know."

As I watched him walk out the door, I looked up at the brochure board again and wondered what brochure could help me cope with the loss of the important person in my life.

Myself.

* * *

Turns out I didn't just have a thing for redheads.

I could also be persuaded by a nice shade of ebony...if it came with enough horsepower.

As I walked around the sleek, black Mercedes sports car that looked like something out of a movie, I couldn't help but grin. And soon that little baby was going to be all mine.

"I'll take it," I said smoothly, trying to remind myself that I could indeed afford such a luxurious item. The old August Kincaid probably would have walked in here without a second thought, plunked down his black Amex card, and been done with it.

But now, the entire place gave me anxiety, and I had no idea why. I felt like an impostor.

A hoax.

I worried that somehow, at any given minute, a team of guards and police were going to rush in, arrest me, and charge me with falsely impersonating another person.

Because this couldn't possibly be my life. Fancy cars and unlimited bank accounts.

But it was, and as I signed on the dotted line and handed over my fancy credit card, I finally saw it. The reality of my life.

I was fucking loaded, and so far I'd done nothing but buy buckets of ice cream, cash in a couple free tickets to the ballet, and take my therapist out for dinner.

It was time to celebrate.

Chapter Thirteen

Everly

It was dark. The apartment had gone quiet long ago.

And yet I still lay awake in our bed, staring at the ceiling, unable to sleep because of the flood of thoughts filling my head.

There were too many, and yet not enough, and then so many I didn't want to face.

Ryan hadn't said anything, but I knew the casual conversation he'd witnessed between August and me the night before had unnerved him.

He wasn't the only one.

It had unnerved me, too. It unraveled me and sent me to a place within my head where I didn't want to dwell.

A place where he became more than the monster I'd turned him into, and I could never allow him to be. Because if he wasn't the monster in this fucked-up fairy tale, then who was?

After that one glance, I'd never once looked back up at our old theater box, refusing to give him the satisfaction of knowing he was on my mind.

Even if he had been.

Instead, I'd followed every twirl, every lift as Sarah flawlessly performed the role of her dreams, bringing the swan princess to life on stage. She had been phenomenal and I'd finally found myself caught up in her brilliance, rather than my own selfish world.

When I met her backstage once again, all thoughts had been firmly back in place, focused on her, as Ryan and I congratulated her. We'd offered to take her out to celebrate but she'd sadly declined, explaining the cast was going out together, but promised to meet up with us later in the week.

On our drive home that night, as I watched the city pass by in a blur, I tried not to envision August and his redheaded date in the back of a darkened car. Ryan had interrupted my dark thoughts, bringing me back to reality.

"You seem better," he'd said, reaching across the seat to grasp my hand. I'd looked over to see a small grin tugging at his lips.

"Better? Than what?"

"Well, you seemed a bit tense after the show started. Did running into August scare you?"

I closed my eyes briefly as the memory flooded back. *Spread your legs...relax.*

"Yes," I had quickly answered, giving a hesitant smile. "Just threw me off, I guess."

Another white lie.

Guilt pulled heavily at my conscience.

"Well, it's a good thing I came when I did," he'd said, giving me a sideways glance as we pulled onto a side street near our apartment.

"You're always there when I need you."

And he was.

I rolled over to watch him sleep. The sound of his even breathing filled me with such peace, I found myself listening to its steady rhythm until I felt my own body drifting off.

Even in sleep, he still was there for me.

What felt like moments later, I was awakened by a noise—a phone, maybe. I sat up, rubbing my tired eyes as I looked over to my nightstand. My cell phone buzzed around next to me.

Why did I insist on putting that thing next to me at night?

Oh right; in case of emergencies.

Suddenly, I looked at the time as I grabbed the phone. Three in the morning—my heart pounded in my chest as I thought of Sarah out late at night with the cast.

"Hello?" I answered, my voice tired and groggy. Ryan's hand reached out for me in the darkness and he too awoke.

"Who is it?" he asked, his head buried in the pillow.

"Miss Adams?" someone asked.

"Yes, this is she."

"This is Doctor Maven from the UCSF Emergency Room. We have August Kincaid here—he was in a car accident."

There were many emotions I should have felt at that moment. Confusion should have probably topped them all as I wondered why I was being called at all, but the second I heard "August" and "car accident" in the same sentence, I couldn't breathe.

"Is he okay?" I asked, taking long, slow breaths to keep my emotions from spilling down my cheeks.

"Yes, a bit banged up. Perhaps a few bruised ribs and a sprained ankle. But he's fine. Or will be."

"Do I need to come down?" I asked, already rising from the bed.

"He will need a ride home—he's pretty out of it from the pain meds."

"That's fine," I answered before hanging up, not even realizing what I was signing up for. I was in some sort of zombie mode, where August was in need and I'd just responded.

Without even thinking of the repercussions or consequences.

Especially the big one sitting on the bed, staring at me right now.

"What was that all about?" Ryan asked, his eyes hooded with concern and doubt.

"August was in a car accident tonight. They need someone to give him a ride home," I answered very casually, pulling out a pair of jeans and a T-shirt from my drawer.

His hand met mine instantly. I hadn't even seen him get up.

"And why does that person have to be you?" he asked. I looked up at him. His expression was full of the same intensity I'd seen at the ballet when he'd pulled me away from August in the lobby of the theater.

"I guess he still has me listed as his emergency contact," I said with caution, stepping out of his grasp to get dressed.

"Damn it, Ev!" he shouted, his voice filling the room. "What is going on with you?"

"Nothing!" I yelled, taken aback by the roaring thunder of his voice. Ryan very rarely raised his voice—especially to me. "Nothing. He just needs someone to take him home. I'll be right back." I turned toward the bed and began pulling on my jeans, the awkward silence filling the spaces where I should have been apologizing—begging for forgiveness for all the stupid mistakes I'd made.

"You know this is way more than just a simple ride." His hand touched my shoulder tentatively, and I turned.

"We knew this would be tricky," I said softly. "We knew if he woke up, it would be rough."

He nodded. "I just expected something much different from casual conversations and rides around town."

"Me too," I admitted.

"I feel like we're drifting, Everly, during a time when we should be growing closer. We're getting married soon and I barely see you."

I looked up into his eyes and saw hurt...pain, vulnerability.

I'd done that and I wanted it gone. All of it.

"It's the wedding planning. It's too much," I blurted out without thinking.

That was only partially the truth. Wedding planning did cause me stress but it wasn't the reason I'd been mentally checking out.

So many lies. So many secrets. When would it end?

"I never said we had to have a big wedding, Ev."

"I know. I just thought that was how it was done," I said.

"Well, who says we have to do it the way it is supposed to be done?" he replied, his eyebrow lifting mischievously. "Let's elope!"

"What?" I choked out.

"Let's just do away with tradition and go away this weekend and get married! We can fly to Vegas, or drive down Highway One and find a little chapel somewhere. Whatever you want to do."

Looking up at him once again, I didn't see hurt or pain anymore. I saw hundreds of possibilities and I wanted to make each and every one of those come true. For him. For us and for our future.

"Yes," I answered.

He picked me up and twirled me around the room while I squealed. It was like our proposal all over again, only I was half-dressed and he was wearing boxers.

"I'll start Googling places while you're gone," he said happily, kissing my cheek with exuberance. "Hurry back."

No more ill feelings about the hospital or August. Just happiness.

And that was exactly the way it should be.

* * *

A little banged up, the attending doctor had said...

Jesus, he looked like he'd gotten thrown into the middle of a boxing ring with one hand tied behind his back.

And the worst part of all? The smug little grin on his damned face.

The "I don't give a shit about any of this" attitude he was sporting.

I wanted to punch him. No, I wanted to kill him...and then punch him.

Asshole.

"Fuck! What the hell is wrong with you?" The words finally burst free from my mouth as we sped down the highway. He'd been discharged with pain pills, directions for how to wrap and care for his wounds, and a future date to check in with his primary care physician...which he didn't have.

Irresponsible asshole.

Silence spread between us after my rather vocal outburst, and he turned toward me. "Can't a guy wreck a car and not be interrogated about it?"

More smug grinning.

Steam billowed out of my ears as I plotted various ways to slap that stupid expression off his damned face. God, I hated him.

No more words were exchanged until we arrived at his house. He didn't bother moving as I pulled into the driveway and got out to retrieve his crutches. As I yanked open the passenger door, he greeted me with his dopey smile.

"You're too good to me," he commented. The drugs he had been given in the emergency room were clearly making their presence known.

"Uh huh," I agreed as I placed the crutches out in front of him so he could use them to stand. He wobbled a little but made it upright. Slowly, we got to the front door.

"Do you have the key?" I asked, looking at him with annoyance.

"Oh, right."

He fished around in his pocket for what seemed like an eternity, until he pulled out a small set of keys. A shiny, new car key was strung next to the familiar house key and I rolled my eyes, trying not to imagine what that expensive car must look like now.

"What thought process did you go through when you decided to buy a car…and then hours later, crash it?" I asked, dangling the key in front of him before I used the other to let us in.

"Hmmm, well…I thought, 'Pretty car…I want,' and that was about it."

At least he hadn't been drunk when he'd crashed. Otherwise, he'd be facing jail time along with those cuts and bruises. Apparently spending two years in a hospital bed had made him a bit rusty behind the wheel. He'd been broadsided when he failed to stop at a light. No doubt he'd be slapped with a fine and have to pay damages for the other driver's car, but I doubted any of that mattered to him now.

"Go sit on the couch. I'll get you some water," I replied curtly before disappearing into the kitchen. Flipping a switch, I watched the large space become illuminated with light.

The room still looked the same—like taking a walk back in time.

I took my time walking around, admiring the beautiful cherry-wood cabinets and polished marble countertops. During the day, light would filter in from the skylights. I rested my hands against the edge of the counter and took several deep breaths.

This had always been one of my favorite spaces—when things were good between August and me.

The inability to decide what I wanted to do with my life wasn't a new thing. I'd been "wandering" for years, trying to find my niche in the world. Before we lived here, I'd dabbled with college—taken a few classes and tried out several majors—but nothing ever stuck.

After August hit it big and I had no reason to seek work, I'd turned to the kitchen, watching cooking shows and copying what their chefs did. It wasn't anything amazing, but it gave me something to do during the day that was my own.

So many good and bad memories were wrapped up in this one space—it was hard to make sense of it all.

Turning toward the closest cupboard, I grabbed a glass and filled it with water, knowing in an hour or two, August would need to re-up his pain meds. I had no plans of being here to help him with that.

I'd already done enough.

Being here, with him, was already too much.

It stirred emotions, made me feel things, remember...

Stepping out into the living room, I glanced around, looking for the large injured man I'd ordered around, but he was nowhere to be found.

"Damn it," I muttered.

Snatching the meds off the coffee table where they had been dropped, I scoped out the rest of the first floor before making my way up the stairs.

If the kitchen brought back a flood of memories, trudging up the stairs to the second floor was like standing on a beach when a tsunami hit. A damned disaster. I didn't bother checking any of the guest rooms. If he was up here, there was only one place he would have gone at this time of night.

The one place I didn't want to enter—the master bedroom.

The double doors were wide open. Moonlight streamed in from the open windows and a breeze fluttered the curtains, filling the air with the smell of the sea. August had always said this one room was the reason he'd bought the house.

From here, it felt like you could see the entire Pacific, right outside your balcony window. Endless turquoise waves crashed against the staggering heights of the cliffs. From left to right, it was nothing but the crystal blue coastline California was known for.

I don't know how many nights we fell asleep listening to the soothing sounds of the waves crashing below us. It was a mesmerizing sound, and for a moment I just stood there and let it consume me.

"I know you're out there," August said, tearing me from my quiet calm.

"I wasn't trying to hide," I answered, walking swiftly toward him, not bothering to hide my annoyance. He'd managed to rid himself of his shirt before falling onto the mattress. He was thinner than he used to be, the loss of muscle taking its toll on his body, but he was still beautiful.

Still August. Still dangerous.

"I have your pain meds and a glass of water," I announced, placing both items on the nightstand beside him.

He watched me, his eyes following my every move in the dimly lit room.

"Can you check my stitches?" he asked softly, pointing to the bandage on his head. Due to a small flying chunk of glass from the window, he'd gotten a nasty cut just above his left eyebrow. Thankfully, he'd needed only a few stitches—it could have been so much more.

"Why?" I asked.

"I think I pulled at them when I was taking off my shirt—can you just make sure they're okay?"

"I guess." I sighed, taking a seat on the bed next to him. Reaching toward him with obvious hesitance, I took a deep breath, trying to calm my nerves. That intense gaze followed me as he watched my fingers reach toward him. Lifting the edge of the bandage, I quickly took a peek under the edge and made sure everything looked as it should.

"Yep, looks good," I quickly answered, pulling back and placing my hands in my lap.

"I'm sorry—I didn't mean to upset you," he said, reaching out toward me but then second-guessing his decision.

A ghost of a laugh fell from my lips as I glanced down at him.

"You didn't mean to upset me? Really, August? After everything tonight—that is the one thing you apologize for? Making me look at your nasty-ass stitches?"

"I—I'm sorry for everything?"

"You're sorry? You're sorry! You fucking asshole!" I screamed, jumping up from the bed. "You have no regard for anyone, or anything! You could have died! Died! You stupid jerk! And you're sorry—for what? You don't even know, do you? You're apologizing for nothing. Nothing!"

Rage, anger, and then tears. It all happened so quickly. I didn't even realize it when the hot salty trails made their way down my cheeks; I just kept yelling and screaming at him.

A volcano can only stay dormant for so long…and mine had enough emotions bottled up inside, it was ready to explode. A timid hand finally touched my shoulder, and I turned to find August standing before me, balancing on one leg.

"I hate you!" I shouted, banging on his bruised chest. "I hate you," I said again, losing my fight. "I hate you, August," I whimpered one last time.

I have no idea which one of us initiated it, but I soon found myself cradled in his arms, sobbing as I held on to him like a lifeline. My body quaked as the pain tore through me. My fingers dug into his skin as salty tears fell from my cheeks.

"I know. I'm sorry, Everly. I'm sorry—for everything."

His voice cut through me, sobering my emotions, like getting hit with a bucket of ice-cold water. I pushed against his bare skin, putting much-needed distance between us. I quickly whisked the moisture from my eyes, sniffling as I tried to control the echoing sobs that still tugged at me.

"Good-bye, August," I said, taking a final glance at him under the moonlight.

"Good-bye, Everly," he echoed, his gaze following me as I fled.

Fled the memories, the man, and the life I needed to forget.

* * *

I wasn't surprised to find Ryan waiting for me when I walked in.

Clutching a cup of coffee between his hands, he sat at the small dining room table, fully dressed for work at six in the morning.

He usually only got up this early when he went to the gym, or when he followed me to work for a free cup of coffee. Neither of which were happening this morning.

"How long have you been up?" I asked, gently setting my purse down on the counter.

"Since you left," he answered, not bothering to look up from his empty cup.

I busied myself in the kitchen, grabbing my favorite mug, then pouring a cup of coffee for myself and refreshing his. When that was done, I had nothing else to do but join him at the table.

Taking a hesitant seat next to him, I took an audible breath before wrapping my hands around the large warm mug.

"We're not getting married this weekend, are we?" he asked, the tone of his voice defeated and shallow.

"No," I answered quietly, taking a slow sip of coffee.

He started to get up, clearly upset, but I stopped him, reaching for his hand.

"Please, let me explain."

Finally, his eyes met mine. Hurt, pain, and distrust met me, and as much as it tore me up inside to know I'd once again caused all of those emotions, I knew I couldn't marry him.

Not right now.

Not just to make things better between us.

Marriage wasn't about fixing a problem—it was about creating a beginning. And I wasn't about to start ours this way.

I watched as he slipped back down in his chair, and I took a moment to collect my thoughts. "I want to marry you, Ryan."

He shook his head in disbelief, but I gripped his hand and pressed on. "I do. Please believe me. There is nothing I want more.

But running off to get married this weekend is wrong, and you know it."

His eyes met mine, and we held gazes—deadlocked until he finally nodded. "Yeah, you're right. I was reacting to the situation last night. I don't know how to handle him in our lives," he admitted.

"I don't either," I said. "And it's something I need to figure out."

He nodded in agreement, but I could see the disappointment—the fear that he would lose me.

"Just promise me you won't let him get to you," he begged. "I know he's different—changed, but he's still the same man who hurt you."

Standing, I took his cup and placed it on the table, stepping into his grasp. His hands instinctively wrapped around my thighs as I settled into his lap, wrapping my legs around his torso.

"I promise, Ryan," I said softly, pressing my body tightly against his. "I choose you. Always you."

No more secrets.

No more lies.

It was time to say good-bye to my past.

Chapter Fourteen

August

It seemed like wherever I went in this life, I always found myself surrounded by boxes.

No matter what I did to hide from them, put them out of my mind…I'd find myself in the recesses of a forgotten closet or the darkest spot in the attic, searching…hunting for something.

Anything.

Ever since that late night with Everly, I'd been on a mission—a sick, twisted manhunt to find anything that would bring me closer to her. Those few precious seconds she'd been in my arms had been the first time, since I woke up, that I'd truly felt grounded—rooted to the earth.

And now I was searching out anything and everything that could possibly give me the same response.

Today I was in the bedroom, with a box of pictures I'd collected. Happy memories of the two of them over the years. I still couldn't say "us."

Even though it was me in those pictures smiling back at the world, it wasn't my memory.

It wasn't my life.

It was like having a twin brother. We looked the same but that was where the similarities ended. The guy in the picture looked like he'd had everything, while I'd been left with nothing but confusion and frustration. Could I really look at all these happy memories and claim them as my own? Claim the woman and the love she'd given as my own?

What about her hatred? And her fear?

I'd have to take that as well.

"Are you aware your front door is unlocked?" a familiar voice called out from behind me. I turned to see Brick, the friendly psychotherapist, standing in the doorway of my bedroom. Holding a pile of mail.

"No, I wasn't," I answered, giving him a curious look as he stepped forward and handed me my mail.

"You missed your appointment. I figured I'd find you here."

"House calls a regular thing for you now?" I asked, placing the mail aside in exchange for something less dismal. He ignored my question and instead pointed at the half-empty bottle of vodka I was now clutching.

"Thought you'd put that particular liquor firmly in the 'no' category," he remarked.

"Well, I might have been a bit hasty with my decision," I answered, pulling the bottle to my lips. The clear, fiery liquid burned all the way down, but it helped numb my thoughts and settle my mind. "So I'm giving it another chance."

"At ten in the morning?"

I shrugged, feeling my body relax a little as the alcohol did its work. "I'm an overachiever. Or at least that's what my report cards say."

He pulled a seat up to mine and grabbed the bottle out of my hand. To my ultimate surprise, I watched as he took a long gulp before placing the bottle on the nightstand beside us. His eyes roamed around the room, zeroing in on the box beside me on the bed.

"The three-million-dollar woman, I presume?" he asked, nodding in the direction of the photo that rested on my knee. I glanced down at the single photo, picking it up and rubbing the crisp edges between my fingers.

"Do you think it's possible to be in love with a woman you don't remember, Brick?"

He took the picture from me, looking it over. I had no idea when it had been taken. No inscription was left as had been on the one in my wallet, but it was obviously several years old—before things had gotten bad between us.

They looked happy—lying in a field, with Everly's hair fanned out around them, making a goofy faces toward the camera above. The image was innocent and lighthearted, and probably captured a moment they had wished to remember for a lifetime.

When had it all gone wrong?

"I think the mind is capable of many things," he said, handing the picture back to me. "Why don't you let me help you with this stuff?" he offered.

I quickly nodded, and we both stood, taking a wide glance over the scattered boxes.

"I just don't understand what happened. How this…" I said, picking up another random happy moment from my long-lost past, "became this." I held my hands out wide, encompassing the room, as if it symbolized everything that was wrong with my life.

And in a way, it did.

This house, this room—it was where it had all fallen apart.

Or at least, that's what she'd alluded to.

If life between Everly and me hadn't plunged into sadness—hadn't cascaded into the dark, dismal existence she'd made it out to be, would I still be here? Or would I be living life like one of these photos? Making memories with the woman I'd loved…

I placed the single photo back in the box, and took a deep breath.

"Have you ever considered asking her? I don't know exactly what happened between the two of you but it's obvious you're hurting. It could be good for you—help you move on, August," Brick said gently, in a tone he very rarely used. I called it his clinical voice and usually the sound of it grated my nerves, making me feel weak and feeble. Right now, however, it just helped normalize me, filtering out the alcohol—like a level finding its center.

"I couldn't. After everything she's been through—everything he's done."

Looking across the room, I found myself instantly correcting my words. "*I've* done," I restated. "I can't put her through that again. She deserves a clean slate from me. A normal life—whatever she chooses that to be. I need to find a different way to sort through all this."

Taking one last glance at the assorted boxes, I only saw one option.

"Can you do me a favor, Brick?" I asked, the very idea of it making my fingers twitch. He nodded once, and I grabbed the nearest box.

"Get rid of it. All of it. I can't be around it—the memories of her. It's too painful, knowing I once had something so precious but wasted it away. I don't care what you do with it, but please—just take it from me."

The words felt like sandpaper against my throat as I spoke. Ever since she'd left that night I'd briefly held her in my arms, I'd spent hours in this room looking over these pictures, analyzing each smile—every laugh, the way my hands and fingers held her—trying to find that moment when things had begun to unravel.

Why? I don't know. Maybe because I just didn't understand why I would ever stop loving someone like her.

But maybe I hadn't.

She'd said I'd locked her away—made her a prisoner in her own home.

Why would I have done that?

Maybe sometimes love isn't pure. Maybe sometimes it's toxic—so toxic it consumes a person until they would do anything to have it.

Like a drug.

If I loved her now, would it be the same as before?

Would I consume her?

* * *

I awoke, the remote falling from my hand as I looked around the living room. The TV flickered, grabbing my attention, and I quickly bent down to grab the fallen remote and turn up the volume.

Another old movie was playing. Back to the Future.

Was I ever going to watch something from this century?

Marty looked down at a picture of his siblings, and watched it slowly fade as he was being erased from existence.

How fucking surreal.

I looked around and nearly jumped out of my skin.

Every damn box I'd given to Brick surrounded me, like a bunch of damned creepy stalkers, staring me down. I stood up, looking out over the tops of the boxes and saw nothing but more boxes.

More and more boxes.

The whole house was filled with them.

I dug my hand into the closest one, pulling out several pictures I recognized. Old, happy memories from a life I didn't remember. I didn't want these memories. I didn't want these reminders of a life I would never have again.

As if a wish had been granted, the color began to drain from the photo onto the floor. Our happy smiles smeared and distorted as the photo disappeared before my eyes. Colors mixed, created dark black streaks on my hands. Soon I was covered in it.

I picked up another photo, and another and they all vanished, like they were being erased from existence.

"Wait!" I yelled. "I want them back! I want them back!"

*   *   *

I'd wasted far too much time, sitting around waiting for my life to start.

No more taste tests or fast cars. No more dwelling on the past or pondering over old pictures or crazy dreams that haunted me. I'd been ignoring far too much, and spending the rest of the time feeling bad for myself. It was time to finally wake up from the perpetual fog I'd been in for the last couple of months and take charge of this life I'd been given.

There were bills stacking up on the counter, a million messages on my outdated cell phone, and the idea of spending the rest of my life living off my fortune doing absolutely nothing was starting to make my skin crawl.

There was so much about this situation I couldn't control, but the tiny amount that I could…It was time I made that my bitch.

Starting with paying the bills.

I took a deep, settling breath, made the biggest cup of coffee possible, and took a long walk down the hall toward my forgotten office—a place I'd never visited much, but which seemed like the perfect location for bill paying and general businesslike stuff.

Flipping the lights on, I took a brief look around. It was formally decorated—dark wood and leather—like something straight out of an old Hollywood set. It even had fancy green lamps that probably cost more than most people's cars. But I guess I had liked that look in the past. It was really quite intimidating.

Maybe it would grow on me?

Taking a seat in the large leather chair, I put my feet up on the polished wood table and leaned back, trying to imagine myself conducting business deals in this space.

Nope, couldn't see it.

Obviously, I had been good at what I'd done. The house and bank account were proof of that, but I just couldn't picture myself in a stiff dark suit, commanding business deals over the phone, while there was an entire world out there to explore.

And the perfect woman to worship.

Bills. Need to pay bills.

It had been three days since I'd asked Brick to take away the photo boxes. Three days, and yet I still couldn't go a few minutes without thinking of her. Even my subconscious was dreaming of her. My mind would drift as I brewed a fresh pot of coffee—the smell alone making me think of her—and I'd start wondering whether she was working, and if she liked her job at that little coffeehouse. Even today, as I grabbed the bills off the counter, I thought about how she'd handled everything for me for the two years I was in the hospital.

She'd given over everything to my lawyer and accountant—making sure everything was taken care of. Even my cell phone bill had been paid, for two years, even while everyone assumed I'd never wake up.

Why? Did she secretly hope I would...or had that just been an oversight?

Whatever her reasons, she'd stopped the moment I awoke. All the bills came to me now, and it was about time I figured them out. I could have simply handed everything back over to the same accountant she'd used for the last few years, but for someone who currently didn't have a job—it just seemed ridiculous. I had plenty of time, and I really needed to understand my own finances.

For someone with no memory of their past—I was the easiest fucking target on the planet right now. I didn't want to be walking around with amnesia and also be poor. It was time to start using all those smarts I'd apparently been blessed with.

First bill on the stack—hospital bill. Easy; paid. Next. Utility bill—check.

I went through several like this—lightning fast—and I thought I'd be done in no time. I'd barely made a dent in my giant cup of coffee, and it was still piping hot.

And then I found the bill from an attorney.

Fuck.

The dude who'd hit me in the intersection was suing for damages and hospital fees. Looked like I needed my lawyer—and fast. Not remembering much from my first few days after waking up in the hospital, I couldn't recall the law firm that had contacted me off the top of my head. Pulling out my phone, I clicked through my old contacts, having previously discovered my former self had liked to list contacts in random ways. Dentist was listed just like that—"dentist." I'd spent several nights looking at this strange organizational system. Some people were just an occupation, while others had names—like Everly. But then some were just a string of initials. Not a single person had a last name, which made the whole listing seem very murky and clandestine. Did he think he was a spy? Whatever the reason, it made me hate myself a little more.

As I made my way down the list, I couldn't help but chuckle at some of the notations—"Everly's hippie doctor"—there had to be a story behind that one, I was sure. One that I'd probably never discover.

Shaking my head as I scrolled down, I found the one I needed: "lawyer."

Who knew what his name was, or if he'd even remember me after all this time, but it was worth a try.

After a few rings, a secretary answered, saying, "Johnson, Doyle, and Platt." The names now sounded suddenly familiar, and I quickly introduced myself. As if I'd said some magic word, she quickly cut me off and placed me on hold.

"August Kincaid—it's Jeff Doyle. Is it really you?" A gruff-sounding older man came on the line.

"Yes, it is, sir," I answered.

"Well, I'll be damned. I thought you were dead," he said, chuckling. An odd response considering the comment.

"Nope, just in a coma—for a couple of years," I deadpanned.

"Oh, that's right—" He cleared his throat, maybe because of a lack of anything to say to that. "What can I do for you, son? Already got yourself in hot water?" There was that arrogant chuckle again.

"Had a bit of a fender bender. Need some representation."

"Not a problem—figured it was something to do with you and Trent, and I can't lie, you had me worried."

I had no idea what he was talking about, so I just made a non-committal noise to move the conversation along. I was sick of telling people my sad story of loss—seeing their sympathetic looks, hearing their apologies. He obviously remembered my coma now that we were on the phone, but had no idea I was still suffering from the after-effects. To him, I was August Kincaid—whatever that meant.

For now, it was good enough.

He'd find out soon enough. But for now, I was just August and he was just my lawyer. No sappy eyes—no sad comments. Nothing.

We made an appointment to meet up later in the week to go over everything and he switched me over to his secretary to finalize everything. Within minutes, I was done with the call and back to the silence of the dark, barren room.

I looked down at the cell phone still in my hand and started searching through the contacts, looking for one specific name.

Trent.

There it was. No initials…no occupation. Just Trent.

Who are you and what missing piece are you to the long-lost puzzle of my past?

Chapter Fifteen

Everly

I'd done everything I could to go back—to create the life Ryan and I had lived before that fateful phone call had changed everything.

Like the personal poltergeist he'd become in my life, August had reentered our lives, and nothing since had been the same. We fought more, argued about trivial things, and there was this tension that had never been there before. But no matter how many movie nights, or passion-filled hours we spent in each other's arms, we couldn't find a way back to the way it had been. Things were just different and I didn't know how to fix it.

I'd said good-bye—I'd made up my mind. No more August. No more favors or late-night trips to the ER. I was done. But deep down, I don't think my heart had agreed.

And wasn't that the ironic part of it all?

It was my heart that had chosen Ryan—my heart that had screamed *yes* when he'd presented me with the ring I now wore on my left hand, and it was this heart still that reached out for him in the middle of the night.

Each night. Every night.

Why would the same heart who loved a man so fiercely keep me from him at the same time?

When I'd asked Dr. Lawrence that day in the hospital how all this was possible—how August could remember how to tie his shoes but not remember his own name—he'd simply said, "The mind is a unique and powerful thing."

Perhaps the heart was as well.

As I opened the apartment door, home from another shift at work, I looked around the empty apartment and wondered what my heart was trying to tell me that I couldn't see for myself.

Blankets lay in a heap, left on the floor after our late-night television binge. Two coffee cups sat empty on the table nearby, and I remembered snuggling into Ryan's warmth as we clung to cups of decaf and watched the latest episode of our favorite show. I'd buried my head into his shoulder at the gory parts and laughed when something funny had happened, and never once had I thought about August or my muddled feeling about his return.

It had just been the two of us, and our simple life together.

And that was all this heart—all I'd ever wanted.

A knock pulled me out of my deep thoughts just as I was considering making a cup of coffee after my eight-hour shift. There was a reason I worked in a coffee shop: I had a serious addiction to the dark brew.

Quickly putting my coffee thoughts aside, I ran to the door to answer it. Outside stood a man I'd never seen before.

Shit—I really should have checked before throwing open the door.

Please don't be a burglar.

Or a rapist.

Or one of those people who hands out pamphlets.

"Hi, are you Everly Adams?" he asked, his voice calm and sweet—the exact opposite of what I would expect from a serial killer.

Maybe that was what he wanted me to think?

"Um, maybe? Who are you?" I asked, my timid voice sounding anything but fierce.

"Sorry—I didn't mean to frighten you," he said, taking a step back. "My name is Brick Abrams. I'm a therapist."

Totally confused.

"And you go door to door?" I questioned lamely.

He laughed, and tiny crinkled lines appeared around his worn brown eyes. "No; not usually, anyway. Although lately it seems to have become a habit. I'm here for a friend." It was then that I noticed he had several boxes next to his feet.

"Do you mind if I show you something? You don't have to let me in if you don't want to," he added as he bent down to open one of the boxes. Curiosity got the better of me, and even though I should have been concerned with my safety and what exactly he had in those boxes, I felt an instant kinship to this man—like I'd known him my entire life. I don't know why, but he felt like a friend I'd always had but never known.

Luckily, nothing scary or perverted came out of the box, only a handful of pictures. But when I got a closer look, I discovered that photos could indeed be more intimidating than my worst fears.

And right now, my worst fears were sitting in those boxes.

"What did you say the name of your friend was, Mr. Abrams?" I asked, tearing my eyes away from the pictures.

"I didn't, but I'm sure you could guess."

Swallowing the lump that had now formed in my throat, I nodded. "Yes, but I don't think I can help you, Mr. Abrams."

I slowly backed away. His sad eyes met mine as I began to push the door closed.

"But what if he could help you?"

"He's already done enough, don't you think?" I said, feeling the anger rising in my veins.

"I honestly don't know—and neither does he. That's the problem," he began, and I slowly pulled the door open, allowing the crazy man to gather up his boxes and enter. If anyone ever asked, I'd deny everything and say it was simply caffeine withdrawal that made me open the door, but really, I was suddenly just interested.

Interested in this man who seemed so much like a friend.

He took a seat at our small dining room table as I began brewing a pot of coffee. Being the old friends we were now, I just assumed he would join me. I didn't hang out with people who didn't like coffee— people like that couldn't be trusted.

"So, you're August's therapist?" I asked, looking over my shoulder as I moved about the kitchen.

"Something like that. I'm a therapist, and I know August. Let's just say I want to help him."

"Okay," I replied, feeling like he'd just evaded that question better than a politician on election day.

"August has no memory of his past—no understanding of who he is or why he became the person he is today. He's truly floundering. You hate a man who doesn't exist anymore."

As I stared at the coffee pot, waiting for it to brew, I let his words percolate and settle as I formed a response. "That doesn't mean I have to forgive him just because he doesn't remember."

"No, but shouldn't you at least give him the opportunity to move on—to find a new life?"

"Why? He destroyed mine," I spat.

"Did he?" He looked around, admiring our quaint little apartment with its secondhand furniture I'd lovingly restored on my days off. I'd used new fabric so it would all somehow match. The place was rustic, the total opposite of the house I'd decorated before, but it was still nonetheless home.

"Seems to me, if this is where you were supposed to be all along, how you got here would have been worth all the trouble."

I opened my mouth to respond, but couldn't form a rebuttal. I'd never seen my years with August simply as a long path to get me to Ryan. There had always been the time in my life with August, and then now. Two completely different worlds—separate from each other.

"I just want to move on." I sighed, taking the two cups of coffee I'd just poured and placing them between us as I sat down to join him.

"And so does he. What if you could do that—together?"

"I nearly gutpunched him the last time I saw him," I confessed. "While he was injured."

A smirk pulled across his lips, "He just needs answers. Maybe by giving them to him, you'll find the closure you need to move on."

"So you want me to just talk to him?"

He nodded, taking a sip of coffee.

"And that's it?"

"That's what he needs, Everly. What he's desperate for. He needs to fill in the blanks."

"And you think by doing this, I'll be able to find closure to all of this pain and anger I've been harboring as well?" I asked doubtfully.

"Talking with him could heal many wounds," he answered.

"Hmm," was all I could manage.

But even after we'd said our good-byes, even after my second cup of coffee had long since gone cold...I found myself returning to that single sentence and wondering whether he was right.

Was I still so wounded? And if so, could I find the healing I needed to move on without the man who'd caused me so much pain?

* * *

"You've got to be kidding me, Everly." Ryan looked up from his spot on the sofa.

"I know it sounds crazy—"

"Crazy? It's insane. No, it's more than insane. You can't seriously be considering it."

My lack of response had his eyes rounding with shock as he stood, ready to pace. He loved to pace. And I loved to flee. Those were our standard responses to an argument. He'd pace...talk, battle it out until everything was out in the open and well-discussed, like a well-functioning person—and me? I just wanted space. I'd learned through counseling and my time with Ryan that normal couples discussed their grievances with each other, but the practice still felt foreign to me.

When August got angry or frustrated—or hell, even just wanted to go out for an evening—I'd ended up locked in my bedroom.

I knew Ryan was different. I understood they weren't the same person, but the need to flee still remained. Even though he never raised his voice, never lashed out in anger, I could still feel his disappointment swirling around the room like a choking fog, and I suddenly couldn't breathe.

I rose to open a window. The fresh air dampened my frantic nerves.

"At first, no," I admitted, "I thought the idea was as ludicrous as you do. But, then I went and spoke to Tabitha."

He shook his head in disbelief, a wayward lock of hair falling over his eyes, hiding his expression from me.

"She wants you to do this?" he asked softly, turning away from me to begin his pacing again.

"She didn't give me an opinion one way or another—she just helped me understand the situation."

"And what is the situation, exactly?" he asked, running a frustrated hand over his face.

"Things aren't the same, Ryan—since August came back. For me, for you. It's different. And no matter how hard we try, it's been impossible to go back to the way things used to be."

"It will just take some time," he stated, grasping at invisible straws.

"No—I don't think simply time will fix this," I said. "Ignoring a problem never solves it."

"Then we'll move," he simply stated. "I can find a job somewhere else, and there are coffee shops all over America. Hell, there's a Starbucks on every corner. Rent is expensive here anyway."

He was rambling now. He felt threatened.

Closing the gap the separated us, I took his hand in mine. "I don't want to move, Ryan. And neither do you. The Giants are here and you have a fantastic career. You love this city—don't deny it."

His eyes met mine. "I love you more."

"I know."

When his lips touched mine, I felt the desperation in his touch, tasted the need in each lingering kiss as he carried me to the bedroom. He was scared—so very scared of losing me. We made love slowly, as if our bodies were memorizing every single inch of each another. Hours later, he still cradled me in his arms as we quietly held each other. Neither of us spoke, too afraid to break the calming spell that seemed to have been cast the second our bodies had met.

But spells are meant to be broken, and real life always seems to find its way back to the forefront of our minds.

"I know I'm different from most men," Ryan finally said, breaking the silence. I turned to face him in the moonlight.

"What do you mean?" I asked.

"I see the difference—between me and August…even now. I'm shy, and reserved. A lover, not a fighter if you will. These are qualities about myself I've known my entire life. My parents were gentle-natured and raised me to be so."

"Ryan—"

"No, let me finish. It's these qualities that first made me so appealing to you, I think—my stark contrast to him. I took care of you in a way that he never did—never would. But please, make no mistake that if it ever came down to it—"

My fingers moved across his worried face as he struggled to find the words.

"—I would fight for you, Everly. Do what you need to do to heal—to find the closure you need, but please know that I would tear apart heaven and earth if I had to—for you. This is not me backing away."

I tenderly touched my lips to his. "I know. Believe me, I know."

And as I surrendered back into his embrace, the taste of his kiss was the only thing racing through my mind that night.

He was my future—and soon my past would be nothing more than a distant memory.

Chapter Sixteen

August

Fifteen minutes had passed, and I was still looking down at my phone in awe.

She'd called me. By choice.

When her name had appeared on my phone I'd thought it was a cruel joke.

Why—especially after she'd walked away that night, making it clear it would most likely be the last time I saw her, would she ever try to reestablish contact with me?

Simple—Brick.

Probably violating every rule in whatever code of ethics he was supposed to follow, Brick had gone out of his way to make sure he broke every damn promise he'd made to me by seeking out Everly and doing the exact opposite of what I'd asked of him.

I'd just wanted her to have the life she deserved, and now here she was—right back where she'd started.

She said Brick thought it would bring us both closure—talking about the past as a way to seek out separate futures. I wasn't sure I agreed. Every path I saw led to her, which was exactly why I needed her so far away.

But I'd been a selfish man for far too long...and sometimes I thought some of those traits had remained when I awoke. If she was willing to see me, I would always come running.

*   *   *

I'd figured we'd meet for coffee, maybe have lunch or do something traditional and public. I had no lofty beliefs that she wanted to be anywhere with me, but I'd sincerely doubted it would be someplace remote.

Now I had no idea why I was meeting her in a trashy part of town, where the only form of art was newspaper flying in the breeze and random gang tags painted on the storefront walls.

Maybe she was hoping I'd get mugged on my way here. Ultimate revenge?

Guy recovers from two-year coma and gets mugged. Again.

After I'd had all the repairs done to that crazy-looking sports car I'd bought on a whim, I'd decided to trade it in for something a bit more sensible after my embarrassing accident. It had been fun for a night, but like so many other things, I'd discovered flashy just wasn't my style. So I'd downgraded to a domestic SUV. It was a lot less strain on the purse strings, and it drank gas like it was Kool-Aid, but it felt like me the second I got inside.

It also had a rack on the top for camping gear, and just the thought of that made me happy somehow as I tried to imagine the old August in his crisp suit driving out to the forest and pitching a tent.

A tap at my window had me nearly jumping out of my seat.

Nearly—I still kept my cool.

Everly tried to hide the grin on her face for catching me off guard as I opened the door and hopped out.

"Another new car?" she asked, taking a long look at the shiny red paint.

"Yeah, traded the other one in."

She nodded but didn't say anything until she noticed what was in my hand. "What do you have there?"

"Oh, I found it when I was emptying out a closet. Thought it looked interesting," I said, holding up the SLR camera. It had been hidden away on a shelf high up in the master closet. I'd done some research on the particular model and it was worth a fortune—basically top of the line, or it had been several years ago.

I'd considered selling it, or donating it to the local high school, but as soon as my fingers touched it, I knew it was mine.

"You used to love taking photos. That's why there are so many boxes of them," she said, looking down at the camera with soulful eyes.

"Why'd I stop?"

"Why did you stop loving so many things?" she asked, then began walking away.

I quickly followed her down the street, noticing her eyes taking in the dilapidated, tiny apartment buildings. "Why are we here?" I asked, unable to stop myself from clicking a few pictures here and there as we walked.

"You aren't the only one with a therapist, August," she informed me. "And when I spoke to mine, this is some of the advice she gave me."

"To drop me off in the ghetto and hope I never find my way back?"

Again, she tried to cover up the small smirk that threatened to tug at the corner of her mouth. The fact that she didn't want to share any joy with me stung, but I understood.

I was still the enemy.

She had done so much for me already, considering what little I had come to understand about our relationship, and it showed what a kind heart she had. I just hoped whatever she hoped to get out of this little experiment worked.

"No," she continued. "She said I should start at beginning. If you and I both need closure, maybe we'll find it along the way."

I nodded, looking around at the unfamiliar area. "So our story begins here?"

"Yes, but it looked much different a decade ago. As did we, I guess."

"I've seen pictures of you from ten years ago. You don't look that different," I said, remembering the one I had found in my wallet at the hospital.

Same coppery red hair, same intense blue eyes. If she smiled now, I was sure I'd find the same beautiful girl standing before me.

But she wouldn't smile—not for me.

Not anymore.

"In 2005, this was a great area for clubbing. I guess there are some nightclubs around here still but it's not quite the same. Back then, this was the place to be and I spent every weekend sneaking into the best clubs with friends."

"And me?" I asked with a questioning gaze.

"You and your coworkers liked to come here after work—something about blowing off steam. I think you just liked to be part of the team. The loud noise and the dancing never really appealed to you."

"But it brought me to you," I stated. She flinched. "Sorry," I apologized, realizing what I'd said.

"It's okay. Brick reminded me that had I not met you, I wouldn't have eventually found Ryan. And Ryan is my everything," she said firmly, each word cutting me like a knife.

"Right," I managed to say.

She abruptly stopped walking and I nearly smacked into her side as she stood looking at a small apartment building to our left.

"This is where I lived." She pointed to the second story, where a tattered old sheet fluttered in the wind, serving as a makeshift curtain. Trash lined the streets and what little paint was left on the building was cracked and flaking. It was the type of place you see when you accidentally take the wrong turn off the interstate, and try not to stare as you quickly wait for your GPS to reroute you to safety. Knowing she'd lived here caused permanent damage to my soul; knowing she'd been so close to poverty—so close to danger.

"How long?" I asked softly.

"Since the day I turned eighteen and wasn't worth anything to my foster parents anymore."

I hadn't known she was a foster kid. I guess there was a lot I didn't know about her.

"What about school? What about a job?"

She shook her head. "This particular couple only cared about the cash—nothing else. They kicked me out and replaced me the same day with someone younger. There are people who do it for the right reasons, but it's far from a perfect system."

"Everly—"

"Please don't talk," she begged, before saying, "I remember being embarrassed to take you here. For the first several weeks we dated, you'd ask to see where I lived, and I'd always make lame excuses—like my roommate had a guy over, or I hadn't had time to clean. But finally you figured it out. Snuck a peek at my license and instead of going to your place, we ended up here."

She took a deep breath as I watched her nearly relive the memory as it played out through her words.

"I was terrified. I thought you'd leave the moment you saw the place. You were four years older than me. For an eighteen-year-girl from the foster system, you seemed like something out of a fairy tale."

"What happened?" I asked, turning toward her as she watched the sheet flutter from the second-story window.

"You took my hand, walked me to my apartment, and held out your hand."

"My hand?"

"Yep, you placed it in yours and shook it and then did the craziest thing."

*　　*　　*

"Hi, I'm August Kincaid."

"Everly Adams."

"Good. Now that we have that out of the way, won't you invite me into your lovely home?"

*　　*　　*

"I thought you were crazy at first, but just that small act of kindness gave me the courage to open that door and let you in—both literally and emotionally. We spent the entire night talking—about life, past and present, and where we saw ourselves ten years from then."

"And where did you see yourself ten years from that night?" I asked. Her eyes suddenly turned away from the apartment building.

"It doesn't matter now," she snapped. "Plans change—for better, for worse. We adapt. And all that matters is what's in front of us."

"And you have Ryan now," I concluded.

"Yes."

Silence followed us as we moved down the street past the old clubs and the dingy storefronts.

"Why do you want to know about the past—about us—so badly?" she blurted out as we reached my car. I turned to face her, and saw red blotches of anger tinting her face. I took a second or two to collect my thoughts before responding.

"Have you ever watched a mystery or a thriller-type movie?"

"What?"

"You know, like *Inception* or *Gone Girl*? Where you just have no fucking clue what's going on until the very end?"

"I know what type of movie you're talking about. And no—not really, if you must know. I'm not a mystery lover—I always see the plot twists from a mile away. But what I don't see is why you're bring-ing up movies—right now!" she huffed.

"I'm trying to explain my answer. Would you just give me a sec-ond," I answered gruffly.

She threw her arms across her chest, and I tried to ignore the way they pressed her breasts high and tight against her shirt. I decided to look at the stop sign across the street instead.

That was safer.

"Anyway, as I was saying—I've been watching a lot of movies

lately—in an effort to discover the new me. Well, I've decided I hate thrillers and mysteries. The intense feeling of never knowing what is going on—that sick, twist-in-the-gut feeling of knowing there is something missing and you just don't know what it is. I hate it—with a passion. That's my life—all that damn time. Knowing there are clues and memories out there, within reach, but having no idea how to get to them."

"Why do you need to know so badly? I mean, couldn't you just start over new?" she asked softly.

"I tried. I am trying, but I'm always pulled back to this dark black hole of nothingness. I need to fill in the blanks. I need to make sure I don't…"

"You don't what?" she pressed.

"I don't want to become that man again," I confessed, turning toward her. Her hesitant eyes met mine, and she nodded.

"Then we keep going. One memory at a time."

No smile of encouragement, no friendly good-bye as she turned toward her car, but she had given me the promise of more.

More time with her.

More memories of us, and more chances to change her mind.

She might never love me again, but maybe she'd find it in her heart to forgive the man I was trying to become.

Chapter Seventeen

Everly

"I don't like this, Tabitha." I shook my head as I copied Ryan's signature move in the middle of her suddenly very cramped office and paced back and forth, really wishing there was a window I could open.

Or a door.

"Are you sure that's the reason it's bothering you?" she asked calmly. I hated calm right now.

Calm could kiss my ass.

It had been two hours since my meeting with August and I was so amped up on coffee and rage and forty other different emotions I hadn't sorted out, calm was just about the last thing I wanted to hear.

"Like what? Like how this was just about the worst idea on the planet? Getting two people together like him and me? Shit, it's like putting the atomic bomb and its detonator in the same room and waiting around to see what happens. So fucking stupid."

She let me take another layer off her carpet before responding.

"Why are you so convinced this is such a bad idea? Is it based on your past? Because of what you've been through together already—or are you afraid of what might happen if you get close again?"

"We are never getting close again. Ever," I answered with a finality that I hoped ended that train of thought.

But Tabitha wasn't afraid of me or my stern voice, and she had a knack for picking on the subjects I wanted to avoid the most. I really hated that trait in her.

"Why?" she pressed on.

"Because I—" I stopped myself, realizing I was lashing out, rather than thinking. Why didn't I want to get close to him? He was a different person—a far cry from the August I'd left in that hospital room two years ago.

"He's too dangerous," I finally admitted.

She nodded, understanding my intention. The old August was dangerous because of the harm he could do to me as a person. The new August—he was dangerous for an entirely different reason, and I wasn't sure my heart could take it.

"So are you giving up? Walking away?" she asked. I got the feeling she knew the answer before she even asked.

"No," I answered. "I agree with Mr. Abrams—that closure could be found for both of us by letting go of the past. August doesn't have any memories of himself, so I am simply giving him that. It doesn't need to be anything more."

"And Ryan agrees?" she asked, watching me finally take a seat in one of the nearby chairs.

"He's agreeable—enough. He doesn't like the idea of me being anywhere near August—nor do I, but considering how things have been between us, he's willing to make the sacrifice. We've never encountered difficulties in our relationship. The biggest drama we had before this was what color towels should be bought for the bathroom and whether the yellow and blue went well together. He knew I was damaged when he and I got together, but I just don't think he ever really thought about when this moment would happen—if it ever would. Neither of us did. We lived in this August-free bubble of bliss, and suddenly it's been blown to smithereens."

"No one ever prepares for these types of things, Everly—whether it be a tragedy or something else equally life-altering. Those who say they do are still never prepared for the battle it takes—on your emotions, your general health and well-being. And your relationships. It's normal to see everything suffer slightly. And yes, this situation is unique, but it doesn't make it any less important. You were a victim of abuse.

"While verbal abuse may not make headlines, it still hurts. There are no scars…no reminders on the flesh, but you have wounds. You have memories and days that you'll relive over and over again. And even though that man is gone, his face, the man you once loved—is still here. It's a hard thing to cope with. Do you trust him—do you not? It's something only you can decide. If he had just woken up as August, with all his memories intact, this would be a much different conversation, but he didn't. So the struggle begins."

The struggle had begun the very moment I saw him walk into the coffee shop, so lost and alone. It was in that moment that I'd truly realized he was gone.

"But what if he comes back—the real August?" I asked.

"Ah, but what if he doesn't?"

And that was the real question—the one I was too frightened to ask myself.

What if this was the real August?

Could I truly hate a man who didn't remember any of the sins he'd committed? If you took away the hurt and the pain I felt for him, what was left?

* * *

"I thought you said you liked where I lived…that it didn't bother you," I said accusingly, my hands opening wide in a mock display as I spun around the small space of my apartment.

"Would you listen to what I'm saying…Jesus, woman," August cursed. "It's not about being embarrassed or bothered."

"So you want to rescue me—that's it." I stomped my foot, turning away from him with resentment. After everything I'd shared— everything I'd told him of my life growing up…

"For the love of Christ—" Hands gripped my waist and spun me around. "I know you don't need to be saved. I just want to be with you—all the damn time. I'm trying to tell you I love you, Everly!"

His kiss was punishing—brutal to the point of pain, our lips meeting over and over. He'd asked me to move in with him and I'd lashed out in typical Everly fashion.

Nothing good had ever happened in my life.

Until him.

His hands wove deep grooves in my hair as our frenzied passion slowed. "Move in with me. Please. Warm my bed, live in my arms…never leave."

"Yes," I answered, finally realizing what it felt like to be cherished. To be loved.

* * *

"Showing me more real estate today?" August's voice cut through the lingering memory…bringing me back to the present. I blinked several times, looking out onto the street where our first house still stood.

The house we'd rented when I'd finally agreed to move in with him.

* * *

"So are you going to move into the ghetto with me? Or do you just expect me to pick up all my things and move into that disgusting bachelor pad with you?" I smiled, running my hands over his naked chest.

He looked down at me, placing a single kiss on the top of my head.

"Hell—we can find someplace entirely new if you want; I don't care. As long as I wake up like this every morning."

And so we had.

I'd planned to make that house my next stop on this little roadmap of the "This was our life" journey, but suddenly it felt too private.

Too real.

And I just wasn't ready to give it up.

"No." I finally answered his question. "Just a meeting place," I explained.

His eyes roamed the street and I studied him, waiting for some sort of spark—a hint of something that would tell me he remembered, but there was nothing.

To him—it was just a street.

Nothing special.

And for some reason, that hurt…just a little.

"So, what are we doing today?" he asked, curiosity piqued as he turned to me. I immediately looked away, crossing my arms in front of myself as I tried to think of a new plan.

With the memories of our first house still haunting me, I needed someplace safe and easy—a neutral zone where I could let these lingering feelings fade.

"We're going to be tourists," I quickly answered, remembering a day when we did the same years back.

"Here?" he asked.

"Well, not exactly here, but in the city—yes. Come on, let's go. I'll drive."

I didn't bother waiting for him. I knew he'd follow. Sheer curiosity had him hooked. As I hopped in the car, he followed my lead and jumped into the passenger side.

My car suddenly felt too small. Like a clown car with forty men stuffed in the back. He was everywhere—his scent, his demanding presence, and I couldn't find enough oxygen to breathe.

"On second thought—how about you drive?" I managed to squeak out before pushing open the door and inhaling a large gulp of air into my lungs.

His gentle voice called out behind me. "Everly? Are you okay?" He didn't touch me, but I could feel the heat from his body radiating against me.

I took a step forward and turned.

"Fine," I answered. "I just don't feel like driving—that's all." I made a beeline to his car and waited for him to unlock it. He watched me, his hazel eyes full of intensity, as if he was trying to decide whether to call me on my bullshit or move on.

Thankfully, he chose to move on and unlocked the doors, giving me a way to escape his heavy gaze.

As he settled into the seat next to me, he placed the camera on the console between us.

"So, where are we going?" he asked, starting up the engine.

"Fisherman's wharf," I answered, wondering if he'd need directions, but he just pulled away from the curb and headed in the right direction.

"I've been studying maps," he explained. "That day I got lost and found myself at your coffee shop—I felt so helpless and alone. It wasn't a feeling I wanted to repeat, so I've been trying to relearn the city, bit by bit."

I nodded silently and then winced. "Well, I hate to tell you this, but you just missed your turnoff."

"What?" he exclaimed, looking up at his rearview mirror. "Shit!"

I held back my laughter, covering my mouth.

"You know," he said, "if you want this to work, you're eventually going to have to start opening up."

"I don't need to like you for this to work," I responded harshly. "You want to know about our past—that's what I'm doing. The sooner we do this, the sooner you can move on. That's my closure."

"Seems like you've got it all figured out then," he replied, his voice trailing with each word.

We didn't speak the rest of the way down to the wharf. The truth was, when I was with August I wanted to hate him—and part of me did. The scared, crying, younger version of me that would always remain locked behind that bedroom door would always hate the man who had promised me forever and decided I wasn't enough.

But the woman I'd become…she had a hard time resenting a man who brought a camera with him everywhere and studied maps. Those qualities reminded me of the man who'd begged me to never leave…to warm his bed and stay there forever.

I had him park as close to the water as he could, which ended up being on a hill. I watched as he squeezed into a space meant more for a two-seater than the giant gas guzzler he had, but he seemed to know what he was doing. He even turned his wheels in the right way—a San Francisco must when parking on nearly vertical streets.

"We both grew up in this area," I said as we stepped out of the car and met on the sidewalk. I kept a sensible distance between us as we made our way down to the water's edge. "And one day, as we were strolling along the wharf, eating ice cream or something like that, we realized that neither of us had actually done anything 'San Franciscan.'"

"Like what?" he asked.

"When you travel, what is the first thing you do?" I asked.

He stopped and looked at me blankly.

"Okay, if you were to travel, what would be the first thing you would do?" I rephrased the question. I crossed my arms over the edge of the wooden rail that lined the dock. Several boats were docked in front of us advertising fishing and whale watching cruises for hire.

"Go online and Google things to do?" he guessed.

"Exactly. But this was about ten years ago, and I was less technically savvy back then, so I probably would have picked up a travel guide—but it's the same idea. We realized we'd never done the 'to-do' list for our own city."

"So you did?"

"Yep," I answered, remembering my excitement for the idea. "In one day."

"How did you manage that?" he asked. "Don't people plan week-long vacations here?"

"We were very speedy," I explained. "Which is why we need to hurry!"

I took off on a run, toward the wharf, knowing he'd follow. There would be no holding his hand through this adventure. We were reliving a memory, but that didn't mean I needed to rekindle the emotions that went with it.

Our first stop was bread. Sourdough bread, to be exact.

No, it wasn't exactly one of the top things to do on a Google search, but the second you stepped into Fisherman's Wharf, you knew exactly why Boudin Bakery had been feeding tourists pounds of sourdough for decades. The bakery took up an entire block, and as soon as we stepped on to it, that savory pungent smell that is unique to sourdough flooded my nostrils and I was in bread heaven.

Bread Heaven—it was a real place.

And I wanted to live there. Forever.

Boudin's had a restaurant, so you could sit down and enjoy a meal with friends and loved ones. For us, though, takeout seemed the most logical. Spending an hour making small talk with my ex didn't exactly sound like a ragging good time, plus we had other stops to make on this grand tour.

As he followed me through the store and we waited in line, I watched him curiously as he looked around, taking in the giant loaves of bread shaped like animals and sports emblems, and the many knickknacks scattered about.

"Is this what we did—originally?" he asked as we stepped up closer to the register.

"Uh—no, we actually ate—up there," I said, pointing through the glass toward the restaurant. "But I figured we wouldn't have time."

He just nodded.

We ordered a loaf of bread and coffee and made our way out of the store. I didn't waste any time breaking into the loaf with my bare hands. Good bread didn't need butter or condiments. It could be eaten plain and still be amazing.

I reluctantly handed over the bag to him to share and we made our way toward some of the other shops. I had one more thing to get before we moved on.

Saltwater taffy.

No self-respecting tourist would be caught dead without a bag of saltwater taffy, and I needed to make sure August got his before we left. So, after a quick trip through another store, I selected several different flavors and colors for him, even ones that made his face distort with displeasure, and handed over the bag as we exited.

"One perfectly mixed bag of saltwater taffy. Start eating," I instructed.

"Now?" His eyes widened.

"Yep. We are only tourists for the day, so it has to be gone by the end of the day."

"I'm going to die."

"Giant baby." I rolled my eyes. "Didn't you know tourists gain like ten pounds during vacation? It's a rule or something." I grabbed a few out of the bag. "I'll help. Okay, let's go."

He stuffed a few pieces of taffy in his mouth as we walked back up toward the car, and I watched him cringe as the orange and root beer mixed together. I should have warned him not to mix flavors. That was a rookie move.

"So where to now?" he asked, his eyes full of curiosity and excitement. He'd stopped beside his ruby red behemoth of a vehicle but I just kept walking.

"Follow me," I called out over my shoulder, digging my legs into the pavement as I climbed the steep hill. My breath quickened and my lungs burned as we made our way up several blocks. I took a moment to turn and appreciate the new view. The wharf stood below us, the water sparkling under the sunny glow of the midday heat. It was a beautiful spring day—much like the day we'd spent together here so long ago.

And yet today was so different.

So vastly different.

I crossed the street, seeing his shadow out of the corner of my eye. "We're going to ride the cable car," I explained, as we followed the tracks that led to a long line of people waiting to do the same thing.

"Along with the rest the city?" he chided, as we took our place in the back of the line.

"Would you rather I just tell you what happened that day, or do it this way?" I snapped, folding my arms across my chest in frustration.

His eyes briefly slid down my body, but quickly turned away as he took in the street artists and view of the water. Still feeling flustered and annoyed, I tried not to think about his mesmerizing hazel gaze and the way he looked at me with such intensity.

Waiting for the cable car took time—time we probably could have spent doing other things, like visiting Ghirardelli Square or driving to the Golden Gate Bridge. But I wanted to try and mimic the original day as much as possible, and on that day…we rode the cable car.

*　*　*

"August! Look at that line…we'll never fit everything in! We still have a bunch of things left to do today," I whined.

"But this is what tourists do, Everly...they stand in lines!" He laughed, grinning so wide his eyes crinkled at the corners.

"Okay, but if I don't get chocolate by the end of the day because of this stupid cable car, I'm blaming you!" I shouted as he pulled my reluctant hand across the street toward the long line of eager tourists waiting their turn to ride a real San Francisco cable car.

*　*　*

We slowly made our way to the front of the line, listening to random conversations around us. Foreign languages, different accents—there were even locals like us making a day of it. People were out enjoying the city, and yet I couldn't find two words to string together to say to him.

So I just watched.

Observed as he walked away and clicked pictures of random buildings, people, and scenery. This was something I'd grown used to years ago, when his photography hobby had really blossomed. He'd just wander off and I'd happily wait while he got stuck in the moment, finding ordinary things that seemed to captivate him in extraordinary ways: the way a finial on the gate curved at just the right angle, or how a woman carried her child down the street. He'd always seem to capture just the right moments.

But those were the photos he never printed. Those were the ones he never focused on.

The boxes and boxes he filled were of us.

Always just the two of us.

Eventually, the camera had been locked away and forgotten, like everything else, and life moved on.

Or it tried.

And yet, here we were, back in line on a warm spring day, waiting for a cable car as I watched him snap photos down the street. Life had a way of circling back around. What else in my life would I find repeating itself?

"Looks like we'll be next," he said, walking back to stand next to me.

"Yep," I answered quickly, having been so deep in thought I'd barely noticed he'd returned.

"This wasn't what we were supposed to do today, was it?" he asked suddenly as we quickly bought our tickets and stepped up on the car, choosing to stand rather than sit. I took hold of one of the bars above to brace myself before we started and he did the same.

"Why would you think that?"

He shrugged. "Seemed like a strange place to meet if we were going to head down here. Why didn't we just start down here? It just doesn't seem logical and—"

"No, okay," I answered finally. "This was not what I'd originally intended for the day. Okay? Are you happy?"

His eyes searched mine until I looked away. The cable car chose that moment to come to life. Children laughed and squealed with glee and it began moving along the track. The conductor said something over the loudspeaker but I couldn't make it out.

"What are we going to do?" August asked, taking a step closer. I knew it was to avoid yelling. We'd waited a long time and for some of these people, riding the cable car was a once-in-a-lifetime experience. My anger was not an excuse to ruin that.

I just shook my head.

"Please," he begged, his body nearly touching mine.

"That street," I said, finally giving in. "We lived there."

He froze as his gaze drank me in. "Why didn't you want to show it to me?"

I swallowed, my throat too dry—the cramped space suddenly too small.

"It's too much," I admitted. "There are too many memories there. I'm not ready."

"Okay," he acknowledged with sad, somber eyes, taking a step back as I felt the air creep back into my lungs. The deafening sounds of the cable car returned as well, and I suddenly realized how focused on August I had been; the outside world had completely melted away.

He didn't press further as we rode the cable car down the loop, until it came to a stop about midway through its run, stopping to let passengers off and on. I chose this moment to flee.

August followed close behind.

"I think I've had enough sightseeing for the day," I commented as I looked around. Hopping off on a random street corner wasn't the best idea, but we were still in the tourist area of the city, so I mostly knew where we were—it just took me a minute to get my bearings.

"We need to turn down here," August said, pointing in the opposite direction from where I'd turned.

I looked around, realizing he was right, which only frustrated me further. I said nothing as I walked past him down the street toward where we'd parked earlier.

It was going to be a long walk.

A camera clicked behind me, and I turned to see August quickly pointing the lens across the street, taking a quick succession of shots of several row houses.

"Where do you think you'll be in ten years?" he asked as we crossed another street in our trek back to the car.

"What? Why?"

"Well, you said you're focused on the future—not the past, so surely you have some sort of plan…an idea of where your life is headed. I know you said it didn't matter anymore, but it obviously does, otherwise you wouldn't be engaged, or planning a life with someone."

He'd caught up to my quick gait and now we were walking side by side, our shoulders nearly touching. I took an obvious step to the right. With a gulp of air, I answered, "Well, I guess I see children. And a house full of laughter—simple things, I guess."

"And is that different from what you wanted before—" he asked.

"No, not entirely. Just—"

"Different," we both answered.

Silence followed as we crossed another street, and another.

Finally the roads began to slope, signaling we were returning back to sea level once again. As we crossed another street, August pointed to a corner sign. "Isn't that Ghirardelli?" he asked, as several people stepped out of the famous chocolate store.

"It's one of them, yes. The one that everyone always goes to is down a bit farther, or down the stairs, if you go inside there," I pointed, remembering how badly my feet had hurt the day we'd walked nearly every inch of the city in our quest to be the best damn tourists San Francisco had ever seen.

*　*　*

"You didn't forget!" I exclaimed as we turned a corner and the huge lit-up Ghirardelli sign filled up my vision.

"Of course I didn't. When my woman demands chocolate—I deliver."

Jumping into his arms right there in the middle of the street, I wrapped my arms around him like a lovesick teenager and said, "My hero."

He'd always be my hero.

* * *

"So, do you want to stop in and get something?" he asked, pausing by the entrance.

I looked up at the sign, just barely visible at this angle, and then back down at him. Closing my eyes briefly, I shook my head.

"No," I answered. "I think we've relived enough today."

And then I walked away.

He was my hero, no longer.

Chapter Eighteen

August

I'd watched her pull away from the street corner ages ago.

Our street—or at least it used to be. We hadn't said a word to each other since she'd walked away from me at Ghirardelli Square. I'd rushed after her, only to find her waiting silently by the hood of my SUV.

She was done, and I guess at that moment I had been, too.

I didn't know what I'd done—or not done, to cause her so much pain in that moment, but I was tired of hurting her. My presence alone angered and upset her and as much as I knew this involvement between us was supposed to be mutually beneficial, I couldn't help but feel like I was to blame for everything.

If I could just move on.

Let go.

I glanced up at the street—a place that should hold so many happy memories in my life. Instead, it looked like any other San Franciscan road—cramped, tight little houses all lined up in a row. Not an inch of grass, but plenty of concrete and a nice path to walk a dog or push a stroller. Driveways were a thing of dreams here, and the only parking was on the street. It was city living at its best and you paid top dollar to live it.

Owners dressed up the area with flower boxes on the windows and pretty plants by the doors. I wished I knew which door had been ours—which house had been our home.

Shaking my head, I started the engine, and noticed the bag of half-eaten saltwater taffy on the passenger seat.

We hadn't finished it like she'd wanted. Just another failure to add to the day.

Pulling away from the curb, I drove around the neighborhood, taking it all in—the buildings I would have passed on a daily basis, the restaurants I would have most likely dropped by after work to pick up takeout.

I could see it.

Life with Everly.

Despite everything, I could imagine it. Her in my life, in my bed.

It would be as easy as taking my next breath.

Swerving to the right, I took the first empty spot on the side of the road I could find and put the car in park, killing the engine. Lowering my head to the steering wheel, I took a long, deep gulp of air.

If my mind could forget everything—every memory I'd ever had—then surely I could train my heart to do the same.

Starting right now.

Feeling determined, I glanced up and spotted the first restaurant I could find—a small bar and grill that was advertising a festive happy hour that had just begun.

Perfect.

I knew just about two people in this city. Three if you counted the redheaded waitress I was currently trying to avoid. It was time I ventured out and met new people.

Tried new things.

And moved on. For good.

*   *   *

Having declined a table, I took a seat at the bar instead and restlessly tapped my thumbs against the grained wood, waiting for the overworked bartender to appear.

The restaurant, one of those fusion places that mixed a million different cuisines in an attempt to create something new, was decently busy for a weekday. The place was steadily filling with locals arriving after work. Mostly coming in in twos or threes, they filled up the tables around the bar and kept to themselves, but every so often a group or a single like myself would take up a couple spaces at the bar.

It didn't take long to order a drink, and once my order for a nice microbrew Brick had gotten me hooked on had been placed, I continued my people watching until I was bored stiff.

It took less than five minutes.

This was why men ate peanuts and watched TV at bars. We didn't people watch—that was a chick thing.

"You look familiar." I turned to my right and saw a beautiful blonde a few seats down, leaning toward me, trying not to shout over the noise.

"Do I?"

"Yes," she continued, grabbing her drink and moving closer. "Have you been here before?"

"Maybe," I answered with a grin. She seemed to take my answer for flirting and she responded with a giggle. I was just being honest, but I liked her smile.

And her laugh. At least I could make someone laugh.

The bartender arrived at that moment with my drink and I offered to buy her another. "Another gin and tonic," she said to the man behind the counter. He nodded and stepped away.

"Hmm." She took the remaining sip of her drink. "Oh, I know where I've seen you!" she said. "Did you used to work at Joey's bar down the street?" she asked, her eyes wide with excitement, like she'd just put the final piece to a very complicated puzzle together.

Honestly, I didn't know what to say.

Everly hadn't ever mentioned me working in a bar, but that didn't mean I hadn't.

Would it be likely for this woman to recognize me from a job I might have had ten years ago?

Not really.

"Uh—" I started, but she cut me off.

"It's Mike, right?" Her hand fell to my arm, and I looked down at it briefly.

"August, actually. But I bet I'm better looking than Mike." I grinned.

She laughed, covering her mouth and turning away. "I could have sworn that was you. But no, you're right. Mike had a giant skull tattoo on his forearm. And you?"

I lifted my sleeve to reveal nothing but the lean muscle I'd been slowly gaining back. My morning runs were paying off.

"Definitely not Mike," she said slowly. Her eyes raked over me in an appreciative manner. "So August, then? That's a nice name."

"Thank you, and yours would be?"

"Magnolia," she answered with a shrug, before adding, "My mother was a florist."

I liked the way she covered her mouth when she laughed, as if she was embarrassed or befuddled. It was sort of cute. "Beautiful name for a beautiful woman."

Her drink arrived and we spent the next few minutes getting to know each other. She worked in the area and liked to stop by occasionally for happy hour. Her coworkers had bailed on her, which explained her current single status. My part of the conversation was slightly awkward.

"I am retired," I explained.

"Retired? How old are you?" Her eyes widened.

"Thirty-one," I answered, with a grin.

"How does one retire at thirty-one? Because I'd really like to do that."

I chuckled, trying to figure out how I was going to explain that. I wasn't ashamed of my situation, but it wasn't one I wanted to tell just anyone.

"I was really good at my job. So good that I made enough to retire—much earlier than expected. So I did, and now I'm just deciding what to do next."

She placed her hand under her chin and just looked at me with wonder. "Wow, that's amazing."

"It's actually sort of boring," I confessed. "But I think I've found something I'm really into."

"Really? What?" Her enthusiasm was genuine and it felt good to be interesting for a normal reason.

"Photography. I used to do a bunch when I was younger and

kind of fell out of it, but now I have the time to pick it back up. I'm loving it."

"That's great. Really great." She smiled, and tiny creases formed at the corners of her eyes. "It's rare to find something you're truly passionate about."

"I agree." My eyes locked with hers. "Hey, do you want to grab some dinner while we're here?" I asked, realizing I didn't want our conversation to end.

Her expression lit up once again, and I felt her hand touch mine.

"Yeah, I'd like that."

"So would I."

And even though it wasn't as easy as breathing, I took that first step and got a table for two, because I needed to move on. I needed a new path that didn't include coppery redheads and little cramped houses.

I needed a new life.

*   *   *

The Haight, or the Haight-Ashbury district of San Francisco, was like stepping into a kaleidoscope. Every walk of life seemed encapsulated in the two-hundred-some acres of space, from wide-eyed tourists wanting to take home a one-of-a-kind treasure to the aged beatnik who'd spent every day of his life here, playing the same song, never regretting a thing.

Things had changed since the crazy days of the sixties—the arrival of new generations and styles, but the vibe was still mostly the same—different was beautiful and creativity was celebrated.

It was no surprise that this was the place Brick had chosen for our next meeting. As soon as I spotted him sitting at the little café, cradling his cup of coffee to his lips, wearing a crazy flowered shirt and khaki shorts, I could see how at home he was here.

"Are we ever going to meet at your office again?" I asked, taking the open seat across from him.

"You didn't talk much in there," he shrugged, taking another sip of his coffee. "And besides, the coffee is better here."

The mention of coffee had me thinking of Everly. Had she worked this morning? Was she behind that counter greeting customers and making cups of coffee just like the one Brick held?

Would she greet me the same way, or give me the same cold shoulder?

I let that thought go and ordered an espresso and a blueberry muffin since I hadn't had breakfast. Sitting back in the cozy chair, I allowed myself a minute to enjoy the warm sunshine and cool California breeze before diving into conversation.

People milled about down the street in front of us, many on their way to brunch or in hopes of some early morning shopping. It was early Saturday afternoon and soon this place would be bustling with tourists.

Turning back toward Brick, I asked, "So, are you ever going to send me another bill?"

I'd begun to notice, now that I had a firmer grasp on my finances, that he hadn't sent me a bill in over a month.

"I haven't really decided yet," he answered with a slight grin.

I shook my head in disbelief. "Anything to do with the new choice of meeting location, or perhaps the fact that you went out of your way to contact Everly on my behalf?"

His eyes crinkled at the corners. "No to the first part—I really do like the coffee here, and I do find you open up more outside an office setting. I would be doing this regardless of…other things. In regard to the second half, well…that was out of the norm, even for one so out of the box such as me. I acted more as a friend than a counselor or therapist, which is why I stopped charging you as one."

"So, I guess if this all goes south, I won't be able to sue you?"

He chuckled, shaking his head at my comment. "No, but you will have me around—as a friend—to put everything back together again."

"And if it just happens to go well?"

"My bill will be in the mail," he joked with a chuckle.

"So much for friendship." I rolled my eyes. My coffee and muffin were delivered at that moment and I dug in, feeling famished. Brick was right; the coffee here was right on and their muffins weren't all that bad either.

"Your Everly makes a good cup of coffee," Brick said as I polished off the last of my muffin.

"She's not mine," I muttered.

"Sorry; you know what I meant. She made me a cup or two that day I visited her. Real nice, very sweet."

"To everyone else," I answered.

"Still giving you the cold shoulder?"

My silence was answer enough for him.

"She just needs time, August."

"Time for what?" I blurted out. "Time to realize I'm not the same guy…because I'm not. I've showed her that over and over, but no matter what I do, I'll always look just like him and that's something I can't change."

"Time," he simply repeated.

Time. Such a funny word for me. It was something I'd lost—so many memories and years gone in a single moment. And yet, here I was with nothing but time stretched out before me to do whatever it was that I chose.

It seemed my entire life always boiled down to that one word.

But what was I holding out for? What would giving things time bring to me at the end of all this with Everly? She'd never be mine... and why did I want her to be? Why did I feel such a pull to this woman I didn't remember?

Looking at the people passing by, I watched them disappear into little boutiques and funky shops. Men would buy their girlfriends and wives tiny trinkets, a necklace or a pretty scarf to remember the special day. If I wandered into one of those shops, I wouldn't know the first thing about Everly—what to get her and what she might like.

And yet, every time she was in a room, I had to be near her.

Why?

Were they feelings left over from a life already lived or did I truly love this woman?

I guess I would never really know.

"Have you seen Magnolia again since I last spoke to you?" Brick asked, pulling my attention away from the busy street.

"Date number three is tonight," I answered.

"So things are going well, then?"

I nodded. "She's beautiful. Nice to talk to. What isn't there to like?"

"Have you slept with her yet?" he asked out of the blue.

"Jesus, Brick." I choked on my coffee. "Give a guy some warning. No—she has one of those five-date rules."

"And you see yourself sticking around until lucky date number five?"

I shrugged. "Yeah, why?"

"Just curious. That's all."

And now, so was I.

What did the good old shrink have up his sleeve?

Chapter Nineteen

Everly

"Here's to Sarah and her ballerina twirling, leap-flipping hard work!" I shouted, thrusting my wineglass up in the air as the three of us cheered and toasted my incredibly successful friend.

It had been a long time coming, but we'd eventually figured out a date when all three of us could sit down and have a celebratory dinner in Sarah's honor. The delay was mostly due to Sarah's crazy work schedule, not ours. But we'd figured it out and here we were.

My two favorite people in the world, several bottles of wine and a house full of home-cooked food.

It was marvelous.

"That was horrible," Sarah laughed, covering her mouth with her petite hand. "We really need to work on your understanding of ballet."

I shook my head as I took a large gulp of merlot. "Nope, I'm fine. And that toast was amazing, thank you very much! It was from the heart!"

We all laughed as we settled in to dinner. I'd really gone all out this time, making all of Sarah's favorites—even though I knew she'd only eat a bite or two from each.

If that.

She might not be a purger anymore, but she was and always would be a ballerina first. Her weight was paramount to her career and she took it very seriously. Fatty foods were the enemy and only consumed on occasion, and I knew she would be spending tomorrow in the gym or on the ballet floor working off the extra calories she'd consumed. The fact that she was even drinking tonight meant that it was a special event. Usually all she had was Diet Coke, black coffee, or water. It was a dedicated life, and she was dedicated to it one hundred percent.

"You're trying to kill me, Ev," she pouted, looking at the table full of food.

"No, if I was doing that, I would have made a chocolate cheese-cake." I grinned.

"You didn't!" she warned, jumping from the table to run to the re-frigerator, where I'd hidden the tempting dessert.

"You evil bitch!" I heard her mumble behind the refrigerator door. She reappeared, licking her finger, and I saw her eyes roll back slightly in her head.

Ryan chuckled. "I think her understudy may need to do the next show."

"No," she answered, coming back to the table to pour more wine. "That psycho has been gunning for my spot ever since the first re-hearsal. I will be limping onto the stage before I let her have the satisfaction."

Ryan and I looked at each other, our eyes wide with surprise.

Wow, dance drama. Who knew?

"Okay, well…that sounds frightening. Anything else going on at work, babe?" I asked, trying to lighten the mood.

"I met a guy," she grinned, a goofy, happy grin I hadn't seen in ages. Not since she'd dated a short-term coworker of mine who'd turned out to be married. That didn't end well.

It did explain why he never saw her outside of work, though. I always thought that was strange and slightly awkward. The rest of us at the shop never knew what we'd be walking into when going for supplies in the stockroom. She thought he was just scared of commitment—turns out she wasn't far off the mark there.

"Who is he? I must know everything!" I said, demanding the details every best friend must have.

"I actually don't want to say quite yet," she explained. "It's really new and different…and I don't want to jinx it."

"So you're just going to announce that you have this new guy in your life that makes you all gushy and weird and then what? Nothing? What's with that?"

"Come on, Ev, give her some slack—she'll come around when she's ready."

"I will," she agreed, turning her head to his in agreement. "I just want it to be real before I tell you anything."

When did they become so chummy?

"Okay, I can live with that," I said resignedly, taking a bit of risotto from my overfilled plate.

"Besides, I want to talk about you," she continued. "I've been so busy with my performance schedule that I feel like we haven't had any time to talk about everything that's been going on with you."

I looked up at her, not really knowing what to say. The time I spent with August felt private somehow. We were reliving past memories. I was sharing a part of myself with him, a piece of me I'd buried away. It wasn't something I really wanted to discuss over dinner and wine with my best friend and fiancé.

"I don't really know what to say," I answered awkwardly, taking a sip from my glass.

"I know it must have been difficult—spending all that time with him. Why do you keep doing it?" she asked, rather bluntly.

I opened my mouth to answer, but found no words.

I didn't really know why I kept going, other than the fact that I just did. I felt some string pulling me toward him, linking us together, and until I figured out how to cut it loose, I would continue to go. And I felt strangely protective of that. Why did I need to explain it?

"Honey." She grabbed my hand from across the table. I looked up at her, meeting her warm gaze. Ryan was silent as he watched the exchange. "You know you don't have to do this—any of it. Just walk away. Come back to us and forget all of this nonsense."

I blinked once, and then again, feeling like I was in some sort of staged intervention. Both of them were staring at me with sad, round eyes that were meant to be comforting but offered nothing of the sort.

"No one is forcing me to do anything," I answered, yanking my hand back from hers.

"We know. We just worry that you put too much stock into what this Dr. Abrams said—that this is the only way for you to move on. I think you just need time to adjust, to get used to this new normal. That doesn't have to include August."

Everything she said was lost after the first word left her mouth.

"'We?'" I asked through my gritted teeth. "Since when are the two of you a we?"

She shot a hesitant glance across to table to Ryan. "Ryan was worried about you," she explained, while Ryan said quietly next to me, "We both were."

"So you just decided to talk about me behind my back?"

Her eyes widened with shock. "Honey—it wasn't like that. We were just concerned."

"So concerned that you didn't think to involve me in these little chats?" I was already rising from my seat, my appetite gone. The need to flee grew by the minute as the room turned into a giant vacuum, sucking all the air right out of its center. I couldn't stand it—the thought of the two of them talking about me, like I was some weak little child.

I was not weak.

I was not powerless.

And I was not going to stand here for one more second.

"I need air," I managed to say, before I grabbed my keys and purse off the table.

"Everly, please," Ryan said, touching my shoulder as I made my way to the door.

"So you *can* speak after all?" I nearly spat, making my way toward the door. I slammed it shut before I could hear another word. They didn't run after me. They knew my routine. I always ran, always fled.

I'd come back; I always did.

* * *

I should not be here.

I should not be here.

I'd driven all over the city, letting my thoughts wander and wander as I tried to cool my heated temper, but nothing had worked and bit by bit—mile by mile, I'd edged closer and closer to the dark blue sea.

Until I found myself at the cliffs, pulling up to the last place in the world I should be.

Why, when I felt the most alone, did I turn to the person I trusted the least?

I shut off the engine and dimmed the headlights, then I sat in the surrounding darkness, deciding upon my next move.

If I were smart I'd start up the car, back up into the street, and go home.

But tonight—after seeing my best friend and my fiancé gang up against me like some adolescent troublemaker, I was feeling less on the brainy side and bordering on something a bit riskier. Which was probably why I was currently sitting in August's driveway... contemplating whether I was ever going to get out of my car.

The decision was made for me when a small tapping at my window nearly had me jumping out of my skin. I turned to see August bent over, his hands in his pockets as he took a step back, waiting for me to respond.

I pressed the button to lower the window before realizing I'd already pulled the keys out of the ignition. Taking a steadying breath, I pushed open the door and stepped out, ready to face the decision I'd made by driving here.

"Hi," I said hesitantly, unable to meet his firm gaze. I instead found a new fascination with the brickwork on the driveway, studying the intricate herringbone pattern that wove beneath my feet.

"Hi," he replied, mimicking my tone. He didn't ask why I was there, or expect anything—just stood there, patiently waiting as I moved gravel beneath me. It was then that I noticed his shoes. They were nice—fancier than I'd seen him wear during our excursions around the city—black, shiny…much more reminiscent of the old August—and in stark contrast to the flip-flops I'd thrown on when I'd run out of my own house. Glancing up, I realized he was dressed up as well—but not like he'd once been, with thousand-dollar suits and designer ties. Tonight he was more understated, in a pair of sleek gray trousers that hugged his trim waist. The dusty green shirt he wore matched his eyes perfectly and I had a hard time pulling my own from his gaze.

"You have plans," I blurted out. "I'm so sorry—I've interrupted something."

Feeling extremely embarrassed, I turned and nearly stumbled into the door of my car. With lightning-quick reflexes he caught me, grabbing my waist and righting me before stepping back. His hand had only touched me for a brief moment but I could still feel the heat of it, grazing the bare skin between my jeans and T-shirt.

"Everly, stop—please," he pleaded. "Why are you here?"

I turned, my hands nearly trembling as I stood before him. "I don't know," I answered honestly.

His eyes rounded as he took in my appearance. "Come on. Why don't you come inside for a while? Maybe you can make coffee for the both of us?" he suggested.

I nodded, but then asked, "What about your plans?" I looked down at the keys in his hands that he quickly stuffed in his pocket.

"Don't worry about it. It wasn't a big deal."

"Okay," I relented.

I followed him up to the door that still had the brass knocker with our initials on it. I tried to ignore the guilt I felt as I passed through the entryway, but it seared a path through my belly nonetheless.

I was not doing anything wrong. This was just another one of our meetings.

An impromptu meeting between August and me—nothing more.

Tonight, I'd become a grand master at lying to myself.

"Why don't you start the coffee while I make a quick call?" he suggested, as he shrugged off the light jacket he had on. I stood there watching him tug his shirt from his pants, until I realized I was staring and quickly scurried into the kitchen.

Nothing had changed since the last time I'd been in here, which made me smile. The kitchen had always been my domain, and it felt good to be able to roam around in here without having to think at all. I pulled out cups while the coffee brewed. I didn't bother listening to August's conversation. He obviously wanted privacy since he'd walked into the other room, and if he was talking to another woman—which I highly suspected he was—I honestly didn't know if I wanted to hear it.

Knowing I was the cause of a possibly botched date was already weighing heavy on my mind.

I was supposed to be helping him move on…not tread backward. And I had enough guilt when it concerned that man.

"Almost ready?" he asked, stepping into the large space, dominating it instantly. The kitchen could have been a football field wide and it still wouldn't have been big enough in that instant. His presence had always seemed larger than life, and that was one thing that hadn't changed—past or present. He could change his clothing style, the way he wore his hair, and even the build of his body, but his invading presence never changed. It always affected me. Invaded me. Took over my senses.

"Just about," I replied, tapping my fingers against the cold marble countertop in a rhythmic motion. The last bit of coffee brewed, gurgling and steaming until the last drop fell. I quickly turned to grab the sugar and milk and returned ready to fix everything up.

Only to realize I had no idea how he took his coffee anymore.

Looking up at him, I opened my mouth to ask, but he smiled. "Just black," he answered.

I only nodded as I pivoted back toward the refrigerator to return the milk. I'd grabbed everything on impulse, ready to dump two spoonfuls of sugar and a slash of milk into his cup like I always had.

How easily I'd fallen back into an old routine.

"I take it that's different?" he spoke up.

"Yes," I answered, "but good. Now you're a purist like me." I gave him the slightest hint of a grin. His eyes narrowed in on my lips, noticing the tiny change in my expression. I quickly wiped it away with a fake cough, using my hand to cover it.

Coward.

I don't know why I continued to treat him so poorly. After the amount of time we'd spent together, I finally understood the difference. He might carry the same facial features, wear similar clothing and hairstyle, but beyond his physical attributes, August had changed.

For the better.

And yet, I was still hell bent on punishing him for who he'd been before.

Maybe it was leftover resentment for the last few years of our relationship—leftover feeling seeping through my psyche. Or perhaps I was too afraid to get attached then suddenly discover one day I'd grown close to a man who'd disappeared yet again because his memories had returned.

All great questions to bring up with Tabitha…if only I had the guts.

Admitting them to myself was one thing. Saying them out loud to someone else seemed drastic…like I was actually owning them—acknowledging August as an important person in my life, rather than just contemplating the possibilities in my convoluted, messed-up head.

Picking up my cup of steaming hot coffee, I glanced up at him as he did the same.

"Do you want to sit in the living room?" he offered. I nodded and followed him into the large, inviting space. I'd designed this room for comfort, going against the stuffy professional designer's idea of style for a more laid-back atmosphere. She'd chosen sleek leather and hard lines. All I'd envisioned were legs sticking to furniture in the summer and backaches year round. I'd told her to try again, and when she'd come back, clearly peeved, she presented a much less formal idea with soft suedes and plenty of places to kick up your feet and relax.

I wondered, as I took a seat in what used to be my favorite spot—an oversized chair that basically swallowed me whole—if August enjoyed this room now as much as we used to. Before work had become his life, and I'd still had pieces of him to myself, this had been the center of the house for the two of us. Board games, movie nights, and many nights of drinking and debauchery had occurred right here. Where the bedroom had once felt like the beating heart, this room had been our own little slice of heaven right in the middle of our home. With grand views of the Pacific that rivaled those from the master bedroom, you could watch the sun set over the water while listening to the crashing waves below.

But even a view like that could feel like prison when you weren't allowed to leave.

"Was she upset?" I finally asked, deciding to jump off the tightrope

I'd been walking, between wanting to know and not wanting to know what he'd had planned for the evening.

"What—" he began to ask as he looked up at me. My eyebrow cocked in amusement, and a small smirk played across his lips.

"No. Not too much," he admitted. "I told you it wasn't a big deal."

Looking around, I tried to imagine him here with someone else. In the place that used to be ours. We had planned to raise our children here, and now he would possibly raise his own. Without me.

"This is stupid," I blurted out. "I shouldn't have come. You were going on a date, and I ruined that for you. This isn't how this is supposed to go." My words were coming out like shrapnel, firing quicker than I could comprehend them as I stood, ready to sprint for the door.

"When did it all go wrong between us? Will you explain it to me?" he asked suddenly, stopping me instantly. I turned to see him, still in his same position on the couch, holding the half-empty cup of coffee I'd made for him, as he looked up at me with wide, vulnerable eyes.

"Why?"

"You know why," he answered. "I hate mysteries."

"Okay," I answered, taking my seat once again, as the adrenaline from my attempt to flee steadied. I took the warm mug in my hands for support and brought it to my lips, savoring the smell, before I spoke.

"There really isn't a specific day…or moment. Like most couples, it happened gradually. Only ours wasn't normal—by any means."

"Why do you think that? I mean, why do you think I changed so much?" he asked, genuinely concerned.

"You found something else you loved much more—money."

"Can it really be that simple? Did I ever seem the type?" He set down his coffee mug and leaned back into the sofa as I tried to study his expression. I couldn't tell if he was upset, confused—or maybe a little sad.

"No—at least not before. When we first met, you were willing to move into my shack of an apartment to be with me. But we decided to rent a house, and even though it was bigger than anything either of us had ever lived in, it was still in San Francisco...which meant we paid double for the ability to live in what was called a house, but it was literally a shoebox, with nice flower boxes and a balcony."

"So why did we move? How did I go from being content in a shoe box to needing all this?" he asked, motioning around the room with his hands.

"You moved up in the world, and with money came more. I think at first it was the desire to give me everything I never had, and maybe in some warped way, it continued that way—I don't know. But after time, it became more about who we were to others than what we were to one another."

"It just makes no sense to me," he said softly.

"Me either, but things happen."

"Then why do I feel so strongly for you still?" he asked, his mouth clamping closed as if he'd suddenly realized what he'd said. "I'm sorry. I shouldn't have said that."

Silence settled between us and even though I knew I should leave, I didn't. I couldn't move a muscle from that chair, and once more...I didn't want to.

"Do you like jewelry?" he asked suddenly, out of the blue.

"What?"

He chuckled to himself, tiny lines appearing around his hazel green eyes. "Sorry, it's random, I know. But just go with it. If you were in one of those small boutiques—like around The Haight, and happened to wander in, what would you buy? A necklace…a scarf, maybe a—"

"A coffee mug," I answered immediately.

"Like an I-Love-SF mug?" He laughed.

"Yes! I don't know, maybe. Don't laugh. It's your ridiculous question. I collect them. Whenever I'm someplace special, I always try to find a coffee mug I can use—to remind me of that specific day or place."

He looked at me, somewhat taken aback…maybe slightly bewildered, until a large grin broke out across his face. "A magnet. Okay."

"What about you? What would you buy?" I asked, throwing his odd question back at him.

"Hmm, nothing probably. I'd rather take photos. Much more meaningful than anything I could buy. Cheaper, too," he said with a wink.

Like the man needed to worry about his pockets.

"You've really gotten back into photography, haven't you?" I commented, setting my now empty cup on the coffee table between us.

"Well, it's all new—now. But yes, I'm really enjoying it. It started out as just something I could do to fill in the hours of the day and now when I wake up, it's the first thing I want to do. In fact, can I show you something?"

I looked around with slight hesitation, and finally nodded. Standing, I followed his lead down the first-floor hallway. My heart sprang into a gallop as we neared the farthest corner, and his hand settled on the door handle of his old office. I hadn't been in that space in years, blaming its four walls for the division between us. So many fights had been started here.

So many battles had been lost as I gave in to his power, unwilling to stand up for myself. Unwilling to let go and walk away.

August had always had a power over me, a certain hold, and it had never been more evident than when he stood behind that mighty desk, like a king surveying his kingdom.

My hands clasped together as sweat dotted my forehead. I would not turn away.

Fear had ruled my life for far too long. It was time to face my demons.

Taking the first step in behind him, it was hard not to notice the obvious changes he'd made. The few windows had been boarded up, covered in dark black cloth, and what once had filled a proud businessman's office had been pushed aside to make room for photography equipment and makeshift tables.

Even a dark cloth and various chemicals covered the priceless desk August had once loved so dearly.

All of it forgotten.

Replaced.

"You've turned it into a darkroom," I stated in awe, looking around at everything he'd assembled in such a short time.

"Well, I've started to," he replied. "It's taking some time, but I've managed to print a few test rolls. Would you like to see?"

"Yes." I gave a small smile, not even bothering to hide my delight. The fear I'd felt for this room was evaporating with every second that passed, like a calming balm, soothing away the haunting memories as August directed me to the other side of the room to show me what he'd captured.

Each photo was better than the last, and I recognized several scenes from our escapade around San Francisco. Several were of strangers, hugging loved ones, caring for their children—moments in time captured forever. Others were more obscure—a random angle of a building or the way a tree's shadow met the pavement.

There were even a few of me.

He tried to hide them but I saw my own expression staring back at me.

If I only knew what I'd been trying to say.

Chapter Twenty

August

I hadn't meant to take her in here.

The words had just flown out of my mouth and here we were, standing in my sacred space, as she fingered through dozens of black-and-white prints I'd exposed over the last week.

If I'd known she was going to be in here, I would have cleaned.

Organized.

Planned.

Hell, I would have at least removed the photos of her. The ones I found myself staring at when the days got long, and the nights became so lonely I couldn't stand the silence any longer. I knew dark-rooms were a thing of the past—now that digital had taken over the world—but there was something cathartic about standing in almost complete darkness, working on a craft, bringing it slowly to life, rather than sitting hunched over a computer screen.

Each photo brought a little bit of life back into me. It wasn't my life, perhaps, but it was something. And I watched it all appear like magic in those processing trays. Like tiny glimpses of hope—that maybe one day, I'd have a life worth photographing.

My eyes turned to the small bulletin board I'd put up on the wall for display, and settled in on the single photo I'd pinned up there. Two smiling faces in the grass, looking up at the camera with nothing but hope and happiness in the future.

Maybe someday, I could turn the camera around again and find someone worth capturing.

"Why do you have that?" Everly's voice asked in the darkness, as I watched the silhouette of her hand stretch toward the bulletin board. In the dull red lights, I saw her finger the photo, her eyes shadowed and her expression hooded as she pulled it from its place on the wall.

"Because you're smiling," I answered honestly. I had a feeling too many lies had been told within the walls of this large house. I wasn't about to add to them.

Not now, hopefully not ever.

"Why is it so important to you?" she asked. I took a step forward to glance over her shoulder. I watched her tense slightly as she felt my approaching presence but she didn't move.

"Why is it so important for you to hide it from me?" I fired back.

"Maybe I've wasted enough smiles on you."

"Fair enough. But it's still something I aspire to see," I answered softly, taking the photo from her fingers and repinning it to the board.

"I thought you got rid of all those photos," she spoke up, turning around, brushing the sleeve of my shirt as she did. "The ones of us, I mean," she clarified.

"I did—or at least I thought I had, but I found that one lying on the bedroom floor. Seems it managed to find its way out of the box I threw it in. That—or a very sneaky, super nosy ex-therapist of mine placed it there."

"Ex?" she questioned, but hardly seemed surprised.

"He's refusing to charge me anymore—keeps meeting me at restaurants and showing up at my door for beers. So yeah, ex-therapist, I guess." I shrugged as I watched her continue to roam around the room. The faint red glow washed away most color, and the usually vibrant copper tone of her hair had transformed into something darker.

In here, there were no in-betweens. No middle tones. Just reds and blacks. I wasn't processing so I could flip the overheads on and bathe us in white light, but here, in this space, I loved the contrast—the separation from normalcy.

Seeing her here, though, made me suddenly aware of just how erotic a darkroom could be. Every curve of her body was accentuated, enhanced by the lack of color and the stark red glare. Her lips appeared heavy, as if they were begging to be touched and caressed along with the rest of her body.

I needed to get out of the room.

"Will you show me how it works?" she asked, looking up from the main table I'd assembled in the middle, where the processing trays and enlarging equipment were set up.

"Really?" I asked, an equal mixture of dread and excitement running through my veins.

"Yeah, I mean—I don't really want to go home yet, and we don't have anything else to do."

"Sure," I answered quickly, hardly delaying the decision I'd just told myself to flee.

I truly hated myself. That or I really was the asshole she thought me to be.

Because damn if I didn't think of bending her over every hard surface and reacquainting myself with every inch of that luscious body I seemed to have forgotten.

"—her name?" Everly's voice yanked me back to reality. Catching the end of a question I'd barely heard, I blinked a few times, trying to clear salacious thoughts from my mind.

"What did you say?" I asked.

"What's her name?" she repeated. "Your date?"

"Oh, um"—my mind searched—"Magnolia," I finally answered, busying myself as I gathered the proper equipment to develop. She watched me intently from the other side of the table.

"Interesting name," was all she said.

A small smirk tugged at my lips. "Her mom used to be a florist over in Half Moon Bay. She grew up on the coast so she's really looking forward to seeing the house."

"I'm sure her childhood home wasn't quite like this," she commented, running her fingers along the cool plastic table as her eyes met mine.

"No, but not all of us can be related to a founding member of SunGlobal."

Her eyes went wide. "I thought you said her mom was a florist! Not an heiress to a billion-dollar company!"

"I did—and I said she 'used to be.' I didn't say what her dad did," I laughed.

She launched a pencil at my head and I managed to duck at just the right time. "Well, you better clean up before she comes. Don't want the place to look like a dump for the princess."

Was that jealousy I detected?

Don't jump to conclusions. That will get you in trouble, August.

"I'll do my best. So, ready to get dirty?" I asked, watching her eyes fly up to mine.

"What?"

"Hands—are you ready to get your hands dirty?" I clarified, clearly missing a key word in my sentence.

"Yes—lead the way," she instructed.

"Okay, first we need to clean the negative, and load it into the carrier." I handed her a cotton ball I'd just soaked with a little rubbing alcohol and the negative.

"I just rub it on there?" she asked hesitantly.

"Yep."

She did so tentatively at first and then, seeing that nothing bad was happening, completed the job back and front. Without thinking, I grabbed her hand and started moving it back and forth to dry the negative. Her hand froze as her eyes focused on mine and I quickly stepped away.

"Sorry—just shake it a bit until it dries. Good," I said, watching her movements. "That should be good."

"Now we put it…?" she questioned, looking around, until she found me pulling out the carrier—a large black frame with handles.

"Slide it in this way." I pointed as she carefully put the negative down.

"But won't it be upside down?"

"No, it will be great," I promised with a warm smile.

And it was. As soon as it was loaded and focused, I had her look down at the photo.

"Wow—is this from the backyard?" she asked.

"Yeah—I hiked down a ways today and got some really great shots. I printed several earlier. This was my next in the set."

Since I'd already done so many like it, and played around with f-stops and aperture, I already knew approximately how long to expose the photo, so I skipped test strips and decided to just go ahead with the entire photo.

"I don't see anything," she said softly, as if the sound of her voice would disrupt the process entirely.

"Ahh—this is where the magic happens," I explained, handing her the tongs for the first tray. "Place our photo in here."

She looked down the line of trays. "That's a lot of steps."

"Just trust me."

Her eyes met mine and she hesitated. "Okay."

She slowly dropped the white paper in the agitator solution. "Move it back and forth," I said, resisting the urge to touch her again.

"There it is!" she exclaimed, as the scene came back to life underneath the liquid.

"Now, the next tray," I instructed, standing so close to her I could feel the heat from her body meshing with mine. She was so entangled with what she was doing I don't think she even noticed just how close we were standing to each other.

She went through the process, placing the photo in one tray after the other, with me closely beside her until it was set.

"Now we use this," I said, grabbing the squeegee from the table. She took it from my hand, brushing the outer curve of my palm as she retrieved it. Every accidental touch or fleeting graze from her body felt as if an atom bomb were igniting in mine. My heart raced, my stomach tightened, and I fought for every ounce of control not to return the favor.

She's not mine.

She's chosen someone else.

Move on.

But no matter how much I reminded myself of those simple facts, I knew that as many times as I'd kissed Magnolia goodnight on our dates, as I'd pushed her against the door of her luxury apartment her father had bought her, I'd never once felt an ounce of what I felt from just a brush of Everly's hand.

"It's beautiful," she said softly, holding up the finished photo.

"Yes," I answered, my eyes never wavering from the real beauty in the room. Even without a speck of makeup on, she lit up a room. Fiery red hair, milky white skin, and those captivating blue eyes that seemed to sink directly into my soul.

I would give everything I had and more for a single moment with her. A single second when she looked at me with those eyes and I felt loved.

"Where do we put it now?" she asked, separating me from my distant thoughts.

"Here," I answered, pointing to the area across the office where I'd strung some wire and clothespins. I heard her giggle slightly as she pinned the photo up and stepped back.

"What's so funny?" I asked.

"I just remembered a time when I came in here and you had a million suits all lined up right here in this very spot—trying them all on for a gala. And now you have clothespins and fishing wire strung up in their place."

I stared at her, trying to gauge her mood.

"Hmm—I'm pretty sure a bunch of suits would be pretty dirty in here now."

She choked out a laugh, covering her perfect smile from me. But it was a smile nonetheless.

I'd done that.

Made her happy—for once.

Even for a second.

*   *   *

After cleaning up in the darkroom, I found her back in the living room, looking out at the dark water as tiny flecks of light caught on the waves that washed ashore. She didn't say anything when I entered the room, just stood there, quietly observing…waiting.

"We had a fight," she finally said, after I'd made my way across the large room to stand next to her. I resisted the temptation to look over, to soak in her expression. Somehow, I gained her trust in that moment, and I knew it was a heavy burden to bear.

"He doesn't like me visiting you. He thinks it's bad for our relationship."

"He might be right," I answered, finally turning to meet her hesitant gaze.

"Do you ever think of me—when I'm not around?" she asked softly, her eyes rounding in doubt.

Stepping in closer, so she could feel the breath of my words as they fell from my mouth, I whispered, "Every second, Everly. Every damn second."

A small gasp escaped her lips as she pushed away from me.

"I should go," she said. "Being here—it's not a good idea."

She was already retreating, her emotions…her physical reactions all crumbling, breaking apart until she was rushing toward the door.

"I'm so sorry for bothering you, August—for ruining your night. It won't happen again."

"Everly—damn it. Wait."

I grabbed her hand, halting her progress. She looked down at our joined hands, her eyes wide with shock.

"Stop running," I urged.

"I'm not running. I'm going home, where I belong. I want to go home."

I shook my head, a disheartening chuckle escaping my throat. "Go home then. But don't tell me a part of you doesn't want to stay. Don't tell me that deep down, a part of you wishes you were still here every morning making coffee in that kitchen and helping me develop film in the office. For a split second tonight, you saw it, didn't you? What life could be like between us?"

Her eyes darkened and suddenly, she twisted her hand from mine.

"No," she answered. "There is only one man I see in my future. And his name isn't August Kincaid."

And then she was gone.

And I was alone once again.

Slamming the door closed, I stomped into the living room and paced, attempting to clear my head.

Why? Why did I do this to myself?

Nothing would ever change.

She was not mine.

Picking up the phone, I did the only thing possible to ease the pain in my heart and the anger I felt toward my own stupidity.

"Hello?" Magnolia answered after the second ring.

"Hey, it's August," I replied, trying to act as casual as possible.

"Didn't expect to hear from you again tonight."

"Hey—I'm sorry to cancel. A friend had an emergency. It's all taken care of. I was wondering how many dates I could possibly fit into one evening if we started...now?" I asked, my voice lowering with each word.

Silence followed before I heard, "Be here in twenty minutes." And then the line went dead.

Everly had left her empty mug on the coffee table. I turned and headed for the front door.

She'd made her intentions clear.

It was time I made mine.

Chapter Twenty-One

Everly

If I were a religious person, I would call what I did over the next several days repenting.

Since I wasn't, I'd just go with calling it reveling in guilt. I felt it in spades.

Guilt over driving to the cliffs when I was angry with Ryan.

Guilt because I'd stayed...because of the things I'd said, things I'd done.

Guilt, guilt, guilt.

I hated the word.

Ryan still hadn't asked where I'd gone after the failed intervention. Part of me thought he already knew, and the other enjoyed the quiet bliss of not knowing. Somehow, in the midst of all this, I'd become that heroine I despised—the one that always made me flip through pages of a book or roll my eyes in a movie because she just couldn't get her shit together.

I'd become someone I couldn't stand.

So now I would make amends.

Starting with the wedding plans I'd ignored over the last several weeks. There was so much to do and with the rift currently brewing between Sarah and me, the only person left to handle them was me.

As I looked through dozens of florist and cake brochures, I suddenly missed my best friend incredibly. We were supposed to do this together. Well, actually, she was supposed to pick out everything I liked while I sat here fooling around, making origami swans out of the dozen brochures she'd painfully gathered.

She loved this type of thing—me, not so much. It was why August and I had never hosted parties at the house and why I much preferred to spend an evening snuggled under blankets, rather than in a noisy club. I'd spent years living in other people's homes and never having one of my own. For a child—having a place to call their own is one of the most precious things on earth. And I'd never had that until August and I moved into that tiny one-bedroom home on that beautiful, crowded street in the city. That was the first time I'd ever had a place to call my own. No roommates, no foster parents—just August, me, and our cute little home.

The walls might have changed, but that feeling still remained. I loved the feeling of coming home.

And even though Ryan and I were back to renting rather than owning a place, I'd still made it ours as much as possible. And being there would always beat a night out at a fancy club. But our wedding would be different and that was something I had to realize. It wasn't going to be a dinner party or fancy soiree. It was going to be our wedding day—and that deserved attention.

So why couldn't I focus?

I'd been diligent in my other groveling duties. I'd cleaned the house from top to bottom after my morning work shift, made a killer dinner each night he'd returned home from work, and yet when it came to planning the most important day of our life…

I couldn't string two minutes together.

Chocolate or vanilla…roses or lilies? It all seemed maddening.

"Ev, I think we need to talk." Ryan's voice broke through the silence as he stepped into the kitchen. I looked up and saw him awkwardly standing before me with his hands in his pockets, staring down at the brochures scattered on the table. He visibly winced and turned away.

"Sure, what's up?" I asked, gathering everything up in an effort to make room for him at the table, but he just turned and began to pace, lacing his hands behind the back of his head.

"I should have known. You shouldn't have to badger and practically beg a woman to date you," he said under his breath.

"What are you talking about?" I asked, suddenly concerned.

"Do you remember how long it took for you to say yes to me? Do you recall how many coffee orders I placed…how many cheesy one-liners and mentions about good hygiene and my impeccable driving record it took before you took a chance on us?"

"Why are you bringing this up?"

"It shouldn't be this hard," he answered. "Love shouldn't require thought or force. It simply is, and as easy as it is for me to feel that for you—I don't know if you feel it back."

My heart hammered in my chest as I jumped to my feet.

"Are you crazy, Ryan? I love you—only you. I agreed to marry you!" I said, holding my left hand out as proof.

"Where did you go, Ev? The other night? When we fought—where did you go?"

Silence poured into the room.

An agonized laugh fell from his lips. "See, the sad thing is I already knew. The moment you left here, I knew where you'd end up—who you'd turn to. It's like he's your true north on a compass. Up until a few months ago, I thought I might be."

"You are," I cried as tears began free-falling from my cheeks.

"No, Everly. I'm not. I filled the void for a while. But your heart was already taken. I don't get it…it's something I'll never understand, especially after everything he did to you. But even after all that, you never gave up on him. And now you need to give that a second chance."

"What are you saying?" I cried out, and wrapped my arms around myself like a protective vise. He finally stopped pacing and turned to me.

"I'm taking the high road—and giving you an out to discover what your heart really wants. Him or me."

I took a step forward but froze when I saw him back away.

"I don't want an out!" I screamed. "I want you!"

"No, you don't," he said softly. "You don't know what you want and until you do—I won't be your second choice."

His eyes met mine and I saw loss and pain, and then finality as he gave a single nod and headed for the door. Panic rose inside of me and I ran after him.

"Please Ryan, don't. Don't do this."

"I'm only doing what you're too afraid to do yourself," he said, stopping just short of the door. He turned to face me, unshed tears visible in his blue eyes.

"I love you—and this is my way of showing you," he whispered. He caressed my cheek and disappeared like a ghost out the door, leaving me alone with nothing but the silence and my tears to soothe me.

* * *

This time when my car pulled up that brick driveway, I knew exactly where I was. And why I was there.

Not wasting a second, I killed the engine and stepped away from the car, intent on my purpose. I had words—plenty of them—and I was ready to unleash them on my enemy.

Because that's what August was. My own version of Public Enemy Number One.

He opened the door almost immediately after I began pounding on it. His happy, surprised expression faded just as quickly as the words began rushing from my lips.

"You've ruined my life. Again!" I screamed, pointing my finger deep into his chest. His surprise gave way to confusion as he let me stumble my way over the threshold.

"I don't understand, Everly. What's going on?"

I grunted out a laugh. "You. You are what's going on. Ever since you woke up, my life has been in turmoil. It wasn't enough that you treated me poorly for years—no, now you have to ruin the best thing that's ever happened to me."

His hands went up in a defensive position as he slowly backed into the living room. My finger was still pressed deep into his chest and the way he looked down at it made me feel like I was pointing a loaded weapon at his heart.

"Ryan left me!" I cried out, fresh tears dripping down my cheeks.

His eyes rounded in sympathy. Sympathy I didn't want or need.

"No!" I yelled. "Don't you dare say anything. You've done enough!"

Stepping out of my reach, his eyes turned hard as he wrapped his arms around his torso. "What have I done exactly?"

I yelled out in frustration, my hands going through my hair as I turned away from him. "He doesn't think I love him. He says I need time."

"To do what?" he pressed.

"To be with you!"

"And you obviously don't agree?" he asked slowly as I turned and met his gaze.

"Look, I get that me coming here, announcing my split from Ryan is like a wet dream come true for you, but let me explain something—it's temporary. We will get back together."

His expression turned heated. "You think I like seeing you show up like this? All wrecked and destroyed over another fucking guy? Do you think this pleases me somehow? Jesus, Everly—if I ever pictured you coming through that door again, it certainly wasn't like this."

"I hate this," I sobbed, "I hate this whole thing. Why did you have to wake up, August? Why now? Why couldn't you have waited? Just a little bit longer? We could have been married—happy. Settled."

He shook his head, shock written all over his face. "Do you think anything would have really been different? Do you think the timing of this would have changed anything, Everly? That somehow marriage vows would have made the big difference in all of this?"

"Yes!"

"No"—he cut me off—"It wouldn't. The only difference would be a marriage falling apart instead of an engagement."

"We're getting back together!" I screamed.

"Please," he hissed. "If that were true, why was the first thing you did after he left to come here?"

I opened my mouth to answer but the words fell flat as he stepped closer, pushing into my personal space. His scent surrounded me as his dark hazel eyes looked down with purpose.

"Exactly," he said softly. "You and I are the same. Both too scared to admit the cold, hard truth—moving on isn't an option for us because we're still stuck right damn here."

Pulling me closer, his mouth closed over mine. His kiss was brutal and hard. My gasp of surprise only pushed him further, digging his hands into my waist as he lifted me from the floor. The more I fought, the more punishing he became. We fought as my legs wrapped around his waist and my jagged teeth sank into his lip.

Hearing him cry out in pain only fueled the fire that was raging uncontrollably in my belly, begging me to go further—to hurt him for everything I'd lost. He grabbed my hair roughly as I pushed us back onto the couch. We ripped clothes from our bodies in mindless frenzy. I had no idea what I was doing, only that he was the reason I was doing it. Time rushed by in a blur, as passion and pain dominated my mind.

He was the reason for everything.

Nothing was gentle. There were no lingering kisses, no words of praise as he pulled a condom from his wallet and quickly slipped it on. No thoughts of whether this was wrong or right passed through my head as we pushed and pulled at each other. His dark eyes met mine seconds before he lifted my naked body and slammed it down on his, culminating our wicked dance into something deeper.

I cried out at the intrusion but he gave me no time to adjust as he moved me up and down over and over on his swollen cock. Every plot of vengeance…every fantasy of getting even was pushed aside as he worked my body over his. I let him own me in those minutes, giving it all up for those few shorts moments of bliss.

My head fell back as he picked me up and flipped me over the back of the couch, spreading my legs wide.

"Shit!" I yelled as he entered me from behind, his relentless pace never slowing as he moved hard and slow into me. I pushed back, feeling the hard line of his pelvic bone hit my ass as he grabbed my hips and pumped in and out.

"Remember this," he said, leaning over, against my ear. "Remember what this feels like when you go crawling back to your fiancé tomorrow, Everly. Remember what I feel like inside you. Don't ever forget how we feel together."

His words had me breaking apart, coming like a tidal wave at each hard thrust. As I tightened around him, his speed picked up, moving faster until I felt him surrender to his own inevitable release and collapse next to me on the couch.

Neither of us said anything as he stood and walked away, heading for the stairs.

There was really nothing left to say.

I could have left. I should have left. That is what a smart person would have done.

But instead, I traced his steps up the familiar staircase.

"Not the master," I said as his hand went to the door handle of the bedroom we'd once shared. Without a single word, he walked until he reached the guest bedroom and waited.

Without a single word, I followed.

*　*　*

The crashing waves did nothing to calm my weary nerves. I watched the early morning sun climb higher up the horizon under the large bank of fog that hung heavy over the city. After sneaking out of bed, I'd found my clothes scattered around the sofa with August's things.

I barely remembered removing them.

Everything had happened so fast.

And yet, when it was over, and the moment had passed…I hadn't left. I hadn't fallen to my knees begging with remorse and chastising myself over the inexcusable decisions I'd made.

No, instead…I made them over and over again. All night long.

Was this what Ryan had expected me to do? When he'd walked out the door last night, leaving me to choose—did he know I'd end up here? Did everyone seem to know me better than I did myself?

Pushing away from the balcony edge, I pulled the blanket I'd grabbed from the living room tighter around my shoulders and headed back inside to make a cup of coffee. I felt no big rush to leave as long as August was still asleep. Today was my day off and it wasn't as if I had anywhere else to go.

I had no home anymore anyway.

I had no home.

That thought lodged in my brain and I halted mid-step in the kitchen, nearly spilling the bag of coffee grounds I was carrying.

Oh dear god, I had nowhere to go. Did I?

Ryan had been the one to walk out, but it had always been his apartment. I'd moved in with him—not the other way around. When we'd made the step to move in together, I had been living in a tiny apartment I'd found after I moved away from the cliffs and we'd thought it best to keep his. It was in a better area and larger.

I couldn't expect him to leave—especially now.

After what I'd done.

Setting the coffee down on the counter, I felt my heart rate double at the thought of being homeless. Visions of ratty sheets and second-hand clothes filled my mind as my childhood raced back.

I couldn't go back. I couldn't.

Running toward the door, I grabbed my purse, ready to race back to the apartment.

I had to plan—pack…something. Oh, god. What a mess I'd made.

As soon as I opened the door, though, I nearly flew into a very surprised Brick, who had his hand up in the air preparing to knock. He righted me with one hand as I stumbled in my haste, bringing me upright to his curious gaze.

"I didn't expect to find you here," he said, balancing a drink carrier with his free hand.

"Really? This wasn't your secret plan all along?" I sneered, hating myself for taking my anger out on Brick—but really, hadn't he orchestrated this all? Hadn't he been the reason we were even seeing each other again in the first place?

If he hadn't shown up at my apartment all those weeks ago, would I still be engaged?

Would I still be sitting in my warm, inviting little apartment planning out the rest of my years with Ryan?

Or would I have eventually ended up in this same position?

Somehow, I already knew the answer.

"You want to go for a walk?" he asked, holding up his drink carrier. "I was supposed to meet August here for a morning hike down to the beach, but I'm guessing he forgot. Plus, I think you could use this coffee a bit more right now."

I eyed the paper cups in his hand and bit the corner of my lip reluctantly. "Okay, but only because you have coffee."

"I always know how to charm the ladies," he chuckled, handing me a piping hot cup of joe. He dropped the cardboard carrier on the table by the front door and we headed out into the brisk morning air. The fog that had settled overnight was slowly starting to clear. Bit by bit, the city was beginning to reveal herself to the world once again, like a mask slowly being stripped away.

The crunch of gravel was the only sound between us for a while as we slowly walked down the street and sipped from our cups. Between each house, I'd sneak a glance at the gray ocean as the fog slowly began to recede over the water.

"You haven't asked what happened—between August and me," I said.

"Considering it's barely seven in the morning, I don't really need to ask, do I?"

"No, I suppose not." I straightened slightly but kept walking.

"You know, I may be old, but I'm not that old." He laughed.

I just shook my head, trying to hide the slight smirk he'd managed to get out of me. "Your jokes aren't making this any better, Brick," I said, giving him a playful shove.

"Jokes always make everything better," he argued, "Besides, who's to say things need to be better than they already are? What if they're already great now?"

I just shook my head in disbelief. "You really are as crazy as August said you were. Life is not great, Brick. It's complicating and confusing and—"

"Real?"

"What?" I asked.

"Everyone's life is complicated and confusing, Everly. It's what keeps us breathing and not falling over dead of boredom. It's the chaos that makes life worth it. Don't deny what you're feeling because it's not simple or easy. Deny something because it doesn't feel right, not because it's complicated."

"You sound like you're speaking from experience," I said as we passed another block. I took my last sip of coffee.

"Nah, what would I know? I'm just a country boy from the Midwest." He winked.

"I'm just scared I'm falling down the rabbit hole again—bound to make the same mistakes with the same man over and over again."

"But he's not the same man, is he?" he reminded me.

"No, he's not—but he could be."

"Yes—he could and that's a risk you have to decide if you're willing to take. Because loving August as he is now doesn't always mean that he'll love you the same way back."

And there it was—my deep, underlying fear. The one that kept me running from him time after time.

If I gave my heart over to a man who then turned into my worst nightmare...?

Who would be there to pick up the broken pieces?

No one, because there would be nothing left to find.

Chapter Twenty-Two

August

Her scent was everywhere.

The sweet strawberry scent of her hair clung to the sheets, the air…hell, I think she'd permanently grafted it to my fucking nostrils. It was the first thing I noticed when I awoke, and damn if it didn't make me want to reach out for her and feel her naked skin against mine again.

But she wasn't here. She wasn't anywhere.

After realizing her scent was the only thing she'd left in the bed, I quickly jumped out of bed and grabbed a pair of boxers, then headed downstairs in search of her.

Her clothes, keys…all gone.

I'd known this would happen. I'd even told her I expected it.

So why did it hurt so damn much?

Because even though I'd expected it, a small part of me—the hopeful, naive part—wanted her to choose me. To decide I was worth the risk.

But she'd chosen him.

She'd always choose him.

At least now I knew what it felt like to have her skin against mine, to taste her lips and feel her breath quicken as I moved inside her. No longer memories of a former forgotten life, these were mine now and I'd carry them to my grave.

Wandering into the kitchen, I paused, seeing the bag of coffee grounds still open on the counter. Fingering the bag, I tried picturing how she'd looked the other day, moving around with ease from one corner to the next as if she owned the place.

"Hi." Her voice nearly had me jumping, and I rotated around to see her standing in the doorway.

"Hi," I answered, looking curiously at the blanket draped over her shoulders.

"I went for a walk—with Brick," she explained, holding up a paper coffee cup.

"Shit!" I exclaimed, remembering the morning hike we'd planned. She just shrugged and kicked off her shoes, tossing the cup in the trash as she moved about the kitchen. I watched as she took over the coffee making once again, and a piece of my heart eased.

"It's okay—it was good to see him. I needed a therapy session." She gave me a weak smile.

I nodded, leaning against the counter as we waited for the coffee to percolate.

"Did you get what you needed?" I asked, not really sure how to phrase what I really wanted to ask.

"I think so," she answered vaguely, eyeing me from across the room.

"Okay."

I didn't know what else to say, but I was afraid to stop talking. Afraid that if there was a long enough lull, she would leave again. And if she left, would that be the end? Would she ever come back?

"I know what you're thinking," she said, tapping her nails against the counter. "You're waiting for me to run—to make a mad dash out those doors and never come back."

"Well, it is what you've done in the past," I reminded her.

"I know—and look where it brought us." She let out a long sigh as her eyes met mine. "I've made a mess of things, trying to come to terms with what I'm feeling. You would think after years of therapy I would have a better grasp over my own mind, but it turns out I'm just as lost and confused as I was then. I don't want to run anymore, August."

"Then don't," I simply said, taking a step forward.

"This scares me," she whispered.

"It scares me, too."

"I don't know if I'll ever be able to forget the past."

"You shouldn't," I urged. "Never forget the man I became, Everly. I don't ever want to become him again."

"I'm not making any promises," she said, her voice soft and low as she closed the last remaining gap between us.

"I'm not asking for any. I just want a chance."

As badly as I wanted to touch her and taste her all over again, I needed her to make the first move. I'd given her no choice in the matter last night when I'd kissed her, but now—now, I needed to know she wanted this as much as I did.

I needed to know she wanted me.

It felt like a slow eternity in hell as I watched her eyes roam my skin, moving over the hollow of my neck, until they lingered on my bare chest. I held my breath as I watched her fingers reach out, barely skimming my torso as she began to explore me with her timid touch.

I was on fire, yet frozen in place, and for the first time since I'd opened my eyes for the first time in the hospital, I felt alive again.

There was no anger, no hatred or ulterior motive between us this time as I reached for her. I'd remember every memory I had with Everly in this new life, but I had a feeling these were the ones I'd dream about.

I lifted her into my arms and carried her carefully back upstairs, remembering her words from the night before. Avoiding the master bedroom, I walked toward the guest room. If that room made her more comfortable, I'd move everything I owned in there just to make her happy.

I set her gently down on the bed. Her vivid blue eyes never left mine. They fluttered closed as I silently dragged my fingers up her bare arm, across the hollow of her neck and down the valley between her breasts. Her hips rose, and her back arched as I slowly lifted her shirt, throwing it to the floor.

There were so many things I'd missed in my haste the night before. I'd been so angry—driven by pure instinct—that I'd failed to stop and appreciate what I had in front of me.

Everly was pure perfection before my eyes.

From the tiny freckles scattered over her creamy skin to the surprising tattoo on her beautiful shoulder, I couldn't have dreamed a more perfect woman if I tried.

Kissing a path down from her belly button, I began unbuttoning her jeans and she helped me slide them off her hips. Her legs went on for days, and I had plans to be buried between them for just as long.

I slid up her body, cradling it beneath mine as my lips left a trail of kisses along the way.

"August," she said softly.

My eyes met hers.

"I need to know, before this goes any further. I can't allow anyone else to get hurt because of us. So I need to know—are you still seeing Magnolia?"

My head dropped to her chest and I shook it back and forth.

"No," I answered. "I tried. Believe me, I did."

"It was the name, wasn't it?" she joked, a slight rumble in her ribcage bringing my head up again. I smirked slightly.

"No, it was you. It was always you," I said, remembering the night I'd gone to Magnolia's after Everly left. Barely thirty minutes and two drinks in, I'd apologized and ended it. For good.

There was only one woman I wanted to be with.

"I don't know why or how, but it's only ever been you since the moment I woke up."

She pulled me closer until our lips met and no other words were needed. My mouth moved with hers, devouring her sweet softness. Touching her tenderly, I wove my fingers into the coppery strands of her hair as our kiss deepened. Her hands seemed to be everywhere at once, as she gently caressed the corded muscles of my stomach, sliding her fingers up my chest as she gripped my shoulders and wrapped her knees around my waist.

A complete contrast from the night before: we didn't rush a thing. Every move, every touch was carried out as if we had an entire lifetime to spend in this bed.

And if I had my way, we would. I never wanted to leave.

When the last of our clothing was shed, I took my time kissing her skin, teasing the tender peaks of her nipples with my tongue until she begged me to stop. I gladly complied, pulling the pink bud into my mouth and giving it a hard suck. Everly screamed out my name and I nearly came just from the sound alone.

My hands were shaking as I grabbed a condom from the nearby table. No more games.

The next time she screamed out my name, it would be with me inside her.

Her eyes never left me as she watched me slowly unroll the condom over my shaft. Whatever feelings of guilt or remorse she may have been feeling earlier, she'd put them aside for now and was solely focused on me. Only me.

That look made me feel like I could take on the entire world.

It gave me a glimpse of the man I wanted to be.

I bent back down and felt shivers race up my spine at the feeling of our warm bodies rejoining. We were like two halves of puzzle interlocking seamlessly. She was my other half—I just needed to convince her of that. And every second she was here in my arms, I'd fight like hell to prove it to her.

Her gaze never left mine as I moved, and I felt the trust she gave with every powerful jolt of my hips. I felt humbled, honored, and weighted by the enormous responsibility of it all. How my former self had neglected such a precious treasure, I'd never understand. But now that I had a second chance, I'd give everything to right my wrongs.

Even if I didn't remember them.

"I know you're scared," I breathed, lavishing her neck with long, smoldering kisses. "But I can't ignore how right this feels when we're together."

She answered by arching her back, as her fingers dug into mine, pulling me closer, deeper. Our lips met in a frenzy—tongues mating as our bodies crested over the edge of delirium. Sweat dripped from our skin as I worshiped her, bringing her to the peak of ecstasy. She writhed and moaned, wrapping her legs tightly around my waist. Running my hand down her leg, I pushed on her thigh, freeing it from its viselike grip around my waist, edging it closer to her chest.

"Oh God!" she cried as I deepened the angle of each thrust.

"Let go," I said, kissing her lips once again until I felt her body tighten around me. "That's it," I whispered.

"August!" she screamed, wave after wave of release sweeping over her beautiful body. I couldn't stop myself from claiming her lips again, needing to taste her as she came apart. Feeling my own climax was imminent, I never slowed the pace of our lovemaking, prolonging her orgasm in spades. She gripped my shoulders and moaned between kisses as I came.

I swear I saw fucking stars.

I'm sure my former self had had more sexual encounters than he could count, but for me—practically newborn, barely alive a few months, I could count them on one hand—the waitress and Everly.

Neither of those encounters had ever brought me to my knees like this. Collapsing next to her, I was sure I'd never move another muscle in my life.

She'd destroyed me.

I only hoped it was permanent, because I never wanted to go back.

*   *   *

"So is this what you do with your spare time then?" Everly asked as I set the sparsely filled tray down on the bed before her.

Laughing, I answered, "Well, besides photography, watching shitty movies, and taking you to bed, yeah, I guess," I answered with a shrug.

"It's just…" She looked curiously at the different types of food. "So weird."

I chuckled and nodded. "I know, but okay…hear me out." She gave me a look that said she was just humoring me as I held out my hands in defense. "Just one minute."

"Okay." A slight grin tugged at the corner of her lip.

"You go to an ice cream shop and look at the various types of sundaes. Each have several different ingredients and based on that, you make your selection, right?" Biting her lip to keep from laughing, she nodded. I ignored her, shaking my head, and continued with my explanation.

"Over your life, you've tried everything on that menu—maybe individually or with something else, but you've made a conscious decision whether you like it. Me? I'm starting from scratch. Looking at a menu like that? I truly don't have a clue if I like caramel or cherries or even whipped cream."

"So, you've decided to do it this way?" she asked, motioning to the tray again.

"Okay, I know…it's weird. But I'm a guy. We're simple creatures. One thing at a time seemed like a good idea when I started and I just haven't been able to graduate to anything else," I admitted. I looked down at my pathetic excuse for a meal, which consisted of plain eggs, sliced cheese, and coffee.

"So," she smirked, "when you discovered you liked eggs and cheese, you never had the idea to…I don't know, combine them?"

"That requires cooking."

"Oh my god," she said, shaking her head. "You're pathetic—like a toddler."

"Yes. Yes I am. You came just in time to save me."

Her hand paused midway as she reached for a piece of cheese. "What am I going to tell Ryan?" she asked, her face falling as the realization of own situation hit her. Laughing over eggs and cheese had suddenly become a serious matter as she came face to face with real life again.

"Why do you need to tell him anything? He left you," I reminded her gently, grabbing a piece of cheese for myself.

"It's not that simple," she answered. "I'll have to go back there. I have to find a place to live."

"Live here," I said, the words leaving my mouth as quickly as my heart leapt at the idea of having her forever.

Her eyes met mine, as fear and doubt seemed to swipe away her features.

"You're even crazier than I thought," she whispered, shaking her head in disbelief.

"Yes, I am. When I'm around you, I feel crazy, delirious, and for the first time since I woke up, I feel truly alive. What I feel for you doesn't make any sense, Everly. None of this does, but if we're going to do this—then let's do it. If there's anything I've learned about life in this little do-over I've been given, it's that there's no time for half-assing your way through things."

Her eyes filled with worry as she busily bit down on her bottom lip, obviously contemplating my words.

Feverishly shaking her head back and forth, she said, "I can't depend on someone. Not again. I can't be that person."

"But I don't want you to be anywhere else."

"So charge me," she suggested. "Make me pay rent."

My eyes widened in shock. "Now you're the one out of your mind! Why would I do that? I am the last person on earth who needs more money, Everly."

"And I am the last person on earth who needs to be dependent on another man. Please, August. Let me do this. I should have never moved in with Ryan, and let him handle the majority of the rent. It gave him power—power he never used, but still it puts me at a disadvantage. I can't ask him to leave and now I'm left without a home. I can't jump from feeling powerless with one man to doing the same with another. Especially—"

I held up my hand to stop her. "I get it," I said, taking her hand in mine. "I don't like the idea of you giving me money, but I understand the need for it. Do what you need to do, as long as it ends with you here every day."

"As long as you agree to me taking over the cooking again." She smiled.

My heart skipped a beat just seeing her smile. It was one of the most beautiful things I'd ever seen. "Deal. But I have one caveat of my own."

"Okay," she said, her eyebrow peaking in interest as she picked at the mostly cold eggs. "I want a fresh start. No more comparing me to the man I was. I understand you can't forget, and I don't want that. I just want the opportunity for you to know me and who I am now. I want you to fall in love with the August that exists today."

"I want that, too," she whispered, pushing the tray away to crawl into my lap. "We'll go out later," she breathed into my ear.

"Good idea," I agreed.

And we did.

Much, much later.

Chapter Twenty-Three

Everly

I needed clothes.

And a toothbrush and, well…everything else that wasn't currently lying in the bottom of my purse—so basically everything but a tube of Chapstick and a stick of gum.

I really wish in August's effort to move on, he'd at least kept a few things of mine. A single shirt. A pair of pants, maybe? In my attempt to move on, I'd left everything from our life here, walking away with very little to call my own. In that moment, I'd never expected to miss any of it.

I'd been camped out here at August's place for nearly two days, and even though I was enjoying lounging around in his T-shirts and sweats, carrying around the smell of him everywhere I went, I was starting to feel like a bum and desperately wanted some things of my own.

Like a razor.

And deodorant that didn't smell like a dude.

Also, I had to work tomorrow. So wearing the rugged August apparel needed to come to an end quickly.

I had two options. I could deplete my savings account and go out and buy an entirely new wardrobe, shampoo, and every other thing a girl needed, or I could muster up the courage and go back to Ryan's apartment and pack up my things.

The coward in me began adding up just how many things I could buy at the dollar store, but I knew I needed to face my fate.

I'd made this decision.

I'd done exactly what Ryan had predicted I'd do, and now I needed to own up to that.

He'd said he wanted me to give this life a chance, and so here I was, doing exactly what he'd asked. I only hoped he'd meant what he said.

God, I was the biggest asshole on the planet.

I don't know how long I spent on the side of the road, looking up at our apartment building. Even though I'd gathered up the courage to come, I'd still chosen a time of day when I knew he most likely wouldn't be home.

I told myself I was doing him a favor—saving him from the grief of having to see me.

But I knew that was a lie.

It was me I was saving. I didn't want the pain of seeing him, because I knew as soon as I set my eyes on him, the wave of guilt and remorse I'd been keeping at bay for everything I'd done over the last two days would come rushing back.

And then where would I be?

Taking a deep breath, I stepped out of the car and walked briskly across the street, keeping my head low to avoid any possible run-ins with neighbors. All I needed was one unnecessary conversation about how wedding plans were going or where our honeymoon was going to be.

Just the thought had me nearly turning around with my tail between my legs. But I marched forward and made it inside without a nosy neighbor in sight. I took the stairs as an extra precaution. No one ever took the stairs. Except for the few health nuts who jogged early in the mornings, we were all slaves to the elevator, and after two floors of climbing...I knew exactly why. Walking up stairs was exhausting.

Also, I apparently needed to work out more.

Something to ponder for another day.

Successfully making it to the fourth floor, I walked down the hallway to our apartment and fished out my keys. With a shaky hand, I unlocked the door and nearly fell in due to my rubbery legs. The stairs combined with my nerves...bad combination.

Standing in the entryway, I listened carefully for any noise. Nothing.

I was alone.

Everything looked exactly the same. Our lives had completely combusted but this little apartment had stayed the same, like a little bubble.

A bubble I was about to pop.

I took a moment to walk around, running my fingers over the soft fuzzy blanket that hung over the back of the sofa. It reminded me of a teddy bear, so plush and velvety smooth. I'd loved snuggling under it on lazy mornings with a good book and an even better cup of a coffee. Ryan and I had made many memories under that blanket as well, I recalled, remembering the many nights we'd fallen asleep under it rather than making the trip to the bedroom.

It had been such an easy life to live. Ryan might think I'd been hard to win over, but it had been him who was hard to resist. After August, I'd sworn off love—sworn off men. They caused me harm and were too dangerous to trust. But then in had walked Ryan—the complete opposite of August. He was sweet, gentle, and patient, and soon I began to see a new path—one that was so easy to imagine. Loving Ryan had been simple and safe.

And perhaps that was the root of the problem.

Maybe love wasn't supposed to be safe.

Maybe it was supposed to be crazy and full of risks.

Yet as I wandered through that apartment, with its little touches we'd done over the year we'd been there, part of me knew I would always still crave the simple and the safe. A part of me would always crave Ryan.

Knowing I'd wasted enough time, I began packing quickly, stuffing as many things as I could into the few suitcases I could claim as my own. I didn't bother folding or organizing anything—everything was just thrown in and would be dealt with later. Running into the bathroom, I grabbed my toothbrush and shampoo from the shower.

The bottle was still wet.

How long ago had he been here?

Seeing the water drip down the sides of the shampoo bottle had me remembering the way he smelled. Like me—he always smelled like my strawberry shampoo because he was too scatterbrained to run out and get his own. I used to make jokes and ask what he'd done before I was around and he'd laugh and hold up a bar of soap.

Looking down at the bottle, I took a deep breath and placed it back in the shower.

I could get more.

Turning back around, I picked up a couple other things and

stepped back into the bedroom, placing them in the suitcase before returning to the closet.

"I figured you'd be coming back soon."

I swiveled around. Ryan was standing in the doorway looking down at me in the closet. His hair was messier than I'd ever seen and his eyes looked lost and tired.

"I'm sorry," I said. "I tried to come while you were at work."

"I took the day off," he admitted. "Been a little off my game."

I stood facing him but had trouble looking him in the eye. The way he looked...the fact that he was missing work—all because of me.

"I hate this, Ryan," I stated. "I wish we could go back to the way it was."

"We always knew this could happen, Ev. He would have woken up eventually. I was just the fool who thought I was enough to help you move past him. But you need to figure that out on your own."

I took a step forward, tears rimming my eyes, but stopped myself. "Ryan, please don't think that. This was never about you or him. It's always been about me. There are so many issues—feelings I pushed aside when he went into that coma. A coma is not a way to end a relationship—no matter how turbulent it may be."

"And now you need time. I understand."

Silence settled between us before he continued, taking a hesitant step forward. "But let me make one thing clear. I may have stepped aside, but by no means am I bowing out. I'll wait, Everly—for however long it takes for you to realize I'm the one."

"Ryan—"

"No, let me finish. You may need time. Time to work out whatever unresolved feelings you have for him, but he'll never be good enough for you—no matter how much he's changed."

"You don't know that," I countered.

"I do. He's hurt you before. He'll do it again."

Shaking my head, I began zipping up bags and swinging them over my shoulder with force. "I'm sorry I've hurt you, Ryan. You don't know how truly sorry I am, but please don't make this harder than it already is."

I needed out.

"Still running, I see. Well, at least some things haven't changed."

He was right. I was still running, but at least this time I knew where I was going.

Stopping just shy of the door, I turned to face him. Wrapping my fingers around the slim gold ring that I'd thought would be there until the day I died, I pulled it off and placed it on the table.

"Good-bye, Ryan."

His light brown eyes were the last thing I saw as I turned to walk out of the apartment we'd shared—the home we'd built together.

The simple life I'd left behind.

God, I hoped I was making the right choice.

*　*　*

"So, this is called a pan…and this large square-looking thing is called a stove. You can cook more than just eggs on it."

August eyed me suspiciously as I placed the pan on the stove and turned the knob to raise the heat.

"Please tell me you actually cooked those eggs on the stove?" I asked, as his eyes darted to the microwave.

"You microwaved them?" I asked incredulously, my hands going to my hips.

"Well, I mean—it worked, didn't it?"

"I have no words. Seriously. No words. This is going to be harder than I thought."

"For a woman of no words—you sure are talking a lot," he joked.

"Shut it." I laughed, slapping his arm as I moved toward the refrigerator.

"Have you used the stove at all?" I asked, pulling open the monstrous refrigerator in search of ideas. I had plans of making some sort of pasta, but I needed ingredients. I found a block of cheese and some shaved ham I assumed he'd been using for lunchmeat. Moving to the freezer, I found a bag of frozen peas, which could work.

"Okay, we're going to make dinner. Are you ready?"

"As I'll ever be." He smirked, his hazel eyes flashing green with amusement.

"Just put this down as one of those new life experiences you're always wanting, okay?"

"For some reason, I somehow already know I'm going to hate cooking. Just call it a sixth sense."

I shook my head and laughed. He'd always been scared of the kitchen. It was why I'd grown so fond of it in the first place. When we first moved in together, I quickly realized neither of us knew our way around the kitchen, much less a box of ramen. After several failed attempts to make meals together, I took the lead, teaching myself during my free time how to prepare simple dishes that were low cost and filling.

Later, when budget was no longer a concern, I branched out and began experimenting more with fancier ingredients and more intricate recipes. August was always proud of me and loved the food I produced.

At least until the end—when he was too busy to care about anything.

Then all he wanted to do was grab a quick bite and rush out the door.

But now, all that was behind us. We were starting new and I needed to remember that.

So, on with the cooking lesson.

"Do you have any garlic?" I asked. The vacant look in his eyes told me that was a definite no. "Okay, tomorrow—when I get off work, we are going shopping. And we're stocking this kitchen. This is horrifying. I refuse to live someplace that doesn't have food."

"I have food. Sort of," he argued. "But yes," he answered, wrapping his large hands around my waist. "We'll go shopping. Together. For *our* kitchen." He placed emphasis on the word "our," releasing a bevy of butterflies in my belly. The idea of sharing a home together—again—made me feel nervous, scared, and exhilarated all at once.

I leaned back into his embrace as his hands began to wander.

"Hey! No distracting me." I laughed. "I haven't had a decent meal in days. Now, go find some noodles."

"Yes ma'am."

He wandered into the pantry while I set my sights on the ham, grabbing a knife to begin chopping. I had a simple pasta dish in mind, but the ham and peas needed to cook through first.

"Any chance you have an onion in there?" I called out. He stuck his head out, holding a package of spaghetti.

"I'm pretty sure if there was, it would have sprouted roots by now."

I laughed and took the pasta from him as he came out of the pantry to stand beside me. "So, what do you want me to do now?" he asked, his voice low and husky next to my ear.

I audibly gulped, thinking of all the ways I could answer that question.

"Get a pot for the water," I answered softly.

I heard him chuckle as he turned toward the cupboard to grab a pot.

Jerk.

"So are we ever going to talk about your outing today?" he asked, returning with a large pot. I watched him place it carefully on the stove, as if he was scared he'd break something, as I tried to figure out how we'd gone from casually flirting to this.

"I don't know...never?" I tried to joke.

"I know I'm new to, well...everything," he said, swiveling me around in his arms, "but according to the many romantic comedies I've watched, we're supposed to talk through our feelings and emotions. Otherwise bad, albeit hilarious consequences follow."

His smile was infectious. "You've based all of your relationship experience on romantic comedies?"

"Well, not all. I threw in a few dramas to keep it serious," he said, laughing.

"Oh boy," I replied.

"Now, come on—I know something happened. You ran upstairs with your things and I didn't see you for hours as you hid in that room."

I sighed, finally resting my head on his shoulder.

"Ryan showed up. It was brutal."

His hands gripped my chin, forcing eye contact. "What did he say? What do you mean by brutal?" His expression had turned dark, defensive.

"He said he'd wait for me."

His face fell as he realized the reason. "Because he thinks I'll hurt you again."

I nodded.

"I will always keep you safe."

"I know," I said.

"No, look at me," he begged, as his intense gaze met mine. Hazel green eyes full of fire and promise met mine and I knew without a doubt he meant every word.

"I'll never hurt you again, Everly."

As my lips eagerly met his, I hoped and prayed I'd made the right choice, because a life with August was going to be anything but simple.

Chapter Twenty-Four

August

I didn't know how long it would be before Everly would be able to move into the master—if ever. So, the next morning, I decided to move my things into the guest bedroom with hers.

I hadn't asked her to elaborate on her fears over the master bedroom, but I had a feeling I already knew based on the lock I'd removed from the outside. Proof that I'd really locked her in there.

Why?

What reason would a man have to lock the woman he loved in their bedroom? I just didn't understand it.

"Why are you up so early?" Everly asked, peeking in at the doorway. She had a towel wrapped around her head and chest and drops of water dripped down her arms. *If she didn't have to be at work in thirty minutes...*

"I wanted to see you before you left...and drink the coffee you made." I grinned.

"Who said I was making coffee?" She laughed.

"If there's one thing I've learned about you in the last few days, it's that you cannot survive without coffee running through your veins. Especially in the morning."

She smiled brightly, something I'd never take for granted. "You're right. I've already had a cup. There's a fresh pot downstairs." I expected her to head back to the guest room and finish getting ready for work, but instead, I heard light footsteps enter the bedroom. It wasn't the first time she'd been in here. She'd wandered in here a few times, only to scurry back out in record time. The first time had been on that evening she drove me home from the hospital after my car accident.

I'd seen the torture and misery then. I had assumed it was all directed at me—and I'm sure a good part of it had been, but I'd never thought about how much a room could affect someone.

How many memories a house could carry.

"Are you happy here?" I asked.

"What do you mean?" she asked as she roamed around the room, looking at some of the pictures I'd recently hung. After I'd purged the house of everything Everly, I'd begun hanging my own photography. It filled me with pride to see her admiring it now.

"I mean—this room, this house...it's filled with so many memories. Would it be easier to just...start over?"

"You want to sell this place?" she asked in shock.

"I would—for you," I said, taking a step in her direction. "I'd do anything to make you happy."

She continued her long walk around the room, stopping at the large dresser by the bed as she silently thought. "This house is filled with memories. So many of them—both good and bad. And sometimes it's overwhelming being here with all of them swirling around in my head."

"So, let's move," I urged.

"Let me finish," she said. "As overwhelming as it is sometimes, it's also soothing. Like therapy. The fact that I can walk into this room right now gives me a great sense of peace. Knowing I can face my fears head on, rather than running away from them like I usually do? I can't tell you how good that makes me feel. I may not be able to sleep here, but at least I can take baby steps for now."

"I just don't like seeing you in any kind of pain. If I could take it away by just erasing it all—"

"No," she said adamantly. "I love this house. Despite everything, it means a great deal to me. Right now, I need to work on fighting the ghosts—not running from them."

Finding my way to her as she fiddled with my watch and other various things that sat in a large ornamental bowl on the dresser, I asked, "Is there anything I can do to help?"

Looking up at me over her shoulder, she gave a small smile. "Yes. Help me make new ones."

"Gladly," I whispered, leaning in to capture her lips. She pulled back, laughing under her breath. "I didn't mean this second—you're going to make me late for work!"

"Very very late," I agreed.

"August!" she yelped, twisting out of my grasp.

"Okay, okay!" I chuckled. "But you owe me—the second you get home."

"Deal," she agreed with a Cheshire Cat grin that nearly had me on my knees forgetting everything I'd just agreed to.

"Hey, can I borrow your watch?" she asked, grabbing it from the large bowl.

"Sure, why?" I asked, looking over her shoulder.

"I usually wear one to work and in my rush to pack yesterday, I forgot mine. I can go back to get it but—"

"It's yours," I said, placing my hand over hers. "But don't just settle on that one. There are a few more in there. Take a look and pick whichever one you want. I was going to donate them to charity since I have no need for six different watches."

"You realize," she said, standing on her tiptoes as she dug through the bowl, "that most people keep these types of watches under lock and key, right? Not in a glass bowl on the top of their dresser? Do you know how much these are worth?" Her eyes darted back to mine with an amused grin.

"Probably a fortune, and I'm sure the old me cared about that kind of shit…but really? It's just a watch. It tells time just as well as something I could pick up at Target."

"I'm pretty sure some people would argue with you on that," she said with a laugh, trying on another bold silver watch. She held out her arm to look at it and then shook her head and moved on.

"Yeah—rich snobby people."

"Like you?" she teased.

"I'm rich, but definitely not snobby."

"No—hey, what's this?" she asked as her hand dug to the bottom of the bowl.

I came to join her and saw her hesitantly pull out the tiny green bead I'd found in my coat pocket when I was in the hospital.

"Maybe you can tell me," I said as she swiveled around to face me.

"What do you mean?" Her eyes were wide, like I'd said something to ignite panic.

"I found it in my belongings when I was in the hospital. It was in my coat, so it must have been there the night of the mugging. I just thought you might know what it is," I said, placing my hand on her shoulder.

"I've never seen it before," she said, jerking back as she eyed the tiny green bead.

"Hey, are you all right?"

"Sorry," she mumbled, averting my gaze. "It's just that night—it was scary. I don't like reliving it."

God, I'm an idiot.

"No—shit, of course not. Come here," I said, pulling her closer. She came into my arms and I felt her shaking against me. "I'm so sorry, Everly. I'll never mention it again."

I felt her nod as she pulled herself back together.

"It's okay—you didn't know. I better get ready for work. I'm definitely going to be late if I don't hurry."

"Sure, of course," I answered, watching her flee for the guest bedroom.

Would she ever stop running?

*   *   *

Over the next few days, Everly and I settled into a happy rhythm. I woke up with her early in the morning, sometimes waking her myself with a dip beneath the covers or a gentle kiss to pull her from her slumber.

Alarm clocks were greatly overrated.

Most days she'd make it to work on time, although I had made her late a time or two. She'd threatened life and limb if I kept it up so I just woke her up earlier. She wasn't too pleased.

At first.

I found Everly was easy to persuade once my mouth was buried deep between her legs. Of course, much the same could be said of me when the situation was reversed and she was in the driver's seat. If Everly wanted anything, it could be hers in those moments when I was buried deep inside her.

But the only thing she asked for was more.

And more was exactly what I gave. Every damn time.

Everly showing up at my house that night, angry and hurt, had changed my entire life. I'd never thought I'd get a single smile from her, much less be able to reach for her without her recoiling in fear. What I thought might have been lingering feelings left over from a former life only intensified with each passing day.

The more I learned about her, the deeper our connection grew... and the further I fell.

It wasn't just the girl in the picture I was falling for; it was Everly, the coffee-addicted, quick-witted woman who always managed to keep me on my toes. She was funny, bright, and she could make dynamite pasta out of basically nothing.

It was a wonder I could keep my hands off her for a second.

It was also the excuse I gave myself for driving toward the café instead of home after running errands early one afternoon, with hope I could take her out to a late lunch.

Parking was a bitch, as was the case in most of San Francisco, so I ended up several blocks away and had to huff it to the café on foot. Luckily, the fog had mostly cleared and the sun was attempting to peek through the clouds, bringing the promise of warmer weather with it. The light jacket I wore hopefully would no longer be needed later in the day. San Franciscans, I learned, loved the sun. They wouldn't live anywhere else. This foggy, cloud-covered city was the only place in their eyes, but when the sun managed to make its way through the gray sky, it was like a damn miracle. People flocked to the parks, bike rentals sold out, and everyone ran out to enjoy the great outdoors.

As the heat from a small ray of sunshine warmed my chilled face, I didn't blame my fellow city dwellers one bit.

Not one damn bit.

Just as I reached the little café, my phone began to buzz in my pocket. Curiosity got the best of me and I reached in to grab it, wondering who could be calling me.

I very rarely received calls. I had been in the hospital for over two years and had not had a single visitor, so I considered myself not exactly popular.

The name "Trent" flashed across the screen, the same name my attorney had mentioned a while ago. Although seeing the name piqued my interest, I seriously wondered if this call wasn't going to be like all the others. This wasn't the first random phone call or blast from my past, as I liked to call them. I'd been naive in the beginning and had answered a few, only to discover that my attorney was quite the talker, and word had gotten out that I had miraculously "risen from the dead." Many of my former acquaintances had called, saying they wanted to check on my progress now that I was out of the hospital. When asked why they hadn't bothered checking on me sooner, I received several colorful answers, including one from a Mr. Parker, who said he knew me from "the club," but who said he hadn't wanted to bother me in my delicate state.

I'd been in a coma.

For two years.

I wised up quickly to the money-grubbing assholes and stopped answering my phone. My former life had been filled with fake people and their fancy shit. I'd had enough. I stuffed the phone back in my pocket and reached for the café's door handle.

Everly had once said she loved working at the coffee shop not only for the endless supply of coffee but also because it was never the same from one day to the next. Because she and her coworkers always divided up the duties, she would end up working the counter one day and barista the next. It kept her on her toes.

As I walked in that afternoon, her smiling face wasn't the first thing I saw—which meant she was the one in charge of the crazy machinery that churned out the caffeine. As I heard her call out a double whipped, extra hot something or other, I began to understand why she took her coffee plain and black.

I had no idea coffee could be so damned confusing.

"Can I help you?" a perky young blonde asked from behind the counter.

"Yes," I answered, giving her a lazy smile.

"What can I get you, handsome?" she winked.

"Actually, I'm just here for Everly. Wanted to see if she had lunch plans."

She looked me up and down. Her caramel brown eyes assessed me before she turned and hollered over the noise, "Everly, you have a visitor!"

"Okay!" she yelled back, and I saw a tuft of her red hair peeking over the tops of the coffee machines.

"And who might you be?" the blonde asked, placing her hands down on the counter as if she had all the time in the world. I looked behind me, realized I was indeed the only person in line, and grinned.

"I'm Everly's—"

"Friend," Everly rushed over and cut me off. "Longtime friend," she stressed again.

"Well…does your hot friend have a name?" the blonde asked, now looking me up and down like I was a large slab of steak and she was a caged lioness just waiting to sink her teeth in.

"August," I answered, holding out my hand in greeting, although my eyes never left Everly's.

"Well, feel free to visit more often, August. Much more often," she purred.

"Will do. And I'm sorry," I said, turning my attention back to her. "I didn't catch your name."

"Trudy," she answered, blushing.

"Nice to meet you." I gave her a wink before Everly tugged me away.

"I'm going to take my lunch break. I'll be back in an hour," she said as we made our way toward the door.

"Okay, hon. Enjoy!"

We stepped out into the fresh air and began walking—no place or destination in mind. Just mindless, silent walking.

"So, do you think you could get me Trudy's phone number?" I finally asked, the bitterness clear in my tone.

"Just stop."

I froze on the street corner, anger radiating through my veins.

"You're angry at me?"

"Yes! Why didn't you call or tell me you were going to stop by?" she yelled.

"Would that have made it better, Everly? Would that have given you time to make up a better story about who I was or why some guy other than Ryan was coming to take you out to lunch? Because that's what this is all about, isn't it? You haven't told them?"

"It isn't any of their business," she said softly.

"It isn't any of their business or it isn't worth telling anyone? Because I remember you telling me you and your coworkers were pretty damn tight, so if you can't admit what's going on to them, who can you tell? Have you told anyone?"

Silence followed, telling me exactly what I wanted to know.

"Is this a joke to you?"

"What?" Her eyes grew wide. "No, August. God, no."

"Then why do I feel like the biggest idiot in the world right now, Everly?"

Her arms wrapped around me and as confused as I was, I sank into her warmth. "I'm sorry. It's still all so new. I'm still working through what to say—what to tell everyone. No one knows about that part of my past. I don't know how to explain you."

"Then don't. The world doesn't need to know every detail. But, I do want to exist in yours. I want to be able to show up at your work and be recognized as your boyfriend, not some guy your coworkers can possibly hook up with."

"I'm not sure the status update will change Trudy's opinion on that." Everly gave a hesitant laugh, her eyes filled with dread.

"I want to matter in your life," I said.

"You do. You always have," she urged, wrapping her arms around me. "I just don't know if I'm ready to tell everyone."

I pushed back in frustration, the back of my hand running across my forehead. "You mean you don't know if you're ready to tell them about me?"

"August—please try to understand. I was engaged two weeks ago. I—"

Taking a step back, not wanting to hear another word, I held my hands up to stop her. "I understand plenty."

"August! Please don't leave!"

But I couldn't stop my feet from fleeing.

Maybe it was time she saw me walking away for a change.

Chapter Twenty-Five

Everly

My leg twitched up and down nervously as I sat alone in the snug little waiting room. It was late in the afternoon and I knew I must be her last appointment of the day. She usually didn't take patients after four, and it was just past that when I saw the door to her office crack open as she ushered out her last client.

She'd made a special appointment for me. She'd extended her day because she knew I'd probably chicken out and avoid coming if I didn't get in today.

She was right.

Damn woman was always right.

That was a classic avoidance technique I'd mastered.

What I called running or my tendency to flee, Tabitha called avoidance. When conflict entered my life, I solved it by avoiding the situation altogether.

Ryan and I argued about my future job prospects? I needed to go on a walk, or take a long drive.

August went into a long-term coma? I avoided the entire situation for years and acted like nothing had happened until it all blew up in my face like a giant atomic bomb.

Yeah.

Avoidance sounded like a good term.

She said her good-byes, waiting until the door settled back into place before greeting me. Tabitha worked solo—no assistant or receptionist. Every appointment was made and handled through her, which was why she kept her patient list so small. Even the waiting area was nothing more than a few chairs and a scattering of magazines.

"Are you ready?" she asked, turning to me, ready to give me her complete attention for the next hour.

"As I'll ever be," I answered, taking a deep breath.

"After you," she said, giving me the lead. I entered the small office, taking in the familiar surroundings as I found my favorite spot—an old red velvet sofa with mismatched flowery pillows that I always held in my lap. Tabitha never said anything about this little nuance of mine but I'm sure plenty of therapist-related stuff had been written down in her notes about me.

I snuggled down in the couch, grabbed the lumpy pillow I favored, and crossed my legs beneath me, ready to talk. I'd gone too long—spent too much time avoiding this place. Being here always felt right, even when I didn't want to admit it. Tabitha helped center me. She brought out the emotions and feelings buried below that surface that I was always unwilling to face.

Admitting to myself that I needed to be here was sometimes difficult. No one ever likes to admit they need help, but I was thankful I'd stumbled upon someone as patient and understanding as she was. I'm not sure every therapist and counselor out there would have stuck by me through everything.

I was kind of a pain-in-the-ass patient.

Hence the reason she was seeing me after hours.

And staring at me as if I was in trouble.

"It's been a while since I've seen you," she commented, looking through her notes as if she needed them to confirm exactly how long it had been. We both knew, without having to check dates, that it had been too long. I'd chickened out, calling to cancel my appointments during the daytime when I knew she'd be with patients just to avoid having to explain why I couldn't make it. Her voice mail was always very understanding.

The reason I'd been avoiding this sacred space? If I came here, suddenly everything that had happened over the last few weeks would become very real. And up until this afternoon, I'd been happily living in my bubble world, ready to live out my existence there for the rest of eternity.

"My life is a mess," I stated with a heavy sigh.

She gave me a warm smile. "Every life is a mess, Everly. It's what we do with that great big mess that truly matters."

"Ryan and I broke up," I said, squeezing the pillow between my arms.

"I know," she answered, nodding.

"How?" But then I realized as the word had barely left my lips. "Sarah?" I asked.

She shrugged, and pointed to my left hand. "You're not wearing your engagement ring. First time in months I haven't seen it on your finger."

I shook my head, refusing to believe she'd figured it out so easily. "How is Sarah?" I pushed.

"You know I can't answer that," she said, unwilling to break her patient confidentiality clause.

"I know. I just miss her," I replied.

"Then you know what to do."

I nodded. "But that means telling her about August. What if she doesn't ever want to talk to me again?"

"Why don't you start by telling me about August, and we'll go from there?"

"Okay," I agreed.

Over the next thirty minutes, I told her the story of August and me. I relived the pain of Ryan leaving me and the anger I'd felt, blaming it all on August. How my anger had turned into something entirely different and somehow, in the midst of all those unresolved feelings, I'd realized I still wanted him.

Not for a night, or even a fling.

"But what about your past?" she asked, knowing everything I'd gone through to get over him the first time.

"It's something I struggle with. But it's getting easier. The more time I spend with him, the less I see him as the man I left in the hospital two years ago."

"And who do you see instead? The old August? The one you fell in love with all those years ago?" she asked.

"Bits and pieces," I answered. "But he's also different. Completely new—and I like that just as much. Learning new things about him... I didn't think it was possible, but it's almost like starting over. He likes his coffee black now, and he loves vanilla ice cream."

"You seem happy," she said.

"I am—I think."

"Then why would Sarah hate you for being happy?" she asked.

I shook my head. "I spent the last few years painting this man as the worst possible villain on the planet. Even though I didn't give her detailed explanations, as my friend—she still hates him. I just don't know if she'll ever trust him."

"Do you trust him?"

I nodded. "I'm beginning to."

"Then she will learn to as well."

"Why are you always so supportive of my decisions? Do you ever want to shake me like a rattle and holler and scream at me for making these decisions?"

She laughed, her bright smile lighting up her tan skin. For a woman in her late forties, Tabitha was stunning. Golden blond hair and still fit from years of yoga, I'm sure she was still turning plenty of heads anywhere she went.

"Sometimes," she answered honestly. "But it's your life—not mine. These are your decisions to make. I'm here to help guide you, and support you, like you said. But the decisions? Those are yours alone."

"Well, damn. It would be a hell of a lot easier if someone else could make them."

"That's the truth for us all, sweetheart," she sighed. "But then, we wouldn't get to enjoy the chaos we make along the way. Time for you to go enjoy yours."

*   *   *

After our very public fight on the streets near the café, I had no idea what type of atmosphere I'd be entering when I got home. I had lived with two very different types of August over the years.

The August before money and the August after money.

These years could also be described as the good years and bad years, although we did have a few good years after the money flowed. It was when the money had gone to his head that life truly became unbearable.

August became unbearable as well.

During those years, we didn't fight. I tried in the beginning, but quickly learned that arguing with him only got me a fast pass to the bedroom, and the click of the lock sooner. Honestly, after a while, there wasn't much to argue about anyway. I didn't understand why I wasn't allowed to leave the house anymore, and he wouldn't explain. Once that was established and no answers were given, it seemed like a moot point. I'd hoped by being cordial and acting more like my old self, he'd ease up on the restriction, but he never did. In fact, the more time that passed, the worst the obsession became.

* * *

"I can't bear the idea of you leaving this house, Everly," he said in a blind panic. "Please, just do as I say and stay in this room until I get back. I need you stay here." His hands shook as he tried to smooth his hair in the mirror and straighten his tie.

"Okay," I whispered, feeling defeated once again. "I'll stay."

* * *

And I did.

I always did.

I don't know why I never left. I could have. So easily.

It's not difficult to pick a lock or break open a door. God knows the things you can learn on the Internet. If I'd had the drive...the true need, I could have found a way. I could have left—if I'd wanted to. I'd always told Ryan and Tabitha—even August himself—that he'd held me prisoner in that room. But really? I think the only person who had truly held me prisoner was me.

Even if I hadn't realized it then, I'd chosen to stay. I'd chosen to remain with a man I said I'd once hated until everything boiled over.

I'd since learned it's better to fight than to hold it all in.

Good things never come from bottling everything inside. But as I turned the doorknob and stepped inside the house, I felt the trepidations of the past following alongside me.

What type of August would greet me?

Would this new August be like the one I'd left behind? Firm and frightening—unwilling to budge a single inch? Or would he be more like the August I remembered, who'd fought as my equal—working through each problem as a partner rather than a ruler?

I seriously hoped the latter, because I was no longer someone's helpless pawn to be played.

"August?" I called out, peering down the hall for any sign of him.

What if he wasn't here?

"In here," he answered. I followed the sound of his voice to the living room, where I found him lighting several candles around the room. The entire space was aglow in a soft light, the light from the wicks of the candles dancing along the walls and ceiling. It was beautiful and romantic—the complete opposite of what I'd expected when I walked through that door.

Our eyes met from across the room and I saw the apology before it touched his lips.

"I will never walk away from you in the middle of a fight again," he promised, walking toward me. "I'm so sorry."

I shook my head. "It's me who should apologize. You deserve an explanation and I did a terrible job of it today."

"No," he stopped me. "I understand I threw your life into chaos. I know it will take some time to adjust."

"You did"—I smiled—"throw my life into chaos. But I was reminded today that sometimes chaos is exactly what our lives need. Ever since I left you in that hospital, I was hell bent on living the most simple, safe life I could. I think that's why I gravitated toward Ryan. He was gentle-natured and I knew he'd never hurt me. But love is so much more than that, and unfortunately he realized that sooner than me."

"Do you think you would have figured it out sooner or later?" he asked.

I blew out a deep sigh. "I don't know. I tend to avoid the obvious, if you didn't notice."

He grinned, chuckling under his breath. "No, I never actually noticed that."

I nudged his shoulder, as he brushed a stray piece of hair out of my face. "Even if you're the most stubborn woman on the planet, I'm glad you're mine. Besides, I don't mind kissing the sense into you every now and then," he said with a wicked grin.

"That was unfair and you know it."

"All's fair in love and war, babe," he said with a laugh. "And in that moment, I couldn't resist you for another second. You were so angry—so full of passion and fire. Deadly combination."

"I'm pretty sure I bit you." I smirked, remembering that first night. "And possibly drew blood? Hey—do I smell French fries?" I asked, getting a sudden whiff of fried food.

His deep laugh filled the room as he kissed my forehead.

"Food never gets by you, does it?"

"Definitely not French fries."

"I'd hoped to have everything set up by the time you got home, but you beat me to it…so everything is still in bags," he explained, turning to point to the several bags on the coffee table.

"Oh, good. You didn't cook," I said, making a grand display of wiping my brow in jest. He rolled his eyes as we walked to the brown bags and I took my first peek inside.

"No. I did not cook. I wanted you alive afterward."

Rubbing his back, I soothed his battered ego. "Don't worry. One of these days, I'll teach you to cook—something, I'm sure."

"Thanks. Grilled cheese, maybe?"

"Ooh, I don't know. That involves the stove. Are you sure you're up to that?"

"Smartass. Why don't you grab some of the food? I know it's your favorite. Or at least, I think it is."

I looked at him in surprise, my eyes darting back to the coffee table with curiosity. "Cheeseburgers and fries? It is one of my favorite meals. How did you know?"

He pointed to the cardboard box by the TV as we grabbed food and sat down on the couch. "When I got home today, I was pretty angry," he said. I bit my lip in regret. "I didn't understand why you would want to keep us—me—secret. And then the more I thought, the more I realized how often since I left the hospital I'd just wished someone… anyone…could understand what it was like to be me. To know what it was like to walk a day in my shoes—to feel what it was like to have all of their memories ripped away from them. I mean, shit—I don't even remember losing my own virginity. No memory at all."

"Sharla Newman. You were sixteen," I interrupted with a wry grin.

He turned to me mid-fry and chucked it at me. "Not the point, but thanks. I'll be sure to look her up on Facebook."

I snorted, taking a bite of my burger as he continued.

"Anyway, as I was saying—so many times I wished someone was there to get me. But had I ever stopped to truly understand anyone else? I was so angry with you, but had I taken the time to figure out why you might have omitted what was going on in your life with your coworkers? I'd been sitting around silently screaming for someone to walk a day in my shoes, but hell if I was willing to do the same."

"So, you went through the box of pictures?"

"Yeah," he answered. "Brick brought them back and I figured if I wanted to understand you better, it was a good place to start."

I smiled, looking over at the box. "And what did you discover?"

"You love the redwoods. And hamburgers. Every birthday picture for several years was taken at the same burger joint. I sat there for hours, trying to see if I could figure out what place it was, but I couldn't decipher it."

"It closed down a few years ago," I said sadly. "We stopped going there when you—the old you—decided birthdays should be celebrated more extravagantly."

Silence followed as he looked down at his greasy burger.

"Well, he's not here anymore—so I say we make new memories."

"I'd like that." I smiled widely, remembering the days when birthdays had been celebrated over fries and milkshakes rather than champagne and caviar.

"There's just one problem," he said.

"What?"

"I don't know when your birthday is." He smiled.

Loud laughter burst from my lungs as I clutched his shoulder, resting my head there as I caught my breath.

"June fifteenth!" I squealed between breaths.

"June fifteenth," he repeated. "Got it. I'm on it."

"So what else did you learn about me in that box?" I asked, picking the pickles off my burger as he watched.

"Apparently not enough." He grinned. "Not a pickle fan?"

"Not on my burgers."

"Duly noted."

"Come on! Tell me more—stop stalling!" I demanded, as he snagged my pickle slices off my paper wrapper and tossed them in his mouth.

"Well," he said, "I noticed that you're extremely photogenic. After an entire box full of photos of your face, I'm itching to get you behind the lens."

Finishing up my food, I threw all of our trash into the brown bag and leaned back into the couch, facing him.

"That sounds kind of sexy," I said, running my fingers down the buttons of his shirt.

His eyes caught mine and I saw just a hint of movement as a tiny smirk pulled at the seam of his mouth. "It could be."

"Would you photograph this?" I asked, slowly unbuttoning the first four buttons of my blouse, until the sheer lace of my bra began to peek through.

"Yes," he answered, his voice dropping an entire octave.

"What about this?" My fingers went to the fly of my jeans.

"Wait. Just one second. Let me get a camera," he said eagerly, running to the other room. He reappeared in record time, with his vintage black and white. He'd also removed his shirt, which gave me a nice view of his lean abs and muscular arms.

"Take off your pants. I want a few in just your shirt and panties." His breath was uneven, as if he'd just been for a jog. Looking up at him caused my legs to squeeze together in need.

Just the mere thought of capturing my image with his lens seemed to be making him nearly wild. I slipped off my jeans and lay back on the couch, dangling my feet off the edge in a flirty position I knew would send him off the deep end.

"Have you done this before? Shit, don't answer that," he said, as the camera started clicking.

I laughed, turning my head away as he hovered above me. "No—I just know what you like."

"Yes, you really do."

"Like, maybe a little bit of this?" I asked, unbuttoning my shirt completely and letting it slip from my shoulder. It fell to the floor in a slinky heap. Pushing up on my elbows, I gave him a sultry look as my cleavage was sent sky high thanks to my new, improved position.

"You are so beautiful," he managed to say as he knelt down on his knees to get a different angle. "Let me just open the windows. I want more light on your skin."

I watched him move toward the large windows that faced the cliffs, pushing back the curtains that were used to block out the sun when it became too bright late in the afternoon. Right now, sunset was just about to take over the sky, the last rays of the day surrendering to the evening stars.

"Perfect." His voice followed his footsteps as he made his way back to the couch. "Now, I think you need to get naked."

I agreed, reaching for the clasp behind me. My bra came undone easily and slowly fell from my shoulders, as the camera clicked away.

Raising one arm at a time, I let it fall to the floor as his heated gaze watched from behind the lens.

Wanting him to enjoy this as much as possible, I slowly stood, widening my stance as my fingers slipped under the thin fabric of my panties. August backed up, readjusting the angle to encompass my new position, as the camera continued to click. With a sensual grace I hadn't known I possessed, I gently slid the last piece of clothing from my body until it hit the floor.

I heard the camera hit the glass of the coffee table as August quickly set it down. His hands shook as his eyes met mine. Dark, heated, and filled with purpose, his gaze was locked and I was his target. His belt and jeans hit the floor and then I watched him move—slowly stalking me, like a predator. My thighs tightened and my breath hitched as his naked body moved toward mine.

As if he were a magnet, I felt his pull and instantly responded, moving toward him without thought.

Without reason.

My body was his. It was made for him.

I would always belong to August. I always had.

Goose bumps pebbled my flesh the instant his fingers touched me as anticipation overwhelmed me. No matter how many times his hands swept over my skin, it would never be enough.

I know now why I'd never left. Even when things got bad. Even when I thought it couldn't get any worse.

Deep down, I was still in love with the monster he'd become. Deep down, I'd always held out hope that somehow…some way…he'd find his way back to me.

And he had.

He was new and different, but he was August.

And he was mine.

My hands slipped around his neck as he lifted me effortlessly; my legs slid around his waist.

"You feel so damn good," he whispered as he fell back onto the sofa with me, his hands ghosting up and down my thighs. I rose up on my knees and my lips found his, kissing deeply as he pulled me closer. His fingers dug into the round curves of my ass as I slowly slid down on his hard length.

"Fuck," he hissed.

Leaning back, I grabbed his camera off the coffee table and handed it to him. "I don't think you're done yet."

He took it from me, his eyes never leaving mine as I slowly began moving up and down on top of him. He flipped the camera around, the lens pointing toward us as he began photographing our lovemaking.

It was erotic and I felt bold and completely brazen as he snapped away. My head fell back as I met each and every powerful thrust.

"It will never be enough. I'll never get enough of you," he said, an almost agonizing quality to his voice.

I was on fire and his words were like kindling, making me burn hotter and brighter.

When he finally couldn't take it any longer, the camera hit the couch and both his hands took over, working their way through my hair, down my bare back, to grip my hips so he could push me deeper onto him. His low groans matched mine as we lost ourselves in one another until we were both breathless and spent.

As he carried me upstairs later that evening, well after the sun had given up to the moon and stars, I couldn't help but remember the way he used to carry me to bed when we lived in the tiny house across the city.

"I'll give you everything someday," he'd whisper.

"I just want you," I'd answer back.

"But you deserve so much more."

Our life had started out so simple. Just a boy and a girl in love. But then August had decided he needed to give me the moon and the stars and everything in between…when all I had really needed was him.

And during the somewhere in between, I lost him, too.

After everything collapsed, I'd desperately gone in search of that simple life again, but I'd gone about it all wrong.

Ryan was right. Love should be simple.

Life may be difficult, but loving someone…whether it's right or wrong, that should be the easy part.

And loving August had always been as easy as breathing.

Chapter Twenty-Six

August

"Go away, woman," I muttered into my pillow, hiding the grin spreading across my face. "I'm asleep."

"No you're not. You are definitely awake," she said, wiggling on top of me to prove her point. A certain part of my anatomy jumped up to say good morning to her as she giggled.

"You're relentless," I laughed, lifting the pillow off of my head to see her beaming smile above me as I lay comfortably beneath her in bed.

"It's morning! Wake up! Coffee time!" she exclaimed.

I laughed, shaking my head as tiny tendrils of her hair tickled my naked chest. "Don't most people zombie their way to the kitchen in search of coffee? I've never seen anyone jump out of bed, practically singing show tunes in anticipation of coffee."

"I'm just in a good mood."

I gave her a hard look up and down, taking my time on the way back up.

"You want something," I replied, seeing through her coy pillow talk.

Feigning innocence, she batted her eyelashes at me, trying to suppress the laughter I felt boiling up inside her like an old furnace about to blow. "I have no idea what you're talking about!"

Grabbing her around the waist, I threw her down on the bed and straddled her between my thighs. "'Fess up, Adams. What's with the happy attitude? I know I'm good in the sack, but usually only caffeine can bring about this level of joy in the morning."

I paused for a second and then looked down at what she was wearing. Leggings and a T-shirt.

"Let me smell your breath," I demanded as she squirmed beneath me.

"What the hell? That is—no!" she squealed, the laughter she'd held inside bursting forth. I pulled her closer, getting the quick whiff of coffee breath I knew I'd encounter.

Traitor.

"You've already been up!"

"I needed coffee courage!" she said, giggling, as I punished her with my fingers, tickling her mercilessly. She squealed, and the sounds of her laughter filled me with a peace and tranquility I thought I'd never have. It was like the sweet sound of angels to my ears, and now that I'd heard it, felt it to the depth of my soul, I knew I'd never be the same.

I'd never be right in this world without it.

"For what?" I asked as she wiggled out of my grasp, begging for mercy—which I granted.

"Well, I've been thinking," she explained, readjusting herself on the bed so that she was sitting cross-legged in front on me. I lay back with my arms behind my head.

"I know how important it is for you to be known among my group of friends."

I stopped her, reaching out to wind a piece of her hair around my finger as I spoke. "I told you it could wait. It doesn't have to happen right away, Everly."

"I know that, but I'm ready," she replied, he eyes closing slightly, as she let herself surrender to the feeling of my fingers in her hair. It made me wonder if it was something she'd always liked.

Had I done this before?

"I feel like the longer we go on not telling people, the longer this won't feel real," she continued. "And I want it to be. I don't want to just be sitting around playing house with you, August. I want my friends to know who you are and what you mean to me. I want you to matter in my life."

My heart quickened in my chest. "I want that, too."

"Good, so that brings me to my next point."

"Okay," I said with an inquisitive brow.

"I want to have Sarah over for dinner."

"Sarah," I questioned, doubt settling into the pit of my empty stomach as I swallowed audibly. "Your best friend who hates me? That Sarah?"

She nodded.

"Wouldn't it be best if you confronted her on your own and we did this in stages...like they do when they introduce someone to a wild animal or something?"

She laughed. "Are you comparing yourself to a wild animal?"

"Who said I would be the one attacking anyone?" I grimaced.

"Okay, okay...I know I haven't painted her in the best light," she said.

"Best light? Over the last two years you basically conditioned her to hate me—not that I blame you, considering the circumstances, but it kind of blows for the new guy. Which is still me, by the way."

"I know," she said, taking my hand. "Which is why I want her here, around you—to show her that you are different and new. Telling her is one thing, but actually having her here? I'm hoping you can change her opinion faster than I can."

"Okay," I agreed, with a reluctant nod. "But if this goes badly—it was your idea."

"Agreed."

"But first, we have a date in the darkroom," I said, a mischievous grin spreading across my face.

Her eyes widened as she remembered the film we'd captured the night before.

"Race you!" she yelled, jumping off the messy bed toward the door. I caught her before she got two feet and threw her over my shoulder as I raced downstairs.

Turns out developing those pictures was just as much fun as it was making them.

* * *

Everly had been in the kitchen all afternoon, chopping and dicing god knows what.

It seems Sarah would be getting the dinner to end all dinners.

I'd heard a lot about Everly's best friend over the last several weeks. I was both anxious and scared as hell to meet her. Besides Ryan and I guess her counselor, Sarah had been the one constant in Everly's life over the last two years. She'd been there for her from the beginning and I know her opinion was highly valued.

I didn't like being on the bad side of that opinion.

I hoped by the end of the evening, she might hate me a little less and by some miracle wouldn't be dragging Everly out by her hair in an effort to knock some common sense back into her.

I'd suggested going out somewhere—neutral territory. Somewhere that didn't scream, "Hey, look at my gigantic house!" But Everly vetoed that idea, deciding that since we were now officially a couple, we should present ourselves as such.

In our massive house—that I'd bought before, when I was a giant douche.

Fuck.

I already looked like an asshole.

I took a deep breath as I pulled out a pair of jeans from a drawer and grabbed a black T-shirt. I was making no effort to dress up. I didn't want to seem stuffy or overwrought with my own self-worth.

Just me—the jeans-wearing, photo-chasing guy. No big deal.

But as I jogged down the stairs on my way to the kitchen to help Everly with any last-minute preparations. I knew it would take a damn miracle for Sarah to see me as anything but the asshole who'd stolen her best friend away.

Walking into the kitchen, I looked around wide-eyed. "Did we invite the entire ballet over for dinner?" I asked as I scanned the counter. It was covered in dishes.

"I went a little overboard, huh?" she asked, biting down on her bottom lip as she surveyed the kitchen.

"A little? It looks like every major holiday combined in here," I said with a laugh, peeking around to see just what was under some of the covered dishes.

"Don't touch!" she scolded. "You'll let out all the heat."

"I thought you said Sarah was like the size of a twig in winter. Why did you make so much food?"

"Guilt," she answered. "I tend to make a lot of food when I'm feeling guilty."

"Good to know," I said with a grin, grabbing her waist and pulling her toward me. "I'll be sure to use that to my advantage when I'm feeling a bit peckish."

She laughed as her lips fell on mine, just in time with the chime of the doorbell.

"Damn bell," I cursed.

"She's here," Everly said, her eyes suddenly going wide with panic.

"Whoa, calm down. Do you want me to go get the door?" I asked.

"No! God, no. She'll skin you alive. I'll go. Why don't you pull out the wine?" she suggested, tossing a towel on the counter.

"Sure."

I watched her smooth out her hair, take a deep breath, and walk toward the front door. I knew she was a bundle of nerves, but she was handling it well. Sarah meant a lot to her and I knew tonight was important to her.

I didn't want to screw anything up.

Turning back around, I looked for the wine she'd mentioned. The only wine I'd drunk since my reawakening had been a glass or two in restaurants. I'd decided I was more of a beer drinker and that was pretty much where my wine days had ended.

Until Everly showed up.

She loved wine. Loved everything about it—the color, the flavor, and the smell. It was like a grown-up version of coffee for her. She didn't drink it every night and she definitely didn't need a cup to wake up in the morning, but she loved drinking a glass with dinner if she could and would always order it on the rare occasions we'd gone out.

Now if I could just figure out where she kept it.

Opening the refrigerator, I scored and found a bottle of white wine chilling inside. I just needed to find the red. Luck was on my side when I found it hanging out by the wineglasses that had been set out earlier.

Now I just had to figure out how to open the damn things.

Looking around, I found the wine opener in a drawer and began the complicated process of opening my first bottle of wine. I started off by staring at the contraption for a long period of time, and then staring at the bottle.

That produced no results.

Shit.

Everly and Sarah were going to walk in here and see me standing around like an absolute idiot because I had no idea how to do this.

Great first impression.

Not willing to waste any more time, I pulled apart the wine opener and placed it on the bottle, drilling in the corkscrew until…fuck— what did I do now?

I tried pulling. Nothing. That little fucker of a cork was permanently wedged in there.

"Do you need some help, babe?" Everly's voice rang out into the kitchen.

I froze, looking up to see her and Sarah staring at me from the doorway.

"I've never opened a bottle of wine," I confessed. "Or if I have, I don't remember. I guess this isn't one of those things that stuck around."

Everly, always patient and kind, walked forward, taking the bottle from me and showing me what I'd done wrong. I watched as she clamped the wine opener down, which allowed the cork to be pulled free.

"So simple," I said, shaking my head and chuckling.

"It's okay," she said with a warm smile.

I glanced up to see Sarah watching our entire exchange. Her eyes darted back and forth between the two of us, analyzing and dissecting our every move and interaction. *She's waiting for me to slip up—to do something she could call me out on. What?* I didn't know exactly, but I guessed she hadn't come here with an open mind. Not that I'd expected any less of someone who loved Everly so fiercely.

No. I actually respected her more because of it.

But it didn't make my job any easier.

"So, have you spoken to Ryan lately?" she asked, her gaze briefly assessing my reaction before she turned to Everly.

"What? No. Why would you ask that?" she said quickly, glancing up at me apologetically. I gave her a warm smile as she passed me a glass of red wine. I handed it over to Sarah as a gesture of goodwill, but she just set it on the counter as she plotted her next move.

"Well, it's just—he was such a big part of your life. I figured you'd at least care how he was doing after all of this."

The corkscrew clattered to the counter as Everly slammed her hands down in frustration. "Listen, I understand you're mad. Things between us haven't been the best. But I didn't invite you here so you could instigate more fights, Sarah. I understand Ryan is probably hurting. Does that upset me? Yes. But let's not forget who started this whole thing. It's not like I left him high and dry."

"But you did leave him," she bit back, her voice rising to match Everly's. The anger in the room was palpable and I suddenly felt caught between them without any idea what to do. I'd heard breaking up a cat fight was a bad idea. I was pretty sure the same logic applied to women.

"I did exactly what he told me to do, Sarah!" Everly yelled. "I gave August a chance, and damn if he wasn't right. I know that hurts, and I know it messes up your precious wedding plans, but can you be a fucking best friend and be happy for me?"

"I just don't want to see you get hurt," she said softly.

"That's not your job! Can't you just be there for me?"

"Yes," she answered, tears leaking down her chiseled pink cheeks.

This was girl drama overload and I was in way over my head. They ran into each other's arms, hugging and crying like weepy teenagers as I huddled in the corner with the bottles of wine, wondering when it would all be over.

"I made you food—a lot of food," Everly said between sniffles. Sarah looked around, her puffy eyes wide with surprise. She'd been so focused on her mission of destroying the evening she hadn't noticed the piles of food stacked everywhere.

"For my entire lifetime?" she asked with a laugh, as she grabbed a napkin and began blotting her eyes in that dainty way women do. Everly did the same, but much more quickly, and then started lifting tin foil off the trays and pulling out plates.

"I was going to put everything on the dining table, but now I'm worried it will all be cold by then. So why don't we just dish up in here and eat in the living room?" she suggested.

"Sounds great," I agreed, pouring myself a glass of white wine as Everly handed Sarah the first plate and instructed her to dig in. As

I looked over everything Everly had made, I realized what a talent she had. I'd known that first night, when I watched her turn the few scraps of food in my kitchen into a five-star meal, that she had potential, but gazing out over the counter now, I saw what an amazing gift she had.

"Have you ever thought about cooking professionally?" I asked as I took a plate from the counter and began dishing up chicken tetrazzini, homemade lasagna, and garlic knots.

"Sometimes, but I have the coffee house," she said with a shrug.

"You'll never get her to leave that coffeehouse," Sarah said. "She loves it there."

"Well, as long as she's doing something she enjoys," I replied. Her eyes met mine and she smiled warmly.

"But don't you think she should be doing more?" Sarah asked as we took our plates out to the living room. Her inquisitive gaze followed me as I sat on the floor in front of the coffee table next to Everly.

"She's trying to bait you, August."

"Everly and I may have made amends, but that doesn't mean I'm sold on you yet," Sarah admitted.

I shrugged, unfazed. "I get that. And honestly, it's not really up to me what Everly does with her life. If the coffeehouse makes her happy—then she should do that until it doesn't. I'm not that guy anymore. Hell, I'm not even employed. I have no right to tell anyone what to do with their life, when I'm not doing shit with my own. I won't bully her—now or ever."

She didn't respond, but her silence gave me a sliver of hope.

Sarah and Everly spent dinner playing catch-up. I listened as they spoke about their jobs, lives, and Tabitha. Sarah loved her life in the spotlight, but it was exhausting.

"You don't even want to see my feet," she said in regard to the brutal schedule she was forced to keep.

"I never want to see your feet," Everly commented with a grin. "They're nasty."

"Well, it's a miracle I can walk some days."

"Don't you have an understudy?" I asked. Both women looked at me like I'd said a bad word.

"What?"

"Sarah hates her understudy with a passion, and has sworn she'll never take the stage in her place."

"Is there a reason? Or is it beyond my realm of understanding as a dude?" I asked, pulling apart a garlic knot to gather up some of the incredible marinara sauce from the lasagna.

"Yes, but it's complicated. It's an old rivalry. Just dance drama." She shrugged as she pushed around a bit of leftover pasta on her plate.

"Even I don't understand it," Everly chimed in.

"But you support the hatred, because—"

"That's what best friends do," they said in union.

"Got it." I held my hands up in surrender.

"Whatever happened to the mystery man you were dating?" Everly asked as she began to gather plates from our feast.

"He's around," Sarah answered vaguely, a smug smile pulling at her lips.

"Why are you being so secretive?"

"I just don't want to screw it up," she confessed. Her fingers played at the rim of her empty wineglass. "He's kind of perfect and I've never felt like this."

"And you think by telling me, that it will end?"

"I don't know," she answered honestly. "I just like having him to myself. When we start involving friends and"—she made a gagging sound, before continuing—"family, I want to know this is real. And good."

"Take it from me, Sarah. It will never be real until you stop hiding."

She looked up at us, taking a big breath, but just shook her head.

"It's different. I can't explain how—it just is."

"Okay, well—I'll be here for you whenever you're ready to show this man off. He is real, right? I mean, it is a real live person?" Everly joked, and laughter followed. Sarah stuck out her tongue, which only made the laughter boom louder.

"Very funny," Sarah said. "Yes, he's real. Wait. Blow-up dolls count, right?" she added, giggling.

I collected the plates for everyone and headed for the kitchen. The sound of their happy reunion followed me and I felt overwhelming joy for Everly.

It was good to see her relaxed and carefree with her best friend. I never wanted her to feel apart from any aspect of her life because she'd chosen me.

I never wanted her to regret me.

Because I know I'd never regret her.

"I've got a couple more dishes for you," Sarah said as she entered the kitchen behind me.

"Thanks. You can just put them there," I said, pointing at the countertop next to the sink, "and I'll take care of them in a minute."

"Actually, I wanted to talk to you alone, if you had a chance."

"Sure," I answered, placing the empty wineglass I was washing in the sink to give her my full attention.

"I came here tonight prepared to drag Everly out of here by my fists if needed."

"You know I'd fight you for her." I smiled.

"I realize that. I'm willing to give you a trial period," she explained, her arms curved tightly across her chest.

"A trial period?" I repeated. I shifted to one side and leaned against the counter, hoping to gauge where this conversation might take me. I understood her fierceness—her need to protect her friend. But I wouldn't back down.

"I've been Everly's friend for two years. I was with her when she picked her life off the damned concrete and put it back together. To this day, there is still shit she won't tell me about what went on in this house. All I know is you were one fucked-up son of a bitch."

Flinching at her harsh words, I interrupted her. Each word could have been branded to my chest from the sincerity I put behind each one of them. "I'm not him."

"I'm beginning to see that. But I still don't trust you completely."

"That's fair," I answered, appreciating her honesty.

Taking her time, she slowly dried her hands on a kitchen towel before looking up at me, her expression resolute. "So, take this second chance, August. Make her happy. Give her the best damn life you can, because if anyone deserves it—Everly does. But I swear, if you hurt her—again—I will make sure you never see her again. Do you understand?"

Nodding my head in understanding, I said, "If I hurt her again, I wouldn't expect anything less."

"Good," she replied, tossing the towel onto the counter. "Now Everly sent me in here for cake. Point me in the direction of the chocolate."

I grinned, loving her ability to change directions with little to no fuss, and pointed her toward the massive refrigerator. Opening the refrigerator, she gasped. This was followed by a slew of expletives from the ballerina's mouth.

"I think my understudy may be paying her to destroy me," she nearly cried as she pulled out a massive chocolate cake, nearly the size of Texas.

"No, she just loves you," I said with a chuckle, eyeballing my portion as she set it down on the counter. It was probably the size of the entire gulf coast side of Texas.

I wasn't a ballerina.

"And I love her. More than you could ever imagine. Never forget that."

"I won't," I vowed, looking at her with a steady gaze. "And Sarah, thank you for loving her when I couldn't."

She didn't say a word, but simply nodded.

It wasn't a slam-dunk but over the course of the evening, Sarah and I managed to see eye to eye and I realized we were both batting for the same team. Team Everly.

And that was all that mattered to me.

Chapter Twenty-Seven

Everly

The crashing waves had once brought a kind of solace to me. The soothing, never-ending back-and-forth cascade of sound was a sure thing—a solid, dependable vibrato that lulled me to sleep when I couldn't, eased my distress, and cured my anxiety.

But now, it just reminded me of where I was.

As each wave crested, hitting the cliffs below, I was gently reminded of the house that had become my prison.

He'd left me here again.

Doing so had become so regular I didn't even bother asking where he was going.

As our eyes met seconds before he pulled the door shut, I swear I saw an ounce of remorse somewhere in those steely irises of his. But then he pulled back into the darkness and I was left alone.

With no one but myself to blame.

I'd once been a strong woman—someone worth loving. But now, I was nothing but a lifeless shell.

The waves continued to crash outside, making the room feel as small as a sardine can. I wiped a trickle of sweat off my brow as I paced back and forth, trying to wish away the hours until he returned.

Twenty-two.

Number twenty-two. That was how many times he'd locked me in here.

At first, I'd cried and screamed for him as he walked away, begging him to reconsider. What had I done? Why was he doing this?

Now, I just let him go in silence. Nothing would change his mind. After twenty-two imprisonments, I'd learned my place.

I still didn't know why. I just didn't care anymore.

Looking around the room, I fiddled with the necklace that rested on my collarbone and studied the pictures on the walls, absently wondering if he even noticed them anymore.

Did he remember when he'd proudly hung each black-and-white photo around the room? I'd been highly embarrassed to see myself everywhere, but he'd just held me from behind, his hands moving up my body as he studied each of his masterpieces.

"I wanted my queen to be well represented," he'd whispered.

Did he remember how much he'd once loved me?

* * *

"Rise and shine!" An annoying voice rang out through the foggy haze of sleep.

"No," I whined, shaking the tormented dream from my memory. August was no longer a ghost of my past. He was here. And he was mine.

"It's not morning," I mumbled.

"Oh, but it is." August chuckled—a dark mischievous chuckle that made me want to punch him.

Hard.

"It is not. Mornings involve sunshine and birdcalls—coffee and happiness." Lifting my head half an inch off the pillow, I peeked out the corner of my eye, seeing nothing but blackness. "And none of those things are occurring right now. So, there will be no rising...and definitely no shining. Go away."

My head fell back onto the squishy pillow in victory.

"You should know, early riser, as well as I do, that mornings do in fact frequently happen in the dark."

"But those are work mornings." The more I spoke, the higher my voice got. Its current pitch was somewhere between that annoying girlfriend Chandler had dated on *Friends* and Miss Piggy. "Work mornings don't count."

"Will this conversation be any shorter if I mention I have coffee?"

"No you don't," I said, my voice growing grumpier by the second.

"How would you know that?"

"Because, Einstein—I would smell it. I work in a coffeehouse and—Is that coffee?" I asked as the vibrant aroma of coffee beans filled the air. My eyes flew open to find a metal travel mug held out in front of me.

"Sneaky," I said, "hiding it behind metal. But why is it in a travel mug and why are you waking me up at the ass crack of dawn...on my birthday, I might add?" I flipped the lip to the mug and took my first sip of the morning, preparing myself for black sludge, considering the man who had made it.

"Wow, this is actually good!" I exclaimed. I looked down at the cup in awe.

He laughed. "I'll try not to be overly wounded by your shock."

"Sorry! It's just really good! But it doesn't explain why I'm not sleeping in right now."

"It's your birthday," he said, as if that were some sort of explanation.

"And?"

"I promised you the best day ever."

"And that day begins at six in the morning?" I said, glaring at the clock by the nightstand.

"Yep! Now get your ass in the shower!" He swatted my ass and grinned. "We leave in an hour."

*   *   *

"Damn it! Why are there already so many people here?" August asked as we made the last turn into the Muir Woods Redwood Forest parking lot.

Which was completely full. At eight in the morning.

"Because it's Muir Woods," I said, a small smile creeping across my face.

"I know, but I thought by leaving at the ass crack of dawn—as you so elegantly put it—we'd avoid the tourists."

I shook my head, trying to keep from laughing. "Nope. You just joined the other crazy ones who rushed up here at the ass crack of dawn."

"Well, shit."

"There's more parking along the street if you keep heading down there." I pointed along the long curvy street that we'd been on before turning into the lot.

"Hope you don't mind a walk." He frowned.

"Here? Absolutely not." I smiled. He continued down the road, finding a small spot a ways down. He parallel parked with little effort and within minutes we were hand in hand on our way to the entrance, August's trusty camera around his neck.

"Thank you for this," I said, taking in a deep cleansing breath.

"I know you love it here, and I said it would be the best day ever," he reminded me with a smug grin. It tugged tightly at the corners of his eyes, creating the tiny little creases I loved to stare at. Gazing at these, combined with his hazel irises and chiseled jaw, I was nearly walking into oncoming traffic before I righted myself and began walking in a straight line again.

"You got a bit of drool…right there," he said with a laugh, commenting on my absentmindedness.

"Shut up."

We made our way to the rustic little welcome center to buy tickets. I'd been here so many times with him, it seemed like our place.

Like coming home.

But to him, it was as if he was visiting for the first time.

So many good memories lost.

It hurt. The knowledge that in order to make new memories, he had to first lose every single memory from his past—a cleansing of sorts, I guess. The guilt that he'd lost every single memory from his childhood—his parents, and family…it hurt. It all hurt.

Had I known that this was the only way to bring him back to the man he once was, before money and power had corrupted him, would I have chosen this life for him? Would it be so selfish of me to wish this existence on someone—just to have the man I remembered?

It was one of those questions I asked myself, but already knew the answer.

I had once been hopelessly in love with a monster and yet I'd gladly become one to bring him back.

Loving someone was easy. Life was the chaotic mess in between.

"Tell me what you like about this place so much," August asked, after we'd purchased our tickets from the elderly man behind the ticket window. August held on to the small map that plotted out the various trails and sights along the paths, while I just breathed it all in. I didn't need a map to tell me where I was going.

I'd been down these winding paths more times than I could count.

"The smell," I answered.

"You like the smell?"

"Yes—take a deep breath," I instructed, looking sideways to wait for him to do so. I watched him shake his head in amusement as his eyes met mine, but he did as I said and took a solid breath into his lungs, letting the mountain air fill his airways.

"What do you smell?" I asked.

"Air?" he answered, giving me a sideways grin.

"Seriously? That's it?"

"Mountain air?" he specified, watching as I did the same, breathing in deeply as we walked down the shadowy path. "What do you smell?"

"Everything," I answered. "The crisp woodsy smell of the trees, the rustic flavor of the earth, and that clean feeling of the water rushing through. It's like the best air freshener money can buy, but it's impossible to bottle, because there is no way we could replicate this."

He didn't say anything, as we continued to stroll along the wooded walkway and he snapped a few pictures. Others walked around us—families, couples and even a few school groups pointed toward the heavens as they looked at the giant redwoods. The drive out from the city was only about thirty minutes, but stepping out here was like visiting another world. So vastly different from the hustle and bustle, the forest breathed solitude and serene tranquility. Even as the school-aged kids ran up and down the wood walkway, nothing could sway the sense of peace I felt when I came here.

"What else?" August asked.

"What?" I asked, looking up at a piece of sky through the trees.

"What else do you like about this place?" he asked softly.

I looked around, trying to pick just one thing. I loved everything, really. The solitude. The way I felt when I was here. The time I'd spent with him in this place so long ago.

"Oh, here—let me show you," I said, pulling him along the path. We came to one of my favorite markers. So many trees had fallen over the years, whether due to drought or storms, and rather than trying to move them the forestry department usually left them where they fell unless they interfered with a path or caused a safety hazard. In this spot, they'd cut one of the oldest fallen trees in half to demonstrate the incredible lifespan of a giant redwood.

"Here," I said, pointing to the many rings within the tree. There were several markers there, designating historical events which went back nearly a thousand years.

"When I look at this tree—stand in this place, I feel almost insignificant."

"What?" he said, confusion crossing his face.

"Let me continue." I grinned. "Before this tree fell, its life span was over nine hundred years. You and I would have been a speck of time—a blip, barely noticeable to its existence."

"This is depressing."

"Shut up. I'm talking." I laughed. "Sometimes, when life is chaotic and intense, and I feel like it just can't possibly be any worse, I like to come here and remember that I'm not the only one in the universe. That in the nearly ten centuries of this tree's life, hundreds of thousands of people lived and died feeling exactly the same way I did at some point in their life…and chances are their lives were worse than mine because I at least have indoor plumbing and a blow dryer."

He chuckled and rolled his eyes.

"There are a ton of reasons I love these woods, but one of the biggest is that one. It puts me in my place."

"And it smells good." He winked.

"Yes, and it smells incredible."

"You just geeked out over air and trees," he said with a grin.

"Yes, and?"

"It was fucking adorable."

"Just wait until you hear me talk about waterfalls. I love waterfalls… oh, and streams!" He laughed.

We continued down the path, talking the entire way as I pointed out my favorite spots and even shared a few memories.

"You kissed me there once," I said, pointing to a tree along the path that had a large hole in the trunk. It was a favorite of the tourists for pictures and usually had a line, but luckily, due to our slow pace, we'd missed the huge rush of people and it was just us as we arrived.

"Right here?" he asked, pushing me against the tree.

"Yes," I answered, gulping audibly as our eyes met.

"Like this?" His hand cupped my jaw as his lips slowly grazed my own. The heat from his breath rushed along my neck and sent shivers down my spine.

"Happy Birthday, Everly," he whispered as his mouth captured mine. Butterflies fluttered in my belly as I clung to him, wishing I was suddenly anywhere but this very public setting. The only thing I wanted for my birthday was him. Alone.

Now.

When he pulled away, his smirk was nearly heartstopping. I saw a few young tourists skirt by us, the blushes on their faces apparent. I looked up at him, my eyes wide with embarrassment. He just laughed it off and held up his camera, showing me the images he'd just caught without my knowledge.

Hell, with that man's lips on mine, a semitruck could have come crashing through the woods and I probably wouldn't have noticed.

"I wanted to get this new kiss on record," he explained as I looked down at our very indecent public scene.

"Those poor teenagers are probably scarred for life," I said.

"Those poor teenagers probably have done that and more," he corrected.

"You're probably right. When I was their age—"

"Stop! Don't need to know." He held up his hands in protest as we roamed back to the welcome center.

"What do you mean, you don't want to know? I know all about your previous escapades."

"Yes—but I don't. And, honestly—I really don't want to know about that aspect of my life. There's you now, and that's all that matters."

"So, the same goes for me?"

He nodded. "Yes. As far as I'm concerned—you had amnesia as well, forgot all other lovers but me, and now we're even."

"That's ridiculous, you know that."

"I'm a ridiculous kind of guy," he shrugged. "And you love me for it."

The air changed swiftly as we both froze.

The look of surprise sweeping across his face led me to believe he hadn't meant to say it, but it had been said.

The "L" word.

Turning to him, my heart beating like a jackhammer, I replied, "Yes. I do."

*   *   *

"I can't take credit for this next trick. Well, at least not all of it," he said quickly as we pulled up to the darkened street corner.

"Okay," I answered, looking around for some sort of clue. "Are you going to buy me some cocaine? Take me clubbing or get me a tattoo?" I asked, glancing at some of the unsavory establishments in the neighborhood.

I wasn't quite scared—I'd lived in an area much like this before. Granted, I'd been slightly harder around the edges back in those days, but I'm sure if it came down to it, I could still throw a punch. Or stand behind August and give him moral support.

That sounded like a better option.

"That would definitely make it a memorable day, but no. Not today; sorry. This is just where we're going to grab lunch."

"Really—you shouldn't have." I laughed, wondering where in the world we could possibly eat around here. I didn't see any restaurants, unless you counted the convenience store on the street.

I wasn't a high-maintenance girl by any means, but I was averse to food poisoning and those nasty hot dogs in the window of the run-down store looked like they'd been there since Bush was in office.

The first time.

"Come on, oh ye of little faith," he said, opening his car door with a grin that basically told me I was a big chickenshit. Taking a deep breath, I pushed my own door open and waltzed out with my head held high. We met on the curb.

"Where to?" I asked, acting far more confident than I felt. We'd gone from my version of the happiest place on earth to the ghetto and I was trying to figure out how this worked into my best day ever.

But I took his hand and followed. Because I trusted him. Finally.

We walked to a little apartment complex a block down. It reminded me a lot of the shoebox hole in the wall I'd rented the year I met August. The one I'd been too afraid to show him. The one he'd never judged me for.

The place I fell in love with him.

There were no curtains in the windows here. Just bars. Rows and rows of bars. It reminded me of a prison—a real one, and I wondered if the people who lived there felt the same way. Jails weren't the only forms of imprisonment. Sometimes life could feel just as cold and endless as those cold metal bars.

I remember staring out through my ratty curtain windows, way back when, wondering if I'd ever find a home of my own—someplace worth wanting. I'd worked a dead-end job with no way out and all I saw were barricades and closed doors ahead of me. August had shown me there was more to life than a pile of no's. He'd taught me there could be kindness in the eyes of others and if I wanted to make more of myself, I could.

Even if it was just as a barista at a coffee shop.

He'd always been happy with me the way I was...until money had driven him to want more. More from life and more from me. Now he was different, and all I saw were pieces of the old August finding their way back again—when life had just been him and me and nothing else.

It gave me hope for the future.

Hope for our future.

I held his hand as we climbed the steps to the third floor. There was no elevator, which made me wonder how they managed to get away with such out-of-date construction. But looking around at the leaky ceilings and the worn carpeting, I remembered what it was like to live in a place like this.

The forgotten zone.

No one cared whether your water worked or if roaches scattered along your floor at night. This was where the poor lived—where they were lost in the system and left to their own devices.

I remembered it well.

It made my heart bleed.

Four doors down, August finally came to a stop. My palm felt wet in his hand as I nervously pulled it away to wipe against my jeans. I waited as he knocked on the door, standing slightly behind him but to the side, as if that made some sort of difference in my pride factor.

It didn't.

I was still practically cowering.

A former street rat. Cowering.

How far I'd come.

A large old man opened the door. His gray hair and long wiry mustache looked strangely familiar to me. As I gazed into his dark brown eyes, trying to pinpoint where I'd seen his face before, I heard his gruff Brooklyn accent. "You August?"

"Yes sir," August answered.

"Come on in," the man replied, stepping aside to let us through the stripped-down, ugly door. As soon as I passed over the threshold and my nose came in contact with the smells wafting through that apartment, I knew exactly where I'd met the man before.

My eyes flew over to August.

"How?" I managed to say, as I turned back to the old line cook who'd once owned my favorite burger spot.

It had closed down years ago and was never heard of again.

"Sarah," August said. "When she was over the other day for dinner, I happened to show her some of the pictures of you at the burger place and she recognized it, too. Only—unlike you, she knew the owner's name. Once I had a name, he wasn't too hard to track down."

"Strangest call I've ever got," the old man said, shaking his head as he turned over a burger on the large electric skillet he was using.

"I'm Everly." I walked over and held out my hand. I watched as he did the same, wiping off the grease on a towel that he'd slung over his shoulder first.

"Joey," he replied. "I remember you. The little redhead who used to come in every month. Twice if it was your birthday," he said with a grin. "I remember Mr. Moneybags over there as well. Don't forget what we agreed on," he warned, which felt a little less threatening with the smile still plastered on his weathered face.

"No sir," August replied. "I intend on paying you every last dime."

"I don't doubt that. Now what do you two want on your burgers?" he asked, making me grin back at him like a damn fool.

"You're cooking for us?" I asked.

"Well, what do you think you're doing here, sweetheart? Did you think you were coming to this part of town just for the scenery? Your man said you wanted my burgers for your birthday. He's paying me a hefty sum, so that's what I'm doing."

"You're insane." I laughed, stepping forward to run my hands up August's neck.

"Maybe a little," he said with a wink. "Tell the man what you want!"

"Okay, okay!" I answered with sheer excitement, listing everything I wanted on my epic birthday burger. Joey just nodded and smiled, not bothering to write anything down as he took the order. He never had. None of the waitresses in his restaurant had ever sent back handwritten orders when I'd visited. Everything had been called out and yelled back for accuracy.

"Hey Joey—why did you close the restaurant?" I asked.

He stared down at the burgers, silently flipping them as I watched the years seem to pass by his tired eyes. "I didn't choose to shut it down. It just happened—like so many things in life. Big chain came in down the street, customer loyalty dropped, and before long I was behind on rent. The restaurant business ain't easy. There's always something out there bigger and shinier, ready to take away your livelihood. That place was my heart and soul. I haven't been able to get back on my feet ever since." He took a deep breath, looking up as his tired eyes blinked several times. "But it's good to know I'm missed. At least by a few."

"You are," I replied. "There was no place quite like yours."

"It was a good little spot," he agreed. "I drive past it every once in a while—there's a damn frozen yogurt place there now. Looks like someone vomited the rainbow all over it."

I couldn't help the snort that escaped my throat. I heard August chuckle next to me as we watched Joey finish wrapping up our burgers and fries. August and I thanked him for the meal, and as we left August handed him a fistful of cash. Joey didn't bother counting it, which meant he either trusted us or didn't care. I knew it was the former. Somehow the old man who lived in the apartment that felt more like a prison than a home had come to trust us in the few minutes we'd grown to know each other.

"Joey, I want you to have this," I said, reaching for the watch that adorned my wrist. He looked down as I unclasped it and slid it over my petite hand.

"Kind of big on you, isn't it?" he asked, looking at the large silver watch.

"Yes, it was given to me, and I just don't think it's a good look. I thought you might like it and if not, maybe you could use it toward your burger joint fund."

"Burger joint? How do you know I even want to go back in business?" he asked, looking down at me as his fingers ran over the shiny metal of the Rolex watch.

"Because you wouldn't look so damn happy when you cooked them if it wasn't still your passion," I answered.

He swallowed deeply, as if he were holding back some deep emotion.

"Thank you, Everly…August. Thank you very much."

"Good luck, Joey," August replied.

I waved good-bye and we stepped out the door, burgers and fries in hand, and as I looked around, the tattered floors and dingy walls didn't look nearly as scary anymore.

If Joey and I could survive this life, there was hope for the rest of them.

As long as we didn't forget.

* * *

"Do you have a place in mind to eat these?" I asked, peeking into the bag as the aroma began to fill the car. My mouth was already watering and I was nearly shaking with hunger as I tried to discipline myself from snagging several of the fries and shoving them into my mouth all at once.

I couldn't believe he'd found Joey and had him make me a burger and fries.

In his house.

On an electric griddle and a tiny deep fat fryer that anyone could pick up from Walmart. It made me wonder why his burgers were amazing and mine were just all right when I had all of the same equipment in my own kitchen.

"Not really—I thought of a few scenic locations along the water, but if you have something better in mind, let me know."

"Turn here," I instructed, and he took a sharp curve off the freeway.

A couple of interchanges later, we were pulling up to my spot—the secret spot I went to when I wanted to be alone. Alone from everything and nothing at all. It's where I went when Ryan became overwhelming with talk of school and careers... when Sarah and I bickered and even when work became too stressful.

Even a barista can feel overworked from time to time.

It had always been my place—until August. He had been the only other person I'd invited here. And now I wanted to do so again.

As he shut the engine off, he looked up at the massive bridge in the background. "I have a picture of the two of us here," he said, lifting his wallet from his back pocket. He pulled out a tattered old photo, obviously worn from being shoved in his wallet, but it was one I recognized immediately.

"That's an old one," I said, smiling, as my hair dipped down in front of me. I leaned in closer to get a better look, flipping over the photo to see the words I'd written so long ago. "We were babies," I said, laughing, looking at the date.

"Will you tell me about this day?" he asked as we dug into the food, not willing to risk the possibility of it getting any colder.

"I think we'd been dating for a few months—maybe longer. We were already head over heels in love. I swear it was that way from the minute I saw you," I explained candidly, a tiny moan escaping my mouth as I bit into the burger for the first time.

He chuckled, watching with amusement as I ate the glorious food with enthusiasm.

"I've been coming here since I was a child. Before I was old enough to be traveling alone, I was riding buses and taking BART to get over to this very spot."

"Why here?"

"I don't know. I was in the car one day with my random foster parent of the moment, and I remember we drove past here. I'd of course seen the Golden Gate Bridge a hundred times before then, having grown up in the city, but from this angle, it looked immense—colossal, like it could engulf the entire ocean. It seemed otherworldly, and at that time in my life, I needed something kind of magical and beyond the realm of what was considered normal."

"So that was here," he asked.

"For my eight-year-old mind, yeah. It was."

He looked up at it, the shiny red cables stretching from one end of the bay to another. "I can see it."

I hid my embarrassed smile and continued. "So, after we'd been dating a while, I decided you were cool enough to bring to my magical spot."

"And now I guess I'm cool enough again?" he asked softly, his eyes meeting mine.

"Very," I answered, food forgotten.

"And what do cool people do in a place like this?" he asked.

My fingers slowly went down his chiseled chest and I bit my bottom lip.

"Very magical things," I answered, pushing him back and showing him just how enchanted a bridge could be.

Chapter Twenty-Eight

August

I no longer missed the memories.

Life with Everly had completed me.

Completed my existence.

For the first time since I'd awakened in that lonely hospital bed, I wasn't searching for something that was lost to me.

With her, I had found it all.

Everything was falling into place. I could see our future, feel it… grasp it with my fingertips. Life was moving forward and I finally had everything I'd been searching for.

Until it all slipped away, so fast I could do nothing but watch it all crumble around me like sand.

* * *

Looking over the giant case of desserts at the local bakery, I tried to make a snap decision and failed.

After weeks of sheer bliss with Everly, I still had no idea what her favorite dessert was.

I guess I could add that to the pile of things left to discover. It had suddenly become my favorite pastime.

"Can I help you?" the old man behind the counter asked. He had kind eyes and bits of flour streaked across his weathered face. Based on the lack of employees and size of the place, I was guessing he was the owner and wore just about every hat under the roof.

As he arched back, stretching his tired old body, I looked over the large case of desserts again, wondering how much time it took him to make each one of them by hand. Every single day.

"What would you recommend for a coffee lover?" I asked with a solid grin as I surveyed his life's work. Each dessert was like a piece of art, and I could see the proud gleam in his eyes as he spoke.

"Oh, well—you can't go wrong with chocolate," he responded, pointing to several different cakes, cookies, and brownies that would go especially well.

"I'll take them all," I said. His eyes lit up in delight.

"Yes, sir!" he answered eagerly, and got to work on boxing up half the store—because that's just about what I'd ordered.

But I didn't care, because tonight Everly and I were celebrating. After submitting my work to several galleries around the city and hearing nothing for weeks, I'd given up hope. I was a new talent— never heard of and really, why would anyone want to take me on? It had been a risky long shot, but after sitting at home for months on end without any other employable skills, I believed it was one I'd needed to take.

Finally, I'd received the phone call I'd been waiting for. A small, local gallery wanted to display a few of my photographs—on a trial basis—but if they sold, it could work out to be something more per-manent.

It was a beginning, a start for something real, and I couldn't wait to share it with Everly. I couldn't wait to share everything with Everly.

With my purchases in hand, I left a very happy bakery owner be-hind and headed for home. Everly would be reaching the end of her shift soon and I wanted to have everything just perfect before she got there.

Summer had arrived without much fanfare in San Francisco. The weather had warmed slightly and the fog had grown thicker, but other than the increase in tourism, not much had changed. It was what made California so desirable—the total lack of seasons. There was no snow to plow, no leaves to rake, and when summer came to the bay, people continued to wear T-shirts and jeans through August, as if nothing changed.

What kept me here, though, was the view—the never-ending coastal views. I would have easily given up every penny I had if it weren't for the panoramic coastline that greeted me every single time I walked in my front door. I may have been a giant asshole back in the day, but I'd managed to get one thing right and that was this house.

Fumbling with packages and cake boxes, I made my way through the front door and set everything in the kitchen. Knowing I had time left before Everly got off work, I grabbed a beer and stepped out on the deck that overlooked the Pacific.

The waves crashed and unfurled below, and the salty spray of the ocean filled my lungs with a sense of peace I'd never thought I'd find. This house finally felt like a home to me. It finally felt like it belonged to me, rather than to a stranger.

Walking in here for the first time all those months ago was like stepping into a life I didn't want. How could I wake up with the same name and yet be so completely different?

I'd known from the first moment I saw her appear in my hospital room. I didn't want to be the August Kincaid she remembered, but I had no idea who I wanted to become, so somewhere in the middle I'd managed to find a common ground. I was still a work in progress, but so far, I was digging the life I'd discovered in the midst of it all.

"Remember when I helped you move in here, and we stood out here like fucking kings on a castle tower?" An unfamiliar voice shot through the crashing tide.

Fuck, I really needed to learn to lock the damn door.

My head whipped around to meet my intruder face to face. He was tall, well-built, with glaring brown eyes and a menacing sneer that might pass for a smile. His wavy black hair matched his tailored suit perfectly. He oozed money and sophistication, probably wearing more money in fashion on his body at the moment than most people made in a year.

I didn't say a thing, just kept my eyes trained on him. No need to give up all my cards at once.

"No greeting? No words of welcome for your old buddy and partner Trent?"

So this was the guy that had been blowing up my phone for the last several weeks. The troublemaker my attorney had mentioned. He was a persistent little shit.

"You called a few times," I said absently, baiting him for more information.

"Well, what the hell was I supposed to do, August? You're released from the hospital and never bother to call? For months? I have to find out from our fucking attorney that you're up and walking around. Do you know how that makes me look? How that makes *us* look?"

"I can't imagine."

Because, really—I honestly couldn't. But it was nice of him to visit me in the hospital. Oh wait…

"What the fuck is wrong with you?" he roared, stepping into my space, his voice filled with venom and ire. "Do you think this is all some sick joke? You did seem to think the world revolved around you, didn't you? Well, let me tell you something, asshole—it doesn't. While you were taking an extended siesta, the rest of us were busting our fucking asses, and it's time you pay your dues."

Dues? Suddenly something clicked into place as memories and conversations aligned. Everly had once said I'd quit my job because of an old fraternity brother, although she'd never mentioned his name. She'd said that after I went to work for him, I was never the *same.*

No words of welcome for your old buddy and partner Trent?

Shit.

No matter how far I reached, it seemed the glaring truth of my past would always find me, no matter what I did with my new life.

"Look—Trent, is it?" I said, beginning the opening line to the speech I'd delivered time and time again to the elite crowd of lawyers and businessmen I'd associated with so long ago. Once they discovered the August of old was dead and buried, now hidden beneath layers of amnesia with little to no hope of being found, they usually moved on quickly. The new August, who spoke of photography instead of stock portfolios and who would rather hike instead of attend a gala function, was nowhere near their speed, and even though I had the money, I wasn't worth the time.

And I was just fine with that.

"What the fuck are you talking about?" Trent lashed out, his words like talons directed solely at me.

"I don't know who you are, but if you let me explain myself, it might clear some things up," I said calmly, before proceeding. I told him everything.

Well, mostly everything. I told him the *Reader's Digest* version, including the mugging, my coma, and the resulting loss of memory.

"So you have no memory of anything?" he asked, seeming almost dumbfounded by the news. *Almost.*

"Nothing before that night; no."

"I'm sorry, man." His bent head shook, as if he felt pity for me.

"It's okay. You didn't—" I stopped myself as I watched his shoulders begin to shake. My mind couldn't process what my eyes were seeing until his gaze met mine and I heard it.

Laughter.

He was laughing. At my pain, at my suffering and all the loss I'd endured.

"You misunderstood, buddy. I wasn't apologizing for your misfortune. I was apologizing because things are about to get a hell of lot worse."

My expression hardened as my fists tightened. "How's that, *buddy?*" I asked, throwing the familiar term back in his face.

"See, you and I have a partnership. It's one of those things that works a lot like marriage—a 'till death do us part' type of thing—not that I've tried that particular thing out—too many fish in the sea and all. But I've heard it works the same way. And well, here's the thing. You're not dead."

I got up into his face, close enough to see the whites of his teeth as his cold, vicious smile reflected back at me. "In case you weren't listening, let me give you the abbreviated version so your little brain can comprehend it. I don't remember a goddamned thing about my former life, including but not limited to a so-called partnership with you. So forgive me if I'm not jumping up and down at the idea, but I think I'll decline."

"Jesus, you really are a total blank, aren't you?" he said, stepping back, his eyes wide with curiosity. "Amazing. For a second I thought you were just playing me, but there really is nothing of you left. Just nothing."

"Now do you understand?" I asked, glaring at him.

"Yes. I understand perfectly." He smiled widely, rubbing his hands together. "It's time to get to work."

"I'm not working for you!" I roared. The words exploded from my mouth like a cannon. "Now get the fuck out!"

He didn't budge. The asshat didn't move a single inch as his arms slowly slunk into the pockets of his thousand-dollar suit, and he began to swagger around the deck. I watched as he took the beer I'd opened before stepping out here, and slowly brought it to his own lips.

"You will work for me, and here's why," he casually said as he set the beer down on the rail. His voice was eerily calm, in vast contrast to the crashing tide below. "Before your little incident, turns out you owed me money. A lot of money, actually."

"I'll write you a check," I interjected, which only made him laugh harder.

"I don't think you're quite grasping the concept here. So let me dumb it down for *you*. You may think you're on the up and up because you have a few million stashed away in the bank. That's chump change to what we dealt with on a daily basis. Did you ever wonder why you could afford a place like this?"

I had actually, but like so many things in my past, I'd just let it go. Obviously that had been a big mistake.

"The reason we could afford shit like this house you're standing in and the crazy huge yacht I own is because we never keep it in one place for a long period of time. We keep our money hidden, from the prying, investigating eyes of Big Brother. It works. Or at least it did until you decided to peace out for two years, leaving behind a huge debt and no one but me to clean up after you. And I hate messes."

"How much?" I said through gritted teeth.

"Fifty million dollars."

I tried to school my emotions, temper my expression, tone down my temper. What the hell had I gotten myself into?

"How do I know you're telling the truth?" I asked.

"Well, you see, that's the tricky part of amnesia, isn't it? But I guess I could always go to your lovely girlfriend and ask. She was around back then, wasn't she? What was her name? Everly? She was a hot piece of ass, if I remember correctly."

He obviously hadn't just been calling. He'd been watching—waiting for the right opportunity to ambush me with this information—and now he knew he'd hit the right button to make me flinch. The right nerve that just might cause me to cave. I had no idea who this man was and what he was capable of, but based on the way Everly cringed at the mere mention of his name and his maniacal laugh, I wasn't taking any chances.

"What do you want?" I asked, knowing he had me. Knowing I'd do anything to keep Everly safe, even if it meant giving up everything.

"You always were a little sensitive when it came to her," he said, a mischievous grin on his face. "You're going to come back to work, like a good little boy, and we'll talk about this amnesia no more. No one ever needs to hear about it. As far as your clients are concerned, you took an extended vacation after your very traumatic hospital stay, and are now well rested and ready to make them as much fucking money as humanly possible."

"And when they discover I have no skills as a stockbroker whatsoever and lose every single penny of their well-earned fortune?" I asked, each word coming out like a dark staccato note, drilling me deeper into hell.

"They won't know their head from their own ass, because I'll be pulling all the strings. As soon as they discover the much-loved August Kincaid is finally back, your beloved clients will come rushing back to us with open arms, and we'll be flooded with so much fucking business we won't know what to do."

"So, I'm just your puppet?" I asked, my eyes darkening as his lightened with glee.

"Yes. You see, you were always the face and I was the brains. People don't like me much, which is why I brought you on board. You, with the good looks and the wholesome ideas. You were exactly what I needed. People believed you when you told them you would make them money, even when we were robbing them blind. And the amazing part…they just kept coming back for more."

His bone-chilling calm as he spoke about robbing people of their life savings was scary. And the fact that I'd once helped him do this, with the same smile on my face, made me ill.

"You know the front door is open?" Everly's voice cut through the tension as my eyes went wide with panic. I turned just in time to see her step onto the patio, her face bright with life until she met Trent's eyes, and then everything seemed to drain from her like water leaking from a sieve.

"What is he doing here?" she seethed, her words barely audible from between clenched teeth.

"It's nothing," I said, frozen in place as I watched her eye him from across the room. "He just came to visit."

"He came to visit?" she repeated, turning to me in horror. "And you allowed him inside?"

"Everly—so good to see you," Trent smiled wickedly, making my fists clench greedily. I hadn't tested out whether or not I liked making a good stiff punch to the face yet, and I was thinking Trent seemed like a good candidate to try that one out on.

"Why don't you go upstairs and wait, while I say good-bye to my old friend," I said calmly, even while rage and panic twisted and turned my gut, making me feel anything but calm.

She froze as my suggestion struck an obvious nerve. All I wanted was for her to be as far away from Trent as possible. I just wanted her safe. I always wanted her safe.

Seeing her standing so close to this man, bathed in fear, made me erratic. In my haste to protect her, her reaction told me I'd uttered the one thing that made her feel anything but safe.

"What did you just say?" she whispered, a tear already leaking from the corner of her eye. I could see her trust dissipating, receding as she took several steps back.

My gaze darted to Trent, who was watching our entire exchange with an expression of amusement painted across his fucking face. Then he focused solely on Everly as she backed away from us, his gaze slowly roaming up her body, and I saw red.

"Please, upstairs. Now." She flinched at my harsh words, turning toward the door and running. I could hear her sobs echoing from the stairwell.

"I want you to leave. Get the fuck out of my house and leave," I said, not bothering to look in his direction.

Trent walked to the slider and stopped. "I'll have my secretary call you on Monday. Don't disappoint me, Kincaid. You may not remember but I don't take kindly to those who owe me a debt—even if that debtor happens to be a friend."

"We are not friends."

"We'll see about that. Make sure you tell Everly I said good-bye— and take care of our girl...wouldn't want anything to happen to her." And then he disappeared inside. I listened for the front door to close before running up the stairs, two at a time, to find her. I skidded to a halt in front of the master bedroom. It was the last place I expected her to be, but there she was, immobile as she stood beside the king-sized bed, looking down at the unfinished project I had yet to show her.

"What is all this?" she asked, focused on the black frames scattered all over the bed.

"A late birthday present. I wanted to give the room life again. When I took all the photos down and put everything in that box, the room lost so much. It lost its light. I just thought these would give it so much more."

Her fingers traced the closest picture—a close-up of our faces as we kissed. The original portrait had been much more erotic, taken from one of the nights we'd photographed our lovemaking, but I'd cropped it because I'd loved her expression—the overwhelming need that seemed to consume her. That alone was eroticism.

"But why here? Why in this place?" she persisted, her voice distant and reserved.

"There were once good memories here. I want to make them again someday."

Her eyes swept over the numerous frames, taking in the dozen or so pictures I'd picked of the two of us, before she silently moved around the room. Stopping at a bare spot on the wall, where the paint was slightly duller, she stared at the square where the last photo had rested. Tears began to stream down her face.

"You're just like him. And I'm going to end up just like her," she said, sobbing into her hands.

"No, no, we aren't. We are what we make ourselves, Everly. Don't you see that—our past has nothing to do with what we are today."

"You're wrong," she cried, shaking her head. "It's already happening. I can see it already beginning."

She was pacing now, her eyes blazing as I tried to follow her rambling.

"See what? You're not making any sense."

"Why was he here, August? Tell me! What was Trent doing here?"

I opened my mouth to answer, but stopped short—my previous vow remaining true. I'd do anything to keep her safe. Even if it meant giving up my own future.

Even if it meant giving up everything.

"I can't do that," I said softly.

"Can't, or won't?"

"Does it matter?" I asked, feeling my heart falter with every false word.

"No," she conceded, her gaze falling to the floor, like all of our hopes and dreams. "But I can't be here if he's back in your life. I won't. That man singlehandedly ruined our life once already. I won't stand around and watch him do it again."

I simply nodded, accepting the fate I knew was sure to come. The fate I'd accepted the moment I realized I couldn't protect her and claim her all in one breath.

What's your girlfriend's name again? Trent's cold words wormed their way back through my mind, making me suddenly very aware of just how similar I might be with my past self. Was this how the old August had felt? When he'd locked her away all those times? Was what he'd done really a desperate attempt to save her, rather than a sick plot to keep her in chains?

"Why are you doing this?" she asked. "Why would you trade everything we have just like that? Just like...before?"

I shook my head, hating myself. Hating that she truly believed I was choosing a life of power and wealth over her. "Sometimes it's not about one or the other, Everly. Sometimes it's just what's meant to be."

"There's always a choice," she said softly.

I watched her gaze around the room in silence, almost as if she was reliving pieces of the past. Each brush of her hand against the furniture felt like a good-bye. Every touch of her fingertips along the bed linens was a farewell. She was leaving and I wasn't going to stop her.

No more shy smiles and coffee-flavored kisses. The memory of her skin would be nothing more than a ghost I wrestled with in my sleep. She would be gone. Forever.

How would I go on? How would I survive?

"Why do you think he did it? Locked me in here? Was it out of cruelty or some twisted fascination—"

"I think maybe he did it out of love," I said, softly interrupting her, as I stepped forward and took her hand. I watched as she flinched but didn't step out of my grasp. "I don't think he ever stopped—how could anyone ever stop loving you?"

"Loving me destroyed you," she sobbed, a salty trail running down her cheek.

"Loving you brought me back to life," I corrected.

"But not for long enough." Her eyes met mine as she tried to pull back.

"Love me one more time," I begged, "Please." I took a hesitant step forward as my thumb slowly skimmed her damp cheek. Her eyes fluttered closed and her breath faltered. It was exactly what I needed to know—she wanted this as much as I did.

I might be letting her go, but first I would drown in this love…this promise of so much more, for one more night.

Before reality set in and I lost her forever.

Pushing back fiery strands of her hair, I cupped her chin and kissed away her tears, which only made her lips quiver and fresh tears appear.

"I want to hate you. I want to push you away and scream and yell. I shouldn't want this—I shouldn't. But I do—God, I do. If this is my last few hours with you—this is how I want to spend them with you. What is wrong with me? We aren't right, August. This isn't right," she cried, her face burrowing into my chest. "I'm so angry," she sobbed.

"I know. I'm so sorry," I said over and over, meaning it more than she could ever know.

"Take it away—take the pain away," she begged, her gaze lifting to mine in a desperate plea for escape.

As my fingers dug their way through her hair, our foreheads touched and I found myself taking a deep breath as I silently asked whoever might be listening for strength. Strength to make it through the night with her body wrapped around mine, knowing it would be the last time. And courage to let her walk away the next morning, knowing she was walking away with my heart in her hands.

This wasn't how this was supposed to end.

My lips met hers as I took my time kissing her, trying to memorize every single moment. Every moan, the color of her lips, the way she arched her neck when I pressed my body against hers—it soon would be all I had.

My life had been a never-ending quest into the past, and now, it seemed, I would have only that.

Nothing but a handful of memories.

As my hands slid around her waist, I lifted her, feeling her strong legs wrap around me. Carrying her to the bed, I paused, remembering the photos scattered about. Knowing they'd only cause us pain later, I carefully sat Everly on the edge of the bed and began the task of making room. The photos I'd carefully exposed and printed fell to the floor in a heap, along with their custom-made frames.

They didn't matter anymore.

None of it mattered.

All I had was this one night.

I ignored the fluttering sound as the photos fell and the frames clattered to the ground. My focus was solely on Everly. It had always been Everly.

I knelt before her and my hands trembled as I drew her blouse above her head, letting it fall to the floor with the forgotten pictures. Her baby blue eyes met mine as she slowly undid the buttons of my shirt, one at a time, letting the tips of her fingers brush against my bare skin.

"I'll always remember how this feels," I whispered.

"Don't." She shook her head. "Don't make promises. You never keep them."

I didn't say anything more, but I knew that it was one promise I'd never break. She'd branded me permanently. I may not have had specific memories of her when I awoke in that hospital room, but my soul and my body had known her instantly.

She might not be mine after tonight, but every piece of me would always belong to her.

Clothes were shed and as I joined her on the bed, I tried to commit to memory every single inch of her body. The soft curve of her hip, the scattering of freckles over her collarbone that reminded me of confetti, and even the winding tree branch that disappeared over her right shoulder.

My fingers instinctively traced the intricate tattoo, following it toward her back, where the birdcage hung. She turned, letting my hands lightly explore her skin.

"It's time for this bird to fly, Everly," I said softly. "It's time for her to dream and explore and find her own path."

Resting her head against the pillow with her eyes trained ahead, she asked, "But what if she's too scared?"

"She'll find her way. She's stronger than you think."

"I don't know if you're right about that. I once said I'd never shed another tear over you," she whispered, her voice breaking as I held her in my arms for the last time. "I guess I don't keep my promises, either."

She turned toward me, her eyes wide with doubt as I bent down and kissed away the tears, until our mouths fused together and no more words were spoken for the rest of the night. We lost ourselves in one another over and over, stoking the fire that would no doubt burn for each another until the end of time.

But sometimes love and passion aren't enough.

When I awoke the next day, she was gone.

And I was left with a pile of pictures and a lifeless house of memories.

Chapter Twenty-Nine

Everly

They say time heals all wounds.

But can it forgive?

It was the one question running through my head over and over again as I climbed the steps to Ryan's apartment that fateful day. After my world had crumbled around me, I'd spent weeks in hiding. Refusing to leave Sarah's house for days at a time, I'd nursed myself back to health after walking away from August for good this time. I should have seen it coming. I should have known.

No one ever changes.

Not that much.

Not for good.

Sarah had taken her role as best friend seriously, never uttering an "I told you so" or blaming me for my own heartbreak. She did, however, threaten bodily harm to various parts of August's anatomy, an offer I'd turned down.

This was as much my fault as his.

At least he had lack of memory as an excuse. I remembered every-thing and yet I'd still gone back begging for more.

August had always managed to bring out the senseless side of me.

But in those quiet weeks, as I cried myself to sleep in her tiny apart-ment, remembering the feel of his body against mine, the words and promises he'd spoken, I realized things about life and about myself. Loving August had been easy. Falling for him had been one of the simplest things I'd ever done. But when it came down to a fight, he al-ways walked away.

There was always something better, bolder, or brighter waiting for him on the other side, and I was never enough. Even after he'd changed—become someone else—he'd chosen wealth, power, and prestige over love. He'd chosen Trent.

And I'd been left with nothing.

Again.

When would I ever learn?

Ryan had once told me loving someone should be simple—as easy as breathing.

I'd had that. Now I wanted someone who would fight for me. And Ryan had been quietly fighting for me all along…waiting for me as I came to the conclusion he'd known all along.

I finally took the last step, my heart running like a bullet train in my chest, on the short walk to the front door. The little purple door decoration I'd made with acrylic paint and a wood cutout from the craft store was still attached. It had been my first attempt at painting and I had pretty much failed at it. The poor little flower looked like something from the kindergarten junk pile, but Ryan had loved it so much he'd proudly stuck it on the door and never allowed me to take it down.

He'd always loved me. Even when it hurt.

Even when it had been nearly impossible to do so.

Holding my hand up, I knocked several times and waited as my heart threatened to catapult out of my body at any second. The door opened and there he was. Gentle brown eyes and a warm, curious smile.

"Took you long enough," he said.

"Yeah." I smiled as I fell into his loving arms, finally feeling like I'd come home, safely in his embrace.

*　　*　　*

It seemed time really was the cure to healing even the deepest of wounds. With each passing day, the damage August had done seemed a distant memory and I felt myself falling more deeply in love with Ryan.

Time moved on.

Love grew once again.

But there were still dark days when I couldn't help but pick at that scar, like a disobedient child picking at a scab. Sometimes I just needed to remember.

To mourn.

On days like this I would disappear and take the long drive to the other side of the city, and submerge myself in the memory of him. The little spot under the bridge was no longer mine. No longer private. When I came here, all I could see, all I could feel was him. The memory of the smooth cadence of his voice haunted me; thoughts of his lingering touch gave me chills.

Did he ever come here to remember? Did he still mourn the loss of my touch?

As much as I loved Ryan, a part of me would always love August. Two vastly different lives and yet I would have been happy in either. How could one heart love two completely different souls?

The gravel crunched behind me, and I turned to see approaching headlights. I wasn't the only one who knew of this spot. In a city of millions, it was impossible to have a place of your own, but this car I recognized. This intruder I'd requested.

The lights dimmed and the car door creaked open. I stepped forward and met him halfway.

"It's been a long time," Brick said, a warm smile creasing his aged face.

"It has," I said. "Too long." I closed the gap, wrapping my arms around him in a long embrace, holding back the tears that threatened to make an appearance.

"It's okay," he soothed. "I won't tell."

A strangled laugh fell from my mouth as the floodgates opened up and moisture gushed from my eyelids.

"I'm happy now," I managed to say through the sobs. "But why does it still hurt?"

He pulled back, his kind eyes finding mine. "It will always hurt. It never stopped the first time. You just had anger to replace the pain."

"I want to be angry at him. It would be so much easier if I hated him," I confessed.

"I know. Me too."

"He's shut you out, too?" I asked, curiosity piquing as I turned to him in the darkness.

"For the most part. Every time I call or visit, he's busy or has an excuse. He's changed and not for the better."

"It's Trent. He's like a parasite. The moment he came into our lives, everything changed. And now he's back, and our August is gone for good."

"August chose his path," Brick said, rubbing my shoulders to ward off the chill in the air. "Now, all you can do is choose yours. The pain will lessen with each day and soon it will feel more like a distant memory instead of a sharp burning ache in your gut. Live your life, Everly. Let him live his."

"You won't tell him about this, will you?" I asked as we both turned toward the bridge. I wrapped my hands protectively around my chest as the breeze whipped around us, making me very aware of the late hour.

"He'd have to return my calls to even make that a possibility... but no," he answered. "What is said between you and me is confidential."

"So, should I expect a bill in the mail?" I joked, nudging his shoulder. He chuckled. It sounded like the gravel had when he'd parked his car next to mine, deep and ragged.

"No. You know I only make house calls for my non-clients. This was strictly one friend visiting another."

"Good," I answered. "Because I'm pretty sure my therapist is strongly against house visits." I looked around, and laughed. "Or bridge visits," I corrected.

"That wouldn't surprise me in the least," he answered, a slight smile tugging at his lip. His arm curved around my shoulder as we made our way back to our vehicles. He stopped short, taking my hand in front of the driver's side door.

"The next phone call I get from you will be a happy one," he said with confidence.

"How can you be so sure?" I asked.

He squeezed my hand and smiled. "Because you are a survivor, Everly. You've been surviving one bad break or another ever since you were little. You will survive August Kincaid as well."

I nodded, knowing he was right. Knowing I'd already taken the first steps. That agonizing pain in my gut that had doubled me over for weeks no longer ruled my life. Slowly, it had reduced itself to a dull throb that flared up from time to time.

And during those flare-ups, I would mourn.

Mourn a life I would never have.

Mourn a man I had lost—not once, but twice.

And then I would move on again and celebrate the new life that had just begun.

Because life was once again full of possibilities. And Brick was right. I was a survivor.

And nothing could take that away from me.

*   *   *

"If you bring another feather dress in here, I will kill you!" I hollered over the dressing room door.

"Hey, you brought me. That was your first mistake!" Sarah yelled back as the attendant began helping me out of another monstrosity of a dress.

It felt like *déjà vu*. Sarah handing me horrible dresses in a never-ending store of white.

I could have avoided the entire episode. I had a perfectly good dress in the back of my closet at home, but somehow it felt tainted now.

Ruined.

After reuniting with Ryan, and after months of getting to know each other once again, he'd gotten down on one knee and proposed once again.

And I'd happily said yes.

This time, we were going to make it down that aisle and when we did, I was going to give my whole heart to the man who'd believed in me…even when I couldn't. Ryan truly was the best of us. He saw love in an unconditional, never-ending way. Somehow he knew by letting me go, I'd eventually find my way back to him.

And now I was determined to find the perfect dress to say my "I do's" in. But Sarah was making it almost impossible, as usual. Deciding to try several stores rather than just one, Sarah had dragged me all over the city today, finally stopping at a shop I recognized from my drive to work. As I stepped out of the latest disaster of a dress, adding it to the huge pile of discards, I began to feel discouraged. Taking a seat in the corner while the attendant made ready the next dress, something much simpler she'd picked out based on my specifications, not Sarah's, I awkwardly waited in my white underwear and strapless bra, trying to do my best not to seem awkward at all.

Which was proving difficult…because who isn't awkward in a bra and underwear?

Underwear models, I guess.

But definitely not normal people. Normal people with flaws and blemishes that showed like neon flashing signs under the bright lights of the three-sided mirror that adorned the large bridal dressing room. I may have been just skinny but I felt like a beanpole sitting there, as my eyes critically picked out each scar I'd managed to pick because I'd never had a parent around to tell me otherwise, every bony rib poking out because I'd always been the last one to receive dinner, and the scared little bird who still sat in her cage on my shoulder because she was too frightened to take the first leap.

I think it's time for the bird to fly, Everly.

Easy for him to say. He didn't bother hanging around to see if I made it off that first rickety branch. Or whether I was still peeking out of the cage door, waiting for the right opportunity to take that first step.

He'd once promised he would never hurt me again.

Nothing but a bunch of empty, useless words.

"Okay, ready to try another?" the bridal attendant asked cheerfully, clearing the moody cobwebs from my mind.

"Yes," I answered brightly, bouncing up from my chair as I stepped up to the dress.

No dark thoughts, Everly, I chided myself.

"This is very elegant, but understated. I know you said you were wary about lace, but I saw this and it had the shape you like. I thought you might like it."

As the fabric fell around me and I got that first look, I had one of those silly moments everyone speaks about. Tears welled up in my eyes as I tried to keep my emotions at bay.

"So, this is a yes?" the attendant asked with a sliver of a laugh.

All I could do was nod as I stared at my reflection, waiting for her to finish lacing the back. The gown gave me curves where I had none, cleavage where there was little, and accentuated my small waist, making it appear feminine rather than boyish. I felt beautiful and glamorous and about a dozen other adjectives in between.

"Do you want to go show your friend?" she asked, moving back to allow me access to the door.

"Yes, please," I answered, taking one careful step at a time behind her as she guided me toward the larger mirrors at the front of the store.

"Oh. My. God!" Sarah shrieked the moment she saw me enter. "If you don't buy that dress, I will beat you over the head with it and force it on you the day of your wedding."

"That's so sweet," I crooned. I rolled my eyes and took a hesitant step up onto the pedestal. The lovely attendant held out a hand and helped me the rest of the way as I took center stage.

"I know this may sound a little self-absorbed, but I think I might just marry myself dressed in this gown."

Sarah chuckled, rising from her chair to stand next to me. She looked small and short as I towered above her on the carpeted pedestal, and the realization made us both instantly laugh. Turning to her, I took her hands in mine and pulled her up to stand shoulder to shoulder with me.

"Now we just need to find your dress," I said.

"I think we need to spend a bit more time staring at this one," she pressed, holding my fingers up high in the air in an attempt to awkwardly twirl me around. We laughed and giggled as we tried to mimic a horrible rendition of a waltz.

"Maybe we should leave the dancing to you," I suggested.

"Or maybe you just need a man." A familiar voice cut through the silliness of the moment like a knife, freezing me in place instantly.

He couldn't be here, I chanted in my head over and over as I turned. I kept my eyes squeezed tightly shut in a desperate attempt to rewind time.

I'd walked away. I'd chosen the safer path and this time, I'd been happy with that decision.

He needed to stay away.

I needed him to stay away.

"What the hell are you doing here?" Sarah's icy voice rang out as my eyes betrayed me and opened, and I came face to face with the one person who could tear my entire world apart.

Again.

"I just came to wish the bride congratulations," he said smoothly.

Everything about him was different. From the way he dressed, in a crisp black suit, to the rigid posture he held. Even his gaze was different—cold, heartless, and almost cruel.

Where did you go, August?

"You need to leave," I managed to say, my voice shaking with sheer effort.

"We need to talk." His eyes briefly traveled toward Sarah. "Alone."

Sarah's hand tightened around mine. "If you think I'm going to leave you alone with her…"

"It's fine, Sarah," I said softly, my words barely above a whisper.

Her wide eyes turned to me. "You've got to be insane. Why would you agree to this?"

Looking up, I caught the curious eye of the attendant and a few nosy customers. "I don't want to make a scene," I said into her ear. "If I just give him what he wants, he'll be in and out and it will be over."

"Ryan will never forgive me for this," she pleaded.

"Let me handle that," I said. "Just go wait outside by my car. I'll meet you out there when I'm done."

I could see she didn't want to go. After she'd lived with me and seen days and weeks go by when I could barely pull myself out of bed, I understood why. August was the enemy—the reason for my pain and heartache. But as much as I agreed with her, I had also put much of the blame on myself. I'd made my decision. I'd chosen one man over the other.

And I'd chosen wrong.

Staring into those cold, lifeless eyes couldn't make that statement any truer.

"If you need anything, call me and I'll be back here in a second," Sarah said, squeezing my hand before she left with her head down, quickly moving toward the exit. Her gaze met mine briefly before she disappeared out the door, and I gave her a quick nod. Then she was gone.

And I was alone with August.

"It's cute how protective she is with you. Although, she did promise to tear off a few of my more precious limbs if things ever went sour between us…"

"You have me to thank for calling her off on that particular promise. She, unlike others, is good at keeping her promises."

He smiled, a menacing smile that made my skin go cold. "That's harsh."

"What are you doing here, August? How did you even find me?" I asked, not moving a muscle, as he took a confident step forward, loosening his tie.

"I told you—I came to wish you congratulations." He grinned, not bothering to answer my other question. "I hear you're engaged. Again. I'm really quite surprised at how quickly Ryan welcomed you back with such open arms, considering how quickly you ran from them when given the chance to fall into mine."

"You son of a bitch," I said, seething.

He ignored my comment as his eyes slid down the length of my body, softening slightly. "You really do look quite stunning."

"If that is all you came for, than you can go." I began to turn away, but he closed the gap between us, making my heart stutter.

"I wanted to show you something," he said, the proximity of his body to mine making my breath rush in and out of my lungs like wind on a stormy day. When Sarah had stood beside me on the pedestal, she'd looked short and goofy. Even though I was still looking down at August, his presence was anything but silly, and I felt intimidated by his size even though I stood over him slightly.

He didn't give me a chance to speak as he delved into his explanation, pulling something out of his pocket but hiding it from view.

"Letting you leave was one of the hardest things I've ever done," he said, but it was said as more of a statement than a proclamation. I watched him warily, wondering where his humanity had gone since that last night I'd spent in his arms.

And only one word came to mind.

Trent.

"I spent days...weeks even, hating myself and the decision I'd made. I'd drowned myself in that damn box, looking over pictures of us, of you, until I was near mad with need. It wasn't normal—what I was feeling—and I knew I'd never be able to exist without you. I needed you back. I grabbed several pictures of you, holding them between my hands for strength as I planned exactly what I'd say to get you back, and then something happened—something in a photo caught my eye."

He stepped up on the pedestal, causing me to stumble backward. His arm darted out, righting my stance before his hands fell back into his pockets. He tugged one out again and produced a single green stone.

"Do you remember this?" he asked.

My heart thundered in my chest as I nodded, my eyes frozen on that tiny bead in his hands.

"Remember how I asked you if you'd ever seen it before and you said no?"

I nodded once again, a single tear slipping from the corner of my eye. I took a ragged breath as I waited for the revelation of the single secret I'd held within me for nearly three long years.

Raising his other hand, he flipped over a single photo—one that had been taken years ago at one of my many burger birthdays. August was crouched behind me, his eyes alive and full of excitement, just like mine, as I blew out the candle stuck in my burger. We looked younger, carefree and happy.

"Do you see the necklace around your neck?" he asked, holding the photo up.

I swallowed slowly as I gave a single nod. "Yes." The word came out strangled and shallow as I stared at the picture. There I was, smiling back at myself with a beautiful green emerald necklace around my throat.

"The strangest thing happened when I saw that green beaded necklace wrapped around your pretty neck. My head felt fuzzy and my vision blurred and suddenly I was on my damn knees, reliving a memory. Only it wasn't a memory of this life—it was from my former life. Can you guess what memory I had, Everly?"

My lips trembled as I tried to keep everything tightly together.

"No? Let me remind you. You and me—in a dark alley? Only there was no one else. No evil muggers or scary robbers, as you conveniently reported to the police. Just you and me. How did I get in that coma, Everly? How?" he demanded.

* * *

"We have to go. We're not safe here," he pleaded.

"No, I'm not safe with you!" I yelled, struggling out of his grasp. He tried to catch me as I moved erratically in his tight hold, until finally I broke free, my fist making contact with his head as I turned. The pain of my necklace being ripped from my body made me swivel back around just in time to see his large body collapse to the ground, his head crack against the pavement as tiny green stones fell around him.

* * *

"Me," I cried. "I did it."

"Yes," he answered, taking my hand in his. It shook as he opened my palm and placed the tiny bead inside. His cold, lifeless eyes met mine as he said the words I'd feared since the night he awoke.

"And I remember everything."

The monster was back.

J. L. Berg's Playlist While Writing *Forgetting August*

Depending on my mood, either I like to write in absolute silence or, if I'm writing a particular scene, I write to music. It helps me concentrate my emotions and really focus on my characters and what they're going through. In *Forgetting August* and *Remembering Everly*, I found myself picking a variety of songs that were upbeat, emotional, and powerful. Each song helped me visualize and learn about my characters a bit more, making the storyline that much stronger.

"I'll Never Forget You" by Birdy
"Habits (Stay High)" by Tove Lo
"Amnesia" by 5 Seconds of Summer
"Misguided Ghosts" by Paramore
"I Should Go" by Levi Kreis
"Over" by Tove Lo
"Devil's Backbone" by The Civil Wars
"Start with Goodbye" by Carrie Underwood

"Leave Your Lover" by Sam Smith

"Dark Horse" by Katy Perry

"Yours and Mine" by Brooke Annibale

"Seven Devils" by Florence + The Machine

"Amnesia" by Justin Timberlake

"Yours" by Ella Henderson

"Lay Me Down" by Sam Smith

"Love Me Like You Do" by Ellie Goulding

"Elastic Heart" by Sia

"One Last Time" by Ariana Grande

"Apologize" by OneRepublic

"Where'd You Go" by Fort Minor

"With or Without You" by U2

"Dancing" by Elisa

"Talking in Your Sleep" by The Civil Wars

"Chains" by Nick Jonas

"I See Fire" by Ed Sheeran

"Photograph" by Ed Sheeran

"Losing Your Memory" by Ryan Star

"Monster" by Paramore

"Fight Song" by Rachel Platten

"Until We Go Down" by Ruelle

"Everyone Wants to Rule the World" by Lorde

"Thousand Miles" by Tove Lo

"The Heart Wants What It Wants" by Selena Gomez

"Hello" by Adele

Bonus Scene

Everly

Five minutes.

I'd made it five whole minutes this time. It was a new record.

Looking down at my watch, I took a deep breath of relief, mentally congratulating myself on this small bit of success.

It had been a few weeks since I'd moved back into the seaside house I'd once shared with August, and since then, I'd been slowly conditioning myself to become reacquainted with the master bedroom. It had once been our little getaway from the world—a place where we'd lose ourselves in each other. But toward the end, it became a symbol of everything that had gone so very wrong between us.

I'm not sure if August noticed me dodging in and out of the bedroom, as my heart raced and panic flooded my veins. If he did, he didn't say a word, knowing I needed solitude in this endeavor.

This was a quest for one. Because the only foe I would be battling is my own damn fear, and this time, it was going to lose.

This room, these four plain walls held so much power over me. It made me feel weak…powerless.

It was a stark reminder of the Everly that had allowed herself to become a prisoner here.

* * *

He'd been distant for two weeks.

Was it my fault?

He'd canceled our weekend plans to Big Sur, and since hearing the news I'd pouted like a child, telling him he loved his job more than he loved me. It was stupid. I knew that now, but how many canceled plans would it take before our life together crumbled?

Ever since our weekend that wasn't, he'd been nearly silent around me, distancing himself further from my touch. The possibility of a breakup seemed more real than I'd ever imagined. My heart ached just thinking of not having him by side when I slept. How would I go on? Where would I go? I'd have no one.

Even now, as we entertained guests in our own home, he seemed to be millions of miles away from me. I glanced up at him as he stood tall and alert at Trent's side. It seemed those two were never too far away from each other anymore.

Instead of August, I caught Trent's gaze, and he sent me a sly, wicked smile. I immediately turned away, feeling like his eyes had carried some dark, sinister meaning. That guy was a total slimeball—in every way imaginable. I'd known it from the moment I met him. Growing up in the foster system, you grew accustomed to picking out the good from the bad. Sometimes it's easy—the deceitful-looking character actually fit the part. But more often than not, the villain looks a whole lot like Trent. Well mannered, devilishly handsome with a charming smile that made women swoon.

"Can I get you another drink?" A deep voice interrupted my thoughts.

I turned to the left to see a tall, handsome man I didn't recognize. His smile was infectious and I couldn't help the tiny grin that tugged at the corners of my lips as he glanced down at my nearly empty glass of merlot.

"Um, sure," I answered, with obvious hesitance. I usually had August at my side during these types of things, and suddenly I felt incredibly vulnerable. Was it okay to take his offer? Was it considered rude not to? I had no idea what the proper etiquette was. I could feel the heat from my reddening cheeks already.

I wasn't shy by definition, but put me in a room filled with snobby-nosed rich people dripping in high-end labels and expensive perfume, and I would disappear into the wall faster than a chameleon could change its color.

Having very little dating experience, I actually had no idea what to do when a guy offered you a drink. Did you follow him to the bar? Stand in the same place and wait around? This was seriously stressful, and as I contemplated all the options suddenly laid out before me, I became enraged and angry that I was even put in this position.

August knew I hated these events. I was a simple foster girl from the wrong side of the tracks. I loved my flip-flops and jeans, and I bought my makeup from the same place I got my prescriptions. Dressing up in fancy clothes, wearing heels, and making small talk with strangers was my idea of hell. But I did it. Because I loved him. I would do anything for that man and the success he wanted. But wasn't it supposed to be our success? Our future?

When did I get booted out of the plan?

Forcing back tears, I made the decision to follow my attentive and handsome drink fetcher to the bar. August had gone all out this evening, hiring a top-notch caterer and enough liquor to supply a small pub for a month. The waitstaff looked like they'd been swiped from a five-star restaurant and the bartenders seemed rather impressive as well.

As I approached the makeshift bar that had been placed near the deck, I took a deep breath as the sharp smell of saltwater filled my lungs, balancing me. Calming me.

Mr. Merlot turned just as I approached, his eye-catching smile still intact. He handed me a fresh glass of dark red wine as I sheepishly accepted, tucking a stray lock of my crimson hair behind my ear.

"I'm Jeff. I don't think we've met before."

"Everly," I answered. "And no, I don't think so either."

"I've seen you, though," he said as his eyes suddenly found their way to his beer. His smiled turned slightly inward, as if the confession had caused him a great deal of embarrassment.

"Oh?" I asked, clearly interested now.

"Last month," he replied. "At the art gala. You were in this beautiful green dress that made your hair look like it was on fire."

"That's a good thing?" I asked, quite unclear if I was receiving a compliment or not.

"Oh, yes! Sorry," he said, laughter rumbling through the deep cadence of his voice. "You looked otherworldly...like you'd stepped out of another realm or something."

"Um, thank you?" I answered. It was an odd compliment. I wasn't quite sure how to react. I also hadn't been hit on in a long time, and my deflective skills were a bit rusty.

"I read a lot of fantasy. Sorry." He laughed, clearly embarrassed. It was incredibly sweet and I couldn't help but smile in return.

I should have said something right then—told him I wasn't available. Anything to end the obvious spark of hope that was igniting in his eyes.

But I didn't.

It was wrong to lead him on. But I'd been ignored for weeks by the only man I'd ever loved, and right now my emotions were running rampant, feeding on the tiny morsel of attention I was being offered by this handsome stranger.

"You attend a lot of these things," he stated, not as a question or conversation starter, but more like a casual observation—something he'd noticed over a long period of time.

"Yes, I guess I do," I answered vaguely, knowing this should have been the moment where I mentioned August's name, where I said why I attended so many functions and galas—I was here because of August. My boyfriend. The man I lived with…in this very house.

But I didn't.

"Sorry, I didn't mean to sound like a creepy stalker," he chuckled, a tiny dimple forming on his left cheek. "It's just that I, too, attend most of these events, and well—they tend to become a little…"

"Monotonous?" I offered. "Boring? What about tedious?"

His chuckle turned into a deep, rich laugh and I, too, joined him, quickly covering my mouth with my free hand.

"Yes. To all of the above. It's why I noticed you. You are definitely the opposite of boring."

Glancing up at him from my now half-empty wineglass had me suddenly feeling that twinge of guilt I should have been feeling all along. It swirled and coiled inside my belly, reminding me I was treading on dangerous ground. Just because August was absent didn't mean I should behave like a child. What if he was going through something? Something awful…

"Sorry to interrupt," August's voice cut through my worry as I turned and found him at my side, quickly sliding his arm tightly around my waist. "But I do believe I need to tear my girlfriend away. So sorry."

He tugged on my hand, pulling me toward the stairs, as several guests watched with blatant fascination in their eyes as I was hauled up to the second floor of our house like a disobedient child.

"What in the world is wrong with you?" I managed to say the second we were out of sight.

He remained silent, his hand wrapped in mine as we stalked down the hallway toward the bedroom. My heart skipped a beat just then. In anticipation, fear maybe. I wasn't sure. But right then, I knew something was about to change.

And from that moment on, nothing between us would ever be the same.

It was eerily quiet when we entered the master bedroom. The only sound was the dull laughter of party guests below and the faint sound of crashing waves. Neither of us spoke for what felt like an eternity. I paced the floor back and forth until my feet ached in my expensive shoes.

I risked a quick glance in his direction and found myself unable to look away. He'd given up pacing and was sitting on the edge of the bed, his hands dug deep in his short hair as if all the frustration in the world lay within his grasp.

"Where have you gone, August?" I asked, finally gathering the courage to speak. Someone needed to, and it might as well be me.

"What are you talking about? I'm right here," he answered, exhaustion plaguing his every word.

I took a hesitant step forward, and stopped myself, worried what needed to be said might get muddled by his touch alone. Even when the world was going to hell, everything was right when I was in his arms.

I needed life to feel like an ugly mess right now. Cold and distant. So for now, I'd stay away, because it's the only way I'd be able to tell him the truth.

And that simple truth was, we weren't working anymore.

"August, I—"

"What were you doing talking to Jeff Bennett?" he asked, his eyes rising to meet mine.

"He offered to get me another glass of wine. It was harmless," I said quickly, knowing I was talking far too fast for it to be anything harmless. I'd known what I had done was wrong. I hadn't cheated, and I wouldn't have if given the opportunity, but I'd purposely withheld information, and led someone on. The intention was dishonorable to August.

And myself.

"But why Jeff?" he asked, pressing once again for information.

"I don't know, August," I answered with a bit of annoyance. "He offered, and since you weren't around and I was basically by myself down there for most of the evening, I took him up on the offer."

He rose from the bed, all six-plus feet of him. I'd never feared August, but in that moment I could see why others might. He was strong. Built like a corn-fed, Midwestern football player, even though he'd never stepped foot anywhere near the Bible Belt of America. His good looks and charm made people feel at ease, but it did no good at hiding his anger. When he was pissed, it showed.

And right now, he was downright furious.

"He works for Trent," he growled.

"What?" I said, trying to understand his meaning.

"He's one of his personal employees. Works on his accounts, and God knows what else."

"Why does any of that matter?" I asked as I watched him circle around the room again, agitated as he spoke about his business partner and friend.

"It matters!" he roared. "I just don't want you around him. Or Trent."

My arms wound tightly across my chest as I chose my next several words carefully. "And what about anyone else? Are all men off limits? Or am I just not allowed to speak to those two?"

August wasn't the only one in the room who was furious. His high-handed way of handling this situation had escalated my mood from mad to a notch beyond irate. A flash of ire swept across his hazel-green eyes a moment before he slowly stepped toward me. It was like watching a hungry lion stalk his ill-fated prey.

"You are mine, Everly," he whispered, as his body pressed against me. "Mine and mine alone. I own every part of you, every inch of your body… every breath in your lungs. You. Belong. To. Me."

I didn't think, I just reacted, reaching up for him in raw, urgent need. Our mouths met hungrily as clothes were shed and pushed aside in dire haste. August pinned my body against the far wall of the bedroom, holding me with one arm as his other reached between us.

His touch was brutal and tender at the same time as his fingers brushed along the sensitive skin surrounding my core. My breath quickened with every stroke of his skillful touch. I cried out as the tip of his thumb grazed my clit. "This, right here—what you're feeling? You'll only ever get it from me."

I was still so angry, as his lips claimed mine but every fiber of my being knew he was right. What we had was between us—it only happened once in a lifetime.

For better or for worse, I would hold on to this man as long as I could, kicking and screaming until there was nothing left to fight for. Because love was always worth it.

He alternated between urgent kisses and making a slow meandering path down my neck and shoulders, forgetting about the dozens of guests downstairs waiting for us. His hand grazed my breast, wandering down toward my waist as his large hand firmly grabbed my ass and pulled me closer.

"No matter what happens between us, never forget this," he said. "Never forget how much I love you."

His words felt like a warning. But seconds later, his body was filling mine and I was lost. Lost in his heated gaze. Lost in his tender, loving touch. Lost in love.

His eyes never left mine as he pressed me against the wall, each thrust more urgent than the last. There was a desperate quality in his lovemaking I'd never seen before, as if at any moment, he was afraid I'd disappear. Sensing his insecurity, I tenderly placed my hands on either side of his face. "I love you, August. No matter what. I'll always love you."

His head fell to my shoulder then, as my arms wrapped tightly around him. A low moan escaped my lips as my body began to quake with intensity. As my head fell back against the wall, August let out a low groan and we came together in perfect unison.

Finally, it seemed we were back in sync.

It felt like an eternity, as we both stood there, breathless against the wall, savoring the moment. But soon the sounds from downstairs floated back and reality settled in.

We needed to get back.

The moment he pushed away from me, I felt empty. Cold.

I looked up and found him gathering up his things, straightening the few pieces of clothes he still had on. Nothing was said. No words, just silence.

Sex had never been so awkward between us before.

I quickly followed suit and picked up my shoes and dress. As I sat on the bed to begin the process of salvaging my outfit, I saw him turn to me. He was already put back together. His tuxedo was straight and proper, not a hair out of place or button undone. He looked like the epitome of a proper businessman.

"I'll be back later tonight," was all he said before he turned, cold and distant, toward the door. I sat there in stunned silence as he walked away, unsure of what was happening until I heard the door close.

And the lock click into place.

It was then that I noticed it.

Running up to the door, I touched the lock and felt my breath fly away.

He'd switched it. When? I don't know. But sometime in the last week or so, he'd switched the lock so instead of keeping people out, it now kept me in.

Like a prisoner.

Falling down on the floor, I listened to the party go on without me. The tears fell freely down my cheeks as I cried.

Where did you go, August?

* * *

Thinking back on that evening, as I cried on the floor, my hand instinctively went up to my shoulder where the tiny birdcage rested. It had taken months, maybe years of therapy for me to realize I'd made myself a prisoner as much as August had. I'd stayed in a toxic relationship because I'd believed it was worth fighting for. What was the old saying? If you love something, let it go? Maybe if I'd had the courage to say what I'd meant to that night, and walked away, some of the pain and suffering we'd both endured over the last few years may have never happened.

Maybe August would still have his memories. But then where would we be?

Looking down at my watch...I counted eight minutes.

New record.

Time to get out of here.

Please see the next page
for a preview of

Remembering Everly

Prologue

Guilt, regret, dread.

Three simple words that had the power to strip a man bare.

To make him feel powerless in the most primitive of ways.

That was what my life had been reduced to. Surrounded by money, unlimited wealth, and affluence, and yet I couldn't protect her.

I couldn't keep her safe.

"Why aren't we taking a hired car?" Everly's voice cut through my spiraling thoughts as I turned to see her sitting next to me in the passenger seat. She was a vision tonight—the way the indigo blue of her dress brought out the crimson color of her hair. She wore the beaded necklace I'd given her so many years ago—maybe as a peace offering, hoping to bridge the gap of silence that had grown between us.

Because of me, and all of my many failures.

"I thought it might be nice if it were just the two of us tonight," I answered, sliding my hand across the center console to reach for hers. She didn't seek mine out, but she didn't resist my touch either.

The thought of my embrace didn't make her draw back in fear. There was still hope in her eyes that I hadn't become the monster she feared.

If only she knew.

"I thought we were going to the art gala," she said in disappointment.

"We were. But I know how much you hate those types of events, so I canceled and decided an evening alone would be much nicer."

Every word was total bullshit. I was still expected at that gala and when I didn't show…

Passing the small restaurant I'd picked out—the one that wouldn't require reservations on a Saturday night—I searched around the block for parking, to no avail.

Sometimes I really hated this city.

Three blocks up, I finally found a tight spot on a steep hill. Climbing out of the car, I ran around to the other side to help Everly out, taking note once again of how beautiful she looked.

Her legs seemed to go on forever as she stepped out onto the street, the deep blue fabric of her dress brushing over her lush thighs as she rose to meet me.

"Looks like we have a bit of a walk," I said, offering my hand.

She looked around, taking in the location. "Where are we? I don't think I've ever been to this part of town."

I shrugged, playing it off as best I could as we stepped to the sidewalk side by side. "A guy at work said he'd taken his wife to this place last week and she still hasn't stopped talking about it. I thought it might be worth a try."

She glanced at me suspiciously as I tried not let the stray graffiti and random bits of trash fluttering in the breeze distract me. I'd once sworn to myself I would always give her the best—nothing less—and here I was taking her to a ratty part of town, to a restaurant I'd never heard of, just so I could get her out of the house for the evening.

All because I needed to explain.

Everything.

And it needed to be done on neutral territory, without threat of interruption or discovery.

Soon, she would understand.

Soon, she would know—everything.

We continued to walk together in silence until she stopped suddenly. I turned to see tears dotting her eyelids as the dim street lights cast a halo on her bright red hair.

"Why are you crying?" I asked hesitantly, stepping forward to offer my hand.

She pulled back, her expression wide with fright as she took in her surroundings. I hadn't been the only one to notice the less-than-stellar neighborhood.

"What's going on, August?" she asked, her tone filled with panic and hostility.

"What do you mean?" I said, trying to remain calm. I held my hands up in a gesture of peace.

"Canceling the art gala…taking me to a place like this? It's not you. It doesn't make any sense."

I ran a frustrated hand through my hair, knowing she was right. None of it made sense, but it was the best I could do and I was hoping she would just go along for the ride.

"Maybe you don't know me as well as you think," I bit back, hating myself the instant I said it.

I just needed her to trust me. But trust had to be earned, and over the last few years I'd slowly chipped away at that hard-earned treasure I'd once cherished more than anything. Now, when she looked at me, there was little left but doubt.

Doubt and fear.

A sob tore through her and I watched her turn and run down a darkened alley.

"Fuck!" I cursed under my breath, chasing after her. The clicking of her heels echoed through the narrow passage, until the sound ceased altogether and I found her with her arms wrapped tightly around herself near the side entrance of a sandwich shop. The flickering light above gave me a glimpse of just what damage I'd done to this poor woman.

The woman I'd loved for so long.

Mascara ran down her swollen red cheeks, puffy from the tears she'd shed over the hurtful words I'd said. How many tears had she cried over me?

Buckets, probably.

I wasn't worth it. But I would be.

"Why don't you love me?" she asked, her gaze vacant as she stared blankly at the wall beyond me.

"I love you, Everly. I love you so much," I pleaded, taking her hand. It felt lifeless in mine, like everything had just been sucked out of her and she was just an empty shell standing before me.

Maybe she had been this way for a long time, and I'd been too stupid to notice.

"You don't," she replied, finally turning to look at me. "You haven't for a long time, and I've just been too afraid to see it."

"No, you don't understand—let me explain. But just not here," I said, looking around at the darkened alley. "We have to go. We're not safe here," I insisted.

"No, I'm not safe with you!" she yelled, struggling out of my grasp. I tried to catch her as she moved erratically in my tight hold, but the slippery fabric of her dress loosened my grip and I lost my balance, sending us both flying. Her fist collided with my skull, and I felt myself falling...reaching.

Green stones fell around me like rain as I tumbled to the ground, and the last thing I saw was her tortured face as I tumbled into oblivion.

I could see it all written on her face.

Horror, pain, fear...but most of all—relief.

Complete and utter relief.

Chapter One

Everly

Secrets.

They had the ability to destroy lives, obliterate relationships, and sabotage even the strongest partnerships. Big or small…it didn't matter. Even the tiniest white lie had the power to corrode—to shatter and dismantle everything you loved.

I'd carried a secret so big, for so long, that sometimes I felt physically weak from its weight. I had thought I could carry its burden to my grave—that eventually its truth would die along with me.

But secrets never die.

They live on far longer than we do, and they always find their way to the surface.

Mine certainly did.

Sitting alone in the apartment I shared with my fiancé, I gently rolled the smooth green stone between my thumb and forefinger, over and over, remembering the day it was returned to me.

In all our years together, I'd never seen August so cold. So lifeless.

It had frightened me to my core.

But I still hadn't told anyone. It had been three days and I had yet to tell Ryan or Sarah about what had taken place in the bridal shop. As far as they knew, August had rudely interrupted my bridal appointment to tell me he had his memories back—that was all.

Nothing more, nothing less.

Why hadn't I elaborated? I didn't want to admit my shame. I couldn't share this secret, my darkest lie. What would they think of me? I was the reason August had been in that hospital bed for two years. And the worst part? I'd lied about it—to everyone.

Even to those closest to me. Even August.

I was the worst kind of human.

I knew Ryan would tell me the opposite. He would comfort me as I told him the truth, holding me as I shared my story about the awful truth from that night.

There was no mugger.

There was only me.

*   *   *

"911 Dispatch. What is your emergency?" The words rang clear through the speaker of my cell phone as I held it with both hands, looking down through blurry, tear-soaked eyes at August's lifeless body sprawled out on the ground.

Oh God, what had I done?

"Is anyone there?" The woman asked again.

"Yes," I managed to say. "Please send help. My boyfriend has been injured." My voice cracked as the words fell from my lips, becoming reality.

"What happened? Was there an accident? Were you attacked?"

Glancing around the dark alley, I felt my head nodding in agreement before I even said the words. "Yes, we were attacked. Please, come quickly."

*   *   *

It had all been so easy. No one ever doubted me. And I never gave them reason to. I was a broken, sobbing mess as they took August away in the ambulance, and then stood by him for days until they broke the news that he might never wake from his coma.

The coma I'd put him in. I'd sat with him in that lonely white room, watching him become so frail as the days seemed to pass without end. His doctor mistook my guilt for grief and suggested I try to move on with my life. I was young. August would want me to carry on without him.

I remembered the doctor rubbing my back as he delivered the *ultimate* truth.

"It would take a miracle for him to wake up at this point," he'd said with utmost care. I'd nodded, thanking him for his candor. I'd looked down at August, wondering whether I wanted a miracle.

Would he be the same? Or different?

I'd decided in that moment, I couldn't wait around to find out—it hurt too much. So I'd taken the doctor's advice and moved on, finding my own apartment and job. And eventually—Ryan.

Gentle Ryan.

He would tell me that horrible night was just an accident and I'd panicked—an intense moment of weakness. He'd soothe my tears and insist none of it was my fault. Everything would be forgotten and swept under the rug and we would move on. Life would go on as usual.

But I didn't want it to. I didn't deserve his kindness or empathy. I needed someone to scream and yell at me for the all the suffering I'd caused. I needed to pay for the life I'd stolen.

Because when it came down to it, I'd taken a life.

And I'd walked away, allowing everyone to believe I was the victim of this story when in actuality, I was the criminal. The perpetrator.

The real monster.

"Hey, I was wondering where you were." Ryan's warm familiar voice filtered through the room as I closed my hand over the stone and slowly sank it beneath the blankets, meeting his friendly gaze.

"Hey," I answered, feigning sleepiness. I stretched my neck back and forth, making an elaborate show of my yawn for effect as the tiny green stone burned hot and bright in my hand. "I was just trying to take a nap."

"No luck?" he asked, leaning against the door frame, his arms crossing his broad chest as he took me in.

"No. I don't know why I bothered. I can never sleep during the day. But I haven't been sleeping well since—" I stopped myself, regretting the words instantly.

"Since the bridal shop. I know. I feel you tossing and turning in the night," he said as his eyes lingered on me.

Nodding, I felt the silence settle between us. I wasn't sure what to say next.

He pushed off from the door frame and walked toward me, taking the empty spot on the bed beside me. I felt the mattress dip as his large body crawled on top. It felt comforting, having his weight next to mine.

Safe and real.

He took his time gathering his thoughts, and I could almost see the wheels turning in his head as he chose each word carefully.

"Do you regret your decision? Choosing me? Now that he has his memories…does it change your answer?"

And there it was.

The seed of doubt that had sprouted and blossomed buds and blooms since I was away with August. He'd walked away—sent me into the arms of another man, and even though I'd come back willingly, he didn't always feel confident in my choice. Would I ever be able to uproot its existence or had the damage already been done?

Were we doomed from the start?

"No—God no," I answered, backpedaling. "That is not what I'm thinking at all," I explained, sitting up further in bed to face him fully. "It startled me, yes. I'm still processing it—still trying to figure out what it means to us. But it doesn't change anything. I chose you. I chose this life. That hasn't changed, and it never will."

I'm really quite surprised at how quickly Ryan welcomed you back with such open arms, considering how quickly you ran from them when given the chance to fall into mine.

My voice quivered as I spoke, betrayed my raw emotions. Ryan saw this and mistook my still overwhelming feelings for passion. His lips met mine, a tender whisper of a kiss with a dangling question mark at the end, begging for more. Knowing he needed the reassurance only I could give, I answered with a kiss of my own, returning his tenderness with passion and fire as we fell back onto the mattress and forgot all about memories and choices, and only thought about one thing.

Each other.

*   *   *

"Two months?" Sarah squeaked loudly in response to my surprising answer. "Two months?" she repeated as I just nodded, keeping my eyes straight ahead as I followed the signs to the first place on the list.

"You're not pregnant, are you?" she asked, and then before I had a chance to answer, lowered her voice and said, "Oh my god, you're not pregnant with... August's child, are you?"

"What kind of person do you take me for?" I questioned as I switched lanes, taking the exit the brochure had instructed. "I know my life seems like a soap opera lately, but damn... it hasn't gotten that bad!" I laughed, feeling a little wounded that my best friend really had to ask that question. I mean, I knew my life had been a little turbulent, but I still knew how to prevent pregnancy.

"You haven't answered the question," she pointed out, crossing her arms over her chest.

"For fuck's sake! I'm not pregnant! With anyone's child! I just want to get married!" I hollered over the radio, nearly laughing.

"In two months? Why so soon?" she asked, still pestering, as she began looking around at the well-established neighborhood. We came to a red light. Mature old trees and meticulous landscaping stretched out as far as the eye could see. It was the kind of place where you could picture yourself raising a family—someday.

"Why not so soon?" I said, shaking the picket fence dream from my mind. I had a wedding to plan. "I've made my decision—and yes, I made of mess of it all, but now it's made and I want to start living my life, so I don't see any reason to wait."

Her eyes met mine a moment before I hit the gas to pass through the green light, and I saw her smirk and give a quick nod.

"Okay then. Let's get this thing planned. Good thing I had you shopping off the sales rack last week at the bridal shop." She giggled.

"You knew this would happen?"

"I figured you would either drag your heels or race to the altar. I was really hoping for some sprinting—it's a hell of a lot more fun."

I let out a gentle laugh as we pulled into the small parking lot of the first venue option, killing the engine and turning to her with a smile. Looking up at the beautiful white church, I smiled.

"Well, let's get this thing started."

*   *   *

"I need caffeine!" I whined, nearly falling into the quaint coffee shop that had served as my employer for nearly three years. The familiar scent that greeted me felt as if a warm, snug blanket was being wrapped around my senses. This place was tiring at times, and the hours sometimes sucked, but it had always felt like home.

"I need new legs!" Sarah cried out. "You're a slave driver!" She staggered into the nearest chair, her head falling to the table with a thud. "So tired," she mumbled against the hard wood.

"I didn't mention we were planning everything today?" I said with a wink as I walked up to the counter to greet my coworker Trudy.

"No—you definitely did not. And if you had, I would have worn different shoes." To make her point, she held out her foot, displaying her very adorable, incredibly high-heeled, wedged sandals. They were tan, with accents of lime green that perfectly matched the bright hues of her sundress.

And she'd bought them on sale—a fact she'd told me with great pride this morning on the way to our first appointment.

But thanks to me and my ambitious schedule, she now hated them—with a passion.

Everything in the world was currently my fault, according to Sarah. But I'd had a plan when we'd left the house today, and I didn't want it ruined by her overachiever brain. So I'd left a few key items out of the agenda. Like the florist appointment…and the bakery appointment…and every other bridal-type duty you would need to handle before a wedding.

I'd finally decided to pick a wedding date—to get married and start my life. I'd been a runner for as long as I could remember, darting as soon as life got rough. When Ryan and I fought, I needed air. When things got too real with August, I made excuses and fled. It was why my own fiancé had been the one to help me come to terms with my feelings for August.

It was wrong. So wrong. And it needed to stop.

From now on, I would have my feet firmly planted on the ground. No more running, starting with this wedding, and to make sure I stayed where I was supposed to be—I'd plan the entire thing from start to finish, so help me God.

However, I wasn't stupid. I realized I would eventually need Sarah's assistance and expertise. There's a reason I work in a coffee shop. The work attire only requires jeans and T-shirts every day of the year, and I barely have to wear makeup. I am a low-maintenance girl. But usually, when I asked for Sarah's assistance, it came in overwhelming waves. So, I'd fibbed a little and told her we were meeting up today to look at one or two venue options.

Okay, I lied a lot.

Did I feel bad? I looked at her hunched over the table, mumbling about her pretty, pretty shoes.

Maybe a little.

"Two of the usual?" Trudy asked, with a wink in Sarah's direction.

"Yeah, that'd be great. Maybe a small brownie, too," I added, biting my lip in indecision. Sweets were always a risk when Sarah was moody. With the strict stage diet she always followed when she was performing, and her lingering issues due to years of eating disorders, I always knew to tread lightly when it came to food. But I decided that for today, the chocolate was definitely needed, and today, I needed all the help I could get.

With coffee and chocolate in hand, I walked back and placed the cups down on the table. The aroma immediately brought her face skyward, as she eyed the coffee first and then the brownie with a frown.

"That whole thing is mine. You don't get a single bite," she snarled, kicking her sandals loose underneath the table.

I grinned, nodding. "Deal."

"So, why didn't you tell me we were planning your entire wedding in a day?"

I shrugged. "I guess I wanted to be in charge of it."

"And you thought I wouldn't let you if I knew?" she asked, taking a long sip of coffee before breaking off a piece of the decadent brownie.

"I don't know. Part of me feels bad for the way I acted before. I never got involved—never played the happy bride."

"And so now you're overcompensating? Are you sure this isn't compensation for something else?" Her eyes met mine as our conversation took a turn toward the serious.

"What do you mean?" I asked, clutching my favorite ceramic coffee cup for warmth. It was the same cup I used on all my shifts. It had a cheesy one-liner that said "Meh." My customers loved it.

"Look, I know you are firm in this decision and I see you're happy, but no one is forcing you into marriage. You don't have to marry Ryan to prove you're over August."

"I know that," I answered defensively.

"I just want to make sure you're getting married for the right reasons."

Looking down at my coffee, I watched the steam rise from the cup, like a memory caught in time.

* * *

The last bit of coffee brewed, gurgling and steaming until the last drop was done. I quickly turned to grab the sugar and milk and returned ready to fix everything up.

Only to realize I had no idea how he took his coffee anymore.

Looking up at him, I opened my mouth to ask, but saw him smiling. "Just black," he answered.

I only nodded as I pivoted back toward the refrigerator to return the milk. I'd grabbed everything on impulse, ready to dump two spoonfuls of sugar and a slash of milk into a cup of coffee just like I always had.

How easily I'd fallen back into such an old routine.

"I take it that's different?" He spoke up.

"Yes," I answered, "but a good one. Now you're a purist like me."

* * *

"It's for the right reasons," I answered quickly with an encouraging smile.

"As long as you're happy. You know that's all I ever want for you."

"I am. I really am."

"Good. Now about those flower arrangements…"

Oh God, here we go.

Acknowledgments

Like most authors, I tend to spend a large chunk of my life in the clouds…my imaginary world, as I like to call it.

In this place, I plan and plot, dream and fantasize about the lives I've created and the ones I'm about to. It's always such a rewarding experience to see this daydreaming come to fruition when I type "The End," and suddenly my imaginary world becomes almost real within the pages of my book.

Each novel I write truly is a labor of love and with every word I type, I have a small army backing me up—cheering me on and waving victory flags at the finish line.

I wouldn't be sane (or somewhat so) without the rock that is my husband. He feeds me when I forget to eat, cleans when I can't, and does just about everything in between. Being married to a writer is a tough job and he makes it look easy. Thank you, babe, for loving me.

I'm lucky enough to have two beautiful girls who fortunately love books. Because of this, they tend to understand why Mommy can't play or take them to the pool even when the weather's perfect (sorry!). Hannah and Emily—you are my greatest treasures. I'm ready for a swim now!

To the rest of my family—Thank you for teaching me to always be myself, no matter how dorky or weird that may be. Your love and support mean the world to me and I promise to come visit more, Mom!

Authors tend to be hermit crabs, burrowing into the sand when books are due. Luckily I have amazing friends who remember this and stick around until I come up for air. Leslie, I love you for being you. I don't need to elaborate. Doing so would be unladylike. Melissa, thank you for being my sounding board. Jill, you're both a friend and my PA—that makes you irreplaceable. Seriously, never leave me.

Tara and everyone at InkSlingers PR—Thank you for promoting me and my work. You keep me calm and that is priceless!

This book would never have made it this far if it weren't for the expert eyes of my amazing agent, Jill Marsal, and my talented editor at Grand Central, Lauren Plude. Thank you, ladies, for believing in August and Everly. I hope I've done them justice.

Lastly, thank you to my readers. You always manage to astound me with your kindness. Thank you for loving my characters, and never stop believing in second chances!

About the Author

J. L. Berg is the *USA Today*-bestselling author of the Ready Series. She is a California native living in the beautiful, historic state of Virginia. Married to her high school sweetheart, she has two beautiful girls that drive both of them batty on a daily basis. When she's not writing, you will find her with her nose stuck in a romance novel, in a yoga studio, or devouring anything chocolate.